RAVE REVIEWS
FOR TESS MALLORY!

HIGHLAND DREAM

"Outrageously funny at times, yet sprinkled with poignant moments, *Highland Dream* will bring you to laughter and tears."

—*Romantic Times*

CIRCLES IN TIME

"Tess Mallory is a superb writer. She infuses her characters with true grit. Passion and sensuality are Ms. Mallory's forte. . . . *Circles in Time* is an exhilarating novel: fast-paced, romantic, and satisfying. Highly recommended."

—*Under the Covers Book Reviews*

"There are lots of new twists to the Robin Hood legend in this delightful story of passionate quests."

—*Louisa's Magical Romance website*

MIDSUMMER NIGHT'S MAGIC

"Ms. Mallory writes a wonderful story blending the magic of Ireland and the chance of finding true love."

—*Under the Covers Book Reviews*

TO TOUCH THE STARS

"Fans of futuristic romance will enjoy the interesting premise and exciting resolution."

—*Romantic Times*

OFF-KILTER

"I don't want to come out."

Chelsea smiled. "It's all right, Griffin. Believe me, I understand, but I'm sure you look fine."

"All right, lass, but I think it's a mistake."

The door swung open and Griffin emerged, his face bright red, his hands folded protectively over his crotch.

"Oh, you tried the chaps on. That's—" Chelsea stopped as Griffin angled sideways and looked over one shoulder, down at his bare behind.

"I canna believe the cowboys wear such a thing," he said, his voice aghast. "How do they ever keep from injuring themselves?"

Chelsea stared at the displayed portion of his lean, hard-muscled bottom and thighs and felt every bone in her body turn to mush. She tried to speak but couldn't. Finally she managed to croak out three words.

"Over the jeans," she whispered.

HIGHLAND FLING

TESS MALLORY

LOVE SPELL NEW YORK CITY

LOVE SPELL®

February 2003

Published by

Dorchester Publishing Co., Inc.
276 Fifth Avenue
New York, NY 10001

ISBN 0-505-52526-7

The name "Love Spell" and its logo are trademarks of Dorchester Publishing Co., Inc.

Printed in the United States of America.

Visit us on the web at www.dorchesterpub.com.

This one is for you, Bill. Thank you for the moonlight, the mermaids, the mouse, and the cheese, and most of all, for your gentle love and your endless support. You are my hero, always.

Also for my mother, Alpha Mae Bowman Casler. I know you are bragging about me to the angels. I miss you.

Mega thanks to:

The Usual Suspects: the fam and friends. You know who you are. If you don't, check my last five book dedications! I love you!

My agent, Roberta Brown—always a pleasure. And my editor, Kate Seaver—you are simply the best.

David Baker of Dancing Waters Inn, Ann & Norm Rolling of the EmilyAnn Theatre, and Nell Graham of the Tote Sack, for allowing me to include you in my book.

Special thanks to Marcia Bennett, children's author (*The Mystery at Jacob's Well*, Eakin Press), for introducing me to the magical wonders of Jacob's Well!

And many, many thanks to Dorey Schmidt, Ph.D., author of "The Betrothal Tree," for allowing me to use her wonderful poem, which means so much to the EmilyAnn Theatre, and Griffin and Chelsea, too!

HIGHLAND FLING

Prologue

The Highlands of Scotland, 1605

"Griffin? Griffin, I wasna through speakin' with ye concernin' the purchase of eleven pigs and twelve goats, nor the spreadin' of the manure on the castle gardens. Griffin? Now where has the man gone this time?"

Griffin Campbell, heir to Meadbrooke Castle, Chieftain of Clan Campbell, winner of an untold number of battles and games, leader of the clan's formidable band of soldiers, warrior of indisputable repute, scholar, poet, and swordsman extraordinaire, cowered under the four-poster bed in his room praying Maigrey MacGregor wouldn't find him.

Not that he was afraid of her, oh no, not at all. Well, not much. All right, if the truth be known, he would rather battle a Sassenach bare-handed than endure another minute of his betrothed's company and sharp tongue. Hardly daring to breathe, he watched her too-large feet slap the floor in their too-large slippers, moving back and forth beside the bed as she impatiently waited for him to return to his chamber.

From the moment she arrived at Meadbrooke, Griffin had tried desperately to convince his father that this was not the woman he should marry. His father and Maigrey had decided to simply wait him out. They both knew that

1

if he didn't marry soon he would cease to be the Chieftain of Clan Campbell. A distant uncle, Mungan Campbell, had already declared his plans to challenge Griffin for the position of chieftain if he did not marry and have an heir growing in his wife's belly within a year.

And even though Griffin had no desire to be chieftain, he would never turn down that singular honor and break his father's heart.

Which was why he had finally agreed upon the date of the wedding. A fortnight from now he would be pledging his love and loyalty to Maigrey MacGregor, a woman he couldn't stand, a woman he couldn't bear to touch. Griffin sighed, and a cloud of acrid dust rose up into his nostrils.

That isna Maigrey's fault, ye coward. Ye can at least be honest with yerself if no' with her. Ye canna touch any woman without shaking in yer sniveling boots.

He pushed aside the unbidden thought just as a tickle began inside his left nostril. Reaction made him inhale, which brought more dust into his nose, and suddenly a sneeze twitched for release. Griffin slapped one hand over his nose and pinched hard, fighting the telltale explosion welling up inside his head.

Ye canna sneeze! he commanded silently, his fingers biting into his flesh. *So it burns like salt in a wound—so it feels as though yer bloody head is about to blow off—so what? Are ye a man or a mouse, Campbell?*

His eyes began to bulge. Sweat dappled his brow and ran freely between his eyes, creating a new source of frustration as he blinked and twitched while trying to lie perfectly still beneath his bed.

Ye are a ridiculous, cowardly twit! he fumed as Maigrey continued to pace back and forth. *And if she discovers ye like this ye'll never live it down—she'll hold it over yer stupid head for the rest of yer bloody life.* A new thought made him perk up. *Or maybe she'd call off the wedding! What self-respecting woman would want ta be married to an idiot who would gae sa far as to hide under a bed to escape his woman's prattle?*

It was tempting. Vastly tempting. But in the end he deemed it too risky. He wasn't willing to shame his father, even if it might be worth personally humiliating himself in order to get out of marrying Maigrey.

Using willpower he didn't know he possessed, Griffin finally got his dusty nostrils under control. He released his breath, closing his eyes in relief, careful not to inhale the dust too deeply again.

Damnation, is the woman going to stand there all the day? But stay—he couldn't see her feet anymore. Perhaps she had gone.

After a long, silent moment, Griffin risked another peek out from under the bed. Maigrey stood a few feet away with her back to him. She stared out the long casement window, the sunlight sending stark shadows across her already stark features.

She was not a beauty. Tall, with the hearty countenance and disposition of many a Highland lass, capable, mature, Griffin knew he should be happy to marry her. He gauged her age to be at least twenty and two. She looked more, but it was not her age he found displeasing, nor her sharp eyes the color of a brindle cow, nor the irritation of her ever practical, dull, methodical personality, nor the fact that their children would be plain, nor that her tongue could lash a man at twenty paces. No, what displeased him was the knowledge that he did not love Maigrey Mac-Gregor, and doubted he ever could. And he couldn't help but compare her to a woman he had almost loved.

The image of Jix Ferguson rose up unbidden in his mind. Jix with her dark red curls and her love of life, her impetuous laugh and her kindness of spirit. Jix, who had come to Meadbrooke posing as Maigrey MacGregor with her "brother," Jamie, in tow. She'd played her part well, but eventually she'd confessed to him that not only was she impersonating Maigrey MacGregor, but Jamie was her lover, not her brother! She'd also told him something incredible. Jix Ferguson claimed to be from the distant future.

Griffin stifled a cough as Maigrey came to a stop in front of his face again. Would the lass never give up?

Jix never had, he remembered. Why he'd found it easy to believe her preposterous claims of being from the 21st century, he wasn't sure. However, he was a man of science, a scholar, and the possibility of such a thing did not shake him as much as it might some less educated Scotsman.

Or was it just Jix herself that had convinced him? Her talk, her way of expressing herself, it was all so foreign. In any case, he had witnessed her and Jamie's sudden and unexplainable disappearance, and if he'd had any doubts before, that event had laid them to rest. Of course, the rest of the castle had deemed the event a result of witchcraft, but Griffin didn't believe in magic. Except the kind that drew a man to a woman.

Yes, he had almost loved Jix. Or mayhap he'd just been smitten with her because she hadn't acted horrified when he confided his deep, dark secret to her.

"Och, Griffin."

The sound of Maigrey's voice pulled him back from his reverie and he glanced up at her, careful to stay hidden. He was struck by the sag of her usually taut shoulders, and by her wistful tone as she spoke again.

"If only ye knew that I dinna want this marriage any more than ye do."

What? He raised both brows and tried not to inhale more dust. Maigrey MacGregor was anxious to wed him—all of Meadbrooke knew it! More wonders: She brushed a tear from her lean, hard cheek! Who knew the woman was capable of such tenderness? Had he been too hasty in his judgment?

She straightened her shoulders with a resolute gesture, and Griffin strained to hear her soft words. "Red Hugh will ne'er betray his son and express the feelings I know he has fer me. If only there were some way . . ." Her voice trailed off, and she stood for a moment in silence before turning abruptly and stalking across the room to the door.

Griffin winced as the heavy wood slammed behind her. As soon as he was sure she was gone, he breathed a sigh of relief and sneezed. He slid out from under the bed, his heart pounding as he stood and slapped dust from his legs and chest, feeling stunned. His father loved Maigrey? And Maigrey loved him? Thank the good Lord! The perfect solution.

Highland Fling

Thirty minutes later Griffin sat astride his favorite horse, Firestorm. Tied behind his saddle was a hastily packed traveling bag containing some food, five books, three parchment scrolls, and his oldest quill pen. His plan was a desperate one, but he could think of no other answer. If he disappeared, his father would likely wed Maigrey and perhaps even become the chieftain of the clan as he had always wanted.

In time, after his father's marriage had been consummated, Griffin would return and give his blessing, then retire to his cottage in the woods to study his books and write his poetry, free at last to be his own man.

The first smile he could remember in quite some time split his face, and, putting heel to his mount, Griffin Campbell fled from Meadbrooke Castle into the Highlands.

As Jix Ferguson would say, he was getting the hell out of Dodge—and not a moment too soon.

Chapter One

The Highlands of Scotland, the Present

"Yes . . . yes . . . oh, *yes!* That's it!"

"Oh, definitely, that is definitely better."

Chelsea Brown stared at her reflection in the mirror. Her latest "makeover" by her two best friends—Jix Ferguson and Samantha Riley—was an unmitigated disaster. Again. She sighed. They always tried so hard. Hadn't they learned by now that they couldn't make a silk purse out of Chelsea Brown?

The three friends sat in front of a wide dresser that sported an equally wide mirror in a guest room at Jix's palatial country manor in Scotland. Although Chelsea had been a bridesmaid at Jix's wedding a year ago, she'd been surprised when a special delivery airline ticket arrived in the mail, along with an invitation to come back to Scotland for the couple's first wedding anniversary.

She closed her eyes, remembering her friend's wedding day. Jix had been a beautiful bride, and although Chelsea had sensed there was something more to the story of how her friend and Jamie had gotten together, she'd been pleased to be included. But she'd been just as relieved when the time came to fly back to Texas, to her doctorate classes at the University of Texas. Seeing Jamie and Jix gazing at one another, so in love, had made her own loneliness that much more acute.

I never should have agreed to come back to Scotland, she realized as she opened her eyes and faced her reflection. A mass of mousy blond curls streaked with a darker golden blond were piled high on top of her head, plastered with hair spray. Chelsea's friends had insisted she have her hair streaked with color and assured her she looked great. She wasn't so sure. Now instead of looking like a shy little mouse, she looked like a shy little golden retriever.

"It's temporary," the stylist had told her, "so you can wash it right out if you don't like it." Chelsea had steeled herself not to run for the shower as soon as they hit the door. She couldn't do that to her friends. They'd worked so hard on her. No, she meant *for* her. Didn't she? She sighed and took another look.

Bright blue eye shadow and thick black liquid eyeliner made Chelsea's eyes look huge, garish. Worst of all, she felt obligated to convince her anxious friends that her horrible reflection mirrored back exactly the look she'd been searching for all of her quiet and exceedingly dull life.

"Great, it's really great," Chelsea said, hoping she didn't sound as tentative as she felt. She squinted again, trying not to visibly give in to the temptation to sag her shoulders. She looked like a drag queen. A petite, ugly drag queen.

"I dunno," Jix said with a frown, her green eyes uncertain, a teasing comb poised between her fingers as she dragged her other hand through her own dark red curls. "I'm afraid we've gone a little too heavy on the eye makeup."

"Yeah, maybe so," Sam agreed. "But remember, she insists on wearing these awful glasses even though she doesn't need them."

She held up Chelsea's outdated, brown-rimmed frames by two fingers, the disgusted expression on her face totally incongruous with the ethereal halo of pale blond hair flowing to her shoulders.

Don't talk about me like I'm not even here!

A pang, completely emotional but so sharp it felt physical, stabbed through Chelsea's chest. Samantha Riley was

7

poised, confident, beautiful, and had just graduated from medical school. She was everything Chelsea could never be. And Jessica Isobel Xavier Ferguson MacGregor—Jix for short—was vivacious, exciting, beautiful, and had a wild sense of the absurd. After marrying Jamie she'd written a sizzling romance novel and sold it, first time out.

But Chelsea Brown . . . well, she was just Chelsea Brown. An unattractive, shy, somewhat boring physicist working on her doctorate, the last in a long line of unattractive, shy, somewhat boring Browns who had automatically embarked on scientific careers and spent their lives in laboratories or classrooms.

She sighed as she stole a look at Jix and Samantha. In all the years they had been her friends, why hadn't any of their charm, their poise, their *personality*, rubbed off on plain little Chelsea Brown?

Jix shot Samantha an exasperated look as she took the glasses from her and placed them carefully on the dresser.

"You act like she planned to be nearsighted just to irritate you."

Sam rolled her eyes. "Why do you wear them anyway?" she accused Chelsea. "You have such beautiful eyes."

Chelsea blinked and fought to keep from sighing aloud. She didn't have beautiful eyes—they were plain gray eyes. Okay, she had nice long eyelashes, but that didn't make her eyes beautiful. She didn't have beautiful anything.

When she and Sam and Jix started junior high school together she'd watched as her best friends blossomed, waiting expectantly for the same thing to happen to her. She glanced down at her mostly flat chest and this time forgot not to sigh. She was still waiting. Jix said Chelsea was just a late bloomer. As far as Chelsea was concerned, at twenty-six she'd already gone to seed.

"I just need them for reading," she admitted, "but sometimes I forget and keep them on." She took a deep breath and plunged on, talking fast so she wouldn't lose her momentum.

"And thanks, really, thanks, both of you," she said, clutching the arms of the chair, feeling a little shaky at her own audacity. "But please, *stop!*"

Jix and Sam turned to stare at her, their eyes wide with astonishment.

"But, Chel," Sam said, "your date is just a little over two hours from now and you're nowhere near ready!"

Chelsea turned to Jix, her lower lip trembling. "Oh, Jix, do I really have to do this? I mean, I really appreciate you and Jamie setting this up, but I just . . . I don't know if I can . . . If I can . . ." Her voice broke.

Jix's eyes softened. She reached over to pat her friend's arm, and Chelsea's face flamed with embarrassment. "Of course, you don't have to do anything you don't want to do," Jix said.

On Chelsea's other side Samantha groaned aloud. "I knew you wouldn't go through with it. I just knew it!" She stormed away from the two and flounced down on the huge four-poster bed taking up a fourth of the large room. She threw herself flat on top of the dark blue coverlet and slapped the material with her outspread arms. "Don't you want to have a normal life? Don't you want to find a nice guy, date awhile, get married, have a few kids—or do you really want to spend the rest of your life cooped up in a musty old laboratory?"

Another flush of heat flooded Chelsea's cheeks. A nice guy. Date awhile. Get married. Have a few kids. She closed her eyes. If only Sam knew. If only she could imagine for one moment how much, how very much Chelsea wanted those very things. But it was impossible. Men didn't date women like her. Men dated women like Samantha Riley. Men married women like Jix Ferguson.

Because they're both beautiful, Chelsea reminded herself. *And you aren't, and you never will be, so why don't you just give up now and save yourself the heartache?* She opened her eyes.

"Oh, look who's talking!" Jix stood with her hands on her hips, glaring at Sam's prone figure. "I don't see you walking up the aisle, Miss-I-Think-I'll-Almost-Marry-an-Ax-Murderer!"

Sam sat up, her eyes wide with outrage. "He wasn't an ax murderer!"

"Well, he might have been! He planned to steal your

trust fund—why not get his bride out of the way and collect the insurance at the same time?"

Sam bounced once on the mattress in irritation, her arms folded over her chest. "Yeah, well, you took care of that, didn't you, and all you had to do was abduct me and send me back to—"

"Sam!"

Jix's sharp tone startled Chelsea, and she frowned as a strange look passed between her two friends. She knew about Jix's wild scheme to kidnap Samantha to keep her from marrying Mark the Rat, but suddenly she wondered if there was more to the story than she'd supposed. How many times had this happened before? How many times had Jix and Sam stopped talking the moment she walked into a room and it just hadn't registered? Come to think of it, the two of them had acted rather mysteriously at Jix's wedding, avoiding answering a lot of her questions about their adventure in the Highlands. An adventure she'd not only been excluded from, but about which she knew only the barest details.

"I never did get to hear much about your trip to that isolated village in Scotland," she said, watching the two of them carefully, looking for clues that they were hiding something from her.

Jix smiled, the grin looking oddly strained. "It was pretty lousy, actually. Sam griped the whole time and was in a pretty nasty mood."

"Yeah, I was," Sam agreed flatly. "And by the way, you don't have any room to talk! Your first foray into marriage wasn't anything to be proud of."

"Hey, I didn't ask the guy to hit me, did I?" Jix demanded. "And besides—"

"Please don't fight," Chelsea interrupted, twisting her hands together. She rose from the chair and laughed self-consciously. "Look, I appreciate the makeover, but really, I think I'll just cancel the date and maybe go down to the village for a quiet—"

"No!"

Chelsea blinked as the two women turned on her in

unison. Jix bit her lower lip and had the grace to look abashed, while Sam simply glared at her.

"You don't get it, do you, Chel?" Sam demanded. "Jix and Jamie asked this guy to take you out—he's an earl or a count or something. Do you know how embarrassing it will be for them if you cancel at the last minute?"

Chelsea turned to Jix, who had squeezed both eyes shut as if willing the two women to disappear.

"Jix, is that true?"

Jix opened her eyes, and her stricken expression answered the question well enough.

"It's all right," Chelsea said automatically. "I'll go."

"Are you sure?" Jix put her arm around Chelsea's shoulders. "It's just that he's thinking about investing in Jamie's idea about designing custom-made swords, but—"

"Really, it's all right, Jix." Chelsea took a deep breath. "It's fine. Although I think Samantha would be a better choice." She couldn't help the slightly reproachful look she cast the blond-haired woman. "Why aren't you the one going on this date?"

Sam flopped back on the bed. "Uh-uh. I'm through with men. Forever."

It was Chelsea's turn to exchange a knowing glance with Jix. The voluptuous Samantha Riley had a more than healthy libido and since their days in high school had never been without a man for long. Still, it was true that since her breakup with her fiancé Mark—a man Jix discovered had planned to embezzle Sam's trust fund—the blond socialite had remained alone and presumably celibate. Chelsea felt a stirring of irritation. Sam didn't mind telling Chelsea how pitiful she was for not wanting a man, but it was perfectly all right for Samantha Riley to take a different path.

"You'll change your mind when you meet the right guy," Jix said.

"Nope, I'm turning lesbian."

Jix rolled her eyes. "No, you aren't. Don't be ridiculous. Just because one guy—"

"Um, I hate to interrupt," Chelsea said, fighting her

growing impatience, "but if I'm going on this date I really need to finish getting ready."

Jix's gaze lit up and she hugged Chelsea tightly. "Thanks, kiddo. I just know you'll have a great time!" She pulled away and peered at Chelsea's face more closely. "Okay, I can see where we went wrong."

Sam was at her side in seconds. "You do? Where? What should we do?"

"Sit down, Chel," Jix commanded. "We're starting from scratch."

Chelsea sighed and sank into the soft cushion of the chair as the two women began to chatter. They were her best friends. How could she tell them they were driving her completely insane? Samantha left the room and reappeared a few moments later with a damp washcloth.

Chelsea closed her eyes and took a deep breath just before Sam started scrubbing. Summoning the last of her patience, Chelsea tried to lose herself in a familiar daydream.

The man was tall, dark, and handsome and he gazed down at Chelsea as though she were beautiful, as though she were precious to him. In real life, she smiled in spite of a sudden pain lacing through her scalp as Jix dragged a comb through a snarl she'd no doubt previously created.

The tall man was still smiling at her. What did pain matter? She could bear it. She could bear anything as long as he was by her side. Who knew? Maybe this date would be the beginning of something wonderful—maybe the earl or duke of whatever would be the man of her dreams. Maybe—

"Oops," Jix said, her voice cutting through the self-induced fog around Chelsea's brain. Chelsea opened her eyes just in time to watch Jix's reflection in the mirror as she pulled a long, gooey strand of chewing gum from the teased blond mess on top of her head.

She met Jix's stricken gaze with her own horrified one. Samantha shook her head and rolled her eyes.

"I'm sorry, Chel," Jix said. "Just sit tight—I'll get some ice and that gum will come right out, I promise." She hurried out of the room, with Sam close behind her.

"I told you to throw that gum away," Sam said, her voice dwindling as they moved farther and farther down the hall. "Why in the world you'd chew gum while we're trying to . . ."

Chelsea stared at her new do in the mirror. Her hair stood straight up on top like the tail of an irate chicken.

Oh, yeah, this was going to be just great.

Griffin pulled back on the reins, sending Firestorm into a skidding halt at the top of a small rise overlooking the valley where his cottage—his refuge—lay waiting for him. He couldn't go there yet, for that would be the first place his father would look. No, he'd have to find a hiding place, at least for a time. He'd managed to steal a round of cheese and a bag of scones from the kitchen before heading for the stables. It wouldn't last long, but he'd deal with his hunger when the need arose. He would hunt for his food.

The stallion moved restlessly beneath him as if chiding his master not to be so impetuous. Griffin smiled. As if anyone could accuse him of being impetuous. If anything, he was known for his restraint.

"Aye, Firestorm, I know, laddie. Ye want to be running free and wild. But we've more important things to be thinkin' of today."

Free and wild. His smile broadened as he gazed out across the verdant green countryside. Jix Ferguson had taught him just a wee bit about not always doing what was expected. God knew she was the most unpredictable woman he'd ever met. Too bad she'd been so daft in love with Jamie MacGregor. No, actually it was a good thing. For although Griffin had fallen half in love with the lass, he knew in his heart it would never have worked.

Not because he couldn't have loved her, but because he couldn't imagine her loving him. Jix would've grown tired of his fumbling and ineptitude in a fortnight. After all, she'd had the choice of becoming his bride and had turned him down in favor of MacGregor.

Griffin sighed and guided his horse away from the sight of the valley below and toward the craggy rocks behind him. He was nothing if not honest about his shortcomings. Oh, he was handsome, he knew that. When he'd first come of age, women practically threw themselves at his feet. But it didn't take long before they looked at him not with lust, but confusion.

Why wouldn't the strong, virile son of Red Hugh Campbell do more than flirt? Why wouldn't he take them to bed?

Why indeed. He sighed. What would those women think if they knew that the great lord of Meadbrooke Castle, the next chieftain of the clan, couldn't touch a woman without becoming physically ill? If they knew his secret, they would kill themselves laughing. And that was the least of what would happen if this damaging information got out. Their laughter and his complete humiliation would be nothing compared to the loss of honor, and the loss of the chieftainship. It would break his father's heart.

He'd told only one person his malady—Jix Ferguson. She'd told him that his problem was something called "psychological." That it was a result of an experience he'd had as a child. He'd seen his father make love to a woman who was not his mother. He tightened his jaw at the memory. If Jix was right, then he was even more of a weakling than he'd ever imagined.

To keep the shame of his "condition" a secret, he had ceased his flirtations with the women in Meadbrooke, claiming it was not seemly to dally with girls he had known since childhood. Instead he let it be known that he was sowing his wild oats in a village some miles away. He made a great show of leaving for a few days of "sport" with his women, while the women at Meadbrooke watched with envy as he rode away. If they only knew. In reality, he simply spent the time at his cottage, losing himself in his studies, fighting the sense of guilt and embarrassment that threatened at times to overwhelm him. With the arrival of the real Maigrey, he had no longer been able to avoid the inevitable threat of marriage.

Firestorm whinnied, bringing Griffin's thoughts back to the present. He'd given the horse his head, and they were picking their way carefully up a rocky hillside. An only child, Griffin had never had brothers or sisters to play with, but he'd had an older cousin who had told him of a cave in this area. A magical cave, the lad had claimed, full of wonders. When he pressed him for details, Duncan had only said he doubted that Griffin would believe it if he told him. One day Duncan disappeared, and eventually was given up for dead. Griffin felt the loss keenly and had never forgotten the young man, nor his tales of a mysterious cave.

Firestorm came to a stop at the peak of the hill. Gray shale stretched up above them, but there was no way to journey further on horseback. The rock was too unstable.

Griffin swung down from his mount and began his exploration. If he could find Duncan's cave, it would make a perfect hiding place. He hated to make his father worry, but he knew no other way to handle the situation. In the few weeks he'd spend on his own, alone, he'd have time to think up a convincing story for the day he returned to congratulate his father and his father's new bride, Maigrey.

"Stay here, lad," he said to Firestorm, glancing back at the sun as it slipped downward in the sky. "I've no' much time."

He almost missed the opening to the cave. No more than three feet high, it was hidden behind a thick, thorny bush. Down on all fours, he managed to crawl through, only bumping his head twice. Once he was inside, the rock sloped upward, creating a cavern over twenty feet high— a magical cavern indeed.

Griffin stumbled to his feet and stared up at the ceiling of the cave in amazement, unable to move. Duncan had been telling the truth. It was unbelievable. The cavern stretched high above his head, covered with moss or some sort of growth that glowed, creating an eerie light. In one place water streamed down the wall in a dark cascade, collecting in a small natural basin on the floor, which in turn poured into a deep pool of blue-green water.

Griffin caught his breath in awe. So this was why Duncan had looked so enthralled when he spoke of the "magical cave." No wonder. And though Griffin considered himself a man of science, even he could not deny the air of su-

15

pernatural powers inside the glittering cavern.

He walked over to the pool of water and knelt down beside it, his hand resting on the hilt of his sword. Clear, cool water beckoned to him. Smooth rocks formed the sides of the pool, which measured about eight feet across and seemed to go down into the earth forever, its depths growing darker and greener, no end in sight. He dipped one hand into the water and felt a slight sensation in his fingertips, not unpleasant but totally foreign.

His curiosity engaged, Griffin leaned closer to the pool, and felt a thrill of wonder rush through him. A foot below the water's surface, on the far side of the pool, a row of emerald-green crystals sprouted like flowers in a garden.

They shimmered and sparkled, although the cave was devoid of sunlight, gleaming in the darkness like emerald-green stars. Feeling dazed, Griffin reached down into the water, his fingers outstretched. Once again his skin began tingling with an odd sensation, and, startled, Griffin snatched his hand away. Just before the feeling ebbed completely, he saw a soft glow in the center of the crystals.

Cautiously, Griffin reached down into the water again, oblivious to the fact his sleeve was being drenched. Some memory gnawed at his brain. He was sure that he'd never seen such an amazing gem in his life, and yet—it was somehow familiar.

This time his fingers connected with the tip of one of the crystals, and a jolt of energy coursed through him. A glow appeared inside the crystal, increasing in power as he stared, dry-mouthed and wide-eyed, memory slamming into his mind.

Jamie MacGregor's sword. That's where he'd seen this before. On Griffin and Jix's wedding day.

In the middle of his wedding to Jix, she had refused to repeat the sacred vows. Jamie had rushed to her side after snatching his sword from Red Hugh. They'd stood there with Samantha Riley, holding the sword between them, and the green stone at the base of the hilt—a stone remarkably like the crystal ones he had just found—began to glow. Jix and Jamie and Samantha had all disappeared. Presumably they had gone back to their own time.

Amazing. Could it be? Could these be the same type of stones, and if so, were they responsible for the miraculous trip through time? Griffin's heart began to pound. If he found the key to the seemingly magical stones, he could journey back to the days of King Arthur, to the days of Wallace and Robert the Bruce, or even to the future. If only he could discover how. As a scholar, Griffin found the possibilities fascinating, thrilling. Much more so than any battle he'd ever fought, or any foe he'd ever vanquished. What an adventure it would be to travel to another time! What a wonderful life would be his!

As Griffin's thoughts raced, he realized he'd best stop touching the crystals until he formed a plan. Who knew what power they held?

At that moment the light in the center of the crystal bloomed against the prismlike sides. Griffin blinked. He couldn't move. He couldn't take his hand away. A tremendous energy suddenly engulfed him, pulling him forward, plunging him headfirst into the dark blue-green water.

If only he had asked Jix more questions about her journey through time. If only she and Jamie hadn't gone to their time so quickly, so unexpectedly, perhaps . . .

The world turned emerald green as the water around him began to whirl, surging around his body, pulling him down, sending him into darkness. Griffin spun, trapped, voiceless, frozen, spiraling past eternity, the darkness consuming him, the deep void pulling him down, down, down into a vortex of green.

Chapter Two

Griffin struggled back to consciousness and opened his eyes, fighting for clarity. Cold and darkness encompassed him. He lay floating on his back in icy water, and when he stretched out both hands they collided with equally cold stone and gave him back his memory. He was still in the cave.

Thank God! One moment he'd been fine, the next—the next he'd experienced something that had driven him to the edge of insanity, then pulled him back just in time.

Just in time. That was an ironic statement. He'd half expected to wake up in another time altogether. While he'd momentarily been swept away by the thought of time-travel, his experience in the water had made him simply glad to still be alive. But why was it so dark?

Expelling his pent-up breath, Griffin pulled himself up over the stone edge of the pool and stood, too quickly. Bright spots danced in front of him, and he almost passed out again. Stumbling forward, he fell to his knees beside the water and tried to catch his breath as he gazed down into the depths. His heartbeat quickened. There were no crystals in the water below. No sharp green gemstones gleaming back at him. He glanced up. Where was the moss shining in supernatural iridescence? The cave was dark, cold, and empty.

"Did I imagine it?" he whispered, the sound echoing back to him. He'd heard of men going mad—seeing things that weren't there. His father had once told him he would go daft someday if he continued to bury himself in his books. Had it finally happened?

Panic seized him, along with an uncontrollable need to get out of the darkness. Griffin took a step forward and fell, almost blacking out again. Struggling to his knees, he started crawling toward the light from the opening. It was still daylight when he finally pulled himself through the opening. The sun hung low in the sky above the misty lavender hills, and an eerie twilight cast an equally eerie light over the countryside.

He must have been inside the cave only a few moments, and yet he felt as if he'd been knocked out for an age.

His vision blurred. Irritated, he rubbed at his eyes with the back of one hand as he tried to push his thoughts through the fog surrounding his brain. With great difficulty he rose from the ground, pushing himself to his knees, summoning strength to find his balance.

He stood, unsteadily. He would ride Firestorm to his cottage, rest for a time, and then find another hiding place—a better hiding place. He blinked.

Firestorm was gone.

Griffin felt the panic inching down his veins again as he searched futilely around the cave, stumbled down the hill, and walked halfway across a meadow. His horse was nowhere in sight. Feeling exhausted, he stopped at the edge of a brook, his breath coming in harsh, angry waves as he bent over, leaning his hands on his knees, water dripping from his hair and clothes.

Firestorm never wandered from the place he was left. Never. That meant someone had taken him.

"Hello? May I help you?"

At the sound of the feminine voice, Griffin straightened, narrowing his eyes. The woman stood in silhouette against the Scottish countryside, the sun at her back. As she walked nearer and the darkness faded from her face, Griffin felt the confusion around his mind lift, as if sunlight had suddenly broken through a stormy sky.

Tess Mallory

She wore a scandalously short skirt reaching just below her knees, and a jacket that looked to be made from an extremely bright tartan. She carried a pouch at her side. Soft, light brown hair with curious golden streaks in it danced in waves around her oval face. Real concern lit her pale gray eyes as she gazed at him. What beautiful eyes. What a sweet, bonny lass.

"Are you all right? Should I get you some help?" she asked, her voice strange, yet oddly familiar. She sounded like—Griffin's mouth dropped open. After he'd learned the truth about Jix and Jamie, Jix had dropped her Scottish accent and begun speaking what she referred to as an "American" or sometimes "Texan" accent.

Understanding—like a fist driven into his belly—made Griffin's knees collapse. He sat down hard, staring up at the woman in stunned amazement as realization took him by the throat.

"What—where—what year is this, lass?" he whispered.

Her beautiful eyes widened, and she hurried to his side. "Did you fall into the brook? Did you hit your head?"

"Where am I?" he asked, still feeling dazed.

"A few miles from Craigmoor, and just over the hill from Meadbrooke Manor." Her voice was filled with concern though there was a wary look on her face.

She reached out and touched his temple, her fingers stroking through his hair. Her brows knit together in concern as she examined his forehead, then lowered her gaze to his. All at once he wanted to capture her soothing hand in his, wanted to press his lips to the soft skin. As if she read his thoughts, her eyes widened and she jerked her hand back, then glanced away, her cheeks flush with color.

"I beg your pardon," she said, avoiding his eyes. "Are you hurt?"

There was something he should be remembering, something wrong about her being so near. The bile rushed to his throat and he jumped up, clapping one hand over his mouth. Unfortunately, the woman rose at the same moment and their heads connected with a hard, painful thud.

Black dots danced across his line of vision, and Griffin felt himself falling. The woman fell too, and as their bodies collided, the last thing he remembered was the sensation of her soft, warm flesh touching his.

Chelsea's head throbbed and her chest ached. Her mother had put too many blankets on her during the night. Just because she had the measles didn't mean she had to be smothered to death. She could hardly breathe. The weight of the wool coverings was comfortingly warm, but so heavy, so very heavy and—

She opened her eyes. A man lay on top of her, his face nestled right between her breasts. She opened her mouth to scream, then remembered.

Of course. She was in Scotland. She'd gone for a walk— well, to be honest, it was more than a walk. She'd been trying to escape.

The lunch "date" had been a disaster. From the moment Lord Bothingwort had picked her up in his brand new Jaguar, his disappointment had been evident. Oh, he'd been polite enough, talking to her about the weather, politics, Jamie and Jix. But she'd seen the bored expression in his eyes, and the way his gaze lit up when a beautiful woman walked by their table at the best restaurant in Inverness. Then when his attention returned to her, the boredom, the disdain, would appear.

He'd ended the date as quickly as possible, bringing her back to Meadbrooke Manor, walking her to the door, making his excuses for not coming in for a drink. Then he'd fled in his bright red sports car as if every hound in hell were at his heels.

Chelsea tried to find the courage to walk through that door and face her anxious, smiling friends, but she just couldn't do it. Jix would be sympathetic and disappointed. Sam would be exasperated and frustrated. Knowing that the combination would likely unravel her already frazzled nerves, Chelsea feared she might do the unspeakable— break down in front of them.

So instead she turned away from the huge front door with its bronzed lion knocker and ran in the three-inch spiked heels Sam had insisted upon across the long lawn, across the gravel road, and into the meadow. She had paused long enough to take off her shoes and clutched them to the front of her pseudo-tartan jacket as she ran, her vision clouded by tears, oblivious to the rocks biting into her bare feet.

Maybe if she ran fast enough, far enough, she could get away from the pain and the shame, from the loneliness quickly becoming her constant companion.

Instead, she'd run smack into a strange, astonishingly handsome man in a kilt, his blue eyes dazed, his expression that of one lost. This same man now lay sprawled across her own prostrate body, and she frowned, trying to make her brain work. They'd bumped heads. The collision had made her pass out for a few seconds, and apparently the same thing had happened to him.

The sound of his deep baritone groan made Chelsea blink as her vision cleared and she realized their position was quite a compromising one. She started to push him off, when she caught sight of his face, her breath catching in her throat as she let him fall back against her once again.

He was beautiful.

From his chiseled jaw and sensuous lips to the long, dark lashes lying in crescents on his cheeks, to the dark, arched brows, the long, naturally sun-streaked blond hair, the broad shoulders—he was all man. And all muscle, if the weight of him pressing her down against the ground was any indication.

Tentatively she smoothed her hands over his white shirt. His thick, muscular arms were hard beneath her fingers. A thrill ran through her veins as he shifted, one leg fitting itself between the two of hers. His green plaid kilt hiked up above his thigh, and Chelsea felt her hormones shift from *Slightly Aroused* to *Oh Baby* in a matter of seconds.

He was marvelous.

He was exactly the kind of man who wouldn't look twice at Chelsea Brown.

She shook her head. What was wrong with her? The man was hurt, he'd been disoriented *before* they'd even collided. She had to get him some help, or take him with her to Meadbrooke. But how? Even if she could roll him to one side, she didn't want to leave him out here alone. Getting him to his feet, unassisted, would take more strength than she ever hoped to have. Still, she had to do something. Before her lungs stopped functioning. As much as she enjoyed the feel of his long, hard body against hers, it was time to take action.

Chelsea cradled his head in her hands and tilted his face toward hers. He moaned slightly, his lips parting.

"Hello?" she whispered, her mouth only inches from his. "Can you hear me? Can you—"

His eyes suddenly sprang open and two ice-blue irises gazed at her, confused, wary.

"Where am I? Who are ye? What has happened to me?" He shoved himself upward, hands flat on the ground on either side of her body, his brows darting down in anger.

Chelsea's heart began to pound fearfully as the reality of her situation struck her as forcefully as the man's skull had only moments before. She was out in the middle of nowhere—well, quite a ways from the manor—lying flat on her back, her body held captive by a man who wasn't wearing a stitch of clothing under his kilt.

She cleared her throat. "Get off of me," she said, trying to instill a ring of authority into her tremulous voice.

One hand suddenly encircled her throat, and Chelsea gasped. "Did ye take my horse?" he demanded.

His horse? She shook her head, trembling all over. If Sam were here she'd have already turned the tables on this guy and been standing with her foot on *his* throat. Jix would have convinced him in a matter of minutes that he had stolen *her* horse. But not Chelsea Brown. She stared up at him, speechless, dumbfounded. She was doomed.

He continued to study her until, as if he had come to a decision, his hand relaxed against her skin and, to her astonishment, gently slid up the side of her neck. Their gazes locked, and his handsome face relaxed into a smile. He touched the end of her nose with his index finger.

"My apologies, lass. Of course ye dinna take my horse." With one smooth movement he rolled away from her and balanced on one knee, his voice weary. "Can ye point me in the direction of the castle?"

Chelsea sat up and dragged in a long, deep breath. "The castle?" she asked, trying to regain her wits after the disturbing encounter. Although Scotland was dotted with castles, the closest one was over fifty miles away.

"Aye, aye," he said, his dark brows pressed together, his eyes closed. "Meadbrooke Castle, ye ken? I . . ." He stopped and opened his eyes. "Did ye say somethin' about Meadbrooke Manor before we, er, ran into each other?"

A slight smile curved his mouth, and Chelsea had a sudden, terrible, horrifying urge to kiss him. She clapped one hand over her mouth as if to stop it from happening and nodded silently.

"What did ye mean? Did ye mean the castle?" He moaned again and closed his eyes. "Ye have the head of a bull, lass—did anyone ever tell ye that?"

Chelsea's face burned. She could feel a lump rising on the side of her forehead, and her entire skull ached. The last thing she needed right now was for this absolutely gorgeous man to be comparing her to a bull.

"There is no castle," she said, forcing her voice to be a little more stern. "I can go and bring help from Meadbrooke *Manor,* but that's the best I can do."

He opened his eyes again and blinked at her. "Why do ye sound like that?"

Chelsea's cheeks were scorching. Now he was going to criticize the way she talked? "Like what?" she asked.

"Like Jix . . ." His beautiful blue eyes flickered and his lids began a slow descent. "Ye sound . . . like . . . Jix."

Jix! Then he knew the MacGregors. Of course—he was probably a neighbor who'd fallen off his horse. No doubt she had arrived just in time to slam him in the noggin again! And here she was wasting time, feeling sorry for herself instead of getting him the help he needed. If anything happened to him it would be her fault, and Jix and

Jamie would probably be furious. Or maybe not—she'd never actually seen either of them furious—but in any case, she had to help him. As much as she hated to do it, there was no other choice but to leave the stricken man there and run to Meadbrooke for help.

Chelsea jumped to her feet and stumbled back a few steps, then rushed forward again and fell to her knees.

"Listen!" she shouted at his now ashen face. "I'm going to get you some help, do you hear me? Just lie here and I'll be back soon!"

He groaned, his marvelous mouth falling open. All she had to do was just lean forward a little farther and . . .

Chelsea gulped and scrambled back to her feet. Turning toward Meadbrooke Manor, she broke into a run.

"Griffin, Griffin laddie, do you hear me?" Jamie MacGregor asked.

"It's no use," Jix said with a sigh. "We'd better take him to the hospital. How on earth could this have happened?"

"We can't do that, Jix, he's . . ." Jamie broke off and glanced at the doorway of the guest room where Chelsea stood. He pressed his lips together grimly. "Let's see how he does in the next hour. In the meantime, where's Sam? What good does it do to have a doctor visiting you if she's not around when you need her?"

Chelsea watched the byplay between Jix and Jamie, growing more and more curious. They sat on either side of the bed where their guest lay moaning and incoherent, worry reflected in their faces. Why didn't they take him to Inverness to the hospital? Why in the world would they even hesitate?

"Sam isn't a doctor, yet," Jix reminded her husband as she reached out to brush one long lock of blond hair back from the unconscious man's face.

"Close enough," Jamie argued. "And don't touch him. He might touch ye back."

"Silly," Jix chided. "Griffin wouldn't do that."

"I havena forgotten the two of ye in the garden," Jamie said, his brogue heavy in admonishment. Chelsea's brows rose. She'd been around Jamie long enough to know that when he was upset or concerned his brogue deepened. He turned and frowned at his wife. "Nor that kiss."

Chelsea's mouth dropped open.

"Don't be ridiculous." Jix's face flushed scarlet. She turned away from her husband, and for a moment her startled gaze locked with Chelsea's wide-eyed stare. She hesitated, and then smiled. "Oh, hi, Chel—do you know where Samantha is? Could you find her for us?"

Chelsea closed her mouth. Now, what had that little conversation been referring to? Surely Jix and Griffin hadn't— she didn't let her imagination take her any further. She shrugged one shoulder in response to the question.

"I think she's out riding. Sure, I'll go check."

She practically ran from the room, her thoughts keeping pace with her. Obviously, Griffin was someone Jix and Jamie both knew very well. Or at least Jix knew very well. She shook away the disloyal thoughts that came on the heels of that idea. Taking the broad staircase two steps at a time, she gulped and came to a teetering halt only inches away from Jamie's uncle, Angus.

"Whoa, there, lassie, what's yer rush?" the burly, gray-haired man said, steadying her before she took a headfirst plunge the rest of the way down the stairs. Angus Campbell was a kindly, gruff old man, and Chelsea thoroughly enjoyed their conversations on science and history. He was one of the few people in Scotland she felt completely comfortable around.

"Oh, I'm sorry, Mr. Campbell," she answered breathlessly. "I need to find Samantha."

"Och, the lass is just comin' in the door, and in a fair mood she is, too." He chuckled, running one hand over his grizzled face. "Seems Finn MacCool dumped her on her—"

"Jamie MacGregor!" The shout came from below, and Chelsea flinched. "I want to talk to you about that devil horse!"

"Yes, I see what you mean," Chelsea said to Angus. "I'd better go and calm her."

The old man laughed again and started up the stairs.

"Ye're a braver soul than I, lass. And mind how ye be tearin' around this house. I dinna want the good doctor to have another patient."

"What patient? What is he talking about?" Sam demanded, now a few steps below them. Angus gave Chelsea a wink before hurrying up the stairs and disappearing in the direction of his own room. Chelsea turned to face Samantha.

She stood in her riding clothes, snapping a long quirt against her knee-high boots, fury written on her features, her blond hair disheveled. She looked windblown, tousled, angry, and as always, beautiful. Chelsea fought down a brief familiar surge of jealousy. If Griffin Campbell were awake and standing beside her, he'd probably pounce on Sam before she could take another step.

And Sam would probably pounce right back.

"Chelsea!" Sam's harsh command brought her out of her reverie. "What is going on? It's bad enough that I have to be thrown by that monster of a horse, but now I come back to find that—"

"There's a man hurt upstairs," Chelsea interrupted, unwilling to bear the brunt of Sam's temper alone. "I think Jix and Jamie want you to take a look."

"Hurt? A man? Who?"

"I don't know, but they seem to know him."

"All right." Suddenly Sam was all business. She jerked off her jacket as she hurried up the stairs, handing it to Chelsea hurrying beside her. "Here's what you do—go ask the cook to boil some water, and get some clean cloths ready."

"He's not bleeding," Chelsea said, slightly irritated by Sam's commands. "I think he has a head injury." She rubbed her forehead unconsciously. The gesture brought Sam's attention to the bruise on her forehead, and she stopped in her tracks.

"Are you all right? What happened?" She brushed Chelsea's hair back from her face with a surprisingly gentle touch. "Do you feel okay, Cookie?"

Chelsea felt sudden tears start into her eyes and she

blinked them quickly away. Neither Sam nor Jix had used that silly childhood nickname in years. The fact that Sam's unexpected use of it had touched her—immediately, deeply—embarrassed the life out of her. Exactly how needy had she become?

Apparently, the slip embarrassed Sam too, for she said nothing more but took her friend by the arm and brusquely propelled her toward the open door of the guest room.

"All right!" she announced as she swept into the room, releasing Chelsea and striding toward the bed. "What is going on? Why hasn't Chelsea's bruise been attended to, and why in the world aren't you on the way to the hospital? I think that I—"

Sam stopped dead in her tracks, her blue eyes huge in her suddenly pale face. Chelsea watched, her scientific mind beginning to form an equation. So Sam knew Griffin too. So far, upon their first glimpse of the man, all three—Jix, Jamie, and Sam—had looked as if they'd seen a ghost. Was that it? For some reason had they believed Griffin to be dead?

"Griffin," Sam whispered, standing stock-still. "But how? How in the . . ." She stopped and turned to Jix and Jamie, her eyes still round. "How did he get here?" she asked. "How?"

Jix lifted her shoulders and shook her head helplessly. Jamie just stared at the unconscious man, his brow furrowed with worry.

This was nuts.

"He got here in the SUV, of course," Chelsea said, laughing a little, hoping to defuse the tension in the room. "Jamie went and got him. I found him up by that big hill, south of the manor. He seemed to be sort of . . . I don't know, confused. Then we accidentally bumped heads and—"

Jix was immediately at her side. "Chel, you didn't tell me you were hurt, too!" she scolded. "Oh my gosh, look at that bump!"

Chelsea felt a warm surge of appreciation for her

friend's kindness, but wasn't about to let her change the subject.

"I'm okay." She paused, glancing first at Jix and then at Sam. "Um, I'm assuming that all three of you know this guy. Is he . . . I mean . . . he didn't escape from an asylum, did he?"

"An asylum?" Sam laughed shortly. "Griffin Campbell is probably one of the sanest men I ever met. Why would you think that?"

"Well, look at how he's dressed—and when I first saw him, he asked what year it was." Chelsea watched their faces carefully.

"A lot of men wear kilts in Scotland, lass," Jamie said. " 'Tisn't unusual."

"But most men don't go around with swords strapped to their sides, do they? Not even in Scotland." She gestured to the long-hilted claymore lying on the floor beside the bed.

Jix looked at Jamie, Jamie looked at Sam, Sam looked back at Jix. Chelsea felt a sudden rush of anger. Something was going on. They were deliberately keeping some secret from her, something they didn't trust her to know. *Again.*

"Is something wrong?" she asked, pressing her luck. "Where is he—"

"You know, I think what he really needs is some rest," Sam said, spinning around and grabbing Chelsea by the arm. "I need to give him a complete examination, and you shouldn't be in here for that."

"What about Jix and Jamie?" Chelsea said, digging her heels in at the door just before Sam shoved her out into the hall. "Aren't they coming?"

Jix rose, a little too quickly. "Oh, of course. Let's get out of here, Jamie, and let Sam look at his injuries."

She hurried toward the door and exchanged another covert glance with Samantha. "Let me know if you need anything." She paused, biting her lower lip before rushing on, "And be sure to come get us if he regains consciousness." She put her hands on Chelsea's shoulders and guided her out of the room.

Chelsea didn't resist. But as Sam closed the door behind them, she made up her mind. For once she wasn't going to be left out of one of the Daring Duo's adventures.

Chapter Three

Silence cloaked the manor at midnight. Chelsea slipped out of her room and stood in the hallway shivering in spite of her flannel gown and thick flannel robe. Although the house had been recently fitted for central heat, the Scottish cold still seeped through the walls and into her bones, even in the daytime. At night she froze, in spite of the fireplace in her room. She hadn't told her hosts because she didn't want them to think her ungracious, but for a South Central Texas girl, Scotland was a little hard to take at times. She wondered absently how Jix had managed to adapt so well.

Chelsea wandered quietly down the corridor. She didn't know what had propelled her out of bed in the middle of the night. She'd retired early and once under the covers, she'd stared at the ceiling for an hour or more, trying to figure out the mystery surrounding Griffin Campbell, her imagination running wild. Was he a spy? Jamie had a lot of strange friends in the law enforcement business. Chelsea had met a few of them at the couple's wedding.

She frowned. Or was Griffin from the other end of the spectrum? Was he a criminal? Someone Jamie had put in jail? That would explain why they were so startled, and not exactly happy to see him.

But, no, she couldn't imagine Jamie MacGregor allowing

31

a man like that to remain under his roof even for a night, even if he was injured. Jamie would never expose Jix, or for that matter, any of them, to danger.

Then what? Maybe Griffin was in the witness protection plan—did Scotland have such a thing? Suddenly she knew she had to find out. Jix was a night owl, maybe she was still up. She and Sam often sat up in the library downstairs laughing and talking. They never seemed to consider that Chelsea might enjoy sitting up with them, too.

Ignoring the pang the thought gave her, she hurried down the icy stone hallway, wishing she'd brought a flashlight. Maybe she could convince Jix that she could trust her with Griffin's story.

Chelsea jumped as a door downstairs slammed shut. If she wasn't careful, she'd start imagining all sorts of ghouls and ghosties in the shadows. For a scientist, she had to admit to being something of a wimp.

She ground her teeth together and walked a little faster. Her parents were still constantly amazed at the sentimental, timid, and yes, creative attributes their only daughter exhibited from time to time. In their world, things were black and white. Fear was a relative term. If her parents were here right now, her mother would be pointing out the strength of the stone walls, and her father would be calculating how far this distant point in the Highlands was from the nearest star.

All Chelsea could think about was a movie she'd seen on television the night before called *The Screaming Skull*.

A noise sounded behind her.

Chelsea froze. Something like a groan, or the cry of a hurt animal—*or maybe the scream of a skull,* her overactive imagination whispered—echoed down the corridor. She flattened herself against the wall, listening fearfully while her heart pounded in a staccato rhythm.

There it was again.

Maybe a cat or a puppy had been accidentally shut inside a room. She took a tentative step toward the noise, and another. It didn't really sound like an animal, now that she thought about it.

Another groan, a little louder. She walked a little faster. Her heart pounded.

No, this sounded like . . . a man.

A sense of relief flooded over her. How silly. Of course. Griffin's room was just a few doors down the hall. He probably needed some pain medication. She'd just slip inside and—

She stopped and glanced down at herself. While she was clad in flannel from neck to ankles, she was still in night-clothes. Immediately her new constant habit of comparing herself to Jix and Samantha reared its ugly head. Neither of her friends would let some out-of-date maidenly modesty keep them from helping someone in need—or pass up an opportunity to flirt with a hunk like Griffin Campbell. Really, she was hopeless.

The groan came again.

She should go and get Jix. Yes, that was the thing to do. She turned away, and suddenly the groan changed to an outright cry for help.

"Laddies! Dinna fall back!" The shout echoed down the hallway. "Forward! *Criadgh mor!*"

Without further hesitation, Chelsea ran the last few steps down the hall to Griffin's room and threw open the door. She slipped inside, her eyes adjusting to the moonlight seeping through the long casement windows. The light from the banked fire in the fireplace illuminated the form of Griffin Campbell as he thrashed back and forth in his sleep.

She moved quickly to the carved wooden bed and sank down beside him. "Griffin," she said, trying to sound soothing. "It's all right. Wake up—you're dreaming."

The man continued to fling himself back and forth until at last Chelsea ventured to place her hands on his arms and lean toward him.

"Griffin," she said a little more forcefully, her fingers tightening around his huge biceps. "Griffin, wake up!"

He opened his eyes, and two glazed blue eyes filled with panic stared back at her. Then his expression softened and he reached for her. Before she could protest, the man had pulled her down to him, flipped her to one side, and covered her mouth with his.

Now it was Chelsea's turn to groan. His tongue delved between her lips, hot, filling her with his need, his passion, his hands moving over her body, his warmth soaking into her like rain into the hard, dusty ground.

"Wait," she whispered, her voice sounding dishonest even to herself. She didn't want him to wait. She didn't want him to stop. His mouth found her throat, slid down to the hollow, then lower. When he cupped her breast she finally came to her senses and with a gasp, sat up, pushing him away.

Chelsea flung herself out of the bed, running her hand through her hair, aghast at her behavior. What was wrong with her? She'd barely met this man and already had been under his body twice in the same day.

"Lass?" Griffin's deep voice sent a new thrill through her. She couldn't speak. "Och," he said, sounding dazed. "I was dreamin'. There was a great dragon tryin' to attack my castle and 'twas gettin' the best of me and then . . ." He cleared his throat. "I dinna hurt ye?"

"I'm fine," Chelsea managed to choke out. "Uh, can I get you anything?"

"Could ye bring me a wee bit of water?"

"Of course." Chelsea hurried over to a table in front of the broad bay window. A pitcher of water sat on a tray, along with a tall glass. She poured the glass full and carried it carefully over to him. When she neared the bed she reached down and snapped on the lamp beside him.

Griffin jumped back, startled, staring first at the lamp, then back at her. She stared too. He had propped himself up against two pillows and sat bare to the waist. At least to the waist. Chelsea ran her tongue across her lips. His chest was broad and muscled, a soft brushing of golden hair across it, tapering downward over his hard, flat stomach to his narrow waist and—

"How did ye do that?" he said, his voice hushed.

Chelsea saw his clenched hands on top of the quilted coverlet and realized he was still in a near state of panic.

"It's all right." She ignored his nonsensical question and

handed him the glass of water. His hand trembled as he took it from her. "You've been asleep," she said, honestly concerned. "I think you must have fallen off your horse, and then when you and I bumped heads, it aggravated your injury."

"Fallen off my horse?" The disbelief in his voice was evident. "I've ne'er fallen off my horse in my life!" he said disdainfully. He turned his attention back to the lamp. "Could ye—could ye make it dark again, lass?"

Chelsea nodded and turned the lamp off. She heard his sigh of relief and watched him take a deep drink of the water as the flickering fire painted his face with a warm glow. He handed her the glass and closed his eyes, leaning back against the pillows.

"This is just a vast bad dream," he said under his breath. "I will awaken in the morn, and all will be as it should be."

Chelsea eased herself to sit down beside him. His eyes flew open, and the two burning blue orbs stared back at her.

"Jix and Jamie were very concerned about you," she told him. "They'll be so happy to hear that you've regained consciousness."

"Jix and Jamie?" His dark brows darted upward. "They're here? Now?"

"Yes, they're asleep but—"

He threw back the covers and climbed out of the bed on the side opposite Chelsea. Her mouth dropped open as he stood, naked and glorious, dazed and confused. The firelight cast golden shadows across his muscled skin, carving the hard planes into stark relief. Chelsea drew in a sharp breath, then blushed and grabbed a blanket from the foot of the bed. She circled around, trying to keep her gaze on his face.

Griffin didn't even seem to realize he was as bare as the day he was born, or else didn't care. Chelsea held the blanket up in front of her, neck high.

"Here—you mustn't be running around like that," she said, aghast at the voice in her head tempting her to take another small peek now that she was close to him. She ignored the wicked voice and wrapped the quilt around

35

his middle. He made no move to help secure it. He simply continued to stare down at her. Then his arms slipped around her waist.

Chelsea blinked as she realized he must have taken the gesture to cover him as an invitation to continue where they'd left off before. She desperately tried to clasp the ends of the blanket together at his back, but couldn't seem to make the tuck in the material hold. She gasped as his hands spread across her back and pressed her firmly against him.

He was big and warm, and his chest felt smooth under her cheek. She accidentally brushed her mouth against his skin as he held her, and she heard his own quick intake of breath.

"Och, lass," he said softly against her hair, "ye are like the sweetness of a summer's day." He slid his hands upward to her shoulders, his thumbs tracing circles through the thickness of her flannel robe. He skimmed his fingers higher, trailing them along the side of her neck to her face. He leaned toward her, and Chelsea lifted her face to him, eyes wide open, lips half parted. She could feel him trembling, and that sent a new surge of unfamiliar desire through her. That a man as handsome as Griffin might feel a little nervous, a trifle hesitant, made her feel suddenly strong.

His mouth hovered above hers for what seemed like forever, and Chelsea closed her eyes, waiting for his kiss. And waited.

And waited.

She opened her eyes, dreading the rejection she knew she'd see in his gaze. Instead he looked stunned, bewildered. He dropped his hands from her shoulders and took a few steps away from her, clutching the quilt around his middle, his face pale.

"Och, lass, forgive me. I dinna know what I'm doin'."

"I don't know about that," Chelsea said, drawing a ragged breath and taking a step toward him. "You seem to know quite a bit about what you were doing." Her skin was on fire, and she ached for him to hold her again. A moment of attention from such a handsome man had unbalanced her—that was the only explanation for her sudden uninhibited behavior.

He glanced back at her, his eyes amber in the firelight.

"Aye," he said, "though I'm a bit out of practice. 'Tis been a wee bit since I touched a woman." His voice was flat, suddenly listless.

"How long?" Chelsea heard her blunt words and was shocked at her lack of tact. "I mean—"

"If Jix and Jamie are here, then I'd say it's been about four hundred years." His mouth quirked up at one corner, and the rueful smile made his handsome face even more incredible.

Then his words registered. "Four hundred years?" Chelsea repeated the words, an uneasiness slipping over her. "What do you mean?" It was probably a joke. Jix and Sam were always saying she needed to cultivate a better sense of humor.

His deep, answering chuckle made her breath catch in her throat as he turned and walked back to her.

"Have they no' told ye about me?" he asked softly. "Have they no' told ye about our adventures together?"

Light shattered the darkness, and Chelsea whirled to find Jix and Jamie and Sam all standing just inside the doorway. Jamie looked grim as he lowered his hand from the light switch. Jix seemed uncertain, and Sam, as usual, completely exasperated.

"No, Griffin," Jamie said, his voice stern. "We havena told Chelsea." His mouth tightened. "And neither will ye."

"Now wait just a minute!" Chelsea said. "Why not?"

"What are you doing in here in the first place?" Sam asked pointedly.

Chelsea felt the heat rising to her face. She opened her mouth and closed it several times, but couldn't seem to speak.

"I cried out in my sleep," Griffin said, coming up behind her, the blanket now tucked neatly around his waist. "The lass heard and came inside to help me." He smiled down at her, and Chelsea's heart flipped over. "I was verra grateful."

Tess Mallory

"I'll just bet," Sam muttered. "Come on, Chelsea, I'll walk you back to your room."

"But I—" Chelsea protested, only to be cut off by Jamie.

"Aye, lass," he said. "Griffin needs his rest, and we can sort all this out in the morning."

"But I wanted to—" Chelsea tried again, but Jix jumped in.

"Hey, kiddo, let's you and me and Sam have some hot chocolate downstairs. I have something to tell the two of you anyway, and it might as well be tonight."

A look passed between Jix and Jamie, and Chelsea sighed. If she'd known there was going to be this much cloak-and-dagger stuff on her trip, she'd have packed her magnifying glass and Nancy Drew decoder ring.

Sam tugged on her arm. "Yeah, hot chocolate sounds good. Let's go, Cookie."

Chelsea had little choice in the matter. It was either be dragged along with her two best friends or cause a scene. And Chelsea Brown had never caused a scene in her life. She wasn't going to start now just because some handsome, blue-eyed, blond-haired Scottish warrior had smiled at her. No way.

"Fine," she said. She looked back at Griffin. "Good night, Griffin. I hope you feel better."

"Good night, lass," he said, "and thank ye for comin' to my rescue."

A thrill ran up the back of her neck, and she couldn't help smiling back at him.

"Any time," she said. She turned and led the way out of the room while an astonished Jix and Sam followed close behind her.

"So it's true, then?" Griffin said as soon as the door closed behind the women. "I've traveled through time."

Jamie gave him a long, silent look and nodded. "Aye. Can we sit down? There's much to discuss." He gestured to a small table flanked by two chairs in a corner of the room. Griffin crossed and took a seat, watching the other man warily.

Jamie MacGregor had changed. His hair was no longer

long and wild and unruly, but cropped short to the base of his neck. But there was more to it than that. His clothing was different. He wore some kind of blue cloth trews and a soft green shirt with uniform white buttons down the front that Griffin instantly coveted. Still, he couldn't quite put his finger on the real difference until he glanced down at his own grubby hands and realized the other man was extraordinarily clean.

"Ye're verra clean," he said without thinking.

Jamie blinked at his remark, then laughed. "Aye, that I am. And ye'll soon be just as clean if my Jix has anything to say about it. We've hot and cold running water here, ye ken."

Griffin's mouth dropped open. "Hot and cold running . . . ye dinna mean to say that it comes inside to ye, in the castle? That is, the manor?" He frowned. There wasn't any castle. What had happened to it? He took a deep breath. He hoped there would be time to ask all the questions piling up in his mind.

Jamie nodded. "I'll show ye in the morning. Ye can have a nice hot shower."

"Shower?"

Jamie waved his questions away with one hand. "Later, lad. First we have to get a few things straight. No one knows about our trip through time, and we'd like to keep it that way."

Griffin released his breath thoughtfully. "Aye, I can understand why, but I thought the girl—what was her name?"

"Chelsea."

"I thought she was one of yer friends."

"Aye, but she doesn't know, and we don't want her to know."

"Why not?"

Jamie cleared his throat and frowned. "It's hard to explain. Let's just say that she's rather scientifically minded and not inclined to flights of fancy. She's a practical woman, and I doubt she'd believe us anyway. Jix made me promise not to tell her, and I plan to keep that promise." He looked at Griffin sternly. "And I plan to make sure ye keep it as well."

39

"Aye, I willna tell her if you dinna want me to do so."

Jamie stood and crossed to the window, his hands clasped behind him. He stared out into the darkness for a moment, then turned back to the other man.

"First, maybe ye'd better tell me how ye got here in the first place, then we'll come up with a story explaining who ye are, to tell Chelsea and anyone else ye may encounter while ye're here." Jamie frowned slightly. "I canna understand how this happened."

Griffin pressed his lips together. It was obvious that his presence here made Jamie MacGregor uncomfortable. He must tread lightly if he hoped to receive any help from his host. He had to figure out how to go back to his own time, and Jamie MacGregor was the only possible answer to that problem.

"I'll tell ye how it came about, and believe me, lad," he said, standing and clapping Jamie on the shoulder, "I'm just as anxious as ye are to find my way back to where I belong."

"All right, we've had our hot chocolate," Chelsea said crossly, folding her arms over her chest. She was sleepy, overstimulated—boy, that was an understatement—and feeling more and more angry over the way her friends continued to keep her in the dark about things. And now to top everything off, Jix had another secret. "So what's your big news, Jix?"

Jix lowered her mug and smiled, chocolate rimming her mouth.

"C'mon, c'mon, what gives?" Sam insisted.

"You mean you don't know either?" Chelsea was surprised. Jix always told Sam everything, usually before she ever got around to telling her second-best friend. A shadow touched her heart as she realized that was exactly how she always felt with Sam and Jix—second best.

Sam shook her head. "I haven't a clue. Tell us, Jix, so we can go to bed."

"Okay." Jix licked the chocolate from her lips. "You both think we asked you here for our first-year anniversary party, right?" They both nodded. "Well . . ."

"Jessica Isobel Xavier Ferguson MacGregor," Sam said, "if you don't tell us—"

"Okay, okay!" Jix paused and bit her lower lip before hurrying on. "Well, you remember that lesson back in junior high, you know, in health class—the one about the birds and the bees?"

Chelsea raised both brows. Sam frowned. In unison they said, "Huh?"

"You know"—a sly smile played around Jix's lips—"how the birds pollinate the flowers and the birds lay their eggs and how when a man and woman fall in love and the little sperm guys swim up to meet the little egg and—"

Sam and Chelsea squealed at the same time and fell on Jix's neck, laughing and hugging and jumping up and down with joy.

"I can't believe it—why didn't you tell us?" Chelsea said, so happy she wanted to cry.

"I just did!" Jix laughed, throwing her arms around both of them. "I'm two months pregnant! And I have a really big favor to ask the two of you." She sobered abruptly, an anxious look crossing her face. "Will you stay with me until the baby is born?"

Griffin and Jamie talked until the wee hours of the morning, and after the lord of the manor went to his own room, the Scot went back to bed and lay awake, staring at the ceiling for many hours more.

According to Jamie, it was the year 2003. Almost four hundred years past Griffin's own time. His father was dead. Maigrey MacGregor was dead. Everyone who'd ever meant a thing to him was dead. No, that wasn't entirely true. Jix Ferguson was alive and well from the looks of her, and she had meant a great deal to him at one time.

Better not think about that. Jix belonged to Jamie MacGregor, and there was no place for him in her life except as a friend. And that was as it should be. Samantha was the same as he remembered, arrogant and confrontational. Then there was that other woman—what was her name? Chelsea.

It sounded like a song. She intrigued him like no woman

in his century ever had. Sweet, simple, beautiful, yet intelligence shone in her shy gray eyes. He smiled. How he would love to teach her a thing or two. His smile faded. How he would love to teach any woman a thing or two. Or let her teach him!

His only instruction so far in the art of love had been at Jix's School of Squash. He grimaced at the memory of the makeshift female Jix had devised during her visit to his time. She had rigged the life-sized doll using available vegetables for various body parts, to teach him how to touch a woman without losing either his wits or his supper. It hadn't worked.

Of course, for a moment tonight he'd thought he might actually be able to kiss Chelsea without something terrible happening. The feeling had lingered until he'd stood with the blanket around his waist, holding her in his arms. That was when the trembling had begun, and he'd had to release her before he disgraced himself.

Wishful thinking. He was doomed to be alone. Resolutely, Griffin turned his thoughts back to his conversation with MacGregor. He'd explained about the cave of crystals, how they'd reminded him of the stone in MacGregor's sword, and how he'd been thinking of Jix and Jamie when he'd been pulled into the water and consumed by darkness.

He closed his eyes. He'd best get to sleep. Jamie had suggested that perhaps Griffin had been so disoriented after his trip through time that he'd imagined the crystals were no longer there. Tomorrow they would go back to the mysterious cave.

At the moment there was a more urgent matter that needed his attention. A matter that had been growing in intensity throughout the night. A matter that could no longer be ignored.

Though his head still throbbed, he managed to slide out of bed and stand without becoming the least bit dizzy. Encouraged, Griffin decided he felt well enough to get dressed. Pulling on his plaid and his shirt, he buckled his sword around his waist and headed out the door in search of a place to relieve himself.

Highland Fling

*   *   *

Chelsea lay in bed staring out the window as the first faint blush of dawn touched the sky. She hadn't been able to go to sleep after Jix and Sam had bade her good night and headed to their own rooms.

She felt inexplicably depressed, and was ashamed for her selfish emotions at this happy, happy time in Jix and Jamie's lives. And yet . . .

She was lonely.

Frustrated, Chelsea turned over and pounded her pillow, angry about her melancholy thoughts. Surely she hadn't become one of those women who believed her life wasn't complete without a man. After all, she'd been lonely all her life. So what else was new?

Growing up with two scientists for parents had been an experience that was hard to explain to normal people. Not that her parents weren't wonderful. They were. Together they had made great strides in research that had aided the fight against a variety of deadly diseases. They were two of the most focused, dedicated, driven people Chelsea had ever known. Their work was their lives, but as a result, their daughter had always occupied second place.

Hot tears burned against her eyelids, and she wiped the moisture away before it could make its way down her cheeks.

Silly sentimental tripe, she thought brusquely. *I'm not a child and there's no reason to act like one.*

After all, she was a scientist too. She'd graduated at the top of her class from the University of Texas with a degree in physics and had been offered a full scholarship to MIT where she'd obtained her master's. She'd returned to UT to work on her doctorate and follow in her parents' footsteps.

Why, then, did Jix's invitation to stay until her baby was born seem so tempting? Maybe because during the short time Jix had been mistress of Meadbrooke Manor she had made it more of a home than Chelsea's modest one-bedroom apartment in Austin had ever been.

Chelsea sat up. A sliver of the sun, as yellow as a fresh

egg yolk, glimmered above the distant Scottish hills. What if she stayed?

Jix and Sam were her best friends. The only reason to return to Austin was to go back to school, and surely she had earned a semester off. Her parents, though unemotional and distant, had provided amply for their daughter, setting up a trust fund for her the day she was born. When she turned twenty-one, she'd come into a nice little nest egg. Why not relax for a while, stay with Jix, and enjoy Scotland?

And Griffin Campbell? a knowing voice inside her head asked.

Even in the cold morning air, Chelsea felt her cheeks burning. Maybe she'd devote her life to finding a cure for the accursed affliction of blushing! Thank goodness no one could hear her thoughts. It was ridiculous to even think that a man like Griffin Campbell could be remotely interested in her.

She flung her legs over the side of the huge four-poster bed and, shivering slightly, hurried over to the small fireplace. She stirred the banked embers, and soon a roaring fire lit the room. Chelsea sighed in contentment. Yes, there were worse things than a summer spent in Scotland.

With Griffin Campbell.

"Oh, stop it," she said aloud in a scathing voice. "The man is gorgeous. He'll never look at you twice!" She moved back to the window, hugging herself. Of course, just a few short hours ago Griffin Campbell had almost kissed her. Hadn't he? But he'd had a head injury and had probably been confused.

She made a face. That figured. It would take a concussion to cause a man who looked like that to make a pass at a woman who looked like her.

Chelsea turned away from the rising sun and stopped in front of the antique dresser with its large mirror.

Her reflection stared back at her, and for a moment, one wistful moment, Chelsea thought that perhaps she wasn't so bad-looking. Her face was oval, not a bad shape. Her light brown brows had a natural arch to them, and Sam had insisted on plucking them during the makeover.

Her eyes were large, her lashes dark and long, her nose nondescript. Her mouth was a trifle too large, and she thought the feature overpowered the rest of her face. Before going to bed she'd showered, and the bright gold in her hair had toned down to a more muted shade that was actually attractive.

All right, she decided, *I'm not exactly homely. I'm just plain. Like a little brown mouse. And men like Griffin Campbell don't go for mice. They go for foxes like Jix, or tigers like Sam.*

Using a word she had forgotten she even knew, Chelsea turned away from the mirror, fighting back tears. She refused to act this way! She refused to fall prey to thinking her worth was dependent on her looks! She knew better, and yet here she was, mooning over a man she'd scarcely met, a man she knew nothing about, a man who had some kind of mystery surrounding him. Here she was worrying that she wasn't pretty enough for him. Shades of junior high school.

Mystery. Maybe that was it. Maybe it was the mystery that attracted her.

"Sure, that's it," she said aloud. "It couldn't be the incredibly muscular chest, the blond hair or those piercing blue eyes, or those arms . . ." She closed her eyes, remembering the feel of his arms around her, the warmth of his skin against hers. Had he thought about her after she left? Had he lain in bed and imagined what might have happened if Jamie and Jix and Sam hadn't interrupted them?

Of course not.

With a sigh, Chelsea pushed the foolish thoughts away and opened the door to her wardrobe. She pulled out a dark brown dress and threw it on the bed. It was just right for a plain little mouse like her.

She dressed and slipped out into the corridor, surprised to find the hallway still dark and unoccupied. Apparently, no one else was awake yet. She hesitated, wondering if perhaps she'd better go back to her room and wait to be summoned for breakfast. But she hated to be alone any longer with her thoughts.

For the first time, perhaps in her life, she wished for the mindless distraction of television to shift her thoughts into

45

neutral and stop her obsession with Griffin Campbell. She'd been raised to view the device as a sinful waste of time, and as a result had scarcely ever watched any programs, not even educational TV.

But lately, listening to Jix and Sam discuss their favorite television shows and movies, she wondered if this wasn't just one more thing that made her different from other women and kept her feeling like an outsider. Maybe Jix and Sam never asked her to sit up with them at night because she never had anything to say outside of discussing the latest scientific discoveries and theories.

As she headed downstairs, the clouds of melancholy threatened to gather again, and Chelsea determinedly pushed the depression away. All right, then, if she wanted to watch television, there was certainly no one here to stop her! Maybe downstairs in the library she'd find a TV. Or in the study. Or why not just explore? Jix and Jamie wouldn't care if she gave herself the unguided tour.

One thing was for sure: If she stayed downstairs she wouldn't be tempted to go back into Griffin's bedroom on some silly pretext like one of the twenty or so scenarios she'd come up with while lying in bed staring at the ceiling.

Suddenly from behind a door she heard the unmistakable sounds of a television or radio. Relieved to find a diversion for her ridiculous thoughts, she made a beeline for the room and opened the door. Sure enough, there was a beautiful big-screen television set. At the moment a western was on, complete with the sound of rifles firing and Indians whooping their war cries.

"Hello?" she called. "Jix? I wondered if I could—"

Her words were cut short as a hard, rough hand clamped over her mouth and someone grabbed her around the waist. Before she could react, she was dragged down to the floor, pressed tightly against a very hard and masculine body. A very familiar hard and masculine body.

"Whist, lass," Griffin Campbell's voice whispered, his mouth warm against her ear. "Stay down! I dinna ken how yon barbarians got inside the wee box, but they willna leave it alive!"

Chapter Four

Griffin disentangled himself from the woman and crouched behind the unusual fabric-covered settee. Cautiously he looked over the pale material at the devil box facing him. Tiny little barbarians on horseback were screaming and yelling as they were chased by other men dressed in big hats and strange clothing.

He'd awakened early and dressed, then set out to explore his new surroundings. The manor house was huge and well appointed, richly furnished with belongings that both amazed and delighted him—until he stumbled across this small room and its horror. When the woman had walked in, he'd known he had to defend her. How on earth had the barbarians gotten into Jamie MacGregor's palatial home? And more importantly, could they get out of the box in which they were encased?

"Thank God they're fairly small," Griffin whispered to the woman lying beside him. She groaned and tried to move to her knees. Gently he shoved her back down to a prone position and patted her head. "Stay down, lass. I'll save ye."

He slid his sword from the scabbard at his waist, and the woman gasped. He sprang to his feet and with claymore in both hands, plunged over the fabric settee to roll across the softness and land on the floor on one knee, his sword

47

extended. The woman screamed from behind him just as he lunged forward and pierced one of the small barbarians.

Griffin blinked. Instead of the man giving up a death cry and falling to the ground, what looked to be a large rip appeared in and extended through the length of the man's body. No blood followed even though the tear gaped open.

"Please stop!" The woman cried. She stood beside him now, twisting her hands, her gray eyes filled with concern.

"Stay back, lass," he ordered. The man in the box was still moving, and oddly enough, the tear seemed to shift as he walked forward. Confused, Griffin lunged again. This time his sword connected with something hard—no doubt the innards of a barbarian—and he twisted the blade. The woman screamed again as a loud "pop" resounded through the room and the wild men disappeared.

Griffin stepped back, dumbfounded. "Where did they go?" he asked, glancing down at the woman. She was a bonny little thing, tiny compared to his brawn and breadth. Thank God he'd been there to rescue her. Or had he simply set the angry hordes free? He looked around anxiously. They were nowhere to be seen.

"Did they escape?" he demanded, pulling the sword from the guts of the box and sweeping it around, neatly slicing a long gash in the front of the settee just as Jix and Jamie rushed into the room.

"What in the . . ." Jamie slid to a stop, his jaw dropping as he saw the smoking box. Jix collided into his back, righted herself, and leaned around him for her own view. Her mouth fell open and her green gaze darted from the destruction to Griffin and back again.

"I dinna think they can have gotten far," Griffin began, then stopped as he realized his hosts stood staring at the demon box, looking shocked and upset. He had a sudden sinking feeling.

"I dinna mean . . ." he said, and then paused, gathering his thoughts. "Ye see there were . . ." He gestured with the sword toward the box, and Jix's eyes widened at the sight of his claymore. He sheathed it and tried again. "There were wee barbarians attackin' us."

"What did you do to my television?" Jamie said, apparently regaining his voice. He moved toward the destruction of the box, spreading his hands apart in obvious dismay.

Griffin drew in a sharp breath. "Yer tellie-vision? Och, I dinna ken wee tellie-visions. I dinna know they had such things in Scotland!"

Jamie sank down on the settee, leaning his head on his hands. "And today was the big game."

"Game?" Griffin glanced at Jix. A giggle escaped her, and he frowned. He'd gotten to know Jix well enough in his own time to recognize when she was amused. Right now the redhead was smiling so broadly she looked fair about to split in two.

"It's all right," she said, crossing to Griffin's side and taking him by the arm.

"No, it's bloody well not all right," Jamie fumed. Griffin shifted uncomfortably as his host glared at the long gash in the settee. "And we just had this couch reupholstered."

"Chelsea, why didn't you stop him?" Jix asked.

The woman—aye, Chelsea was her name, soft and sweet like the lass herself—lifted her shoulders in a helpless shrug, and Griffin's sense of chivalry rose with them.

"It wasna her fault," he said, feeling less sure of himself than he had in his entire life as Jix led him out of the room. "I—I'm sorry, Jamie MacGregor," he called over his shoulder to Jamie, still staring at the ripped furniture. "I'll repair it, I promise—and I'll find the wee laddies and put them back in the box if ye want!"

"It's all right, Griffin," Jix repeated, patting his arm and pulling him along. "You couldn't have known."

Dazed, Griffin tried to understand her meaning. "I couldna have known what, lass?" She led him into a bright and sunny room. The walls were a pale cream color with cheerful yellow and red flowers painted all over them. In the center of the room stood a large wooden block, as high as Jix's waist. In the middle of that was a shiny silver tube, curving up and over an equally shiny silver basin. On each side of the tube were silver knobs.

He paused to examine the flowers, amazed to find they were all exactly the same.

"It must've cost ye a pretty penny to have these drawn and colored on yer walls," he noted.

"Griffin," Jix said as she released him and turned, hands on her hips, her head tilted at an all-too-familiar angle. "You must realize that you are not in your time anymore." She glanced behind him and lowered her voice. "You're in the twenty-first century now, and trust me—we don't keep miniature barbarians in boxes in our home."

"But—" he started to protest, gesturing toward the other room with one hand. Jix took the opportunity to step over and grab the hilt of his sword. His hand closed over hers, and he glared down at her. She grinned up at him.

"Give it up, laddie," she said. Griffin considered refusing, but after all, she was his friend and it was her home. He gently took her hand from the hilt.

"I won't take it out again," he said. "Ye have my word."

"Unless there are wee barbarians loose in the house," she said, amusement coloring her voice.

"But . . ." Griffin released his pent-up breath and shrugged, feeling helpless. "I dinna understand."

Jix reached up and patted his face. "It's all right. I'll explain it to you. In the meantime, you have to remember that things are different here. Remember when I first appeared in 1605? No, of course you don't, because you thought I was Maigrey at the time." She paused, a thoughtful look on her face. "Well, take it from me, you can't just travel through time and adjust all at once. It takes a while to understand how things work and what you should and shouldn't do." She cocked her chin up at him. "I mean, face it, Griffin, you've journeyed four hundred years into the future. You can't just jump in with both feet!"

"Four hundred years into the future?" a feminine voice squeaked from behind them.

Jix closed her eyes. "Oops."

Griffin turned to find the bonny Chelsea staring at the two of them, her pink lips pressed together tightly.

Jix took a step toward her. "Hi, Chelsea, what's up?" she

asked brightly. Griffin had to smile. Leave it to Jix to pretend nothing at all had happened.

But Chelsea didn't seem to be having any of her friend's usual chicanery. Her voice was soft and sad. "I knew when you got back last year that something strange had happened to all of you, but you didn't trust me." She shook her head, looking stunned. "You and Samantha and Jamie all had this incredible adventure through time and you didn't trust me enough to tell me."

Jix laughed but the sound was hollow and insincere. "Adventure through time? Chelsea, what are you talking about?"

The hurt in Chelsea's eyes intensified, and Griffin almost crossed the room to comfort her. After all, she had come to his aid during the night when he cried out. A picture of the woman sitting on his bed, in his arms, flashed through his mind. He'd been groggy with sleep. Had he kissed her? How was that possible? He looked at her with new eyes. She looked away, her lower lip trembling.

Impossible, Griffin thought. *If I had kissed her I would remember growing ill, wouldn't I?*

"I thought you were my friend, Jix," Chelsea said, her gray eyes filled with accusation. "I've always known that you were closer to Samantha than you were to me, but I never thought you didn't trust me." She spun on her heel and walked out of the room.

Jix moaned and slapped one hand against her forehead. "I'm such an idiot!" she declared and started after the woman. She reached the door and turned back, rushing to Griffin and grabbing him by the hand. "Come on," she said.

"Where are we going, lass?" Griffin asked, resisting her urgent pull.

"To save a friendship."

Chelsea ran up the two flights of stairs to her bedroom and burst through the doorway, tears flooding down her cheeks. She slammed the heavy door and tried to pull her rampaging emotions under control before she threw herself across the wide bed and wept like a petulant fourteen-year-old. Taking a deep breath, she forced herself to walk slowly across the room and sit down in the brocade-upholstered easy chair near the set of long windows in her room. She stared out at the Scottish countryside with unseeing eyes.

What a dummy she was to have said such a thing to Jix! Why had she reacted so emotionally? It was Jix's business if she and Jamie and Samantha had traveled through time and left her out of it, not even bothering to tell the tale of their adventure. She had no right to—

She stopped her mental tirade as the truth of the situation sank past the hurt and into her brain. Traveled through time? *Traveled through time!*

Chelsea jumped up and crossed the room to the ornate cherry wood wardrobe in which she'd stashed all of her clothes and her carry-on bag after arriving at the manor. She opened one of the double cabinet doors and reached down for the black satchel bag containing her computer. In a matter of minutes she had the laptop on and her latest scientific paper displayed on the screen, the title in bold-face lettering.

Time Travel: Probing the Possibilities of the Impossible.

Chelsea's gaze flickered over the familiar words below the heading. She'd spent the last three months on the dissertation, planning to submit it to a university publication. Suspicion darted suddenly through her mind. Was it possible that Jix knew about this paper? Had Jix staged the whole scene with Griffin as some elaborate joke on her shy and unworldly friend? But why? Jix wasn't a malicious person. Chelsea couldn't imagine that she would pull such a stunt. Samantha, on the other hand, had the temperament to play a prank like this, but even she wouldn't ridicule Chelsea's professional endeavors. Would she?

Distracted by her thoughts, Chelsea jumped when a loud knock resounded on her closed door. She shut the laptop and, composing herself, walked unsteadily to admit her hostess—and Griffin Campbell.

She swallowed hard. She hadn't expected Jix to further

humiliate her by dragging this stranger upstairs into her room. Really, enough was enough.

"Jix, I really don't think—"

"Wait, Chelsea, before you say anything else," Jix interrupted, bursting past her friend and pulling Griffin with her. He tossed Chelsea an apologetic smile, and the tight knot of hurt still in the pit of her stomach relaxed. Jix released Griffin's hand and turned to her friend, an imploring look on her face.

"I am so sorry," Jix said, twisting her hands together. "I should never have said that downstairs—you are my friend, Chelsea, and I do trust you!"

Chelsea waved one hand to stop Jix's frantic apology. "It's all right," she said tightly. "I shouldn't have gotten so upset—it's just that sometimes your and Samantha's jokes are pretty hard to take. How did you find out about my paper?"

Jix frowned and shook her head. "Jokes? Paper? What are you talking about?"

Chelsea laughed, the sound weak and pathetic even to her own ears. Crossing back to the desk and her computer, she felt Griffin's gaze on her. She yearned to glance back at him, to see what expression lay in those beautiful blue eyes. He had smiled at her sympathetically but not with pity. Maybe he didn't think she was a total loser. She opened the laptop.

"You know what I'm talking about." She glanced up. Griffin's eyes held only curiosity, but Jix's were filled with confusion. "Time travel, right?" Chelsea smiled ruefully. "Sam always teases me about my scientific theories, but you've always been so supportive. I guess it is kind of funny when you think about it, but, well, it's real to me."

Jix shook her head and rushed across the room to Chelsea's side, grabbing her friend by both arms. "Chel, what are you talking about? I think your theories are incredible, you know that!" Jix hugged her tightly and Chelsea hugged her back, frowning over her shoulder at the bemused Griffin.

"Then why the joke?" she asked. "Why stage such an elaborate hoax with Griffin and the television and the—"

"Och, lass, I told ye that I've never seen the wee tellievisions before." He shrugged. "I only thought to protect ye."

Chelsea closed her eyes, trying not to get angry all over again as she stepped away from Jix. "Okay, I get it—it was probably Sam's doing. She thought if she brought this hunk of a guy to the manor and made fun of my theories, humiliating me in front of someone she knew I'd go goofy over, that maybe I'd loosen up and act like a human being instead of a computer, right? But, Jix"—she met her friend's gaze—"how could you let her do this to me?"

Jix's mouth dropped open and her eyes widened. She glanced down at the screen of the laptop, and her auburn brows lifted as she turned back to Chelsea.

"Chelsea," she said in a hushed voice, "it isn't a joke. I met Griffin when Jamie and Samantha and I traveled back in time to the year 1605. Now he's come forward in time to . . . to . . ."

"To what?" Chelsea asked, suspicion edging her words.

Jix bit her lower lip and looked up at Griffin, her eyes filled with sudden perplexity. "I don't know," she said. "Griffin—why have you come forward in time? And how did you manage it? Jamie brought his sword back with him when we returned."

"Oh, it was Jamie's sword that let you travel through time," Chelsea said flatly, proud that for a moment she sounded a bit like Samantha Riley. "Of course, I should've known that a magical something or other would show up in this story sooner or later."

Griffin shook his head. " 'T was not a sword that brought me here, and frankly, lass, I dinna ken why I'm here. I went for a wee swim, and the next I knew, I was stumbling down the hill and into yer arms."

Chelsea felt the burn creep up her neck. "Yes, and that was planned so well, although how Sam knew I'd be coming back early from my date . . . on second thought, I guess that wasn't much of a stretch of imagination, was it?" Tears burned at her eyes again, and she took a step backward. "Fine. I'll just pack and—"

"What's going on?" Samantha said as she strolled into

the room. "And who tore up the television? Or do I even need to ask?" She shot an irritated look at Griffin. "Are we going to have to take your toys away from you on your very first day here?"

"Oh, drop it, Sam," Chelsea said, brushing the moisture from her face. "I know about your funny, funny practical joke."

Sam frowned. "What funny joke?"

"I told her about Griffin, and she thinks it's a joke," Jix said.

Sam rolled her eyes. "Why do you always do this, Jix? I thought we agreed not to go blabbing this around."

"She overheard me talking to him about it."

Yeah, that's right, Chelsea thought bitterly. *Don't tell your lame friend the truth just because she's your friend! And it isn't the truth!* But Sam's next words sent a wave of doubt through her.

"Well, I don't blame her for thinking it's some kind of stupid hoax. It sounds like one of your jokes."

"One of *my* jokes? *You're* the practical joker in the group," Jix said.

Sam turned to Chelsea and patted her arm. "I know it's hard to believe, but it isn't a joke. It's the gosh-darn truth."

"Please, Sam, don't tease me." Chelsea glanced over at Griffin, and he flashed her a hesitant grin, his ice-blue eyes melting her anger. "Just admit it's a joke and we'll forget the whole thing."

"Chelsea, it's true," a voice behind her said. She turned to find that Jamie had joined the kitchen confab. In his hand he held a long, beautiful sword.

"Jamie!" Jix shouted, one hand to her throat. "What are you doing? Put that away right this minute! Are you out of your mind?"

It was at that moment that Chelsea began to believe the crazy story. The frightened look on Jix's face was too real, and she supposed that deep down she wanted to believe that her friends would never humiliate her like this for the sake of a laugh. Jix rushed across to Jamie's side. "I don't want to take a chance on losing you," she said, flinging her arms around his waist. "Put it away!"

"Aye, I will, love," he said, holding her against him with his left hand as his right held the sword up vertically by the hilt. "I just wanted to show Chelsea so she'd believe you and not think we were havin' a wee joke at her expense."

Chelsea took a step forward, mesmerized by the sword. It was all shining silver with intricate etchings of Celtic knots down the blade and around the hilt, but the crowning glory of the piece was the luminous green stone set at the base of the hilt. The stone shimmered and shifted, its light internal, not caused by the sunlight beaming down through the kitchen's skylight. Magic. Suddenly it didn't seem so unbelievable anymore.

"Saints preserve us," Griffin whispered. Chelsea turned and moved instinctively to the man's side. His face had turned ashen, and he looked as if his knees might crumple beneath him at any moment. He reached one hand out toward the sword. "I was right. The crystals are the same. My crystals in the cave and this—they're identical, Jamie."

"Your crystals? What are you talking about?" Jix asked, her voice hushed.

Chelsea felt the man beside her tremble. She put her hand on his arm for a brief second before dropping it back to her side. What was wrong with her? She'd never been so bold in her life around a man. But with Griffin, she felt comfortable. Safe.

"Aye, in the water cave. I told Jamie about it last night. I went there to"—he broke off, frowning—"to be alone. I found a wee grotto there, and under the water were these beautiful green crystals, embedded in the sides of the stone. I remember thinking, 'These look like the stone in Jamie's sword.' I touched them, and the next thing I knew, I was here."

"Jamie, put the sword away," Jix implored her husband.

"Wait," Chelsea said, her gaze caught by more etching on the blade of the sword. "What does that mean?" she asked, squinting to see the words engraved on the blade more clearly. "*S'Rhioghal*—"

"Don't say it!" three voices screamed in unison.

Chelsea's mouth dropped open, and the rest of the

words died in her throat. Even Sam looked disconcerted, and Sam was never disconcerted.

"That's what sends you back in time!" Jix said, her voice filled with anxiety. "Now will you put it away, Jamie MacGregor, or do I have to start with the ultimatums?"

"Aye, perhaps ye're right, love," he said, solemn-faced. Jamie backed out of the room, holding the sword at arm's length.

"But if saying *S'Rhioghal*"—Chelsea broke off as Jix and Sam took a step toward her—"if saying those words," she corrected, "is what sent you through time, then how did Griffin come through time? Did he say the same words, and even if he did, how could rocks know what he was saying? They're inanimate objects." Chelsea was in full scientist mode now. She shook her head. "It makes no sense." She glanced up at Griffin, whose gaze followed Jamie out of the room. "Did you say those words, Griffin?"

He shook his head. "Nay, I did not. I was merely thinking of when Jamie and Jix left my time, using the sword with the green stone."

Chelsea walked away from the three and back again, then away. She always thought better when she could pace. "So probably saying the words didn't have anything to do with it. Probably it was the fact that he was thinking about the two of you when he touched the crystals that triggered the transference of energy."

She halted in mid-stride near Griffin and glanced up, startled, to see him studying her with an admiring look on his handsome face. A warm rush of hope surged through her, and evaporated with his next words.

"Aye," he said with a nod, " 'tis what I believe as well. Ye are quite bright, lass, for a woman."

Jix laughed, the tension in the room broken only slightly with the sound. "Now, Griffin, don't you remember the talks we had back in 1605 about women and intelligence and not being a chauvinist?"

Griffin looked immediately abashed. "Now I've put my foot in it, have I? My apologies, lass. It isna that I dinna think woman are intelligent, nay not at all. But to find one that is no' afraid to speak her mind, who isna worried she'll no' find a husband if she says such things,'tis a rare thing." Jix giggled, and he glanced at her, then at Samantha, then back to Chelsea again. "Well, mayhap no' so rare a thing here, but in my time it is."

"Your time," Chelsea said. "This is too crazy!" She pushed past the man and went back into the study, her mind racing as she began to pace again. The ripped television screen sat there as a monument to the incredible story she'd just been told. No wonder Griffin had attacked it. How frightening would it be to walk into a room and see tiny people contained in a box? She paced a little faster.

Could it be possible? Of course it was possible. Her own research had proven it, well, beyond much doubt. There was always doubt when you worked with abstract ideas. But her theory dealt with space travel and the theory of relativity and Einstein. This was something vastly different. How could a man have actually traveled through time simply because he touched a certain kind of stone? There had to be a scientific reason for it. If it were true.

"Chelsea?" Jix hovered uncertainly at the doorway, her features contrite. Jamie stood behind her, Griffin and Sam at her side. "So do you believe us?"

Chelsea stopped in the center of the room and spun toward the four. "Not quite yet," she said, hands on her hips, feeling the sudden heady exhilaration of demanding information from Jix and Sam and getting it.

"But Chelsea—" Jix began.

Chelsea held up one hand and focused her gaze on Griffin.

"Take me to the cave. I want to see those crystals."

Chapter Five

Chelsea felt like flying as she trudged up the hill. Where had this new courage come from? How had she ever had the strength to stand up not only to Jix, but to Samantha as well?

The wind picked up as they climbed higher and her hair slapped into her face, the ends stinging her eyes. Unconsciously Chelsea reached back and pulled her runaway tresses into a ponytail. The length of her hair made it possible to simply loop the thickness into a knot at the base of her neck, and she quickly took care of her messy mane.

Thank goodness she hadn't let her friends cut her hair as they'd wanted. It was easier to tie it back than to bother with styling it every day. She glanced over at Jix and Sam and saw them look her way, then at each other.

So I'm slipping back into my nerdy homely scientist mode, she thought. *So big deal. Like streaks in my hair or make-up will ever change who I am.*

She stole a peek across at Griffin as he trudged up the hill beside her. Jix and Jamie and Samantha lagged behind, but the man who claimed to be from 1605 had kept pace with her ever since they left the manor. She tried not to read anything into such a small thing, but after all, given the circumstances, he could've fallen back with the others. So why hadn't he?

His face was grim, his mouth held in a tight line. Was he afraid his joke would be found out? Why would he care? He didn't know her from Adam.

"Are you all right?" she asked, suddenly intrigued by his silence.

He shot her a startled glance and then nodded. "Aye, I am well, as well as a man can be in such a situation."

Chelsea smiled. "You didn't expect me to call your bluff, did you?"

"Call my bluff?" He frowned and shook his head over her words. "I'm no' sure what ye mean, but it concerns me that ye dinna believe yer friends."

"Why should that concern you?" A sudden hard gust of wind blew a long lock of hair from the neat knot, and Chelsea brushed it back from her face, feeling self-conscious. Griffin stopped walking, and she did too. She glanced up and their gazes met, his searching hers for a tantalizing moment until he nodded, as if something had been settled.

"Ye are not a vindictive lass," he said with certainty. "Nor are ye given to speakin' yer mind. But on matters of science, ye dare to take a stand." His eyes flickered with sudden comprehension. "Or on matters of the heart. Ye are hurt," he said with a nod. "I dinna realize it before. Ye think yer friends dinna trust ye with important information, and it pains ye."

Chelsea blinked up at him. His insight was uncanny. She laughed nervously and started up the hill again. "Don't be silly. I always say what I think. Well, not always, but . . ." She turned on him in exasperation. "Wouldn't you be offended if your friends were always leaving you out of things? If they treated you like you were a child who didn't have any sense at all? If they tried to remake you and remodel you every time you turned around?"

A corner of his mouth rose in a sympathetic smile. "Aye, lass," he said softly, reaching out to take her hand, " 'Twould offend me somethin' fierce."

Chelsea stared down at his hand, large and strong, holding hers so warmly, so safely. Heat surged into her face, but she didn't pull away. Her heartbeat quickened, and she looked up. He stared back, seeming just as amazed as she.

"Lass," he said, "I wish . . ." He broke off, still staring down at her.

Chelsea willed the words to break free of her lips. "What?" she asked, feeling breathless. "What do you wish?"

"I must return to my own time, but I wish . . ."

For a brief, brief moment he leaned forward, and she thought he was going to kiss her; then a strange look crossed his face and he dropped her hand, stumbling backward, away from her.

"We—we'd best hurry on," he stammered, his sun-streaked hair flowing back from his broad shoulders. He turned and broke into a half-run, leaving Chelsea behind.

She sighed as she watched the man stumble and almost break his neck trying to get away from her. For a brief second she'd thought he was about to say he wished he could stay and get to know her better. She had imagined the whole thing, of course. What would a body-building hunk like Griffin Campbell—or whoever he really was—want with a pale nothing nobody like Chelsea Brown? She shoved her hands into her pockets and followed Griffin's path.

Griffin made it to the top of the hill leading to the crag faster than he'd thought possible. He bent over, slightly winded from his mad rush, and thought for a moment he might pass out. Not from the exercise but from the realization of what he had almost done. Again.

Daft. He was daft. He'd taken the woman's hand and felt the warmth of her touch, felt a rush of desire course through him like none he had ever known. She'd looked up at him with her beautiful gray eyes, and he'd seen the answering response in her gaze. He'd leaned forward and all at once realized he was touching a woman, about to kiss a woman, and what would follow would be quick, disgusting, and humiliating. The last thing he wanted was for the fair Chelsea to see him vomiting into a nearby bush. So he had run like a coward.

It was just as well, he thought as he straightened and

took a deep, quelling breath. He was going back to his own time. He had to concentrate on getting home again, not on becoming enamored with a woman he could never hope to attain.

Jix and Jamie came to a breathless stop beside him, with Samantha close behind. Griffin gave an approving glance to Jamie's choice of clothing. He'd changed into his MacGregor kilt and had his sword strapped to his side, no doubt to compare the green stone in the hilt with the green crystals in the cave. Jix's eyes kept shifting to the claymore, a worried expression on her face, and Griffin didn't blame her. That sword was anything but safe.

Chelsea held herself slightly apart from the rest and refused to meet his eyes. Obviously, she was embarrassed by the near kiss. He sighed. The sooner he showed his friends the crystals, the sooner he would be home again and the sooner he would stop making a fool of himself.

He still felt bad about the tellie-vision, even though Jamie had assured him he hadn't killed any kind of living thing. The moving-picture box was just one of the awesome and amazing creations of the time in which he found himself. It would be interesting to stay awhile, to learn more, but after Chelsea's demand to see the crystals, Jix had pulled him aside and cautioned him that it would be best if he went on back to his own century as soon as possible.

"You never know what those stones will do," she'd said. "They have a mind of their own."

Griffin had dismissed her comments as strange but not uncommon for Jix Ferguson MacGregor. But now as he motioned for the four to follow him across the jutting limestone, toward the magical cave, he wondered. Maybe her words had more meaning than he'd initially granted them. Was it possible that the crystals, the stone in Jamie's sword, were part of some divine plan, some conscious administration by the Almighty?

"Is this still familiar to you, Griffin?" Jix asked. He shook himself from his reverie and glanced back at her. The wind picked up her red hair and tossed it in the air. Beside her, Samantha's long platinum tresses also rose in abandonment. Chelsea had pulled her hair back tightly again, but a few stray locks had escaped.

The three women were stark contrasts to one another. Jix, the fiery and flamboyant one; Samantha, cool and sultry; and then Chelsea—her face clean this day, no longer showing traces of the "make up" as she called it—gentle, timid, and absolutely beautiful. Not brashly exotic like Jix, or knowingly seductive like Samantha. Chelsea's face was like porcelain, her lips naturally pink, her lashes soft and brown, her features even. His heart beat a little faster, and he silently admonished himself for his foolish thoughts.

"Griffin?" Jix said again. "Which way do we go?"

"Up here." He led the way, grateful for a distraction. The entrance to the cave was just as he had left it four hundred years ago, half hidden by a boulder, safe from the casual glance of someone passing by.

"That's awfully small, isn't it?" Sam asked, glancing down at her white blouse and short pants. Griffin felt quite scandalized by her clothing but knew it would be rude to say anything. "I'm going to get filthy."

"I told you to wear jeans," Jix scolded. "You can stay out here."

"I think *you* should stay out as well," Jamie said, catching his wife by the arm as she started to flatten herself on the rocky terrain.

"What? I will not! This is the most exciting thing that's happened since . . . well, since—"

"Since you found out you were pregnant?" Jamie asked softly, putting his arm around her. Jix smiled and relaxed against him, patting his chest with one hand.

"Yes, since then," she said.

A baby. Griffin's heart suddenly ached at the sight of the two, so happy, so in love. He mentally gave himself a kick. He didn't begrudge them their happiness, of course he didn't, but he envied them. Aye, he did.

"Congratulations," he said aloud. "I dinna know there was to be a blessed event."

"We just found out a few weeks ago ourselves," Jamie said, shaking Griffin's extended hand.

"I'm happy for ye, lass." He reached out and lightly

brushed one hand over Jix's tangled curls, then dropped it back to his side, shifting his gaze to Jamie. "For the two of ye."

"Thank you, Griffin." Jix's arms went around Jamie's waist and she gave him a tight squeeze. "We're very happy."

"And to keep us that way—happy, pregnant, and not dashing backward in time—I think we should stay outside and let Chelsea and Griffin go inside," Jamie said, hugging Jix in return.

"What about a compromise?" Jix offered. "We all go inside, but I promise not to get within ten feet of the crystals." Jamie frowned. "Puh-leeze, oh, high and mighty husband of mine?"

"Like he would ever deny you anything," Samantha said dryly. "Come on, let's get this show on the road before I get nauseous."

Griffin went first, dropping to his knees and making his way through the two-foot-high, three-foot-wide opening. A few feet inside, the ceiling of the cave gradually began sloping upward until he was able to stumble to his feet in a crouch and finally stand erect. Jix came next, crawling carefully on her hands and knees, followed by Sam, Jamie, and Chelsea.

When they all stood together at last, Griffin was gratified to see that the reactions of his friends matched his own the first time he'd walked into the cave. It was just as he remembered, the cavern stretching high above their heads. He was glad to see one difference. The moss was back again, glowing with its eerie light. Perhaps the crystals were back as well. Water streamed down the cavern wall in the same dark waterfall, pooling in the natural basin on the floor, pouring down into the deep blue-green water below.

"Wow!" Jix said, staring up at the huge rounded dome of a ceiling.

"Double wow!" Sam agreed.

Chelsea didn't comment, but Griffin saw how her gray eyes flickered over everything, taking in each unique aspect of the grotto. She walked to the edge of the water and knelt, leaning close to the dark depths. Griffin crossed quickly to her side.

"Careful, lass," he cautioned, laying one hand lightly on her shoulder. "If ye go in headfirst, there's no tellin' what might happen."

Chelsea tensed under his touch and then lifted disillusioned eyes to his. "Oh, I think I could tell you. I'd get exceedingly wet." She shook off his hand and stood, turning to her friends. "There aren't any green crystals in the water. You lied to me." She glanced back at Griffin. "You all lied to me."

"Nay, we did not!" Griffin said, spinning around and dropping to one knee beside the limestone pool. The reflection of the algae above sparkled in the green depths of the pool, but as Chelsea had said, there were no green crystals shimmering a few inches below the surface, studding the limestone rocks beneath the water.

He hesitated only a moment, then took a deep breath and plunged headfirst into the water. His view was murky, dimly lit, just as he remembered from before, but this time the underground spring buoyed him up, making him fight to stay below the surface; this time when he reached out to the limestone walls for purchase, his hands closed not around sharp, beautiful crystals, but around solid rock.

The crystals were gone, and with them any chance he had to return to his own time.

Chelsea watched as Griffin threw himself into the pool and dove beneath the surface. She could see his long, white-blond hair billow around his face, and for an instant the whole scene seemed surreal. She could imagine him emerging from the water, bare-chested, clad in his kilt like some Celtic god, or perhaps sporting a merman's tail, straight out of a Scottish folktale. Drawing in a quick breath, she shook the silly thoughts from her mind as Griffin did indeed emerge from the water, not like a god or a fantasy creature, but like a man with the weight of the world on his shoulders.

He dragged himself over the edge of the rock and knelt, his hair dripping in front of his face, his clothes soaked, his knee-high leather boots darkened by the water. His hands were clenched, and when he lifted his face and she saw the pain in his eyes, Chelsea suddenly knew in her heart that Griffin had been telling the truth all along. After all, she'd written a dissertation on time travel, so why was she having such a hard time accepting the very thing she'd sought so hard to prove?

Because this isn't some experiment in your lab, something deep inside her said. *This isn't some abstract theory. It's affecting your life, your friends . . . a man you're attracted to.*

Chelsea shook herself mentally. *Now, don't go getting carried away, letting your hormones do your thinking for you. You believe Griffin because you want to believe him. It would solve everything—it would mean that your friends had been telling you the truth and that a real live time traveler had dropped into your lap. A true scientist would gather more evidence before accepting any of this as fact.*

But what if it was true and Griffin had to remain in this century? A thrill rushed through her, and she quickly squelched it, berating the selfishness that would cause her to be happy at another's expense. But if he really was a time traveler and he really was stuck here, how wonderful to talk to him, to learn about his time, his customs, his history! Why, it was something every scholar dreamed of! It had nothing whatsoever to do with her interest in him as a man—of course not. She could view him strictly as a scientist, examining a . . . a . . . specimen from a bygone era. Yes, that was it. That was why she was so excited at the thought of Griffin staying for a while. She just wanted to probe his mind.

Yeah, right.

"I know ye dinna believe me," Griffin said as he rose slowly from the cave floor, "but I am tellin' ye the truth. In my time the crystals were there. I dinna ken why they are not here now."

Jix walked up to the downcast man, her gaze stricken. "I'm so sorry, Griffin. Maybe this is the wrong cave."

"Maybe the stupid things don't want to be found," Samantha said, folding her arms over her chest. "I wouldn't doubt it a bit."

"Well, in the meantime," Jix said, "welcome to our world."

"Not so fast," Jamie said, coming up beside Jix and hugging her to him, his eyes on Griffin. "If you want to go home, there still may be a way."

Chelsea saw the light return to Griffin's face as he responded eagerly to Jamie's words. She waited just as breathlessly for his answer, though for totally different reasons than Griffin.

"Aye? What way?" Griffin asked.

Jamie pulled the claymore from the scabbard at his side and extended the long sword to Griffin, hand on hilt, blade flat against his palm. "My sword. After all, that's how we did it—why shouldn't it work for you?"

"But ye would have to give up yer sword," Griffin objected. "Forever." He shook his head. "Nay, I couldna ask it of ye."

Jamie shrugged. "Aye, but 'tis for a good cause. I wouldn't keep ye from returning to yer own time for the sake of a material object, no matter how long it's been in my family."

"Thank ye, Jamie MacGregor," Griffin said, relief evident in his voice. Chelsea took a step back from the four, trying to distance her heart even as she distanced herself physically.

Griffin took the weapon from Jamie and looked down at it with awe on his face. " 'Tis a beautiful sword," he said, and gave it a swing, slicing through the air away from Jix and Jamie. He grinned. "I promise, I will one day find the MacGregor I can trust to hand this down in yer family. Mayhap ye will still receive it one day."

"Wait a minute," Sam said, coming up beside them. "If Griffin uses the sword and takes it back to the year 1605, then what if it doesn't get handed down through history to Jamie? What would happen then?"

"It could change reality," Chelsea said before she could stop herself. "It could possibly destroy the world as we know it."

Griffin frowned at her. "What do ye mean, lass?"

Chelsea thought for a moment how best to explain the

incredible paradoxes that actual time travel could create. "For instance, the fact that you have come to our time changes our lives, but no more than, say, the birth of a person would change it. But when Jix and Jamie went back in time and revealed who they were to you, and some of the inventions of the future"—she cast Jix a disapproving look, really, how could she have been so irresponsible— "they could have caused you to change things in your time which could have had repercussions on the future."

Griffin shook his head. "I still dinna understand."

"Me either," Jix said. Jamie frowned, looking thoughtful, while Sam continued to brush dirt off her white shorts.

"It's like this," Chelsea went on. "Suppose Jix had taught Griffin how to build, oh, a steam engine." She held up one hand as Jix opened her mouth to protest. "Just suppose for a minute in this hypothetical situation that Jix knew how to build a steam engine and she showed Griffin. Then what if after she went back to her own time, Griffin started building steam engines and doing other experiments with the new power source? It's possible that the industrial revolution could've happened two hundred years sooner than it did!"

"Industrial?" Griffin blinked, looking confused, and Chelsea resisted the urge to hug him. Probably one of those all-brawn, no-brain kind of guys. Well, she could stand that, couldn't she?

"What I'm trying to say," she explained, "is that if Griffin takes the sword back to 1605, if it never reaches Jamie MacGregor in the present, then none of this would have ever happened."

Jix frowned, looking perplexed. "Then what would have happened?"

Chelsea shrugged. "I don't know. You and Jamie would've met but never married? The sword could've gone to someone else who discovered its time-traveling capabilities— someone like Genghis Khan or Hitler who would've used it for his own gain. There are a thousand possibilities."

"So you're saying he shouldn't use the sword to go back in time?" Jamie asked. Was it Chelsea's imagination, or did

Jamie look totally unhappy at the thought of Griffin remaining?

"I'm saying I think we should make sure we know what we're dealing with first," she said. "Let me work out a few equations, figure out some probability factors." She turned to see what Griffin thought about the idea, only to find the man staring at her, his blue eyes wary and troubled.

"Ye are quite an intelligent woman," he said. Silently he returned the sword to Jamie and walked away, his hands behind his back as he stared down into the watery depths of the pool.

"Yes, well, that and a dollar will get me a cup of coffee," Chelsea said with a sigh. No doubt he wouldn't be interested in her now. Once men found out she had a brain they just quietly slipped away. But she just couldn't play the "be a dummy" game. She couldn't. And she couldn't respect a man who would want her to play it.

Sam walked up to her, her face smudged with dirt and filled with impatience. "Look, here's an idea," she said. "Why don't we get out of this hole, go back to the manor, and plan your anniversary party, Jix?"

Chelsea frowned. "What anniversary party?"

"Oh, I haven't had a chance to tell you," Jix said. "Sam suggested that to celebrate the baby we have a big party and invite all of our friends." She smiled at Griffin. "Now we have another cause to celebrate—Griffin's staying with us for a little while longer."

"And then after the party maybe Griffin can tell us all bye-bye and use Jamie's sword to whisk himself back to his own century," Sam said, ignoring all their concerns with her usual condescension. "How does that grab everyone?"

"But—" Chelsea began.

"We can discuss your fears about the space-time continuum later," Sam cut her off.

Chelsea caught herself before she said something scathing. Leave it to Sam to make her feel like an idiot for pointing out a completely logical point of view. And leave it to Jix to once again leave her out of the loop. Still, if the plan would mean that Griffin stayed longer, she was all in favor of it.

"Sure, that sounds great," she said.

Griffin continued to stand with his back toward the rest of them. After a moment he turned and gave them all a subdued smile. Chelsea drew in a sharp breath as his gaze locked with hers and the blue of his eyes seemed to darken, to fill with heat. All at once Chelsea forgot to breathe until he turned to Jix and spoke.

"Aye," he said softly.

Chapter Six

Chelsea opened the doors of the beautiful tall wardrobe in her room and wondered if there was any possible way to beg off from the gala anniversary party. No, of course there wasn't. She was trapped, stuck, up against a wall. She had to appear a week from today at a fancy dinner party, and in her usual fashion, she had neglected to bring anything remotely appropriate. She pushed the hangers on the wood pole lethargically, feeling more depressed than usual.

She hadn't seen much of Griffin lately, to her disappointment, except sometimes at supper and on occasion afterward when he would invite her to take a walk. So far she had declined, too afraid to be alone with him. Afraid she would do or say something to make a fool of herself. Her emotions where Griffin was concerned were so intense, so consuming, that she feared what she might do if he so much as looked her in the eye.

At least he still seemed somewhat interested in her, and seemed genuinely disappointed when she opted not to walk with him. Maybe at the party she would try to sit next to him and flirt with him a little. The thought made her heartbeat quicken. Oh, yes, she was going to make a fool of herself sooner or later, that was almost a certainty.

Time was ticking by, though, and if she didn't do something soon it would be too late. She suspected that Jamie would eventually ignore her warning and let Griffin use his sword to go back to 1605.

It figured. Not only did most men seem to find her unattractive, but now the minute she met one who showed any interest at all, he had to hurry back through time before he turned into a pumpkin. If only he wouldn't go back! She felt a rush of shame. How selfish! How wrong of her to wish that Griffin wouldn't return to his home and his family and friends.

And who knew what his staying would do to the future? Besides, she couldn't imagine anything that would convince Griffin not to return to his own time. Suddenly her breath caught in her throat as an incredibly wicked thought hit her.

What if he could be convinced?

Maybe she hadn't imagined his interest in her. After all, he had kissed her quite thoroughly in his room that first night. Granted, he'd been half asleep, but still, would he have done such a thing if he found her totally abhorrent? And was the heat in his eyes sometimes when he looked at her a figment of her imagination?

It was possible, likely even, so how could she even consider what she was considering, i.e., seduction pure and simple? Except it wouldn't be pure and she wasn't sure how simple it could be, because she'd never done it before. And just how far was she, a virgin, willing to go to keep him in her time? Was she willing to be like Samantha or Jix—a woman uninhibited and unafraid of the opposite sex? *Sex.* Just the word made her face grow warm and brought to mind visions of Griffin standing naked beside his bed.

On one of the few dates she'd ever had, a man had tried to convince her to have sex with him. When she explained she was still a virgin at the age of twenty-six he had laughed right in her face. It had not only embarrassed her, but she'd been infuriated. Why was a woman's decision to abstain from casual sex viewed as comical or even puritanical? Was it wrong to dream of having one love, one man, one life together, and keeping that special treasure for him and him alone?

"Pathetic," she said aloud, jerking open a door of the wardrobe. "I am pathetic, old-fashioned, and destined to be an old maid if I don't get with the program. Besides," she said, staring into the closet, "what have I got to lose? If he turns me down, at least it's likely I'll never, ever see him again."

With that thought Chelsea began rummaging through the few things she'd brought with her. After a minute she sighed and leaned her head on the side of the closet. Her choices boiled down to a brown checked blouse and knee-length brown skirt, a brown short-sleeved dress—why had she ever bought so much brown?—and a dress she'd never have the nerve to wear. She straightened and pulled the last garment in question off the hanger, holding it out in front of her.

It was hopelessly out of date, but she'd hoped to revamp it somehow. Even Jix and Sam didn't know she had a passion for vintage clothing. Her closet at home was full of beautiful finds from thrift shops and garage sales that she'd never worn. Her secret self. Seized with a sudden longing, Chelsea discarded her jeans and T-shirt and pulled the dress over her head. She modeled it in front of the full-length mirror, and her spirits sagged.

The only reason she'd bought the dress was it reminded her of something Audrey Hepburn might have worn in a movie. But it would never do for a seduction, or even just to appear in public in! Hardly your basic little black dress, it was made of black lace that reached from her throat to her knees and from her shoulders to her wrists. A large black lace ruffle cupped her face, making it look like the pale center of a very strange black flower, and another, longer ruffle touched her knees. The dress was bell-shaped, and underneath was a sleeveless bell-shaped under-dress.

Although the lace was in perfect condition, it was hot and scratchy. The whole effect was wrong, dowdy, old-fashioned, and shapeless.

Chelsea sighed and backed away from the mirror. When

the back of her knees touched the bed, she threw herself backward, arms spread, feeling more hopeless than ever. Forget it. She'd wear one of her stupid brown dresses on the night of the party and watch Jix and Samantha shine and flirt, and she'd remember again why she just didn't have what it took to have a real relationship with a man.

She sat up and groaned as a loud ripping sound accompanied her movement. Standing, she looked down to see that the ruffle at the hem had ripped away. "Great," she said. "Now I can't even resell the dumb thing." In frustration she reached down and grabbed the lace ruffle and the hem of the dowdy under-dress and pulled them both roughly over her head.

She emerged from the garment frustrated and hot and tossed it aside. Inadvertently she glanced into the long mirror opposite her. She blinked. She angled her body sideways. She turned away and looked over one shoulder.

Beneath the loose under-dress had been still another dress, no doubt meant to protect the proper 1950s lady in case the bell-shaped fashion statement got blown about in a heavy wind. The second under-dress was like a tight black slip, and Chelsea's mouth fell open as she looked at her reflection.

This dress sported tiny spaghetti straps, a low-cut neckline, and a thigh-high hem. She could never wear such a revealing outfit. Could she? She didn't have the body for it. She wasn't Jix or Sam or—

She stopped in mid-thought, suddenly realizing how truly pathetic she sounded, even to her own mind. So she wasn't Jix or Sam. So what? She wasn't the Hunchback of Notre Dame either. Okay, so her body wasn't perfect. But her legs were good because of all the hiking she did, and although her breasts weren't silicone-enhanced, they weren't small by any means. She had a curve to her abdomen, but hey, so had Marilyn Monroe. Her upper arms had no definition and she wasn't model-thin, and all in all, she would never make the swimsuit cover of *Sports Illustrated*. She could stand to lose a few pounds. Still, it could be worse.

She turned back to the mirror and drew in a quick

breath. She could do this! She could, if only she had the courage.

And what if he turns you down? The question resounded through her brain.

"So what?" she said aloud. "Even if he rejects me, at least I won't have to live with the fear of ever seeing him again! He's going back to his own time, probably."

And what if he doesn't turn you down? The second question was harder to answer than the first. *What if you have one incredible night and then he leaves you, forever?*

Chelsea's lips trembled and she pressed them tightly together. "Then at least I'll have one incredible memory," she whispered, "with someone I know I could have loved."

All at once she heard a commotion downstairs. She crossed to the door and opened it, then caught her breath in a sharp gasp as a masculine voice shouting "*S'Rhioghal Mo Dhream!*" echoed through the manor and sent a shudder through her soul.

"Jix is going to kill me," Jamie said, shaking his head as he pulled the claymore from its sheath.

Griffin stared down at the sword, resisting the urge to touch the glittering green stone at the base of its hilt. The two stood in Jamie's private study. Griffin had taken advantage of the chance to speak to Jamie alone, while Jix and Sam were sequestered in the library to discuss the "dinner party" and Chelsea was taking a nap.

He didn't have to talk long before Jamie agreed to let him use his sword and try to return to the past. The man seemed almost eager, at first.

"I must go back," Griffin said as Jamie seemed to hesitate. "Ye know that I must. And ye have my word that I'll never tell a soul about the things I've seen in this time."

Jamie shook his head again and rubbed one hand across the back of his neck. "I know. I just keep thinking about what Chelsea said. What if it does change something if ye return? What if we change our own futures?"

"And if I stay here it may change something, too," Griffin reminded him. "Either way, something may happen, but doesn't it make sense to send me back to the time in which I belong? Besides, although ye've been a wonderful host, I know ye dinna want me here, so here is yer chance to be rid of me."

Jamie had the grace to flush at Griffin's words. He cocked one dark brow at his guest and smiled sheepishly. "Is it that obvious? Forgive me. I confess, it's been somewhat hard, for I know that ye loved her, too."

Griffin smiled. "I think a man would have to be blind, deaf, and dumb not to fall a wee bit in love with yer wife, but I assure ye, my feelings for her now are completely platonic." He clapped the other man on the shoulder. "Ye have my word on that."

"Then stay," Jamie said all at once, straightening as if a load had been lifted from his shoulders. "Let me make my childishness up to ye by showing ye more of this century. The sword will always be here, later."

Griffin hesitated. He was tempted—tempted to stay, to see more of the wonders of this world—but he dared not. Already he felt too much for Chelsea Brown. Wanted her too desperately. If he stayed much longer he might never want to return, and that would be wrong. He had to return to his own time. He was destined to be the Chieftain of Clan Campbell. Besides, no matter how much he cared for Chelsea, he could never touch her, never possess her. At least in the Scotland of 1605 he knew his place, knew where he belonged.

"No," he said at last. "I need to go now."

Jamie nodded and held out the sword to him. Griffin grasped the great claymore by the hilt and took a deep breath.

He regretted not being able to bid Jix and Sam and especially Chelsea goodbye, but it was easier this way. And as he and Jamie had agreed, if the women knew, they would no doubt have something to say about his return to the past. Griffin privately feared that if he waited, if they told the women, Jamie would give in to his wife if she protested. After all, she was carrying his child. What man wouldn't do whatever was necessary to keep his wife happy and unworried during such a time?

"What were those words again?" Griffin asked, sliding

the fingers of his left hand over the sparkling emerald. Jamie silently pointed to the engraving on the blade, and Griffin nodded. "Tell the women . . ." He paused. "Tell Jix and Sam goodbye, and tell Chelsea that I wish I'd had more of an opportunity to talk with her."

Jamie lifted one brow, sudden understanding flashing into his eyes. "Aye," he said, taking a step back. "I will. Godspeed, lad."

Griffin closed his eyes and clutched the hilt of the sword tightly. *"S'Rhioghal Mo Dhream!"* he said in a loud, clear voice, expecting the world to turn inside out and upside down.

Nothing happened. He opened his eyes to find that he was still in the twenty-first century. He tried again.

"S'Rhioghal Mo Dhream!" he shouted. From the other room he could hear the sounds of footsteps and doors slamming. The women were coming. Quickly he tried one last time.

"S'Rhioghal Mo Dhream!"

The door to the study burst open, and someone came flying across the room to fling herself against him. Startled, he dropped the sword and grabbed her.

Chelsea Brown looked up at him, half clad, her fingers clutching his arms, her gray eyes wide with panic.

"Don't go without me!" she cried.

Chelsea hid herself away from everyone for the rest of the day and took her supper in her room. After her embarrassing display, she had thrown one dismayed look at Griffin before running out of the study and up the stairs to her own room, where she bolted the door. Jix had come knocking, trying to convince her that Griffin had been flattered, not annoyed, but she had refused to come out.

The next day, after a night of tearful self-recriminations, she sucked it up and made her way downstairs in time for lunch. Everyone acted as if nothing strange had happened. Even Griffin didn't say a word to her about the episode. He gave her a wink as she reached for the bowl of salad in front of him, and she quickly looked away, still too embarrassed to meet his gaze.

The only good thing about any of it was the knowledge that the sword hadn't worked! Griffin hadn't gone back to the past, and maybe he would never be able to leave. Now more than ever, she had to find the strength and the courage to put her plan into action, which, thanks to her ridiculous display, was going to be much, much harder. As the week passed, her embarrassment faded and things got back to normal, relatively speaking.

She helped Jix and Sam plan the party, and felt happy over the way Jamie seemed to have finally lost the chip on his shoulder and taken Griffin under his wing. He took the man with him everywhere—his karate class, tai chi, a rugby game, even to a computer club meeting. She personally thought that exposing the time traveler to so much of their modern world was a mistake, but no one was listening to her, as usual.

The day of the anniversary bash dawned bright and beautiful. Sam and Chelsea spent the morning decorating the large ballroom on the third floor, after agreeing that Jix shouldn't lift a finger on this, her celebration day. Neighbors and relatives from all over Scotland had been invited, and as the time approached for the festivities to begin, Chelsea put her own problems aside as she realized how much it meant to Jix to have her friends there with her. Jix's own family couldn't attend, and as the afternoon wore on she seemed to cling to Chelsea and Sam more and more.

"You look beautiful," Chelsea assured her friend. She pulled the belt on her bulky flannel robe tighter as she tried to help Jix get ready for the party.

"I feel so bloated and miserable," Jix said, sliding a clingy green dress over her head. She smoothed it into place, looked into the mirror, and grimaced. "How is it that a human being can actually turn green? Maybe it's the dress."

"No, it's the morning sickness, which you insist on having all day," Sam said. "Why don't you wear this blue one?" She tossed a ruffled blue gown on the bed.

Jix frowned. "Why? Do you think I need to cover myself up that much? Do I look as fat as I feel?"

Chelsea slipped away as the two began to squabble in their familiar manner. She just couldn't handle Jix complaining about the way she looked, not when she felt so insecure about her plans for the party. Chelsea hurried to her room and locked the door behind her, leaning on it to catch her breath. It was time to get dressed, and her heart was pounding so hard she thought it might burst.

Thank goodness Griffin had been gone since just after breakfast. If she'd seen him throughout the day she probably would've been twice as nervous. Chelsea moved to the wardrobe and opened the door, unable to keep from thinking about the beautiful Scot and how he had disappeared earlier.

He'd looked so depressed at the breakfast table. He hadn't eaten a thing, but had announced just after pancakes were served that he was going riding. Where he'd taken off to on horseback she hadn't a clue, and even Jamie had seemed a little worried. But she knew that Griffin wouldn't miss his friends' party. He was too kind, too sensitive to do such a thing.

She closed her eyes, remembering again the way it had felt to be in his arms that first night when, half asleep, he'd kissed her. A thrill rushed through her, and she felt like a teenager daydreaming about a movie star. Of course, when she was a teenager she'd been more interested in chemicals than chemistry between girls and boys, so maybe that was why this was hitting her so hard now. A late bloomer. A very late bloomer. But now that Griffin was stuck here—what better time to bloom?

Chelsea reached into the antique mahogany wardrobe, and the negative thoughts slipped away as she lifted a hanger from the wooden pole and laid the chosen garment carefully on the bed.

After her disastrous attempt to salvage a dress out of her vintage Audrey Hepburn purchase, Chelsea had made a momentous decision. She would hurry into Inverness and buy some new clothes for the party. The black slip dress had been a good trial run, but even with her lack of fashion sense, she realized it wouldn't do for a gala event like this. Still, the short, sexy garment had given her an idea on which to build.

So yesterday morning, while Sam was busy talking to the caterer and Jix took a nap, she'd begged off, saying she had errands to run, and had driven into Inverness.

The result of her trip was shining on her bed. She picked up the hanger again and admired her choice. Dangling from the smooth metal was the sexiest, naughtiest, most wonderful number she'd ever owned in her life.

It was Red. Scarlet. Gypsy Red. Blood Red. Red like the lipstick Monroe had worn in all her movies. Short, dazzling, the material glittered and shone with an iridescence that sent a thrill up her veins. She tossed the dress back on the mattress, slipped off her robe, and stood naked a moment, staring at the dress, summoning her courage.

"Okay, Chelsea," she whispered. "Here's where they separate the women from the girls." She knelt down beside the bed and, reaching under it, pulled out a paper sack. From the sack she pulled out a bright red, lacy bra.

The saleswoman in Inverness had called it a Wonder-Full Bra and it looked as if it could stand alone without any help from her at all. Chelsea had always been a little lacking in the bust department, and the woman had assured her that this bra would take what she had and reposition it so that any man within sight of her would be drooling in seconds flat.

She didn't want Griffin drooling—he had too much dignity for that—but she did want him to notice her, so she'd bought it. She put the bra on, slid into the matching panties, and before she could chicken out, pulled the dress on and turned to face the mirror.

Her mouth dropped open. The red silk fit her like a second skin, the material shimmering with an allure made all the more evident by her own provocative curves. How had she missed the fact that her body was pretty darned sexy? The hem ended about four inches above her knee. A slit, cut slightly off center, ended high on her left thigh. One smooth leg kept making its appearance as she turned this way and that. The neckline of the dress was low-cut, and the Wonder-Full Bra had certainly done its work. Her cleavage was spectacular, and for a minute her courage faltered. It was too much, wasn't it?

Don't wimp out now.

She twisted around to see how the back looked. Pretty darned good.

But could she really pull it off? She lifted her hair and bunched it up on top of her head and tried to imagine what she'd look like with makeup and jewelry. She'd even purchased some dangling earrings and eyeliner.

Chelsea sighed and let her hair fall back to her shoulders. What was the worst that could happen? Griffin would take one look at her and run for the hills. Griffin would laugh in her face. Griffin would ask her to dance and tell her she was the most ravishing woman he'd ever met.

It could happen. One good scenario out of three wasn't bad odds. Of course, there was always a fourth possibility: She would walk into the ballroom, trip and fall flat on her face, her dress would split, and she'd be left lying naked on the floor while the snobby elite of Inverness danced around her.

It was a chance she'd have to take.

Griffin knelt behind a fallen log in the middle of thick woods. Jamie MacGregor had given him access to his stables, and being able to ride was one of the few things in this place that kept him sane. He'd spent the morning in this glade in solemn contemplation.

The last week had been like a dream and he a sleepwalker being led, usually by Jamie, into this previously unimaginable world made of switches and buttons which when pushed or pulled started whirring motors and gadgets which played music or ground garbage or sent water gushing into a dry sink. He seemed to encounter an amazing terror on almost an hourly basis.

Since his attempt to use the sword had failed, Jamie MacGregor's jealousy seemed to have completely disappeared. Suddenly they were friends, and his new friend had tried to help him adjust to his surroundings in a way that made Griffin deeply thankful.

Jamie had been particularly excited about showing him

the wonders of something called a com-poo-ter, but Griffin had quickly asked him to turn it off. There were some things he was not yet ready or willing to understand. Besides the tech-nah-logy, he'd discovered something even more incredible—a remarkable access to history. The MacGregors had a wonderful library, and late one night, when he couldn't sleep for lying awake thinking of how it would feel to caress every inch of Miss Chelsea Brown's body, he had gone downstairs and found a book of Scottish history.

It was a big book, well worn and well read, the publishing date 1795. Fascinated, Griffin had thumbed through the book and found a detailed historical account of several clans, including the Campbells and the MacGregors.

He would never forget how he felt that night as he sat in the library, running his forefinger down the list of names of Chieftains of Clan Campbell until it came to rest on that of Red Hugh Campbell. Griffin had blinked away hot tears of pride and gratitude. At long last his father had gained that which he'd sought for so long. After Griffin had disappeared, his father had been made Clan Chieftain.

Which brought a new question to his mind: If he could find a way back to his own time, would his return destroy his father's newfound position? But that was a moot issue now. The crystals were gone, and the sword hadn't worked. Initially he'd thought he would like to have time to examine the year 2003, to enjoy the strange delights of the future. But now his curiosity had ebbed and faded, leaving him empty.

Somehow he had to find his place in this strange century, but he had no idea how to go about it. The shadows had deepened as he'd sat there, surrounded by the silence of nature, and in frustration he'd risen and gone out to hunt. It had taken him most of the morning to find any prey, and the rest of the afternoon trying to bring down one of the three deer he sighted, to no avail.

Now, as the fourth buck of the day moved into range, Griffin felt a sureness born of experience that this time he would be successful. The thought brought a sudden lifting of the shadows pressing on him.

The buck twitched his left ear, and Griffin's hand tightened around the hilt of his drawn sword. It was unusual even in his own time for a man to take down a deer with his sword. Most used the bow or spear to catch the fleet-footed animal, but Griffin had learned the art of patience. He didn't like killing, but in his time it had been a necessity at times—the killing of men, the killing of deer. Since he couldn't bed the women of his village, he'd made a show of being a good hunter. At least that was something he could do that proclaimed his masculinity loud and clear.

And besides, just now he felt a great need to do something, anything that would make him feel like he was still Griffin Campbell. Still himself. He remembered the night he had returned to Meadbrooke Castle from a hunting trip. He'd seen the candlelight from outside the bailey and heard the laughter. There was a party going on. Ever mindful of a chance to make a show for the sake of his father and the sake of his manhood, he'd thrown the carcass of the deer he'd slain over his shoulders, making a face as the stench of the blood hit him fully in the nostrils.

Pinning a broad grin on his face, he'd kicked open the huge double doors leading into the hall and strode inside, bringing the music and laughter to a stop as he threw the animal down in front of his father and the beautiful red-haired visitor, Jix, masquerading as Maigrey. She had gazed at him with awe and amazement in her eyes. Everyone had cheered.

It had been a rare night. For the first time he'd felt as though he wasn't faking his claims of being a man. For the first time he'd felt that perhaps there was hope for him. Then he'd learned that Jix loved Jamie, and his adventure with the two had begun.

The deer's nose wriggled, and Griffin knew he had to make his play. He leaped over the log and pierced the animal's side with his blade. The deer never felt a thing. That was one thing he made sure of in his hunting. He hated to see any living being suffer. He'd seen enough suffering in his time. A sudden sadness swept over him as he gazed down at the bloody, now blank-eyed animal. It was pitiful that a man felt the need to prove himself by taking a life, even if it was an animal's. Anger suddenly surged inside him.

Now what was he going to do, now that he had proven he was a strong and virile male by killing a defenseless animal? He couldn't bear to leave the carcass behind, even though he felt sure that Jix and Jamie didn't need any venison for their table. It was wasteful. If he had to flaunt his manhood by killing the creature, the least he could do was to make sure its death served some nobler purpose.

The memory of the night in Meadbrooke Castle flashed back into his mind, and a slow smile crossed his face. His horse gently nickered a few yards away, and his smile broadened. He bent down and heaved the deer up on his shoulders.

"Dinna ye worry, laddie," Griffin said to the slain animal. "Ye'll soon be the center of attention and the very highlight of the evening."

Chelsea hesitated at the top of the stairs. It was one thing to primp and pose in front of the mirror in the safety of her room, and quite another to face the throng of people below.

All right, it wasn't exactly a throng, but there were a lot of neighbors and well-wishers below, and the bright red dress wouldn't exactly allow her to fade into the woodwork like she usually did. She turned back to an ornate gilt-framed mirror at the head of the stairs and checked her appearance. Without the help of her friends, her application of makeup seemed a little subdued and amateurish, but she didn't think it looked terrible. The eyeliner was a little uneven, her brows a trifle dark, and her mouth extremely red. Her hair had been difficult, but she'd managed to pin it up in a kind of French twist, then lacquered it with hairspray. It was staying in place but did slightly resemble cotton candy.

Chelsea smoothed the dress over her thighs, her hands damp. It was awful to not even be able to judge how you looked. She needed another opinion, but she was afraid that if she asked Jix or Sam they'd try to redo her makeup or suggest another dress, and for once she wanted to be in charge of her own makeover.

"All right, Chelsea," she muttered, "either go on downstairs or run and hide in your room like a coward."

She took a deep breath and started down the stairs, hoping she could be graceful enough to walk in the matching red pumps without taking a tumble headfirst. The thought of such a disaster made her grip the railing and slow her pace, setting each foot carefully in front of the other until she reached the next to last step. Releasing her breath explosively, she looked up to meet the horrified gazes of her best friends.

"Chelsea!" Jix cried, moving quickly to her side. "Oh my gosh, honey, why didn't you ask us to help you?"

"Cookie, this is definitely not your look," Samantha added, darting a quick glance around. "Let's go back upstairs and I'll find something in my closet for you."

Chelsea felt the two closing in on her from either side, and her heart sank as they gripped her upper arms and whirled her back toward the second floor. Then something inside of her snapped, and she froze in place.

"No." She shook off their hands and turned to face the room below. "I'm going like this."

"But, Chelsea," Jix said, her eyes filled with consternation. "I really don't think you should. I mean, it's a beautiful dress, but, I mean, don't you think it's a little . . . well, red?"

"And short," Sam added. "Very short."

Chelsea smiled through the pain clamping around her heart. "Yes, it's very red and very short. That's why I'm wearing it. Shall we go in to the dining room? We're eating first, right?"

"Right." Jix exchanged glances with Sam, and Sam shrugged. Jix smiled brightly. "Well, then, let's go in."

Chelsea held her head high, her cheeks burning as she led the way into the formal dining room. Suddenly every eye was on her, and she felt the perusal of each and every guest as she made her way to her seat, designated by a delightful place card she and Sam had made that afternoon. She seated herself between her friends and ignored the whispers going around the long table covered in white linen, decorated with ornate silver candlesticks and flower arrangements.

Jamie sat opposite Jix, and there was an empty seat next to him for Griffin. Jamie stared at Chelsea with his mouth open, and when she sat down he snapped it shut and smiled at her, a dazed look on his face.

Chelsea wanted to sink into the floor. She wished the earth would open and swallow her whole. She hoped the ceiling would collapse and bury her in a pile of rubble—anything to hide herself away from the staring eyes of these people!

"You look lovely tonight," Jamie finally said to her. She acknowledged his politeness with a tight smile and mentally began reciting the theory of relativity verbatim from her college textbook. When she finished that, she started on the multiplication tables. Maybe if she kept her thoughts occupied she could somehow manage to get through this evening without completely breaking down.

What had she been thinking? That she could compete with Jix and Sam? She stole a look at her friends. Sam looked like a queen in an ice-blue gown dripping in glass beads. Her cleavage was ample without the help of a Wonder-Full bra, and though her hair was softer, it was a little lacquered, like her own. Sam's lipstick had been put on hastily, and Chelsea frowned, trying to process the fact that the beautiful Sam did not look perfect. She turned to glance at Jix. The pregnant woman looked flushed and happy, her green dress complementing her eyes. But it looked like she'd cried off most of her mascara during one of the emotional crises that she seemed to have so often lately, and she resembled a very soft and slightly nervous raccoon.

Chelsea leaned back in her chair and reached for the glass of champagne at her place setting. She took a sip, her thoughts running wild.

Her friends had told her she looked awful, but did she really look that bad, or was it just that they weren't used to her looking like this? Was it possible that seeing her in anything other than her usual dowdy plumage would always send them into spasms, unless, of course, they were responsible for the makeover? It was something to think about. In the meantime she would use the possibility to buoy up her sinking self-confidence.

"Where's Griffin?" she asked Jamie and took another sip of champagne. The fizzing drink tickled her nose, and suddenly the evening didn't look so grim.

Jamie's expression changed from rapt adoration of his wife to worry as he shifted his glance to Chelsea. "I don't know. He took off this morning, and I haven't seen him all day. I hope he's all right."

"Maybe the party made him feel uneasy," Jix said with a little frown. "We should have told him it was fine if he didn't want to come."

"I did tell him," Sam interjected from the other side of Chelsea. "He said it would be ill-mannered to miss your celebration."

"Then where is he?" Chelsea said.

Suddenly the tall double doors leading into the formal dining room burst open, revealing a startling spectacle. Griffin Campbell, wearing his green plaid and no shirt, his sword belted at his side, held the huge dead buck encircling his shoulders by its hooves and grinned at the gathered crowd.

"Happy first wedding anniversary!" he cried, crossing to the end of the table where Jix and Jamie sat in stunned astonishment. He bent and dropped the carcass to the floor, then put his foot on the deer and his hands on his hips.

"The conquering hero returns," Sam muttered. "Oh. My. God."

Chelsea stared at the man, a rush of heat beginning at her toes, rising to her knees, pooling between her legs and flooding upward to her breasts. Griffin's blond hair waved back from his strong, rugged face. His arm muscles bulged, strained from having carried the deer, and sweat trickled down his chest. Then a triumphant smile spread across his face, and Chelsea fell in love. Just like that. She fell. Completely. Utterly. In love with a man from the past. How crazy could she be?

She didn't care. She wanted to kiss him. She wanted to lead him out of the room and take him somewhere away from curious eyes and make love to him. He was incredible, and she wanted him.

Chelsea blinked. *Shades of adolescence—what is wrong with me? Get a grip. You can't be in love with him. You just met him. I won't allow you to fall in love with him!*

The entire dining room had started buzzing. Voices were raised. Questions were asked. Two women who were charter members of the local animal-rights groups got up and stormed out. Three men jumped up and started examining the deer, asking Griffin where he had killed it and how. Two more men sharply told the time traveler that it was illegal to kill deer now, they were out of season.

"Outrageous!" one woman said, her voice carrying. Chelsea saw Griffin flush with the comment and watched the realization flash into his ice-blue eyes that he had extremely miscalculated the appropriateness of his gift.

As more and more people crowded around Griffin and the talking grew louder and louder, he began to withdraw, backing away, the expression on his face becoming ever more strained. Chelsea pushed through the crowd now chattering in agitated excitement, until she reached Griffin's side.

"Och, lass," he said, sounding relieved to see her. His eyes widened as his glance swept over her, and he frowned. Chelsea wished once again the floor would dissolve beneath her feet. "Ye look . . . different," he said.

Chelsea felt her hope evaporate along with the last of her self-esteem. "I know, I know. I look awful."

His gaze slid over her again, this time like silk, like very hot silk. "Nay," he said, "ye dinna look awful. Ye look like a pagan goddess. As though ye should be dancin' beneath the moon."

Warmth rushed to her face as Chelsea tried to decide if his words were a compliment or an insult. But before she could force a response past her tight throat, he shook his head.

"I'm a fool and an idiot," he said, glancing around at the partygoers staring at him and talking animatedly. "Can ye get me out of here?"

"It's all right, really it is." In spite of his reaction to the "new Chelsea" she wanted to reassure him. It wasn't his fault. In 1605 no doubt bringing carnage into the dining room happened every day. She began leading him through the throng of people and didn't speak again until they reached the door. She paused, hoping he would change his mind and stay for the celebration. "Look, Griffin, Jix and Jamie understand."

He shook his head. "They understand because they're kind friends, but there's no excuse for my ignorance. I should have known better, but I felt the need to prove myself, to act as though I am someone in this time instead of the nobody that I truly have become."

Chelsea placed one hand on his arm and felt his muscles tighten beneath her grip as she gazed up at him, wishing she could tell him just how important he was in her life.

"That isn't true, Griffin. You are the same person you've always been. It isn't your fault that you're displaced. It's just going to take a little—"

"Time?" Griffin interrupted, a cynical smile lifting one side of his mouth. "Aye."

"Why don't we—"

A scream stopped her from finishing the sentence and she turned, her heart pounding as she watched an ashen-faced Jix collapse to the floor.

Chapter Seven

Griffin sat beside Chelsea Brown, trembling. He wished he could lie to himself and say his fear was just for Jix MacGregor and the possibility that she might lose her baby; he wished he could say he trembled out of guilt over his part in the catastrophe, for he felt sure that the shock of the bloody deer in her dining room had contributed to Jix's current physical problems.

But the truth was, he was scared to death, because he was sitting in a giant iron bird that was about to fly up into the sky and take them to the States United.

His mouth was dry and he swallowed, wishing he'd accepted a drink from the woman walking up and down the aisle. He'd declined, determined to face this new terror with his own courage, not that from a bottle.

The disaster at the anniversary celebration had only proven to him once again how much he didn't belong here. He was helpless, useless, and stupid, unable to chart his own course, unable to eat or drink or sleep or travel without the aid of his friends. Unable to attend a dinner party without making a fool of himself.

He smoothed his kilt down over his knees, glad he had insisted on wearing his own clothing this day. Though he'd garnered a few curious stares in the air-o-port, according to Jamie it wasn't all that unusual to see a man from Scotland in a kilt. Of course, even his kilt was different from those in this time period. His kilt consisted of a long piece of woolen material in a muted green and cream plaid. A man wrapped the plaid around his waist several times, then pulled the rest of the long material across his chest and over his shoulder. Sometimes it was held with a brooch.

The kilts of the twenty-first century were completely different, totally foreign to him. More civilized, he guessed. In comparsion his plaid was barbaric. He didn't care. At the moment it was the only evidence of his past left to cling to. His sword could not be brought aboard the air-o-plane; he learned that it had been taken with the baggage somewhere below. Without it he felt naked, helpless. There was that word again. He clenched his fists, his nails biting into his flesh.

Though Jix, Jamie, Sam, and Chelsea had all assured him that Jix's sudden cramping and bleeding couldn't have been from his unorthodox "gift," he wasn't so sure. He would never forgive himself if Jix lost her baby because of him.

Restless, he glanced back over his shoulder. Jix, Jamie, and Samantha sat a few rows behind him and Chelsea. Jix had her eyes closed and looked pale. Although Jix had refused to go to the hospital that night, Samantha had insisted she see a doctor in Inverness the next day. The news wasn't encouraging, and they had gained permission for Jix to fly home to Texas, to see something called a specialist.

Griffin shook his head and turned back around. To *fly* home. Unbelievable.

Now he sat beside Chelsea trying to keep his fear a secret, wondering if the heavy air-o-plane could really fly over the ocean to the New World. No, he corrected himself, to the States United. No, the United States of America, the country of the three women. Within its borders lay many other countries called states, and Jix's state was called Texas.

According to Chelsea, they would "land" in a town called Austin in a matter of hours. He had laughed when she first told him they would be spanning the globe in such a short time, but she'd assured him it was true. It was at that point that the churning in his stomach had begun.

The ride in the huge bird, Chelsea had assured him, would be simple, although actually getting on board the beast involved a great deal of preparation. Griffin had to have something called a "passport," and after seeing the frustration the item caused Jamie, he begged the Mac-Gregors to simply leave him behind. Jix and Jamie, and to his amazement, Samantha, all refused his request. Chelsea had remained quiet but looked worried.

"Who knows what kind of trouble you could get into?" Sam had said to him in her usual sarcastic way. "We'd better take you along." She'd turned to Jamie, fixing him with a steely eye. "Jix doesn't need to be worrying about Scotty boy here, so why don't you call up one of your underworld connections and take care of it?"

Jamie had glared at her and stormed away, but the next day he'd handed Griffin a small thin book. Griffin opened it to find his own image staring back at him in diminutive form. While the captured image of his face was disturbing, the name inscribed made him frown even more. Ian MacGregor.

"For the rest of yer stay here ye're my brother, lad," Jamie had informed him. "Don't ask questions, and don't talk about it outside the five of us, ye ken?"

Griffin did indeed. Jamie had done something against the laws of this time to help him, and Griffin wasn't about to do anything to get his host in trouble.

Samantha had tried to prepare Griffin for the upcoming trip, but after his tenth question she gave up in exasperation and turned him over to Chelsea. With Chelsea as his teacher, Griffin had managed to relax a little. She'd answered all his question patiently and hadn't chided or ridiculed him even when he'd turned pale at his first sight of the air-o-plane. After his earlier experience with what she called technology involving the tellie-vision, Griffin had steeled himself to expect anything. And yet he had never expected to sit in the belly of a great iron bird and trust it to lift scores of people into the air and bear them without incident across a vast, wide ocean.

How could it be possible?

He glanced over at Chelsea. She had a curious contraption balanced on her lap. She'd explained that it was like the com-poo-ter at Jamie's house, but much smaller. Closed, it looked like a large black book. She was bent over it, her fingers flying back and forth across tiny rows of hard black squares. He could see words forming on the inside of the open case. Griffin had to look away. It was too strange, and he felt strange enough already.

He was glad she was busy working on something and hoped she wouldn't look up at him and see the stark terror he knew must be on his face as they wanted to fly into the sky. What kind of warrior was he? What kind of Scotsman?

"Get hold of yerself, laddie," he whispered to himself, his fingers clenching the arms of the seat. Unfortunately, Chelsea heard his muttering.

She glanced up and turned to him, closing the small com-poo-ter, giving him her full attention. "Are you all right? I know this has to be unnerving."

"Aye," he admitted, " 'tis fair difficult to believe, let alone understand."

She gave him a long, calculating look, and then nodded. "I suppose it would seem like some kind of magic to a man who claims to be from the seventeenth century."

"Aye, it . . ." He stopped abruptly as the slight inflection on the word *claims* sank in. "Are ye sayin' that ye still dinna believe me or the MacGregors or Samantha?" He shook his head. "Surely ye dinna think they would keep up such a charade in the midst of what is happenin' to Jix?"

Chelsea had the grace to blush, and she shook her head as she looked away. "No, no, of course not. And I suppose Jamie would never think of breaking"—her eyes widened and she quickly lowered her voice to a whisper—"breaking the law unless it was a unique situation."

"So ye believe me?" he asked, knowing her answer was suddenly very important to him.

She hesitated, tapping the edge of her short nails on the top of the closed case. Was she nervous? Did being close to him make her ill at ease, or could her edginess possibly mean she felt the same physical attraction he felt whenever she was near?

An image of Chelsea in his arms flashed into his mind, followed by another of the beautiful woman running into Jamie's study and throwing herself against him, asking him to take her with him to the past. Then there was the way she had looked in that scandalous red dress. He shifted uncomfortably in his seat.

Stop it! he commanded his thoughts. *Ye canna get involved with this woman no matter how ye may long to do so. Ye must return to yer own time. Besides, ye daft man, ye canna touch her, and ye know it!*

At the moment the possibility of touching her was even more remote than his own time. Chelsea held herself stiffly beside him. Today her face was clean and devoid of makeup. She wore a brown suit with her hair pulled back in its usual small bun at the nape of her neck. She wore spectacles, dark-rimmed ones, and her attitude toward him was mild and only slightly friendly.

"You must understand, Griffin," she said, removing her spectacles and peering at him with a small frown, "I'm a scientist. That means—"

"Aye, I know what it means," he said, folding his arms across his chest, feeling slightly irritated. He glanced over at the elderly woman sitting next to him. He'd cheerfully exchanged his window seat for the middle one after they'd boarded the air-o-plane. He lowered his voice. "In my time I was considered a man of science and literature myself."

Chelsea raised both brows, her surprise and doubt reflected in her eyes. "Really? In what way?"

Griffin shifted in his seat again. Did the girl think he was an idiot?

"I studied the works of Pythagoras and Galileo, as well as other forward thinkers in my time. I know as well as ye that a man"—he paused, then gave her a nod—"or woman of science views a situation such as this quite differently than a layman would."

He waited for the look of disdain she would no doubt feel for his paltry attempt at appearing as educated as she. Samantha had told him of Chelsea's degrees from the University of Texas, and he had been dumbfounded by her accomplishments, and yet at the same time, not surprised in the least.

But instead of disdain, Griffin saw respect and understanding dart suddenly into the depths of her gray eyes. The acceptance he saw there was quite intoxicating. He leaned toward her almost unconsciously, drawn to her. A sweet perfume, like that of the roses in his castle's flower garden, wafted gently to him. The respect in her gaze disappeared, and in its place was, amazingly enough, desire. She stared at him as though mesmerized, her small pink tongue darting out from between her lips to unconsciously wet them.

Griffin wanted to capture that small, sweet tongue, to possess her kissable mouth, to take her in his arms and keep her safe forever. But if he dared to kiss her now, not only would he risk humiliating himself in front of a vast number of people, but she might think him a barbarian with no restraint. He did not yet know enough of this century's customs to risk such a move.

Still, he couldn't help but continue to drown in her eyes. A smile curved his lips as he watched embarrassment color her face, watched her realize how she felt to have him so near, and saw her bring those feelings rapidly back under control. She sat back in her seat and cleared her throat.

"Well, I had no idea you were a person of studies," she said finally, replacing her spectacles on her nose and opening the book in her lap once again. "I'll make a note of that."

Griffin was still grinning with the pleasure of knowing the lass had been disturbed by his nearness, when what she said fully registered.

"Note?"

She nodded, and her fingers began to fly again. Amazing. Fighting the distraction, he focused on her words.

"What do ye mean, lass? What kind of notes?"

"Notes on you, of course. I'm writing down all the information you give me about yourself, your time, your customs. After all, if you're a"—she glanced around and lowered her voice once again—"time traveler, then as a scientist I've got to take advantage of this opportunity."

"Aye," Griffin said flatly. So he was nothing more to her than an insect in a glass case, an interesting bug for her to examine! He smiled in spite of his irritation. Or maybe that was just what she told herself, to keep her feelings in check. He might be a virgin, aye, he might be celibate, but he was still a man and he still knew when a lass fancied him. He smiled and leaned toward her. "Ye have my permission to take advantage of me in any way ye would like."

Chelsea shot him a startled look and blushed again, the faint pink color creeping up her throat to her jaw. How he longed to trace that path with his lips. He groaned aloud as he realized he might have finally found a woman with whom he would be willing to risk looking like a weakling, like a mewling pup, in order to taste the sweetness of her mouth, even for a moment.

She glanced at him, and he realized he'd been staring quite rudely. Throwing caution to the wind, he started to tell her how beautiful she was, when all at once the great beast in which they sat began to move forward.

His body went rigid as he looked through the small window just beyond the elderly woman seated next to him. He watched the ground move faster and faster beneath them, and he clenched the seat arms so tightly he thought they might snap. He dared not look at Chelsea for fear he would reveal what a coward he really was.

Suddenly her hand covered his, and warmth stole through him as she leaned against his shoulder and whispered in a tone only he could hear.

"It's all right, Griffin. A lot of people are afraid to fly. Just relax, take a deep breath, and trust me. We'll be all right."

In that moment something amazing happened. Griffin released his fear and trusted that if Chelsea Brown said the air-o-plane was safe, then it was safe. The tension in his neck subsided and he unclenched his hands, turning one over to cradle hers.

"Thank ye, lass," he said, rubbing his thumb over the softness of her skin. So far, so good. No nausea, no trembling. "I do trust ye."

His trust was tested further in the next few minutes as the iron bird tilted backward and rose up into the air. He gasped, and Chelsea laughed aloud. His face burned with shame as he darted her a quick glance. To his relief, she didn't appear to be laughing at him.

"I love to fly," she confided, giving his hand a squeeze. "It makes me feel so . . . so free, you know?"

"Aye," he said, swallowing the lump in his throat and trying to get into the spirit of the whole experience. " 'Tis grand, 'tis wonderful, 'tis—"

Bile rose to his throat, followed by the breakfast he had wolfed down in the MacGregor kitchen. He clamped one hand over his mouth and turned to Chelsea, more panicked than the day he'd led a charge against a band of English infiltrators. The belt around his waist held him trapped in his seat, and in about two seconds he was going to make an utter fool of himself.

Without a word, without a disparaging smile or anything worse than a look of sympathy, Chelsea handed him a brown paper sack, just before it was too late. After thoroughly disgracing himself, Griffin leaned back against his seat, certain he had just lost whatever small chance he'd had to woo the gentle Chelsea Brown.

Chelsea sat beside Griffin and tried to ignore the heat coursing through her body by focusing on her sympathy for the Scotsman. How hard it must be for a man of strength to face these strange obstacles of the future. Things like airsickness didn't exist in his century. He was used, no doubt, to solving any problems with a sword. A chill darted down her back as she realized she believed his incredible story of time travel.

And not just because she knew that Jamie would never keep up a charade in the face of Jix's possible health problem. She believed Griffin Campbell because she knew what kind of man he was.

Another chill. Perhaps she was feverish. She lifted the back of one hand to her forehead. No, her skin was cool. Perhaps the thrill of flying again, the possibility of going home again, the fear of what might lie ahead for Jix . . .

Oh, cut it out. The scientist succumbed to the woman inside, and she released her breath in a long, shuddering sigh as she let her honest feelings take voice inside her head.

You aren't sick, and your heart isn't pounding because of flying or Jix or anything like that, and you know it. For the first time in your life, you've met a man who shakes you, who thrills you, who strips away your shyness and makes you want to be bold and daring, who makes you want to give yourself to him completely.

Chelsea dared a glance over at Griffin. He'd finally relaxed after the takeoff and was sleeping. He'd been delighted when she showed him how to use the earphones and tuned the device to classical music. It had calmed him, and once again she'd been surprised by the complicated man Griffin Campbell appeared to be.

Warrior, scholar, music lover? At first she'd categorized him as the seventeenth-century version of a jock. All brawn, no brain. Which wasn't really a problem in the beginning, since she had viewed him through the eyes of a woman whose sexuality was apparently being awakened from a long winter's nap. But now, after spending the last few days with him, Chelsea felt ashamed of her initial reaction to Griffin.

He was rather shy himself, she'd noticed, and gentle to a fault when dealing with any of the women. At the same time, she'd seen his strength of character when he knew that Jamie was going to have to forge a passport for him. A lesser man, a man of lesser integrity, wouldn't have cared. And then there was the way he gazed at her when he thought she wasn't looking. With a flame of desire in his eyes, and yet, something more besides lust.

Appreciation? Respect? She wasn't sure, but at some point she had known that her own thoughts bordered on turning Griffin into a sex object.

That was when she'd resolved to get to know Griffin as a person, not just a body under her scientific scrutiny. She hadn't gotten the chance to try out her vamping skills on him the night of the anniversary party. When Jix had fainted, all thoughts of Griffin and sex had been automatically banished from her mind as she rushed to Jix's side and reassured the frightened woman while Sam cleared the room.

Chelsea glanced over her shoulder at Jix. She hoped that once they reached Texas and Jix saw the specialist Sam knew, everything would be all right.

"Jix will be all right," Griffin said, jarring Chelsea from her thoughts by echoing them aloud.

She looked at him, startled. "How did you know I was thinking about Jix?"

A smile curved his firm lips, and Chelsea found herself temporarily mesmerized by his mouth, remembering that one hot kiss.

"Ye had a little crease right in the middle of yer forehead," he said, reaching up with a finger and lightly touching her skin. Chelsea drew in a sharp breath. The mere touch of the man's finger made her almost faint. What would happen if he ever touched her intimately? "And also," he went on, apparently unaware of the sudden pounding of her heart, "I knew because ye looked back at Jix with such concern in yer eyes. It was obvious."

"You—you're very observant," Chelsea said. "And I *am* worried, but I feel sure the doctor Sam wants Jix to see in Texas will help her."

"Aye, Samantha has told me that medicine has made great strides since my century." He frowned, folding his arms over his chest. The gesture made his biceps strain against the pale cream-colored shirt from his time that he'd insisted on wearing, and Chelsea caught her breath again at the magnificence of the man sitting beside her.

You have got it bad, Chelsea Brown.

"I had often wondered," he said, his gaze thoughtful, "if I would even allow my wife to bear a child."

"Really? Why not?" Chelsea said, ignoring for the moment that word "allow."

He shook his head, his mouth a grim line. "In my time, most babies dinna live past a few weeks, and many mothers die in childbirth. I had resolved that if I ever did find a woman who could love me, I'd never risk her life in that way."

Chelsea's mouth went dry as he looked down at her and

their gazes locked. How could such ice-blue eyes hold so much heat? she wondered. And how could he ever doubt that a woman could love him?

"Have you ever been in love?" Chelsea blurted, then quickly dropped her gaze to her laptop.

"Nay," Griffin said, sounding as though her question wasn't at all inappropriate. "I thought for a time that Jix might be the lass for me, but it soon became apparent how much she loved Jamie."

A flare of jealousy burned briefly inside of Chelsea, and it astonished her. The emotion wasn't completely foreign to her. She'd felt jealousy before, mostly where Jix and Samantha's friendship was concerned, but never over a man.

"Do you . . ." She cleared her throat, afraid to say the words, but knowing she had to find out. "Do you still have feelings for Jix?"

His silence stretched out so long that at last Chelsea forced her eyes to his. What she saw there made her breathless. He lifted one finger to brush the edge of her chin.

"Och, lass, when I look at ye, I swear I can barely remember her name."

Blue eyes held her frozen in place as Griffin leaned toward her, his gaze caressing her face, one hand lifting to tilt her chin very slightly. Chelsea slanted to meet him, feeling as though she were floating outside her body and watching as they moved through time and space toward one another. It was all so surreal; then she was slammed suddenly back into her body as his mouth came down against hers. His hand cupped her face as she gave in to the fire between them and parted her lips, the heat flooding her soul as Griffin touched her tongue with his.

Chelsea raised both hands to his chest and leaned into the burning, passionate kiss, closing her eyes, when all at once she felt his strong hands around her upper arms and shoving her away from him. Her eyes flew open, and she had a brief impression of Griffin's handsome face turning slightly green. She reached for another airsickness bag only to find she had given him the last one.

"Uh oh," she said, grabbing him by the arm and pulling him to his feet. "Come on, Griffin!"

Griffin slapped one hand over his mouth and stood, just as the elderly woman next to him removed her earphones and looked up, her eyes widening with delight and recognition.

"Why, my goodness, to think I've been sitting here beside you the whole time and didn't realize who you were," she said, opening her huge black pocketbook. She snared him by the shirtsleeve and pulled out a pen and an old-fashioned autograph book, thrusting them into his face. "Just sign it 'To Mabel from Fabio,' " she cooed.

Griffin grabbed the pen and scrawled something across the page, handed it back to her, and as she beamed up at him, threw up neatly in her lap.

Chapter Eight

"I'm sorry, Griffin."

Griffin looked up from his crossed fingers into the sympathetic eyes of Jix MacGregor.

She lay quite comfortably on what she'd referred to initially as a "couch" in the sprawling living room of Samantha Riley's large home. He sat in a soft chair beside her, trying to process the last hour of his life.

They'd arrived at the Crazy R Ranch after "landing" at the Austin Bergstrom International Airport and enduring a terrifying journey through what Jamie called "traffic" in the curious beasts known as "automobiles," which he'd unfortunately encountered in Scotland.

Griffin had thought he would disgrace himself yet again when finally the automobile in which they rode had seemed to burst out of the pack of other automobiles onto a fairly deserted road. He'd breathed a sigh of relief, perking up as the scenery rushing by the windows much too fast revealed they were traveling into the country, away from the frightening hustle and bustle of the city of Austin.

The sight of cows and horses had cheered him enormously, and by the time the automobile stopped in front of a huge, rambling home made of stone, Griffin felt almost human again. After getting Jix settled, Jamie and Samantha immediately left to drive back to Austin. They'd asked Chelsea and Griffin to look after Jix while they convinced an old friend, Dr. Ethan Ellington, to accompany them back to the Crazy R Ranch.

"I don't want you to have to go to the emergency room," Jamie said to Jix as he leaned down to kiss her goodbye. Griffin felt an increasingly familiar pang in his heart as he watched the gentle way Jamie treated his wife.

Will I ever find a woman to share my life with? Griffin wondered.

"I hope we can talk him into coming back here with us," Jamie said on his way out the door.

Samantha rolled her eyes. "Keep your fingers crossed."

To Griffin, asking a physician to come to your home was a perfectly normal request. After all, wasn't that what doctors did—visit homes and attend to the sick? It was confusing, as was her parting remark; still, he resolved that if crossing his fingers would somehow help the situation, he'd be happy to do it. Perhaps it was some cultural ritual, or could it be linked to yet another kind of tech-nah-logy he'd yet to discover?

He sighed and risked a glance across the room. Chelsea sat in the chair farthest from him. Her brown-trouser-clad legs were crossed at the knees, her arms folded tightly across her chest. Every fiber of her body seemed tense, uneasy. Because of what had happened on the air-o-plane?

Griffin felt the heat rise to his face just thinking about the embarrassing incident. After his disgusting display, Chelsea had calmed the woman beside him and offered to give her some clothing out of a bag she had carried aboard. The woman had taken Chelsea's bag and with a loud "Humph! And he isn't even Fabio!" had squeezed past him and headed down the aisle toward the back.

Somehow Chelsea's matter-of-fact attitude had helped him get through one of the most mortifying moments of his life, and he had told her he would be forever grateful.

So why did she look so angry now? No, not angry. She looked as though a rope had been strung through her body and then pulled tight. She wore all brown again today. While she looked just as beautiful as always to him, he couldn't help but wish she would wear bright colors and silky cloth. They would suit her. Her body attitude and her choice of garments suggested an attempt to blend into her surroundings. Their gazes met, and Chelsea smiled ever so slightly before looking away.

Of course, she was embarrassed in spite of the kindness she'd shown him on the air-o-plane. He'd humiliated both himself and her, and he didn't blame her for avoiding him. Any ideas he'd had about pursuing a romance with sweet Chelsea had been destroyed the moment he'd disgraced himself by ruining Mabel Cunningham's new silk skirt.

In spite of everything, in spite of all he had experienced in his own time and this one, he was still a pathetic excuse for a man, unable to touch a woman without his fear winning out and sending him running for the nearest bush. Thank God she'd thought it was the airsickness that had made him ill. If she knew the truth . . . He'd thought he was willing to risk his pride for Chelsea. Now he knew he was still too big a coward.

"Griffin?"

He turned his attention to Jix, realizing he'd never acknowledged her comment. "Aye, lass? What are ye sorry about?"

"I'm sorry that the crystals weren't in the cave," she said. She leaned over and patted his clenched hands. "I'm sorry that we had to drag you away from your homeland and everything familiar to you, so suddenly."

Griffin eased away from her touch as inconspicuously as possible. He hadn't had any problems with being near Jix since his arrival in the twenty-first century, but he was guarding his behavior very closely. He'd been a fool to risk kissing Chelsea, and he wasn't about to take a chance on getting ill again.

"And I'm sorry the sword didn't work either," Jix went on, darting a quick glance at Chelsea. "But we'll do our best to help you adjust to living here, Griffin."

Griffin stared back down at his crossed fingers. "Aye, thank ye, lass. But I hope to find a way to go back to my time. Perhaps when we return to Scotland, the crystals will be there."

Jix nodded. "They are certainly persnickety things. They seem to appear and disappear at will, don't you agree, Chelsea?"

Chelsea sighed, and Griffin looked up sharply. Their eyes met, and she looked away before he could discern what was wrong. "I don't know what to think anymore," she said. "It's all very confusing."

"You can say that again! When we were in 1605 . . ." Jix broke off, her brows knitting suddenly together as she pressed one hand to her abdomen. Griffin leaned forward, and Chelsea jumped from her chair to hurry across the room.

"Are ye all right, lass?"

Jix drew in a sharp breath and released it, nodding. "Yes, I'm all right. Chel, would you mind fixing me a hot cup of tea? I'd really appreciate it."

"Of course, honey, you just rest."

Griffin couldn't help letting his gaze follow Chelsea as she walked across the large room toward the kitchen. He noted her grace, the way her hair hung softly over her shoulders, and the way she looked back once to meet his eyes as she hurried into the other room.

He sighed and turned back to Jix. She was watching him, a broad smile on her face.

"Boy, you've got it bad, don't you?"

"I beg yer pardon?" he said. Jix's words still often confused him, as did all of the Americans' speech patterns at one time or another.

"You like Chelsea!" she squealed. "That's great! Go for it!"

Griffin started to deny it, but what was the use? He knew Jix well enough to know she was like a dog with a wee bone when she thought she was on the track of a secret or mystery. Better to admit it and swear her to secrecy.

"Shhh," he cautioned. "Ye canna tell anyone." He gave her what he hoped was a quelling look. She laughed, and Griffin stood, suddenly weary. He might be a helpless, mewling, time-traveling coward, stuck in the future, dependent on his friends, but he still had some pride left.

105

"I'll be outside," he said abruptly. Jix grabbed his hand as he walked by and stopped him.

"Oh, stop it, laddie," she said. "I wasn't laughing at you, so take that Scottish pride and put it away. I was laughing because everyone already knows!"

Griffin's eyes widened as panic surged through him. He sat down on the low chair next to her before his knees collapsed.

"What do ye mean?"

Jix gave his still-crossed fingers a firm pat. "I mean that it's obvious to Sam and Jamie and me that you're already half in love with Chelsea. We think it's wonderful."

"Are ye tellin' me that Chelsea knows that I"—he groped for the right words, meager and understated as they seemed—"that I *like* her?"

Jix glanced toward the kitchen door, then back at Griffin. "Well, I'm not sure *she* realizes it yet. You see, Chelsea is sort of a late bloomer and doesn't really know much about men. Which is a good thing," she hastened to add, "because you really don't know that much about women either."

Griffin nodded grimly. "Aye, that I don't. But please hear me, Jix." He clenched his jaw, hoping his words could pierce Jix's excitement and reach her brain. "In spite of yer hopes to make a match between us, I must tell ye that it willna happen, so please dinna embarrass me by attempting to throw the two of us together."

Jix raised one hand to her chest. "Me? Would I do that?"

"Aye, and more if ye thought ye could get away with it." He smiled, shaking his head. "But ye know full well that I canna be with any woman. And I must return to my own time, where at least I belong."

"Of course you can be with a woman," Jix said, her voice scolding. "Don't you remember our lessons with the Squash Lady? You just need practice."

Griffin groaned. "Och, now don't be startin' that nonsense again. I dinna want to come into the kitchen later and discover ye've assembled a woman out of vegetables for me to fondle."

"Poor laddie," she said, shaking her head. "I know it's

hard, but Chelsea is just the person to see you through this. She'll understand, Griffin. She's a scientist. Just explain how when you were a little boy you caught your father dallying with the maid the very night your mother was dying, and it scarred you in a very unusual way. Give Chelsea a chance—it'll work, Griffin."

For an instant Griffin was tempted to do just that, but reason stepped in and kept him from making a fool of himself again.

"Nay, lass, I dare not. Besides, what if I do find a way to return to my own time? 'Twould no' be fair to begin something I canna finish. I dinna belong here."

Jix leaned forward and tucked a long strand of hair behind Griffin's ear. "Don't be hasty," she said softly. "Maybe you came to our time for a reason. Maybe you aren't supposed to go back."

Griffin captured her hand in his, feeling a rush of gratitude for Jix's friendship and understanding. Recklessly he pressed a kiss into the palm of her hand, just as a silver tea tray slammed down on the table next to him. Tea in dainty cups sloshed over into the saucers below, and a small stack of bread that appeared to be filled with meat or cheese collapsed. He looked up, startled, into Chelsea's reproachful gray eyes.

"Here's your tea, Jix," she said. "I think I'll go up to the guest room and unpack."

Jix seemed unperturbed by the tone of Chelsea's voice and waved one hand toward a door across the room.

"Sure, there are three or four down that hall, just pick one and make it yours. But as soon as Jamie gets back I have a big favor to ask you, Chel."

Chelsea turned back, folding her arms across her chest, a pained look on her face. "Yes?"

Griffin had to steel himself not to rush to her side and take her in his arms. He wanted to kiss away the sadness, the constant loneliness he saw in her eyes. And now what must she think of him? Could that possibly be jealousy in her expression? Did she think he was interested in Jix? That he would dare to try to usurp Jamie's place? Surely she couldn't believe that of him. And yet—if she was jealous, didn't that mean she had feelings of some kind for him?

"Griffin really needs some new clothes," Jix was saying, her words jarring him from his thoughts. "He and Jamie aren't the same size—Griffin's shoulders are much broader and he's a good inch taller. He needs his own things. Besides, we don't know how long we'll be here, and he can't keep wearing his kilt or he'll get his face pounded."

Griffin frowned and glanced down at his green and beige covering. "I dinna see what is wrong with my plaid. 'Tis clean."

Jix rolled her eyes. "Trust me, sweetie, if you set foot out of this house in that, the first redneck that caught sight of you would be calling you a sissy and then the next thing you know you'd be punching him or pulling out that sword and then you'd end up in jail and—"

"All right!" Chelsea said. "You've made your point." She slumped, looking totally dejected. "What do you want me to do?"

"I want you to take him shopping."

Chelsea stared at Jix as if she'd lost her mind. "You want me to what?"

"Take him to Austin, buy him some jeans. Whatever." Jix reached for her purse on the floor near the sofa and drew out a silver-colored card. "Here." She handed it to Griffin. "The sky's the limit."

He stared down at it. There were words on it he could barely make out. Platinum Mastercard.

"I dinna understand—" he began.

"I don't think—" Chelsea said at the same time.

"Oh!" Jix pressed one hand to her stomach again. "Oh, please," she said, a little breathless. "It would mean so much to me, Chelsea. I want to feel that even though we had to drag Griffin over here and keep him from finding a way home again, the trip isn't a complete loss to him."

"But why can't Sam take him?" Chelsea asked, shifting her feet and glancing over at Griffin in obvious discomfort. "I don't have any fashion sense—or at least that's what Sam has told me most of my life."

"Please, Chelsea?" Jix said, imploring her.

Griffin almost chuckled aloud. Watching the auburn-haired lass work her magic on her friend was almost as much fun as watching the . . . what was it? . . . the tellie-vision. In spite of the fact that Jix was playing matchmaker when he'd expressly forbidden it, he was glad. Perhaps he and Chelsea could yet get past the fiasco on the air-o-plane.

"Besides, I really would like Sam to stay here with me," Jix said. "After all, she knows the doctor and everything, and I want both of you to have some fun," she rushed on. "I'd really like it if you'd take him to Austin."

"I can't leave you now," Chelsea said, sinking down on the sofa beside her friend and taking her hand.

"Well, to tell you the truth, it would really help me if there weren't so many people here when the doctor arrives."

Chelsea dropped Jix's hand and stood, the color draining from her face. Griffin's heart immediately went out to the woman, and he felt the first real anger toward Jix he'd ever known. Jix's words had hurt Chelsea deeply. Why, he wasn't quite sure, but he knew it as if he had endured the pain himself.

"Oh," Chelsea said, stepping back another step. She took a deep breath and released it raggedly. "If I'd known, I would've stayed in Scotland. The last thing you need right now is unnecessary people hanging around."

Jix had the grace to blush, Griffin noted. He raised one brow. What was the lass up to? Since his arrival she had treated Chelsea with utmost consideration, and he couldn't imagine Jix saying something to purposely hurt one of her friends.

"No, no, I didn't mean it like that," Jix said, as if realizing she'd gone too far. "It's just that . . ." She glanced over at Griffin. "Griffin, could you give us a moment alone?"

"Aye, of course," he said, rising from the soft chair. "I'll just walk outside and wait for Jamie."

"Oh, and Griffin—"

He stopped halfway across the room. "Aye?"

"You can uncross your fingers now."

Chelsea gave him a curious look and glanced at his fingers, then smiled the first real smile he'd seen all day. He blinked and uncrossed his fingers. Jix and Chelsea giggled in unison as he frowned and headed out the doorway.

Women! No matter the century, they still had the power to drive a man absolutely daft.

"Nay, none of that finery! I want to be a cowboy!"

Chelsea turned away from the rack of silk shirts to stare at Griffin. "You want to be a what?"

When Griffin left the room at the ranch house, Jix had quickly confided the real reason she'd wanted Chelsea to take the man shopping. Jamie, it seemed, was slightly jealous, and after seeing the way Griffin had kissed Jix's hand, Chelsea could scarcely blame him. Jix wanted the handsome Scot out of the way while the very important issue of her baby's safety was under discussion.

She didn't want to hurt Griffin's feelings, Jix explained, but she'd really prefer some privacy for herself and Jamie tonight. So even though Chelsea wanted to stay when Jamie and Sam arrived with the doctor in tow, Chelsea hustled Griffin out of the picture and into Samantha's blue Tahoe to go to Austin.

At least Jix didn't want to get rid of me, Chelsea thought as she sorted through another rack of shirts. *I hope.*

She also hoped that someday Jix would realize what a sacrifice she was making. The last thing Chelsea needed was to be around the handsome Scot. After helping him through his difficulties on their flight, Chelsea knew she was headed for heartbreak unless she put some emotional distance between herself and Griffin.

His reactions to the marvels of the twenty-first century had ranged from amazement to fear, to delight, to awe, and every single naïve reaction endeared him to her more. He had tried so hard to hide his trepidation over flying, and Chelsea's heart had gone out to him. She was sure he had deemed his airsickness a weakness and knew he'd been deeply embarrassed. All of it, including holding his head over a paper bag, had only served to convince her that Griffin Campbell was the man she'd been waiting for all of her life.

How stupid could she be?

"Chelsea, I dinna like these clothes," Griffin was saying, and she blinked and gave him her attention again. He pointed through the plate glass window of Foley's to a tall man striding by wearing dark jeans, a soft checked shirt, black boots, and a Stetson. "I like those clothes. Ye know, like that of a cowboy. Jix and I watched them on the tellievision last night and she explained them to me. 'Tis the closest I've seen to my own culture."

Chelsea blinked and hung the mauve silk shirt with the French cuffs back on the rack. "Cowboys are the closest things to Scottish warriors?"

"Aye," Griffin said, nodding emphatically. "From what Jix has told me, the cowboys protect the land and its people and are greatly admired and respected in Texas."

"Yes, I suppose that's true, but—"

"So if I have to give up my kilt, then I want to dress like a cowboy," he said, his tone almost petulant.

Chelsea bit her lower lip to keep from laughing out loud. He had a look on his face that reminded her of a small boy who desperately wanted his way. Well, why not? If it made Griffin happy to dress like a cowboy, who was she to argue?

"All right," she said, "but we'll have to go to a different store. I know just the place."

As they walked through Barton Creek Mall, Chelsea tried to keep the conversation going, asking Griffin what colors he liked best, but the farther they walked, the quieter he became. When they rode the escalator up to the second level, she glanced back at him and wondered what he was thinking. His jaw was tight, almost clenched, and she made a mental note not to assume that just because Griffin didn't complain about the new world in which he found himself, it wasn't affecting him.

She helped him step off the escalator and turned to ask if he wanted to stop by the food court first. The look on his face brought her up short.

"Griffin," she said, pulling him to one side. "What's wrong?"

His gaze searched hers, and Chelsea felt a quick dismay at the troubled look in his blue, blue eyes.

"I dinna belong here," he said softly. He glanced around at the people hurrying past them and shook his head. "How will I ever find my place?"

Chelsea watched the anguish wash across his features and wished, not for the first time, that she were Jix or Sam and could reach out to him, comfort him somehow. Jix would make a joke right about now, and Sam would flirt with him, but Chelsea Brown could only stand there in silence, her heart aching, groping for words that wouldn't come.

"I'm sorry . . ." she began haltingly.

Griffin's hesitant smile caught her unawares and she had to close her eyes to keep from grabbing him. "Och, lass, listen to me, whinin' like a wee bairn. 'Tis I who am sorry."

She opened her eyes and took a quick, steadying breath. His smile was strained, but she loved him for the effort he was making.

Loved him. There was that word again. Chelsea Brown, are you out of your mind?

Impulsively she laid one hand on his arm, felt his muscles tense beneath her fingers, had one brief intoxicating moment of being close to him, of touching him, before he pulled away. Whatever sizzle she'd thought she felt evaporated as he took a step back, putting even more distance between them. He couldn't have been more obvious if he'd turned his back.

"Shall we make me a cowboy, lass?" he asked, his voice gentle. Chelsea nodded, feeling nine times a fool.

"Sure," she said, lifting her chin. "Just follow me."

"Country Classics" was just around the corner from the food court, and Chelsea led him there, determined to keep her distance, and Griffin's feelings be hanged! She had a few feelings of her own and she was tired of having them trampled underfoot.

They reached the store and Chelsea went immediately to the jeans department, chose four pair of varying sizes—

she would not dare look at Griffin to gauge his waist size, among other things—and thrust them into his arms.

"Here," she said, pointing to the changing rooms at the back. "Go back there and go into one of those little rooms and try them on, one at a time."

Griffin gave her an apologetic smile. "Lass, I dinna mean to pull away from ye, it's just that . . ." He hesitated.

Chelsea mentally filled in the rest. *It's just that you aren't attracted to me. Yes, I get it.*

"I'll get you some shirts," she said, marching off and leaving Griffin to stand gazing blankly after her. When she looked back again, he was headed for the changing rooms.

Good, this is great, she thought briskly as she pawed through a rack of checked shirts.

All she had to do was be businesslike, be professional, be his personal buyer, and everything would be fine. She chose five shirts of varying shades of blue—they would look so wonderful with his eyes—*no, wait, don't go there*—and headed for the rear of the store. On the way she picked up a pair of black boots size 13, a black Stetson hat, and on impulse, a pair of rough leather chaps. She snagged a pair of tartan plaid boxers, too, not allowing herself to think too much about how cute the blond Scot would look in them. Her mind turned of its own accord to Griffin's dilemma as she weaved through the racks of clothing.

Maybe Samantha would let Griffin stay at her family's ranch indefinitely. Maybe he could really learn to be a cowboy and find his place and a sense of belonging; maybe he could find a way to still be a warrior even in this day and age. Maybe . . . She broke off the chain of thought and knocked on the door of the dressing room.

"Griffin?"

"Aye," was the less than enthusiastic response.

"Here are some shirts and things to try on. Just come out after you have them on, okay?"

He stuck his head out the door, looking morose. He took the clothes from her and sighed. "Aye," he agreed. He perked up at the sight of the leather chaps, smoothing one hand over the roughness and giving her a wink. "Thanks, lass."

As Chelsea waited for him to change, a sharp trilling sound went off inside her purse, startling her. Jix had insisted she take her cell phone and anxiety swept over Chelsea as she pulled the contraption from her bag and frantically tried to find the right button.

"Jix?" she said into the small phone.

"It's Jamie," a deep voice echoed back to her.

"Is Jix all right?" Her heart pounded painfully and guilt struck her, heart-deep. Here she was feeling sorry for herself over Griffin's lack of attention when her best friend was in the middle of a major life crisis. She resolved from that moment forward to stop putting her trivial concerns ahead of Jix and her situation.

"She's fine. The doctor said the baby is, too."

Chelsea could hear the relief in his voice. "I'm so glad, Jamie. What did he say she should do?"

"He said . . . wait a minute, Jix wants to talk to you."

"Chel? Did Jamie tell you? I'm all right! The baby's all right!" Jix cried.

Quick tears started in Chelsea's eyes. "Oh, Jix, that's wonderful!"

"I just have to take it easy until my third trimester, so we're going to stay here in Texas until I deliver."

Chelsea's thoughts immediately turned to Griffin. "In Texas? But what about Griffin?"

"Chelsea? I can't hear you—the phone is breaking up. Listen, don't rush back. You and Griffin have fun, and I'll talk to you later!"

The phone went dead, and Chelsea dropped it back into her purse, smiling. Jix was okay. Jamie's baby was okay. The answer to Griffin's dilemma would work itself out somehow. Suddenly she realized it had been an awfully long time and the Scot still hadn't come out of the dressing room.

"Griffin?" she called outside his door. "Did you try something on?"

"Aye, lass," came his response, the sound strained.

"Well, come on out and let me see."

"I dinna think so."

Chelsea smiled. "It's all right, Griffin. Believe me, I understand, but I'm sure you look fine."

"I don't want to come out."

She released her breath impatiently. "Griffin, come out! I want to get back to Jix and I can't do that until we buy you some clothes."

"All right, lass, but I think it's a mistake."

The door swung open and Griffin emerged, his face bright red, his hands folded protectively over his crotch.

"Oh, you tried the chaps on. That's—" Chelsea stopped as Griffin angled sideways and looked over his shoulder down at his bare behind.

"I canna believe the cowboys wear such a thing," he said, his voice aghast. "How do they ever keep from injuring themselves?"

Chelsea stared at the displayed portion of his lean, hard-muscled bottom and thighs and felt every bone in her body turn to mush. She tried to speak but couldn't. Finally she managed to croak out three words.

"Over the jeans," she whispered.

Griffin faced her, his dark brows knit together. "Over the—och, ye mean the heavy blue trousers." He nodded. "Aye. That makes much better sense."

He turned and walked back into the dressing room, offering Chelsea one last look at the scenery.

Chapter Nine

"We'll have lunch in Wimberley," Chelsea said brightly.

Griffin gave her a curious look. Ever since his mistake with the leather chaps, she'd been acting very strange, but who could blame her?

He flushed as he remembered again what a fool he'd made of himself, exposing his bare arse to a lady such as Chelsea. She must think him the worst kind of barbarian. He had apologized over and over again, and she had insisted that he shouldn't worry about it, that it was an honest mistake, but he still felt foolish.

And in spite of her assurances, ever since that moment she'd assumed a different attitude, still friendly, still polite, but distant. As if she had been hired as some sort of guide instead of someone he had kissed.

He released his pent-up breath, daring to stare at her openly, drinking in the pure sight of her. She wore her hair, her soft wheat-colored hair, in that accursed bun at the nape of her neck. If only someday he could take the pins from the luscious waves and spread her hair across his pillow as he gazed down into her eyes and made love to her. Today her garments were just as staid and proper as always, but the heat of the Texas sun had finally pushed her to remove her ugly brown jacket.

His gaze roved over her slim arms, now bare to just

above the elbow. She wore a cream-colored blouse, just sheer enough to drive him crazy, just low enough in the neckline to give him the barest hint of cleavage. The soft garment clung to her curves, and it was all he could do not to reach out and touch her.

She shot him a sudden, startled look and frowned. Griffin jerked his gaze back to the road ahead, feeling like a knave. He cleared his throat.

"How much farther is it?" he asked.

"Not much," she said, her voice sounding cautious and a little confused. "Just over this hill." Then as if she realized she'd been silent too long, she launched into a description of Lone Man and Lone Woman mountains, the two peaks named after two Tonkawa Indians.

She was holding him at arm's length, he realized suddenly, and a wave of depression swept over him, even though he knew it was better this way. She kept talking, telling him about the town they were headed for, which was near the Riley ranch. Her voice seemed forcibly cheerful as she described the quaint village of Wimberley nestled in the hills, called "A Little Bit of Heaven" by its inhabitants.

She gave him the historical background of the settlement, beginning with the building of the mill and the settling of the valley by men named Winters and Wimberley. She chattered on about places called Blue Hole and Jacob's Well and Mount Baldy, then expounded on the "cuteness" of the town square where unique little shops kept tourists captivated through the summer months, and told him all about something called "market days," which reminded him of the market in his own time where items new and old were sold. She described the nearby town of San Marcos and told him of the university there.

At last she seemed to have run out of historical and local references and came up for air. She glanced at him, the tour-guide persona fading, a hint of melancholy appearing in her eyes.

"I'm sorry, I must be boring you silly," she said, averting her gaze back to the road as she slowed to make a turn.

"Nay, I love history," he assured her, wondering what had caused both her sadness and her feigned cheerfulness.

"I'm glad you found some clothes you liked."

Griffin glanced down at the soft black and gray checked shirt he wore, tucked into black jeans and topped with a black belt and silver buckle that sported a strange animal on it and the word "Texas" curved above the armored beast.

"Aye, I suppose I will fit in better now, though I still dinna quite understand about the army-dilla."

Chelsea laughed, and the sound sent a wave of happiness through him. How he would love to hear her laughter every day of his life.

"It's just a symbol of Texas," she explained, her gray eyes warm now, the sadness and false cheer gone. "I don't really know why, except that there seem to be so many of the little guys wandering around."

"Do ye think my boots are a bit too garish?" Griffin frowned at his footwear. With so many options to choose from, it had been a hard decision, but he had finally settled on what now seemed a rather whimsical choice. He'd selected a black pair made from some kind of giant bird called an emu, Chelsea had told him, and the shining leather gleamed. He pulled up the leg of his jeans, exposing the ornate stitchwork on the sides of the boots, which depicted a silver thistle, emblem of Scotland.

"I think they're perfect for you," Chelsea said, her voice soft. He looked up in time to see a longing in her eyes just before it gave way back to efficiency.

"Now," she went on briskly, "we're coming into Wimberley. Would you like to have lunch at the Cypress Creek Café or the Town Deli?"

Griffin leaned back against the soft leather of the seat and prepared himself for an afternoon of what Chelsea had called "sightseeing." If only he could tell her the only sight he was really interested in seeing was the woman herself, soft and yielding in his arms.

They had lunch, a strange combination of spicy meat, tomatoes, and something called a tortilla. Griffin enjoyed it tremendously, but was growing rather tired of the nonstop recitation Chelsea seemed bent on giving him about the Texas Hill Country. He wanted to talk to her about the history of Chelsea Brown, but he couldn't quite find the nerve to make the conversation more personal.

They visited the "square" and the sundry little shops there, and just down the road, the Tote Sack (where he met a fascinating woman named Nell who told him he should be in movies), the Old Mill Store, and what seemed like a dozen others. They stopped at the Pink Flamingo for a snowcone. As far as Griffin was concerned, this one stop made the entire visit to the twenty-first century worthwhile. He ordered something called Tiger's Blood, and the look on his face must have been close to rapture as he tasted it, for Chelsea laughed out loud at his obvious delight and ordered a striped one with coconut, peach, and raspberry for him to try next.

After almost making himself sick on the sweet and icy concoctions—how they kept the ice frozen in the Texas heat he could not understand—they got back into the automobile and headed down the road again.

"This is a wonderful place," Chelsea said as she turned down a dirt lane. "There's someone here you should meet just because she's so nice."

They stopped beside an arch over which a mounted sign read "The EmilyAnn Theatre." Chelsea explained that the nonprofit theater had come about as a tribute to the daughter of Ann and Norm Rolling. A few years earlier, seventeen-year-old Emily Rolling had been killed in an automobile accident just a few days before Christmas.

The story saddened Griffin, and when he met Ann Rolling, his heart ached for the sweet, smiling director of the theater. She welcomed him with a friendliness and kindness that deeply touched him. Her tour of the grounds included waterfalls, ponds filled with water lilies, a butterfly garden, a puppet theater, and at last the outdoor amphitheater, created to resemble what she called a "Shakespearean theater." Her explanation of the program, *Shakespeare Under the Stars,* intrigued him, though he had no knowledge of the plays she listed or the author.

"It's too bad our program is only for high school students," she said with a smile. "You look like you walked right out of the medieval ages. Now there's one more thing I want to show you."

She led the two of them up the hillside to where a gnarled oak tree stood to one side of the winding path. On the ground was a carved sign that read "Betrothal Tree." Next to the tree was a framed sign on which a poem was printed.

Griffin paused in front of it and began to read. "Here, with our hands joined in this living tree, standing on this hill beneath God's sky, I pledge myself to you and you to me with love that will not die, everlasting as the stone on which we stand and ancient as this oak. With arms entwined our lips so softly touch, and by this act we vow our love is blessed, both now and till the end of measured time."

Chelsea had moved to stand beside him, and as he finished reading the poem she glanced up at him. He turned at the same moment, and their gazes locked.

"Measured time," he whispered. "I'm not sure what that is anymore."

"Oh, look," she said. "This is the most interesting part." She circled the tree and stepped up on the large rock behind the trunk. One of the tree's branches had grown back in on itself, creating a circle. She thrust her hand through the knotted natural opening. "I can put my hand right through."

Griffin stepped over to the tree and without thinking, reached up and took her hand in his. "And now I've caught ye," he said.

"The legend says that couples used to come to the Betrothal Tree to swear their love to one another," Ann told them. "In olden times that pledge was considered the same as a wedding vow. So look out," she teased. "I might have to declare the two of you betrothed if you stand there for very long."

Chelsea gazed down at Griffin from her perch, and once again he saw that touch of sadness so frequently evident in her eyes. She bit her lower lip and looked away. The moment grew awkward, and he tried to ease the silence with a jest as he released her hand.

"I dinna think so," he said. "I think the lass could do far better than the likes of me."

"Nonsense," Ann said. "Have you looked into a mirror lately?"

Griffin chuckled. "Thank ye, Mrs. Rolling, but remember, beauty is only skin-deep."

"And sometimes not even that," Chelsea said.

Griffin turned to see her jump off the rock and brush a few dried leaves from her brown trousers, her eyes downcast.

"We'd better be going," she said, moving past him without a glance. "Thanks so much, Ann." Her voice warmed as she spoke to the petite woman. "We'll try to make it to one of the performances."

"That would be wonderful," Ann said, giving her a hug. She turned to Griffin. "And you—don't be a stranger. We can always use some strong backs out here."

Griffin smiled at her and gently took her hand, raising it to his lips with a bow. He brushed his mouth against her skin and squeezed her fingers slightly. "It was an honor to meet ye."

Ann's mouth fell open. "Oh, my, Chelsea, you'd better grab this one quick! He's straight out of one of those hot thigh books."

Griffin grinned, but saw with dismay that Chelsea's face had turned beet red. She turned and rushed down the hillside, leaving him to smooth things over with Ann, explaining that Chelsea had complained of feeling the heat earlier and no doubt wanted to get back into the air-conditioning of her car. Griffin silently congratulated himself on his grasp of all the new words, like car and air-conditioning, that he was able to remember and use without sounding too awkward.

Ann nodded, though her brows met in puzzlement as she laid one hand on his arm. "I hope I didn't say too much," she said, "but honestly, Griffin, I thought the two of you were together. There's just so much . . . there . . . between you."

"Aye." He nodded and covered her hand with his. "And ye're a bonny woman for seein' it. I only wish it could be, but unfortunately, I must return to Scotland."

Ann shook her head. "Scotland will always be there," she told him with an arch of a brow, "but Chelsea may not be." She reached up and touched the end of his nose with her finger. "You think about that, laddie."

Griffin watched Chelsea as she hurried away, her hair coming loose from its knot and falling like warm sunshine over her shoulders.

"Aye," he said, his throat tight with an uncomfortable feeling, "I will."

When he reached the car, she was inside, fiddling with the air-conditioning knob, acting as if everything was fine. He followed her lead, talking casually about the theater and the charm of Mrs. Rolling as Chelsea backed the car out of the gravel parking lot and drove back to the main road.

"There's one more place I want you to see," she said. "I forgot to take you there when we were in town." Retracing their path, they were soon back at the square. Chelsea parked the car and led him down an alleyway to a large house that had been converted into a store that sold rocks. The shelves were filled with gems and artifacts such as fossils imprinted with leaves and small insects and snail-like creatures.

"You said you were a scientist," Chelsea reminded him as she picked up a slice of agate and held the beautiful thin jewel-like slab of rock to the light. "I thought you might get a kick out of this."

Indeed, a "kick" was exactly what he was getting, Griffin decided as he roamed around the shop while Chelsea looked at pieces of glittering amethyst. He loved studying the different fossils, for it reminded him that there was still something in this day and age older than he was. He smiled wryly and picked up a stone with the imprint of a fish in it. No matter how many centuries passed, some things remained, documenting history and the passage of time. It was somehow comforting.

He moved on to the pieces of quartz, beautiful in their

bins, then picked up smooth green pieces of malachite and puzzled over sandstone carved into shapes of frogs and turtles. He had circled through the three adjoining rooms of the store and ended up at the glass counter where the owner sat, peering at a stone through a curious glass strapped around his head, lapping over one eye. The man glanced up at Griffin as he hesitated in front of the counter.

"Hello," the man greeted him with a wave of his hand. "Name's Dan. I own this place. If you see anything you want, just let me know."

"Does that help ye see the stones more clearly?" Griffin asked, his curiosity getting the best of him.

"Yes. Would you like to see the one I'm working on?"

Griffin nodded eagerly, and the man gestured for him to come around the counter. Dan rose and pushed Griffin into the chair and looped the eyepiece over his head.

"There you go, just look at this." He placed a smooth stone in his hand. "Do you see the streaks of gold?"

"Aye, I do," Griffin said, peering through the glass. It was amazing how it made the details of the stone so much larger, yet still clear. "What is it?"

"I'm not certain. I'm trying to break it out of there and examine it more closely. But here"—he took the stone from Griffin's hand and turned away for a minute, then spun back—"this is a real sight under the magnifier. I found this at Jacob's Well just a few weeks ago." He held up a glass box. The object inside was blurred by the magnifier Griffin wore, and he bent to get a closer look. He almost fell out of his chair. He ripped off the eyepiece and stood, his heart pounding furiously.

In the bottom of the glass box were three beautiful emerald-green crystals.

"Where . . ." Griffin swallowed the dryness from his throat and tried again. "Where did ye say ye found this?"

The man frowned at him. "At Jacob's Well. Are you all right?"

"May I buy this from ye?" Griffin asked, trying to keep the excitement from his voice.

"I'm sorry, but it's promised to another buyer. I have

someone who wants to do research on it. There's something odd about these crystals. They put out some kind of energy field. Doesn't register on a Geiger counter or anything, but it's still pretty eerie. I only handle them when I'm wearing gloves."

"Do ye have any others?"

The man shook his head slowly. "No, these are the first I've ever found, the only ones. They're unique to the area."

"Please," Griffin said, feeling a little frantic. "I'll give ye . . ." What could he give him? He had no money. He looked down. "I'll give ye my boots," he cried, starting to tug one off, jumping up and down on one foot. "They're brand-new. I just bought them."

"I don't want your boots," the owner said with a hesitant laugh. "I'm sorry, but the crystals are spoken for."

"What's going on?"

Griffin looked up from trying to pull off his second boot. Chelsea stood frowning down at him, and he supposed he must look a sight, standing with one boot off and jumping up and down to wrench the other from his foot. He stopped hopping around, settling both feet firmly on the floor, and smiled sheepishly.

"I—I wanted to buy something and realized I had no money," he explained.

"Griffin, I have plenty of money," she said, shaking her head and swinging the leather bag she carried from her shoulder. "What do you want?"

"I've already explained that the crystals aren't for sale," Dan said, shooting the two of them a curious look.

"Crystals?" The color drained from Chelsea's face, and Griffin rushed to her side, limping the few steps. He caught her by the elbow.

"Chelsea, are ye all right?"

"What crystals?" she whispered. "You don't mean—"

"These right here." The man indicated the box. "But they're already spoken for. If you'd like, though, David Baker might let you look for similar ones at Jacob's Well. That's where I found these, in the well."

"Jacob's Well?" she echoed faintly, then seemed to mentally shake herself. "Yes, yes, I know David." She pulled her arm from Griffin's grasp and straightened, lifting her chin in an oddly vulnerable gesture. "It's all right, Griffin," she said. "We'll go to Jacob's Well and talk to David. Don't worry."

Griffin was loath to leave the crystals, but he had no choice. He managed to pull his boot back on and, bidding the store owner goodbye, followed Chelsea out the door and to the car.

Once inside the automobile he turned to her, to ask more questions about Jacob's Well, but the words died on his lips. Her face was chalk-white again, and her lower lip trembled.

"They're the same kinds of crystals, aren't they?" she asked him. "And if you find them, you'll leave me and go back to your own time." She drew in a sharp breath, her eyes widening. "I mean, you'll leave *us*—Jix and Jamie and Sam and me—and go back."

Griffin nodded, feeling a sharp ache in his chest at her obvious distress. "Aye, lass," he said softly, "if I find them."

She answered his nod with her own. "Well, all right then. I'll call David tonight and ask him if we can come by to-morrow." She ran her tongue across her lips. "Is that soon enough?"

"Aye," he said with a sigh, " 'tis soon enough. But I must tell ye, I dinna know if they are the same crystals."

"Really?" Chelsea asked, brightening. "Do you think so?"

Griffin laughed. "Unfortunately, there's only one way to find out—by touching them." He hesitated, trying to form the words he wanted to say in his mind first. Wanting to say the right thing. "If I do find them, and if I do return to my time, I'd like ye to be there to see me depart."

Chelsea looked up at him sharply. "You would?"

"Aye." He moved closer to her, his gaze fixed on her lips. "As a fellow scientist, ye ken, I think ye should be there to document what happens."

"Yes," she said, her voice a whisper, "I think I should definitely chronicle what happens . . ." She swayed toward him, and Griffin leaned forward to touch those kissable lips with his own . . . and stopped himself just in time. He cleared his throat.

Chelsea blinked and sat back abruptly in her seat. "I mean, of course I'll go with you to find the crystals." She started the car and backed out of the parking lot, a dazed expression on her face. As they pulled onto the main road, she turned to him, her gray eyes clear again.

"Why don't we stop at the library?" she suggested. "They have a lot of history books about Wimberley and this area. Maybe they'll tell us something about the crystals. Maybe they've been sighted before."

"The man at the store said they had not," Griffin reminded her, then frowned. "What library? At the ranch? I dinna know that Sam was a collector of books."

"How could Dan know for certain?" Chelsea said, answering his first comment. "And the library is a public library, where anyone can come and look at books and take them home with them."

"Take them? Ye mean buy them."

"No, they borrow them. It's a lending library," she explained.

Griffin shook his head, dumbfounded. "Amazing."

"Besides, it doesn't hurt to investigate. After all, that's what scientists do, right?"

He smiled at her, once again letting his gaze travel over her. Och, she was a sweet one. He knew she didn't want him to leave, had known it ever since she first expressed her concerns about the space-time continuum.

Chelsea Brown liked him, just as he liked her. The thought filled him with sudden warmth, and all at once he didn't care if he ever went back to Scotland, or to his own time.

"Here we are." She pulled up in front of a nice building made of stone. Griffin had been greatly impressed by the architecture in Wimberley, as even the businesses seemed to design their buildings so as to detract not from the beauty of the valley.

Griffin followed her inside, and she directed him to a table. He stumbled to the smooth wood surface and caught himself as he stared around in awe at the wealth of books surrounding him. " 'Tis amazing," he said, shaking his head. "And all for the takin'."

"Here," Chelsea said as she dumped a stack of books onto the table. "These will get us started."

Griffin picked the first one off the top and read the title: *Clear Springs and Limestone Ledges.*

"That's a good one," she said, sitting down beside him and opening another book. "It has a lot about the history of the entire area."

Griffin started reading. Minutes ticked by as he flipped through the first book, then moved on to another, and then another. The library was quiet, cool, and peaceful. Griffin looked up from his book and realized that he felt more at home than he had since his arrival in this century.

A sharp, sweet wave of homesickness came over him as he sat there, thinking. In his little cottage, his hideaway from his father and the pressures of being his son, he had assembled over many years a nice little collection of books. There among them he felt at peace both with himself and the rest of the world, as he knew it. But now he had discovered that the world was vastly larger than he'd ever dreamed, filled with people and wonders he'd never imagined. And yet, sitting here amongst the books, he felt such comfort, as if perhaps he belonged.

"Now, this is interesting," Chelsea said, breaking into his reverie. He turned to her, dismissing the purely sentimental thoughts from his mind.

"What is, lass?"

"There was a Duncan Campbell that lived in this area in 1882," she said, her head bowed over the large tome. Her finger traveled across the page, keeping her place in the small print. "It says he was arrested for murder and hanged without a trial." Chelsea glanced up and gave him a half smile. "I hope he wasn't anyone in your family tree," she said. "Pioneer justice—it wasn't always fair." She turned a page and stopped. "Oh, look, there's even a picture, a tintype it says, that was made the day before the man was hanged. It was his last request. Maybe he was one of your ancestors. He looks a lot like you."

She held the book out to Griffin, and he took it. It was a large volume, and he pushed the other books in front of him back before he slid it onto the table and glanced down.

He froze.

Two familiar eyes stared up at him, captured forever in the brown shades of a hundred-year-old photograph. Familiar eyes that seemed strangely relieved, given that the man was to be hanged the next day. A cynical smile played about the man's lips as he gazed up at Griffin from the pages of history, from the pages of Texas history. The man, the murderer hanged by a crowd angry for justice in the year 1882, was his cousin Duncan Campbell. Griffin blinked. It wasn't possible. His cousin had disappeared in 1601, never to be seen again, presumed by all to be dead. Duncan was the one who had told Griffin about the "magical" cave, and then one day had disappeared forever. Of course. It was simple. Duncan had found the crystals, too. Duncan had traveled through time. But how had he traveled from the Scotland of the past to the Texas of the future?

"Griffin, are you all right?" Chelsea asked, her voice anxious. "What is it? What's wrong?"

He smoothed one trembling hand over the page as he pushed himself to his feet, his gaze locked on the photo. "Chelsea, lass, we've got to get to that place, the place the man spoke of."

"Jacob's Well?"

"Aye." He turned to her, his heart pounding painfully against his chest. "Ye've got to help me, lass. Ye've got to help me travel back in time again."

Chapter Ten

Chelsea dragged Griffin out of the library before one of the many people staring at them complained to the librarian. Once outside, she put her hands on her hips and shook her head at him, feeling the blooming joy inside of her start to wither.

She didn't know why discovering there was a man named Campbell in a history book about Texas should make Griffin so upset, but it all boiled down to the same thing: He wanted to go back to his own time. Of course he did. For all she knew, he had a wife and ten kids waiting there for him. But there was still one little problem with his plan.

"Griffin, I can call David Baker and we can go out to Jacob's Well, but even if you find the crystals and use them to travel back in time, you won't end up in the Scotland of that time period, right? I mean, from what you and Jix told me, you were still in the exact same *place*, just a different time."

"Nay, lass, ye dinna understand. I must go back in time here, in Texas." Griffin paced back and forth across the St. Augustine grass, his hands clasped behind him.

"Uh, Griffin, would you walk on the sidewalk, please? They just planted that grass."

Griffin moved to the cement sidewalk without slowing

down. She watched him continue to stride back and forth and at last sighed. "All right, would you please tell me why in the world you would want to return to the year 1605 in Texas?"

He shook his head and kept pacing. " 'Tis not 1605 I must go to, but 1882."

Chelsea blinked. "I'm sorry, you've lost me. Why 1882?"

Griffin darted her an impatient look. "Did ye no' see the photo of my cousin Duncan? Did ye no' see that he was hanged for murder?"

"Your cousin? But, Griffin, that man wasn't your cousin—he couldn't have been. He was just a man named Campbell." Chelsea grabbed him as he strode by and brought him to a halt. "What are you talking about?"

Griffin took a deep breath, and Chelsea realized he was practically shaking beneath her hand. Why in the world was he so upset about seeing a photo of some long-dead ancestor?

"He is my cousin," he said at last, "and he did not belong in 1882 any more than I belong in 2003!" He shouted the last words, and a man walking out of the library gave them both a frowning glance and a wide berth as he headed for his car.

"Griffin, calm down," Chelsea said, trying to put a soothing tone in her voice, trying to be patient. "Let's get in the car and we'll talk about it." She led him to the parking lot and had to practically push him inside the car. "All right," she said, once she was back behind the wheel. "What are you talking about?"

Griffin's ice-blue eyes glittered with pain as he turned toward her, his hands clenched against the dashboard as if to steady himself as he spoke.

"Duncan Campbell is my cousin. We grew up together in the Highlands, and I know his face as well as I know my own. He is the one who told me about the hidden cave—the magical cave, he called it—when we were young. One day he went out hunting and never returned." He shook his head, his brows knit together. "I searched for him, along with many others, but he was nowhere to be found.

After a time we assumed he was dead or perhaps captured by the Sassenachs."

Griffin lifted his gaze back to Chelsea's. "I have missed him every day since, and now—now in this time, in this place—you show me an obscure history book and in it is a photograph of my cousin and an account of his hanging in a time that would be the future to him and me but which is your past." He took a breath. "Dinna ye see? This is why I've been sent here. This is why all this has happened. To bring me to this place, this time, that I might go back and save Duncan."

"Oh, Griffin," Chelsea said softly. "I understand how you must feel, but how can you know for certain that it was a picture of the same Duncan? Perhaps he's descended from your family, but—"

"Nay, lass, 'tis Duncan." He turned in the car seat, his gaze fierce and determined. "Do ye not see? I had no reason any longer for being alive, but now I do. Now I have a purpose, and it's an important one. Will ye take me to Jacob's Well, or must I find it alone?"

Chelsea felt her throat tighten. If Griffin went back in time to 1882, what if he didn't return?

She wanted to say no, that she wouldn't take him to Jacob's Well, but she couldn't. The eagerness, the desperation in his eyes would have been enough to convince her to help him, but her love for Griffin was what made up her mind.

"I'll take you there," she said, "but first, let's go back to the ranch so I can change clothes. We can pick up some swimsuits and take a dip while we're there."

Griffin frowned. "Ye wear a suit when ye swim? Like the one I tried on earlier with a tie and all?"

Chelsea couldn't help smiling in spite of the possibility that very soon she might be telling the handsome Scot goodbye forever.

"You ever been on a horse before, son?"

Griffin looked up from the large leather saddle he held into the amused eyes of Samantha's head groom, a man called Pete. The grizzled mouth of the sixty-something

131

cowboy twisted around a brown-bowled pipe in what Griffin could only guess was supposed to be a smile. It was hard to tell. The man's face resembled the ground, cracked and lined after too many days without rain. But it was a good face, and Griffin found himself liking Pete in spite of his open amusement.

After Chelsea told Jix their news, Jix had suggested that Griffin and Chelsea take what she called a picnic lunch and cross the Crazy R Ranch on horseback to Jacob's Well. Jix hadn't seemed to hold out much hope that they would find the crystals, but she had encouraged them to explore the possibility. At first Griffin had been impatient with the idea of taking the time to leisurely ride to the site, but once he saw how much it meant to Jix—and, he could tell, to Chelsea—he gave in. After all, he reasoned, he had all the time in the world. He might not ever come back, and he had to admit he'd like to spend a little more time with Chelsea before he had to go.

"It's okay if you ain't never been on a horse," Pete said, a thin stream of sweet-smelling smoke bringing Griffin's attention back to him.

Pete leaned against one of the stall doors, pipe sagging from his mouth, arms folded loosely over his chest. He was a small man, but the corded muscles in his arms showed a wiry strength Griffin could respect.

"Aye, I ride," Griffin said, hefting the saddle. "Though I've never used one of these before."

Pete's bushy gray eyebrows darted up, and he removed the pipe from his mouth. "Never used a saddle? You part Comanch? Nah, not with that hair."

Griffin frowned. "I dinna ken yer meanin', but in my ti . . . that is, in Scotland, we dinna ride with this kind of saddle."

The man nodded and replaced the pipe between his teeth. "Well, there ain't much to it," he drawled, straightening away from the stall door and crossing to Griffin's side. He took the saddle easily, lifting it to his shoulder. "Who you ridin'?"

"Samantha told me to take out a horse called Twilight."

"Twilight?" Pete sneered the name. "Now, ain't that just

like Miz Riley to put a man on a silly little mare like that."
He cocked one brow toward Griffin. "I hear tell you wear
a skirt sometimes, but surely you don't want a little-girlie
pony like Twilight."

Griffin cleared his throat and silently thanked Chelsea
for taking him to buy clothing more suited to Texas. In
his jeans and boots he felt at least somewhat at ease,
though his footwear was obviously new. He could imagine
what would have happened if he had appeared in front of
this crusty cowboy in his kilt.

Out of habit he'd brought his plaid anyway, rolled up
and tucked under his arm. Even in his own time, if a man
chose to wear braes, he brought his plaid along just in case.
As if reading his mind, Pete pointed to the material with
his pipe.

"What you got there?" he asked.

A sudden inexplicable anger rushed through Griffin. In
his own time, in Scotland, he was a warrior. He'd fought
a dozen battles, wielding his sword in fights to the death,
vanquishing the foes of Meadbrooke Castle. He didn't like
violence, but he was no stranger to it. He was respected by
all who lived on his father's lands. He had been hand-
picked to be the next chieftain of the clan. But here, in
Texas, in this time, he was nothing, reduced to standing
before a wizened old man for inspection, feeling insecure
because his boots were too new.

"My skirt," Griffin said, straight-faced. "I thought the
urge to put it on and dance among the wildflowers might
come over me while we're out on the ranch."

The older man stared at him, his wrinkled lips pressed
together. After a second he burst out laughing.

"That's a good one, son. All right, I apologize for the
girlie remark. You're obviously not a wimp, not with those
hands." He reached over and took one of Griffin's callused
hands, turning it palm up. "You've done a day's work in
your life."

"Aye, I have worked with my hands." Griffin pulled his
fingers away and narrowed his eyes. "Listen, laddie," he
said, "I have ridden warhorses into carnage that ye couldna

133

even imagine. I dinna want a 'girlie pony.' Back home I had a stallion named Firestorm, and I miss him sorely. Do ye have a stallion, or are all the Crazy R nags made up of mares and steeds without ballocks?"

Pete almost lost his pipe, to Griffin's great satisfaction, but the man recovered quickly and grinned.

"Well, well. All right, then, if you're sure about it, I'll put you on Sinbad."

"I'm sure," Griffin said.

"All right, fine with me. Want me to show you how the saddle goes?" A twinkle danced in the old man's eyes.

Griffin sighed. "I think I can manage," he said. "Thank ye very much."

"No problem at all. Sinbad is in the last stall. And speakin' of carnage, if you don't treat him right, that's what he'll turn you into." Pete laughed and winked and strolled away, humming as he went.

Griffin walked toward the back of the stable, gritting his teeth.

"Thank you, sweetie." Jix put down the tiny cap she was crocheting to accept the cup of tea Chelsea handed her.

Jix lay on the black leather sofa in the living room while Chelsea tried to relax in the comfortable matching chair. She couldn't. When Griffin had left to go to the stables, Jix had asked Chelsea to stay for a minute. Now Chelsea sat fidgeting as Jix sipped tea and did everything but tell her why she'd wanted her to stay. Chelsea was impatient to be with Griffin, heading out for Jacob's Well. What if he left without her?

Chelsea watched her friend start crocheting again and closed her eyes, releasing her breath in one long sigh. It never failed to unnerve her when she saw Jix doing something so maternal. Who would have ever thought the scatterbrained, free-spirited woman would ever settle down and have kids? Chelsea opened her eyes. Still, if Jix could do it . . .

She glanced back at her friend, and her mood took a nosedive. Jix could do it because Jix was beautiful and vivacious and had a crazy sense of humor and was Jix. No wonder Jamie had fallen for her. Every man that ever met Jix fell for her. Including Griffin. Jix looked up just then and smiled, so happy and contented that Chelsea felt a rush of shame.

How selfish she had become! Instead of rejoicing with Jix that her baby was fine, that Jix was healthy and happy, she was fuming with jealousy. Well, enough was enough. If this was what falling in love did to a person, she didn't want any part of it!

"Chel, are you okay?" Jix asked, jarring her from her reverie.

"Oh, I'm fine, I'm great," she said with forced enthusiasm.

"Oh, yeah, you're wonderful." Jix gave her a knowing look. "Listen, just because Griffin is hell-bent on looking for the crystals doesn't mean he's going to find them. Remember, they weren't in the grotto in Scotland when he went back, and even Jamie's sword didn't work. I'm telling you, those things have minds of their own."

Chelsea frowned, lifting her cup to her lips and taking a sip.

"Jix, I know you think that, but it's impossible. The crystals are matter—solid objects. They don't think; they don't disappear and reappear."

Jix raised one auburn brow. "How do you know? Griffin says they're magical. If they're magical they might have all kinds of strange abilities."

Chelsea shook her head. "There's no such thing as magic, and they don't have abilities because they aren't alive."

A smile split the expectant mother's face. "How can you say there's no such thing as magic, knowing what you know about me and Jamie and Sam? How else do you explain our trip through time?"

"Scientifically, of course," Chelsea said, setting her cup down in the matching saucer. "Obviously, those crystals have some sort of property that displaces the space-time continuum and somehow is patterned to react with human thought waves. It has nothing to do with anything supernatural."

"Ever the scientist, eh, Chel?" Jix said, gazing at her friend. "If you'd experienced it yourself, you might think differently."

"If I'd experienced it myself, I'd have broken up the Jix-Sam continuum, and that might have meant the end of mankind as we know it," Chelsea said, making a rare joke. But Jix didn't laugh.

"You think we left you out on purpose, don't you?" she asked, setting her cup down and picking up her crochet work again.

Chelsea hesitated. "I felt that way at first," she said honestly, "but I wasn't there. You invited me, but I had to teach. If I'd been there I'm sure I would have been included."

"For a change."

"Excuse me?" Chelsea shook her head. "I didn't say that."

Jix glanced up from the tiny cap. "You didn't have to." She leaned over and took her friend's hand. "Chel, I'm sorry. I know that sometimes Sam and I can be exclusive, but we don't mean to be. It's just that since I lived with the Rileys for a time, she became . . . well, more of a sister to me than a best friend."

"Well, the two of you certainly argue like siblings," Chelsea said, summoning a smile.

Jix laughed and squeezed Chelsea's hand, then released it and leaned back. "No kidding! And believe me, that includes all the downsides of having a sister, as well as the up. I love Sam to pieces, but you must know she drives me nuts, and vice versa. But with you, Chel"—she paused, her gaze thoughtful—"well, with you it's different."

Chelsea closed her eyes. Of course it was different. She wasn't part of Jix's family, not like Sam.

"You always make me feel good about myself," Jix said.

Chelsea opened her eyes, too shocked to speak. Jix was leaning toward her, her green eyes earnest.

"That's a rare quality, and it means a lot to me. You're kind and patient and loving and the very best friend I could ever hope to have. I'm sorry if I've ever made you feel like you didn't mean as much to me as Sam. That just isn't true."

A warmth rushed through Chelsea, and quick tears smarted at her eyes. "Thank you, Jix," she said, her throat tight. "I—I love both of you very much."

"In spite of the makeovers?" Jix laughed. "Don't bother denying it, I know how bad it was! Now, come and give me a hug before you head out with that big Scot. By the way, he's already told me that under no circumstances would he allow you to go back to the past with him."

Chelsea hurried over to give her friend a hug, but puzzled over Jix's comment. The memory of throwing herself against Griffin as he held Jamie's sword flashed into her mind. Her cheeks burned as she tried to sound casual. "Why would he think I'd do that?"

Jix shook her head, looking exasperated. "Maybe because he sees what we all see, you silly girl. You're in love with him."

Chelsea's mouth dropped open. "I am not."

"Yes, you are."

"I am not!" She shook her head vehemently.

"Fine, fine." Jix held up both hands in surrender. "Whatever you say. Of course, most best friends are willing to confide in one another, but if you say you don't love him, well, then, you don't love him!"

Chelsea started to deny it again, then sank back down in her chair, silent. This was Jix, her friend. If she couldn't tell her the truth, who could she tell?

"Of course I love him," she said, almost groaning out loud. "How dumb is that? I'm in love with a man who would make Brad Pitt look like a goon. And not just a breathtakingly handsome hunk of a man, oh, no, not for Chelsea Brown! He's got to be a time traveler who needs to rush off and rescue a long-lost cousin and who . . ." She broke off before she could reveal that in spite of Griffin's kindness, he obviously wasn't attracted to her. Even she had a little bit of pride.

"He's not in love with me, Jix," she said softly. "And never could be. You know that."

"Honey, I don't know anything except that I've never met two people better suited for one another than you and Griffin. Except me and Jamie, of course." Jix's sympathetic voice broke down Chelsea's last defenses.

To her chagrin, tears burned in her eyes and streamed down her cheeks. "Oh, Jix," she whispered, "what am I going to do? He's going to leave me forever."

Jix put the crocheted cap aside and reached out for Chelsea's hand, squeezing it tightly. "Then don't let him."

"But he won't listen to me. He's determined to go back and save his cousin Duncan."

"No, I mean, don't let him leave you behind."

Chelsea caught her breath as Jix's words rushed over her. "You mean, go with him?"

Her friend shrugged, her green eyes gleaming. "Why not?"

Chelsea shook her head and started to tell Jix she could never do such a thing, never give up her home and friends to journey to another time, but Jix cut her off.

"Chelsea," she said, "I know this sounds crazy, but I trust the crystals. I mean, I trust them and I trust God—now, don't give me that look," she warned, and Chelsea shook her head. Jix should know by now that Chelsea didn't subscribe to any real belief system. Science was her religion.

"God made those crystals, and He can use them however He sees fit," Jix went on. "The crystals took me and Jamie and Sam to the past, then brought us home again, and believe me, it was all for a reason. The crystals brought Griffin here, and if they *are* at Jacob's Well when you get there, then I believe that whatever is supposed to happen will happen."

Chelsea clung to Jix's hand, suddenly wishing she had her friend's simple, childlike faith.

"Okay," she said. "Just as a hypothesis, what if what you say about the crystals is true and they take us back to 1882, where Griffin wants to go, but they don't bring us back?"

Jix's gaze registered the fact that this possibility hadn't crossed her mind, but she quickly recovered.

"In that case," she said, "your destiny, your happiness,

must lie in the past." She reached out and hugged Chelsea. "Oh, but I hope it isn't. I hope it's here, with Griffin, in this time."

Chelsea closed her eyes and returned the hug, her pulse racing with her thoughts. "I hope so, too, Jixie-Pixie," she said. She pulled away and smoothed her friend's hair back from her now anxious face. "Don't worry. You wouldn't dare have that baby without me."

Jix smiled, but there was concern in her eyes. "Be careful. Be very, very careful."

"I will," Chelsea promised, and rose to meet her destiny.

Chelsea's bottom bounced up and down on the back of a gelding named Pancho. At first she'd tried to beg off and suggested they just take the car. But apparently Griffin had bonded with the wrinkled little old stable master named Pete, and she now found herself bumping along on horseback—not one of her favorite places to be—at Griffin's side—which unfortunately *was*.

She was lagging behind, and Griffin glanced back. He smiled, and Chelsea felt her heart contract with longing. He slowed his huge stallion until she caught up, and then he set his pace beside her. Chelsea racked her brain for something scintillating to say as the silence stretched between them.

She didn't want to talk about the crystals. If she didn't talk about them, maybe they wouldn't be at Jacob's Well. Now, that was new thinking for Chelsea Brown! Was she becoming superstitious on top of everything else?

The history of Wimberley and San Marcos and the surrounding area had been just about exhausted, and she had a feeling that Griffin was sick of listening to her discourses on the subject. What she really wanted to say was something unorthodox, something absolutely shocking, something like, oh, maybe, "You're magnificent and please can I jump your bones?" She didn't have the nerve, of course, to say that, so she kept quiet.

Griffin sat his horse easily, like one born to the saddle, his hands strong and sure on the reins. His new jeans fit him like a second skin, and she admired the muscles in the thigh closest to her, even as she noticed he'd brought his sword along, shoved into a place on the saddle meant, no doubt, for a rifle. She'd never been attracted to macho men before, but Griffin's odd brand of it tugged at her heart.

"Nice weather we're having," she finally managed to choke out, and almost slapped her palm against her forehead. Duh and duh-er. How lame could she be?

"Aye," he agreed, not seeming to realize, or choosing to ignore, her lameness. "It feels good to have a horse beneath me again."

A brief image of what it would be like to be beneath Griffin flashed through Chelsea's mind, and she scolded herself for such wanton thoughts.

"Do ye like to ride, lass?" he asked.

"Oh, uh, yes, sure," she lied, hoping the sedate gelding she rode wouldn't decide to expose her by breaking into anything more dangerous than a fast walk. As if reading her mind, Griffin nudged his mount into a trot, and Pancho followed suit.

Please, please, please, don't let me make a fool of myself, she pleaded with whatever higher force might be listening. Desperately she tried to remember the directions she'd received the few times she'd been on horseback. Samantha's father had given them all lessons when they were kids, and even now Chelsea remembered his deep voice booming, "Keep your heels down!" as the three bounced around the corral.

"Keep your heels down!" she repeated now as Griffin's stallion broke into a gallop and Pancho, not to be outmatched, hurried to catch up with the huge beast that surged ahead of them. They raced across a long, flat stretch of land, and Chelsea clung to the saddle horn, her fingers wrapped around the leather reins in an effort to at least appear as though she had some control over her horse.

Griffin glanced back and grinned at her, and she summoned an answering smile, only to see him frown and quickly pull back on the reins, grounding to a stop as Pancho obediently stopped beside him.

"Are ye all right, lass?" Griffin asked, his blue eyes dark with concern. "Ye look a bit green about the gills."

Chelsea gulped air for a moment before even trying to answer. "I—I'm fine . . . really, I'm fine."

He nodded. "That's good. I'm a bit out of practice myself. Would ye like to walk for a time?" He dismounted and circled around Chelsea's horse, while Sinbad complacently chomped grass.

"Oh, yes, that would be . . ." She caught her breath as Griffin reached up and slid his hands around her waist, lifting her out of the saddle and to the ground. His fingers lingered against her skin for a moment, and the heat was so intense that Chelsea could only gaze up at him, spellbound. He seemed as transfixed as she, and she watched as his ice-blue gaze quickened, his jaw tightened, and he leaned toward her. Centimeters away from her mouth he stopped, dropped his hands from her waist, and stepped back.

"I'm sorry," he said. "I'm no' usually such a rascal, but somehow every time I get near ye, I want to touch ye. I canna help it."

Chelsea blinked, her chest tight. "You . . . you can't?" she said. "But you . . . I thought . . ." She hesitated. Griffin stood staring at the ground, looking miserable, and she pushed herself to keep talking. "Griffin, I wanted you to kiss me."

He looked up, a half smile on his lips. "Did ye, lass? Och, if only the wanting was enough."

Chelsea shook her head. "I don't understand. If—"

"Yeeeeeee—haaaaaaa!!"

Griffin spun around at the abrupt sound, and Chelsea silently cursed the two men riding up on horseback until it occurred to her that they might have been sent by Jamie or Jix or Sam to fetch them back. Was Jix okay? Chelsea's heart pounded fearfully as the men's horses slid to a stop beside them.

"Is everything all right?" she asked, overcoming her natural shyness to speak to the strangers. "Is Jix all right?"

"Jix?" One of the men paused to shoot a fine stream of brown juice into the dirt at her feet. She took a step back and was glad when Griffin moved beside her. The stranger swayed unsteadily on his horse, his homely face twisted into a leering smile. "I don't know no Jix, darlin'. Me and Tucker here, we was just on our way over to the Rileys' to see if old man Riley is ready to pay what he owes us."

Chelsea glanced up at the man's companion. The one called Tucker appeared to be a little more sober than his friend, but his eyes held a steely glint she found unnerving. There was a rifle tucked into a sheath on the saddle. She knew that ranch hands often rode with such weapons to guard against rattlesnakes, but the sight of it in the hands of these men made her extremely nervous.

Griffin moved away from her to stand beside his horse. He adjusted a strap on the saddle, seemingly unaffected by the two men. He spoke without looking up. "I think ye'd best be on yer way. We're guests of the Rileys and want no trouble."

The drunker of the two men laughed. "You talk funny," he said. "Don't he, Tucker? He talks damn funny."

"Yeah, Casey, damn funny." Tucker peered down at them through lank black hair. "You may not want trouble, but trouble is exactly what you got," he said. "And if you're guests of the Rileys, then you can give them a little message for us—that is, after I beat the hell out of you."

He smiled, revealing a mouth full of missing or discolored teeth. Chelsea shuddered, suddenly terrified. "What's your argument with the Rileys?" she asked, swallowing her fear and trying to distract the man.

"Old man Riley owes us money," Casey said, stuffing more tobacco in his jaw. "We worked a whole damn week for him, and he stiffed us."

"Well, I'm sure if—" she began, only to be stopped with a word from Griffin.

"Chelsea," he said. She froze, the tone in his voice seizing her attention. His gaze was fixed on the men on horseback, but he had one arm draped over his saddle. If one didn't know him, one might think he was at ease, loose, planning to do whatever would keep the peace. But

Chelsea knew him. It thrilled her to know his power, even as the knowledge of what Griffin might do chilled her to the marrow.

"Get on yer horse," Griffin ordered.

"Chel-seeee," the drunk cowboy sang, leaning toward her. "Now, that's a pretty name if ever I heard one."

"Don't get on your horse." Tucker said. " 'Cause I'll just have to pull you off again."

"Do as I say, lass," Griffin said.

Tucker turned back to Griffin, and Chelsea took the opportunity to hurry over to Pancho and awkwardly mount. Her heart pounded as Griffin stood, unyielding, in front of the angry man.

"Would you like to see just how drunk I am?" Tucker asked through gritted teeth.

Griffin shook his head. "Nay. I'd like to see ye climb down off yer horse and face me like a man."

"Heee-heee!" Casey shouted. "You shouldn't oughta say somethin' like that to Tucker. You'll be sooor-ry."

"Come on, Tucker," Griffin said, his voice soft.

Chelsea took a deep, shaky breath as she watched a single muscle in Griffin's jaw contract as he gazed up at the cowboy.

"Face me like a man, unless, as I suspect, ye aren't a man at all, but just a coward full of a great deal of manure."

Tucker turned beet red as Casey laughed hysterically beside him. "Yeah, yeah, go on, Tucker, teach the funny-talking bastard a lesson!" he cried.

Tucker held Griffin's gaze for a long moment, and Chelsea held her breath, waiting, until finally he dismounted.

The minute Tucker's feet hit the ground, Griffin pulled his sword, hidden from sight, over the saddle horn, swinging the blade with both hands toward the man, stopping the point an inch from Tucker's throat.

The blood drained from the cowboy's face, and Casey's laughter cut off abruptly. Chelsea felt as though her heart had stopped as she watched Griffin in all his six-foot-four glory, his broad-shouldered, warrior-king glory, stand with the four-foot claymore balanced easily in his hands, death scant millimeters from Tucker. She could imagine the Scot on a battlefield, wearing his plaid, his white-blond hair dancing in the wind. She swallowed hard, wishing she were worthy to stand at his side.

"You son of a bitch!" Tucker shouted, stepping back only to have the blade follow. His back hit the side of his horse, and he stopped. Gone was the arrogant, self-assured bully. This man was sweating, his Adam's apple bouncing up and down like a yo-yo. "You said to fight like a man," he blurted, "and now who's the coward, huh? Who's the coward?"

Griffin narrowed his ice-blue eyes, and Chelsea couldn't breathe for a second as the Scot suddenly whipped the blade of the sword around in a wide arc, this time bringing the side of the blade to a halt against the man's neck, barely touching his skin. A faint trickle of blood traced its way down Tucker's throat. Griffin slowly lowered the blade. He reached out and knotted one hand in the front of the cowboy's blue work shirt and jerked him forward until their noses were almost touching.

"I dinna waste my honor on a bastard like ye," he whispered. "And I dinna risk the safety of my lass in order to play by the rules. Now, get out of here and dinna come back. Ever."

Griffin shoved Tucker backward into his horse, and the man lost no time in scrambling up into the saddle. He paused long enough to glare at Griffin, prompting the Scot to swing the sword again. Then Tucker's mouth curved up in an evil grin. Too late, Chelsea thought to warn Griffin about the gun in Tucker's saddle. In horror she watched as the man turned and leveled the rifle at Griffin.

"No!" she screamed, digging her heels into her horse's side and sending Pancho leaping forward in between Tucker and Griffin.

Tucker's horse danced away from Griffin's rearing mount, and for a moment all was confusion. Then Chelsea saw Tucker steady his rifle and take aim on Griffin.

She didn't wait to research the situation or form a hypothesis or correlate an equation. Chelsea Brown threw herself at the man with the gun, even as a shot echoed across the Texas Hill Country.

Chapter Eleven

"Chelsea!" Griffin shouted.

The shot went wild as Chelsea slammed straight into Tucker, taking him down onto the hard Texas earth. Luckily, she landed on top of the man, letting him take the brunt of the fall.

As he lay there with the breath knocked out of him, she suddenly remembered the six weeks training in self-defense she'd taken at the local YWCA. The teacher had been impossible, refusing to give her a certificate, claiming it might make her think she was actually able to do the things he'd been trying to teach her. Now was her chance to prove him wrong.

She jumped to her feet and placed one foot carefully over Tucker's windpipe.

"Don't move!" she shouted.

He grabbed her by the ankle and twisted. Hot fire laced up her leg, and the man shoved her, easily tossing her to the ground.

Well, that's what I get for trying, she thought, rolling to her knees to get away from the man who was no doubt pretty angry by now. But before Tucker could rise and do worse, Griffin was beside her, lifting his blade once again to the man's throat.

Chelsea scrambled to her feet and ran behind Griffin's

broad back. Trembling, she peered out from behind him to see Tucker glaring at the two of them from his sprawled position on the ground.

"Get up and get out of here," Griffin said, "or I'll make ye wish ye had, laddie."

"Come on, Tuck!" Casey shouted, whirling his horse around. "Let's get away from these nuts!"

Griffin dropped the point of his sword and gestured with it toward the horse. Tucker rose slowly and Chelsea ducked behind Griffin again, not trusting the gleam in the cowboy's baleful eye. Tucker wiped a trickle of blood from his mouth and began backing away from them until he reached his mount. Without taking his gaze from them, he pulled himself into the saddle.

"I want my rifle," he said flatly.

"You can pick it up from the Rileys," Chelsea told him, feeling safe again, stepping out from Griffin's solid protection. "I'm sure they'll want to talk to you about all of this."

The man cursed her roundly, turning his horse to follow Casey's. But when the two were a good fifty yards away, Tucker spun back around. Apparently, Casey had a rifle in his saddlebag as well. Chelsea gasped as the younger man pulled the weapon out and fired several shots into the air.

Pancho reared up on his hind legs, almost striking Chelsea where she stood beside him, and she fell flat on the ground, the breath knocked from her lungs. Sinbad plunged and snorted, jerking the reins from Griffin's fingers. The two horses set off in a wild race across Texas as Tucker and Casey's howls of laughter could be heard in the distance, dirt rising from their speedily departing hooves.

"Chelsea! Lass! Are ye all right?" Griffin cried. He rushed to her side and knelt beside her, turning her over and half lifting her in his arms, his face close to hers, his ice-blue eyes filled with fear as he gazed down at her.

Chelsea looked up at Griffin. She knew she was crazy. Knew she shouldn't do it, but she couldn't help it. The wind whipped his hair around his strong, lean face, and as if sleepwalking, yet with every fiber of her body pulsing with life, she slid both hands up the front of his shirt, wrapped them around his neck, and pulled his mouth down to hers.

He tasted of salt and wind and heat, and Chelsea moved her lips across his, melting against him, knowing that her inexperience must show, but for the moment not caring in the least.

His arms went around her, and her heart soared as he pulled her tightly against his hard body and devoured her mouth for five beautiful seconds before pulling abruptly away. He stumbled to his feet and backed away, his eyes wide with something akin to horror. Chelsea began to tremble as she realized what a terrible mistake she'd just made.

"I—I'm sorry," she stuttered, her face burning with embarrassment. "I just wanted to thank you. You were so brave and . . . and . . ."

Griffin turned and ran a few feet, then stopped in his tracks and doubled over. Chelsea turned away as the sound of retching brought sharp tears to her eyes. Suddenly it all made sense. On the plane, he'd kissed her, then vomited. She'd assumed it was airsickness. Anytime he touched her, he quickly pulled away. It couldn't be possible—she couldn't be that disgusting, but the evidence said otherwise!

Apparently, she made Griffin Campbell literally sick to his stomach.

Griffin trudged behind Chelsea silently cursing himself, Texas, and the world in general. What was wrong with him? Had traveling into the future reduced him to the kind of man that had to be defended by a woman? Chelsea could have been injured. What if she'd been killed?

He shook his head, his heart aching at the thought. He was a sad excuse for a man, in every way. When sweet Chelsea had wrapped her arms around him and given her mouth to him, he'd soiled the moment yet again. At this rate he would die a virgin and leave no heirs behind, not even in the twenty-first century.

What a weakling. As a child he'd caught his father making love to another woman besides his mother—so what? Well, not so what, of course it was unconscionable that his father would do such a thing, and his mother was dying at the time, but still—why had it affected him so deeply? It made him feel vulnerable silly, childish. He had to overcome this malady or face being alone the rest of his life. Without Chelsea.

I'll be without her soon anyway. He frowned at the thought.

There was no other choice. He had to save Duncan. And yet, the last thing he wanted was to leave Chelsea. Perhaps he would be able to return to 2003 after he saved Duncan. Perhaps he wouldn't return to Scotland at all.

He glanced over at the woman walking beside him. She looked, if possible, even more miserable than he felt. Of course, that might be because their horses had run away and they'd ended up completely lost. Fortunately, one of the canteens had fallen from Chelsea's saddle as her horse bucked or else they'd have been in serious trouble. His own horse had thrown his knotted plaid from behind his saddle and he carried it under his arm, balancing his sword over one shoulder. They were both tired and dirty and sweaty.

"I'm sorry, lass," he said for the fifth time since their horses had bolted and they'd begun their long trek in an attempt to find the Riley ranch house.

She didn't answer, and he sighed. He'd explained that his stomach had been upset ever since the plane ride, but he knew she didn't believe him. He'd hurt her and he wanted to make it right. Jix's words came back to him suddenly, "Tell her the truth—she'll understand." Was it possible? Would Chelsea understand and perhaps give him the time he needed to overcome his illness? Or would she see him as weak and ridiculous?

Chelsea stopped and twisted her shoulder-length, honey-colored hair back from her face and into a knot at the base of her neck. The Texas sun beat down on them from above, and even Griffin was beginning to feel the effects of the heat.

"I think I know where we are now," Chelsea said, looking across the rocky meadow in which they stood.

"Lost?" he replied, smiling, trying desperately to recapture the camaraderie they'd had a few short hours ago. She gave him a wan smile in return and pointed to a rise ahead of them.

"I think if we climb this hill we'll find Cypress Creek on the other side and we can follow it back. The creek runs behind the Riley's house." She released her breath wearily, and once again Griffin felt a sharp pang of regret.

If only he hadn't jerked away from her and become ill; if only he wasn't such a weakling they'd be rolling in the grass right now, making love under the hot Texas sun.

That sure of yerself, are ye, lad? He answered the wee voice in his head: *Nay, just that sure about my feelings for Chelsea Brown.*

He stopped in his tracks as the realization hit him. He was in love with Chelsea Brown.

"Are you all right?" she called back, a few feet ahead of him.

"Aye, aye," he said, setting his feet in motion again as the wonder of his feelings swept over him. "Never been better."

How had he allowed this to happen? He couldn't be in love with Chelsea. Not only was he unable to do anything about his feelings for her, but he had to find a way to return to his own time, didn't he? Wasn't he obligated to go back and not mess up the space-time contingent or whatever it was Chelsea termed it?

His heart sank as they walked together in silence up to the top of the knoll. He loved her. This was it. This was the love he'd been waiting for all his life, and how could he possibly claim it?

Feeling completely overwhelmed, Griffin was grateful when they paused at the crest to gaze down at a totally unexpected, mesmerizing sight. In the "hill country" as Jix referred to it, there were hills and trees, but also a lot of rocks, bushy trees called cedar, and sparse vegetation. But the view that greeted him from below was completely different from anything he'd seen so far.

A beautiful green-blue stream about twenty feet wide bubbled and tumbled beside grass the color of meadows

in Scotland. Huge, gargantuan trees rose up from the banks to stretch their gray-white limbs to the sky, their trunks measuring easily ten feet around and their height fifty feet or more. Griffin and Chelsea made their way down to the water, and he caught his breath again in wonder. Across from where they stood were stark limestone cliffs rising thirty feet or more above the clear green-blue surface of the water. It all reminded him of home.

"This is Jacob's Well," Chelsea said, relief in her voice. "We are no longer on the Riley ranch, but at least I know where we are. We're actually where we wanted to be."

"This is incredible." Griffin knelt beside the creek and dipped his hand into the coolness, in awe of the beauty of the place.

"Yes, it is," she agreed. "When I was a kid this was one of our favorite places to come and swim. The owner, David Baker, is a great guy. He started a foundation to stop the pollution of the creek and river here in the county. Come here, I want to show you something."

He followed her eagerly. It was the first indication he'd had in the last two hours that she might be willing to forgive him. She walked a few yards beside the creek bank, then turned and smiled. Her face lit up, and Griffin had to restrain himself from running to her, sweeping her up into his arms, and kissing her senseless.

She was so beautiful. Her eyes so soft and gray, so filled with kindness. Maybe she would understand. Maybe he would tell her.

"Look down there," she was saying. Obediently he peered over her shoulder to the spot she indicated. In the center of the creek, beneath the water, was a deep, cavernous hole. It led downward, growing smaller in layers of stone until at the bottom it appeared to be only a few feet wide. A sudden shiver slipped over his skin. It was like the pool in the grotto in Duncan's cave back in Scotland. The crystals had to be here.

"Isn't it wonderful?" Chelsea said.

She gazed down at the water, and Griffin marveled at the intelligence in her eyes. In his time, women were interested only in cooking and clothing and their children, or at least so it had seemed to him. This woman was interested in so many things, and he was so very interested in her.

"This is where the spring comes up out of the earth," she explained. "It's really the opening to a series of caves that stretch far down beneath the ground, eventually leading to the source of the water, a spring, though no one has ever explored that far. At the bottom of this pool there's another opening that leads downward, and then another and another and who knows how many more? It's only been partially mapped." Her voice softened. "Eight divers have died in the last thirty years trying to search it fully. I've always wished I could explore it," she added. "I'm a good swimmer but I'm too chicken."

Griffin frowned at her use of poultry in the conversation, and she smiled at him.

"That means I'm too afraid," she clarified. "There's even a legend about an outlaw who died here. He was convinced that a treasure was hidden in the bottom of the pool. He drowned trying to find it."

Griffin stared down into the blue-green depths, mesmerized. It reminded him of his watery grotto in Scotland, the one that had sent him spinning through time.

" 'Tis wondrous, lass," he said. "And in there, perhaps, are the crystals."

She nodded and, to his surprise, unbuttoned the top button of her jeans. "Let's go find out," she said.

"Nay, we will not."

Chelsea looked up, her gaze questioning. He shook his head and explained.

"I willna take a chance on yer being caught in the time whirlpool. It might suck ye down along with me even if ye weren't touching the crystals. I'll go into the pool and see if they are there."

"But you won't touch them until you tell me, will you, Griffin?" she asked, and her voice was so anxious that it gave him hope. Perhaps she still cared in spite of his embarrassing behavior.

"I promise," he said softly. "Now, where is my suit in which to swim?"

Chelsea's mouth fell open and she clapped one hand to her head. "Oh, no! They're in the saddle bags with the horses."

Griffin smiled, unable to keep from imagining Chelsea without a swimming suit.

"Och, I suppose we'll just have to swim, as the French would say, *au naturel.*"

Chelsea looked away from him, her face slightly pale. "Oh, well, uh, say, aren't you wearing the boxers we bought you?"

He frowned, trying to remember what the strange word meant. "Boxers? Oh, ye mean the short braes ye bade me wear beneath the trousers? Nay, they were too binding."

And at the moment his already tight black jeans were growing even tighter. She looked up at him anxiously, and Griffin the gentleman took control. He would not only probably frighten her with the appearance of his naked, now thoroughly aroused body, but if she were naked too, there would be no way he could keep from touching her. Then he would desecrate the water and the moment with his wretched malady and once again make her feel rejected.

"I have my plaid," he said, suddenly remembering.

"Oh." Her voice sounded rather breathless, and was there a touch of disappointment as well? "All right," she said, giving him a brief, detached smile and pointing to a clump of bushes. "We can take turns changing over there. Will it embarrass you if I wear my underwear? I wouldn't swim at all," she added hastily, "but I'm just so miserably hot."

Griffin released his breath in a long sigh of relief. "Of course, lass. I would be a gentleman and say for ye to change first, but I must go into the pool before ye and I dinna want ye to have to stand half clad on the bank."

"No, we wouldn't want that," she said, turning away from him. "But why don't you let me change first and get into the water a little farther downstream? I'll just avoid the pool."

He frowned. He wasn't about to take a chance with Chelsea's safety, but he didn't want her to feel that he was trying to push her away from him either.

"Verra well," he agreed, "but when I go into the pool, I'd rather ye pulled yerself up on a rock, just to be on the safe side."

"Fine," she said shortly. "I'll let you know when I'm in the water."

She waved and disappeared behind the clump of bushes. For a moment Griffin struggled with his baser instincts, but the chivalry that was part of his character won out. He remained where he was until Chelsea called out to him.

With a sigh he shed his jeans and shirt and unrolled the long plaid. He shook it out and wrapped it around his waist twice, flipping the leftover material over one shoulder. He started down the hill, stopping as the sound of splashing water sent a wealth of images into his mind.

He could imagine how soft and white her skin would look under the glassy sheen, imagine how it would feel to bring her mostly bare body next to his, her breasts touching his chest, her warmth encasing him. How would it feel to make love to her in the water, the coolness churning around the fire they would ignite between them?

Griffin glanced up at the hot Texas sun beaming down upon him and sighed. He had to be a gentleman. He had to do the right thing. He had to—

"Och, to hell with it." He walked to the edge of the creek, stripped off his plaid, and dove in.

Chelsea lay on her back, floating in the creek near Jacob's Well, feeling languid and cool and slightly embarrassed. It was really silly. Her bra and panties revealed no more or less than a swimsuit would have, but just the fact that it was underwear made her blush. And what was sillier was the fact that what she wanted to do was strip the lingerie off and skinny-dip with Griffin.

How lovely it would be if he would forget about Duncan, forget about time travel, forget about everything except being here with her. For a moment she'd seen a glimmer in his eyes—a regret? No, that was foolish of her. She was simply reading into his expression what she wanted to see.

He didn't care for her that way. How could he when it was obvious that she made him ill? It was a hard thing to accept, but she had to do it.

She was still glad she'd worn the new underwear Jix and Sam had insisted she buy during their last makeover attempt. The soft lace-covered, teal-colored bra and matching panties made her feel beautiful, even if she wasn't. Maybe Griffin would sneak a peek when she got out of the water to wait on the rock. Maybe Griffin would be overcome with lust and take her in his arms and not throw up but make mad, passionate love to her at the edge of Jacob's Well.

She closed her eyes, willing her brain to stop entertaining such ridiculous thoughts. Jacob's Well was one of her favorite spots in the whole world, and she resolved to stop thinking about a lost cause like Griffin Campbell and concentrate on the beauty of the spring. Swimming had been one of her few active pastimes growing up, and she'd become an expert swimmer and diver at a young age. She still swam at least twice a week, sometimes at a local gym in Austin, sometimes in the Riley pool, but it was one of the few physical joys in her life.

She frowned as she floated, gazing up at the underside of the huge cypress branches on the south side of the creek. Maybe that was her problem with Griffin. Maybe she was just too boring for the man. If the crystals weren't in the pool, if Griffin didn't go back in time, maybe she could change his mind about her. She could take him into Austin to enjoy the most exciting hot spot in the capital city. Would exposing him to clubs filled with the young and the beautiful convince him she wasn't drab and mundane? She sighed, the water buoying her up, holding her in its cool comfort.

Why do you keep doing this to yourself? she demanded as she floated in the still water. *You make the man sick—isn't that obvious? Physically sick! There is no chance at all that he will ever want to be with you.*

Then why did he kiss me? her logical side countered. *Why did he kiss me that night and on the plane and—*

Give it up, her snide side whispered. *Just give it up.*

The battle in her brain was interrupted as suddenly something hit the water beside her, sinking like a rock into the creek, water geysering up around it, sending what felt like half the spring into her mouth and up her nose.

"Acck!" she cried, spitting out water and trying to keep afloat. She coughed a few times, clearing her throat, then opened her eyes to find Griffin's face grinning at her just a few feet away. "You . . . what . . ." She stopped sputtering and looked over at the bank of the creek. His jeans and shirt lay crumpled on the ground, and Chelsea drew in a sharp breath.

Griffin ducked down in the water until his blond hair fanned out behind him. He looked like a merman in a fairy tale, his blue eyes gleaming with a wicked delight she'd never seen before. The long plaid drifted out behind him and seemed to be tied around his neck.

"Griffin?" she said, laughing. "What are you doing? Why is your plaid around your neck?"

"I told ye I would wear it," he answered, his voice dark and soft.

A thrill rushed through Chelsea's veins as he ducked lower in the water until only his eyes showed above the surface, and he started toward her, looking like some water-borne predator with evil on his mind. A delicious kind of evil.

Chelsea backed away, treading water, her hands sending a few ripples between them. She felt suddenly shy and inept. Even more than usual, she thought wryly.

"Griffin . . ." A giggle slipped out and she smiled with the shock of it. "What's gotten into you?"

"Och, lass, I hope ye'll soon turn that question around and the answer will be 'me.' "

Chelsea blinked at the sexual innuendo, and another giggle, girlish and totally foreign, slipped past her throat. Embarrassed, she dove beneath the surface. That was a mistake. Below the water, Griffin was bare and gloriously naked. Her breath left her lungs, and for a moment she floundered, fighting for air, her arms flailing in the water. Then strong hands reached for her, pulling her up out of the green into the soft, hot Texas air.

She gasped, drawing sweet oxygen into her lungs even as Griffin pressed his skin against hers. She slid both hands up to his shoulders and clung to him for dear life. Their gazes locked as he held her and slowly began to pull her through the water to one of the stark limestone boulders at the side of the creek. His hands on her waist again, he lifted her up onto the smooth stone.

"Are ye all right, lass?" he asked, his hands lingering on her legs as he bobbed up and down in the water below her. "I dinna mean to frighten ye."

Chelsea took another deep, sweet breath and looked down at him. Gone were the seductive look in his eyes and the impish grin. In their place was an honest concern, a gentle protectiveness.

"You didn't frighten me," she said, leaning down toward him, feeling the cool muscles of his shoulders beneath her hands, sliding her fingers up the corded slopes to his throat. She felt the warm, still air above the water touch her cool, wet skin and shivered at the pure sensuality of being alive. "You could never frighten me."

Griffin's hands moved up her side and over her ribs, and she felt him shiver too, watched his eyes darken with passion and need.

"Chelsea," he said, "I must tell ye somethin', lass. Somethin' shameful. Somethin' that will probably cause ye to run from me forever."

"No," she whispered, cupping his face between her hands. "Nothing you could say would ever make me do that."

His lips parted, and impulsively Chelsea bent down and brushed her own against his. A few drops of water clung to his mouth, and she touched her tongue to his, the sweetness of his touch and the moment making her throw caution to the wind. She deepened the kiss, and Griffin groaned against her lips, then slid his mouth to her throat, to her collarbone, to the lush vee between her breasts. He stopped there, his breath coming hard, his hands holding her tightly against him.

She could feel the tension in his fingers, his shoulders; his entire body pulsated with taut awareness, and she thrilled at the thought that she had made him feel this way, that her skin, her body, her desirability had brought him so out of control that he'd had to pause to gather his senses.

"Oh, Griffin," she whispered, her arms closing around him. His fingers pressed into her skin, and all at once Chelsea realized something was wrong. He wasn't trying to control his passion, she realized. It was almost as if he were in some kind of pain.

"Griffin?" She pushed him away from her, lifting his face to hers. His eyes were squeezed shut, his face contorted in agony. "What is it?" she asked, feeling frantic. "What's wrong?"

"Lass . . ." the word was faint and trembling. "I canna . . . I wanted . . ." His throat convulsed, and he slapped one hand over his mouth, pushing away from the boulder at the same time, then turned and swam for shore. Chelsea sat on the rock, stunned, as Griffin pulled himself over the embankment and ran up the hill to a copse of bushes where she could hear him puking his guts out.

Chelsea closed her eyes, willing the swelling of pain and anger and rejection to leave her chest, fighting for her usual emotionless calm, but she couldn't find it. It wasn't there anymore. Griffin had broken through her wall that had kept the world at bay for so long. And now, with his latest—and, she swore, last—rejection, he had broken her heart.

With a sob she stood, and arching, plunged into the deep pool, pushing downward, slicing her arms through the depths, fleeing into the comfort of Jacob's Well. The natural buoyancy of the water pressed up against her, and Chelsea fought it, sweeping her arms out in a wide arc that would pull her deeper under the water.

A sudden current swept her against the side of a limestone rock, and Chelsea steadied herself, one hand against the sharp sides of the stone. Sharp? Limestone was smooth under water, worn down by the flowing of the spring over hundreds of years.

She peered through the clear water, and her eyes widened as she saw beautiful shimmering shards of emerald-green crystals beneath her fingers.

They're here. Now Griffin will really leave me. He'll go back to 1882 and help his cousin and never return.

All at once she realized she was touching the crystals. Touching them and thinking of another time. The green-blue of the water darkened, shimmered with an eerie glimmer, and Chelsea felt sudden panic sweep over her. She couldn't let go of the crystals! A surge of water, like the ocean's undertow, pulsed up and around her legs, pulling her downward. She had to get to the surface. She had to—

The churning water held her suspended, captured, the movement encompassing her body, beginning at her feet and moving steadily upward in a strange, uncanny swirl of power. She couldn't move, she couldn't swim, and the last of the air left her lungs just before the green darkness descended.

Chapter Twelve

Chelsea groaned as consciousness returned, accompanied by a raging headache. She opened her eyes slowly, feeling as though she'd been run over by a truck. Maybe she had. She blinked, trying to focus her eyes. She was lying on a large slab of limestone on the banks of Jacob's Well. Memory rushed back, and she sat up too quickly and looked around for Griffin as her head throbbed.

"Griffin!" she shouted, and winced. Her voice echoed off the stark limestone cliff in front of her and faded into silence. She shifted uneasily. Jacob's Well was always somewhat still, serene. It was one of the reasons she loved to come there so often. She could sit and stare into the cold, mysterious water and recharge her batteries. Remember who she really was.

But the stillness hanging in the air at the moment was different. There was an eerie calm sending prickles of apprehension across her skin. And the fact that Griffin was nowhere in sight only added to her trepidation. Had he dragged her out of the spring and then gone for help? She released her breath in one long sigh of realization and relief. Yes, that had to be it.

The throbbing in her head made her dizzy and she lay down again, letting the coolness of the stone help her gather her thoughts. If only everything didn't seem so hazy, as if she were trying to recall a dream. She remembered kissing Griffin; then he had pulled away and been sick. She closed her eyes against the pain that particular memory evoked and forced her mind to press on. Humiliated, she had dived into the water and . . . and what? She frowned and pushed herself upright again, fighting a wave of sudden nausea.

What had happened? She couldn't remember, but she must have been caught in one of the infamous Jacob's Well undertows, or perhaps she'd hit her head. In any case, Griffin must have saved her and gone for help. She just had to wait for him to return. Yes, that was all there was to it.

But after waiting what seemed an eternity, Chelsea had to reconsider her hypothesis. The sun was beginning to set, and although the summer heat lingered long after dark in Texas, there was a chill descending on Jacob's Well that had nothing to do with the weather. Chelsea gazed at the winding stream stretching out in front of her and listened to the sounds of crickets and frogs chirping and churrumping in the twilighty stillness. As the darkness grew, here and there tiny twinkling lights appeared in the thick underbrush beside the creek.

Chelsea smiled. "Fireflies," she said aloud, then remembered the childhood name for them. "Lightning bugs." She watched them, somehow calmed by the familiar sight as she tried to decide what to do.

If she left, Griffin might come back and he'd be worried if he didn't find her there. On the other hand, it was possible he had gotten lost. Did he even know how to get back to Samantha's ranch? No, of course not. Had Jix taught him how to use a phone? Probably not. So really, Griffin was not going to be a lot of help, and she would probably end up having to find him after she managed to get hold of Sam or Jamie. Better to get going while there was still a little daylight left.

In the back of her mind was the niggling thought that perhaps Griffin hadn't gone for help. Perhaps he'd abandoned her. She dismissed the idea as unworthy. Griffin would never do that to her. He might get sick at the sight of her, but he'd never leave her alone and hurt.

With a sigh Chelsea stood and made her way across the limestone ridge toward the bank of the creek where she'd left her clothing. She made the last step onto the soft green grass and squinted in the dusky light. Her clothes were gone. She knew exactly where she'd left them, but now they were nowhere to be seen. She searched the area and, aghast, realized she might have to go for help in her underwear.

"Oh, brother," she said aloud, her voice echoing across the stream. The owner of Jacob's Well wasn't home. She knew that, because she'd called and asked David Baker's permission to go to the well. He'd given his ready assent and mentioned he'd be out of town for the next week or so.

She glanced across the stream. That meant she'd have to climb the path leading through the limestone cliff opposite where she stood, and make her way across David Baker's property until she reached the main road. Then she'd have to walk into town. In her underwear.

"Great," she said, her voice hushing the cacophony of crickets and frogs. "Just perfect."

Griffin dragged the back of his hand across his mouth and cursed himself roundly, fully, emphatically to the trees, the sky, to God Himself, not caring that Chelsea could hear him. Let her hear. Let her know that Griffin Campbell, warrior, soldier, heir to the Campbell chieftainship, was a mewling, cowardly weakling. For a moment Griffin thought he might sink to his knees and howl his frustration, but he checked the impulse in time. Even a weakling such as himself must cling to whatever scraps of honor he had left.

He'd grabbed his plaid and now pulled the wet wool around him. The kilt lay heavy against his skin as he absentmindedly pulled on his leather cowboy boots and then bowed his head in shame. Put aside the fact that he had ruined whatever chance he might have had to woo Chelsea. Put aside the fact that he had begun to think he might like to stay in this time forever, if only he could be with her. Now he knew—he had no place here. Though he had seen passion, desire, perhaps even love in Chelsea's eyes, it would not be fair to tie her to a man such as he. A man who could not touch her without growing ill. It would be better for her, and for all concerned, if after he rescued Duncan, he simply returned to his own time.

And what will you do there? The question came to him sharply, and he dragged one hand through his wet, tangled hair in despair. What indeed? If he returned—that is, if he could find a way to return—he would possibly prevent that which his father had longed for so dearly, to become chieftain. And what if Griffin did become chieftain? What if his father would prefer that his son attain that which he desired himself?

Once Griffin was made chieftain he would be expected to marry and produce heirs. Actually, he would be forced to marry Maigrey once he returned. If he couldn't even touch his wife, how would he ever consummate the marriage? It wouldn't be long before the truth would be discovered, and then not only would Griffin be shamed and disgraced, but his father as well.

But there was still an option. If he found a way to return to his time, he could simply refuse to marry Maigrey MacGregor and he could refuse to be chieftain. His father would be angry, but then perhaps the council would name Red Hugh as the leader instead. Yes, of course they would. If history told that once Griffin had disappeared Red Hugh became chieftain, why wouldn't the same thing happen if Griffin refused?

He would retire to his cottage in the woods and study his books and write his poetry, and everyone would be happy. Well, perhaps he'd not be happy. He couldn't imagine ever being happy without Chelsea, but at least he could live knowing that she hadn't bound herself to a man unable to give her the love she deserved. She would find another, of that he was certain.

The thought of Chelsea with another man, being touched by another man, sent a rush of fury through Griffin that almost sent him to his feet, almost brought him rushing down the hill to the water, to find her, to take her in his arms. He steeled himself against the urge and with a groan leaned his head in his hands. A wave of despondency swept over him as he viewed the loneliness awaiting him in his future. But he had no choice. If he could find a way to return to his time, he must take it and leave Chelsea behind, let her discover joy with a man who could love her fully.

For a moment Griffin allowed the peace of the creek bank to envelop him, to shelter him from his own feelings of despair. After a time he became aware of the silence. He knew that Chelsea had to be angry with him, but suddenly realized that he had half expected her to come after him.

He lifted his head from his hands. From his vantage point he had a good view of the creek below. Chelsea wasn't there. On his feet in an instant, Griffin hurried down the hill and paused at the edge of the river, his throat tightening with sudden premonition.

"Chelsea?" he called, his voice echoing off the limestone cliffs. Griffin scanned the smooth, clear water of the creek. She wasn't there. Perhaps she had swum farther downstream. He walked quickly along the bank, his gaze searching the stark white stone. "Chelsea?" he called again, a touch of panic in his voice.

What if she had gotten hurt somehow? While he sat feeling sorry for himself, nursing his ego, she might have been in trouble. What if—his heart pounded suddenly against his chest as he whirled around—what if she'd decided to look for the crystals herself? Or simply decided to explore the caverns of Jacob's Well? She'd said she'd always wanted to. Would she be that foolish? Had she been so upset with him that she had impulsively dived into the watery depths alone? He hurried back toward the deep pool, calling her name as he walked.

"Chelsea? Chelsea!"

No response. Griffin wasted no more time in speculation. What if she was trapped below the water, or . . . no, he wouldn't allow himself to think past that. She was all right. She had to be all right.

He sat down and frantically tried to pull the heavy boots

from his feet. The water had swollen the leather, and they wouldn't budge. Griffin stood, unwilling to risk more time. He jumped into the creek and swam as quickly as he could, hindered by the heavy boots, across to the dark grotto beneath the water's surface. He took a deep breath and dove.

Muscles straining, Griffin sliced through the water, kicking with every ounce of strength he possessed until he reached the floor of the underwater cavern. There was only time to touch, glance, and see that Chelsea was not there, not trapped or drowned. There was another opening which, he knew from her explanation, led down beneath the earth, but there was no way she could have gone farther than this. She would not have had the air to go on. Therefore, probably angered by his actions, she had simply left him there and headed back to Samantha's ranch. It was what he deserved. He did not care, as long as Chelsea was safe.

Griffin pushed off the bottom and swam up toward the light. But as he reached for the surface he realized he might be in trouble himself. The heavy wool of his plaid and the weight of the boots pulled him downward, making it difficult to swim. Fighting a sudden sense of panic, he headed for the side of the well, planning to push off from the limestone surface. He reached out for the stone and winced as something sharp bit into his hand.

Then he saw it. Saw them. A shelf about two inches wide running around the circular wall of Jacob's Well. A shelf containing glimmering green crystals. The same kind of crystals he had touched in Scotland. The same kind of crystals that had sent him spiraling through time.

He wouldn't be able to hold his breath much longer, but Griffin didn't move. He had to touch them; he had to go back to 1882 and save Duncan. He would never see Chelsea again, but that would be best for her. If he truly loved her, he would let her go, he would help Duncan, his cousin, and later, perhaps, return to the place and time where he belonged.

Griffin reached his hand toward the crystals, his heart pounding, his lungs close to bursting.

If I touch them, I will leave Chelsea forever.

His fingertips were an inch away.

If I leave her, I will never love again.

Half an inch.

Chelsea, sweet Chelsea, I will never stop loving you.

A quarter of an inch.

I wish you a wonderful life, filled with a love you deserve, a love I wish I could give you.

He felt the sharp crystals against his skin.

Goodbye, sweet Chelsea.

Anguish rushed through Griffin even as the last of his air slipped away and the water swirled about him, caressing him, pulsating against him, taking him down into a tantalizing darkness.

"Ouch, ouch, ouch, OUCH!" Chelsea hopped up and down on one foot, which was a bad idea because she promptly stepped on another sharp stone, which made her stumble, one-footed, and fall flat on her face in the middle of the dusty road.

Her hair, jarred from its usual knot at the base of her neck, came loose and spilled over her face and shoulders, and for a minute she considered simply lying there until some teenager in a pickup truck barreled around the corner and put her out of her misery. But that would be quitting, and Chelsea Brown was not a quitter. Not even if she was lost, exhausted, starving, and as close to being naked as a girl could get.

She pushed herself up from the road and wearily stumbled over to the shoulder, where she promptly sank down onto more rocks. After swimming across the creek and climbing up the trail that led to David Baker's home, Chelsea had been so tired, so discouraged, that she'd resolved to sit and wait for someone to find her. If no one came, she'd find somewhere to sleep and wait until morning. Baker's property also housed a bed-and-breakfast called Dancing Water Inn. Maybe someone would be in one of the stone cottages he rented out, someone who had a cell phone! She had perked up at the thought and kept walking.

The trail had seemed different as she trudged up the

hill. She'd thought there were manmade steps leading up from the well, but maybe she'd been mistaken. When she reached the top it was almost dark, but the tall oak trees flanking the path were still visible. She hurried through them, anxious to get to Baker's private home, a huge round stucco affair which the artist had transformed out of a silo.

Chelsea stopped in her tracks once she made it through the sparse woods, her mouth dropping open. There was no house. There were no stone cottages. She didn't even see the little manmade pond filled with water lilies she had always loved. There was nothing except trees and rocks and grass and a few prickly pear cacti.

Somehow, some way, David Baker's house and his bed-and-breakfast were gone. Poof. Vanished into thin air.

Now Chelsea sat with her elbows on her knees, letting her hands dangle over her bare feet, letting her head fall back and her eyes close as she contemplated the strangeness of her situation.

She should have just waited until morning to start walking, she knew that now, but the thought of strolling into Wimberley in broad daylight in her underwear was just too awful to contemplate. Besides, the moon was almost full, illuminating the road almost as though it were daytime. If she'd just had a pair of shoes, she'd have made it into town to the nearest phone in no time. Instead she had "ouched" her way down the dirt road for the last hour or so and couldn't tell if she was any closer to civilization than when she started. She might even be lost again.

That was it. Somehow she'd gotten turned around when she came out of the creek. She'd gone up the wrong path and missed David Baker's home and bed-and-breakfast. That was the only explanation.

Chelsea dragged herself to a standing position and started walking again. She'd only gone a few agonizing steps when she decided she could truly go no farther. The bottoms of her feet were in shreds. If she could just sit down and rest for five minutes somewhere that wasn't covered in rocks or prickly grass, she might be able to form some kind of coherent plan. She brushed a long lock of hair out of her eyes and stood with her hands on her hips, surveying the land around her. Back behind a clump of trees she caught sight of something large and gray and started toward it, hopping and wincing every few steps. As she got closer, she saw it was an old barn.

Tentatively she opened the huge double doors that were practically rotting off of their hinges and found the structure to be completely empty. No hay, no horses, no tools or equipment, nothing. The only items in the entire building were two old blankets slung over the rail of one of the empty stalls. Chelsea pulled them down and realized they were saddle blankets, itchy, dirty, and smelly.

She didn't care. She spread them out on the dirt floor and collapsed on top of them. Within minutes she was asleep. When she awoke, it was to the sound of jingling bells and loud singing. Chelsea opened one eye and saw faint sunlight glimmering through the cracks of the old barn. It must be dawn. She had slept several hours and now would have to finish her walk to town in full view of anyone who might drive by.

On the other hand, she had a blanket, even if a horse had used it last. It would be foolish to pass up an opportunity to get a ride into town.

Summoning her courage, she wrapped the stiff blanket around her shoulders and headed outside. Across from the barn were two men on horses, pausing on the road. It wasn't unusual to see people riding their horses down the dirt roads in the hill country. Chelsea wondered briefly if Pancho and Sinbad had made it back to the Riley stables. If they had, Samantha would have immediately initiated a search for her two missing guests.

Chelsea sighed. Riding into town half naked on a horse wasn't her idea of a fun morning, but she had to get in touch with her friends. Poor Griffin might be halfway to Abilene by now. She started toward the two men, picking her way across the rocks and grass stubble. The closer she got, the more wary she became.

One of the two had obviously been responsible for the loud singing that had awakened her. She watched as he threw back his head and belted out a slurred version of something about sweet Betsy from Pike. Chelsea noticed that the other man wore spurs that jingled as they knocked against his mount's side. For a moment she thought they were the same two men that had wrecked their picnic, but when she stopped beside the road she could see they were not. Thank goodness.

"Excuse me," she said hesitantly, looking up into a set of bloodshot brown eyes and a cocky grin. Uneasy, Chelsea wasn't sure how to proceed. The man with the spurs had dark, heavy eyebrows, and one beady eye wandered as he stared down at her. She unconsciously took a step back and pulled the blanket more tightly around her. He reminded her of a lizard she'd once seen in a zoo—a chameleon. The creature's eyes had rolled and bulged and made her dizzy.

Except this reptile didn't have a benign expression in his baleful gaze. He raked his one good eye over her from head to toe, pausing to stare at her bare legs, one side of his grizzled, unshaven face twisting up into a leering smile.

"Well, well, well, Joey, what do we got here?" he said, his voice like ground glass. His companion stopped singing long enough to look over at the woman, and he groaned. "Ah, hell, Dead Eye, we ain't got time for no women."

Chelsea blinked. The man called Joey looked to be about sixteen or seventeen years old, but was just as dirty and grizzled as the one he called Dead Eye. Dead Eye? It had to be a joke. But on whom? She laughed nervously.

"You guys wouldn't know how far I am from town, would you?" she asked, wishing the blanket were longer so she could hide her legs. As it was, the stiffness of the thick covering made it hard to keep the ends together and they kept slipping apart, exposing her half-naked body. The sight didn't go unnoticed by either of the men, and Chelsea started backing away.

"Why, sure, honey," Dead Eye said, his gravelly voice sending a shiver up her spine. "Yo're about twenty miles from San Marcos. Why don't ya let me and Joey here give ya a ride?"

Chelsea smiled stiffly. "No, that's all right. I don't want to go to San Marcos. I'm walking into Wimberley. If you could just point me in the right direction . . ." Her voice trailed away as Dead Eye swung down from his horse, rotten teeth gleaming yellow beneath his mustache as he leered at her.

"Wimberley ain't no real town, honey," he said, "come on into San Marcos with us and we'll show ya a fine time."

Her throat tightened as the man came closer. She could smell him now, and the stench almost made her retch. Good grief, were these guys homeless? Just out wandering the countryside on their horses? Who did they think they were, part of the cast of *Young Guns* or something?

"Aw, come on, Dead Eye," the younger one called, still on his horse. "Ya remember what happened the last time we messed with one of Miss Lola's girls? She purt' near took yore head off."

Chelsea seized the words as though they were a lifeline. "That's right," she said, taking another step back. "You wouldn't want to upset Miss Lola. Why, one time I saw her kickbox a man into unconsciousness."

The man called Dead Eye frowned. "What the hell is kickboxing?" Without waiting for her answer, he grabbed her by one arm and jerked her against his smelly, sweaty, nasty chest. She gagged as the man seized her face, his fingers biting into her skin, forcing her to look at him.

"I ain't skeered of nobody," he growled, "and I surely ain't skeered of no woman, even iffen it is that two-bit whore."

Chelsea's throat tightened with fear. This was her chance to really use those techniques she'd learned in self-defense. She should stomp on the man's instep, slam her knee into his groin, and pump her elbow into his fat gut. Instead she trembled in place, frozen by terror.

"All right, Dead Eye, let her go!"

The brusque order came from behind them, and Chelsea spun around. A woman sat in the seat of a wooden cart pulled by two mules. She wore dark red lipstick, too much rouge, and heavy black eyeliner. Chelsea blinked. Her white-blond hair was swept up in an elaborate curled affair, topped by a huge, wide-brimmed hat sporting feathers, flowers, and fruit. Her ample bosom almost overflowed the tight, low-cut red dress she wore, and for a moment Chelsea thought she'd been transported into an old western movie.

"I said let her go," the blonde threatened, "or you'll answer to Mr. Peyton."

That did the trick. Dead Eye let go of Chelsea's arm and backed away. The woman in the wagon gave him a narrow-eyed glare and then turned to Chelsea. "You must be one of the new girls that ol' Cactus Pete was sending over. But how in the hell did you get way out here in the middle of nowhere?"

Chelsea brushed her hair back from her face and shook her head. "A better question might be where am I, and why in the world are you dressed like Mae West?" she said faintly.

The woman laughed. "Why, honey, you're in Hays County, Texas, and I haven't got the foggiest notion who this Mae West might be, but she sure must be a woman of excellent taste." Her voice was cultured, more Southern than the Texas accents Chelsea was used to, more refined than the two louts on horseback.

"Howdy, Miss Lola," Joey said with a sheepish grin. "I tried to get him to leave her alone, but ya know how ol' Dead Eye is."

"I sure do, Joey Kincaid," the woman called Lola said, fixing him with a stern eye. "You're too young to be running around with this trash, and way too young to be drinking."

The boy blushed to the roots of his shaggy blond hair. "Aw, hell, Miss Lola, I only had a little whiskey. Just a little."

Chelsea glanced back at the man who had grabbed her, noticing for the first time that he wore a gun in a holster at his side. Her mouth went dry.

"C'mon, Dead Eye," Joey said, "let's get on to San Marcos." Chelsea's gaze snapped to the boy's thin waist. He wore a gun at his side too, a pearl-handled revolver gleaming from the leather holster strapped to his leg. Ranch hands might carry rifles on the huge ranches like the Riley spread, but even in Texas, men didn't ride down open roads sporting low-slung guns on their hips. What was going on?

Dead Eye grumbled under his breath but mounted his horse, glaring at the woman in the wagon the whole time. Joey tugged at the brim of his sweat-soaked brown hat.

"Ma'am," he said, his voice slurred slightly. "Guess we'll be pushing on now."

Joey laid the reins across his mount's neck, clicking his tongue in encouragement. Dead Eye followed without another word.

Chelsea watched them go, feeling stunned. She should tell the police, she should call someone. There were two armed men wandering around Hays County accosting innocent women. She spun back around to the woman.

"Do you have a cell phone?"

The woman frowned. "Do I have a what?"

Chelsea glanced at the bed of the wagon the woman was driving. There was a barrel marked "flour," a huge bag that had "sugar" scrawled across it in an uneven hand, a bag of rice, and a huge bag of potatoes. Women didn't haul supplies in the back of wagons, not even in Wimberley. Chelsea felt a wave of disbelief sweep over her as her scientist's logic went to work.

David Baker's home and bed-and-breakfast did not existe. Men riding horses and wearing guns had accosted her, talking as if they'd been pulled from the pages of a cheap western, she was face to face with what for all the world looked like the queen of a nineteenth-century bordello, and Miss Lola herself had never heard of a cell phone.

Chelsea swallowed hard. "What day is this?" she said, her throat tight and dry.

Miss Lola frowned again. "Why, honey, it's Thursday."

Chelsea shook her head. "No, I mean, what's the date?"

"June twenty-second. Tomorrow the stage will hit town with a buttload of politicians coming for that silly convention the mayor's holding, and me and my girls have got to be ready. Why don't you climb on up here with me?" Her heavily madeup gaze drifted over Chelsea as she stood immobile beside the wagon.

"And I have to tell you, luv, that while I admire your spunk, you're going to have to wear a little more at my establishment than you may be used to."

Chelsea blinked. "What year is this?" she whispered.

Miss Lola's mouth fell open and she clucked her tongue. "What year is it? Land's sakes, you must have been out here longer than I thought. Get up here, child, and have some water from my canteen."

"What year?" Chelsea said again, feeling all at once as though she couldn't quite get her breath.

Miss Lola stopped her attempt to find her canteen, her long lashes blinking in confusion. "Why, honey, it's 1882. Don't you know that?"

Chelsea nodded, smiled, and fainted dead away.

Chapter Thirteen

Griffin was drowning. He kicked his feet, fighting to escape from the hands clawing at him, the forces trying to drag him down, trying to defeat him. For a moment he thought he was truly lost; then he made one last savage thrust and felt his body rising up, propelled to the surface. He broke through the water gasping for air, gulping great amounts as he reached out blindly for something, anything, to cling to.

His hands collided with stone, and he dragged himself up the side of the rough limestone, tearing his hands, collapsing on the flat outcropping. He lay there, how long he didn't know, just thankful to be alive and breathing, but when he opened his eyes, it was night, a bright lopsided moon hanging above him. Griffin rested there a moment more, trying to reorient himself, trying to remember.

He had dived into Jacob's Well, searching for Chelsea, fearful she'd been hurt, then realized she must have simply left him there to brood, since, thankfully, she was not trapped below the water. He had started to surface when . . . what had happened?

Slowly he sat up, trying to recall what had happened next. There had been a pull, an undertow perhaps? He'd felt twisted under the water, and the rest was a blank. He pulled in another long breath of air and tried to think.

Chelsea had departed hours ago. He couldn't imagine that she would leave him stranded, but perhaps she'd been angry enough to do exactly that. Griffin dragged himself to his feet and leaned against the limestone, pushing his long hair from his face.

What was he, some stray yearling needing his mother to lead him home? He was a warrior, a Scot, and even if he was in a strange place, he could use his tracking abilities to find his way to the Riley ranch. And once he got there, he would ask Jamie MacGregor to send him back to Scotland. It was the last request he would ever make of the man or his family.

He would return to the cave that had sent him to this crazy time period and sit there until the crystals reappeared and took him home again.

Chelsea Brown would no doubt say "Good riddance."

Griffin slicked his wet hair back and squeezed out the water, then stood with his hands on the soggy plaid still wrapped around his hips. He glanced down, remembering he'd left his shirt and trousers on the creek bank. His feet were cold and squishy inside the cowboy boots as he walked up the hill to the spot where he'd sat such a short time ago, trying to be a gentleman, trying to give Chelsea her privacy. If only he'd listened to his better instincts and not joined her in the water, they'd both probably be sitting in the huge Riley family room, drinking iced tea and laughing with the MacGregors and Samantha.

His clothes were gone. His sword wasn't there either.

Griffin closed his eyes. Wonderful. Now he could embarrass his hosts again as he walked all over the Texas countryside clad only in a kilt and boots. And his sword—a family heirloom lost because of his neglect.

He would cross the creek and head back the way he and Chelsea had come. All at once he remembered she had said something about the owner of the well living on the premises, beyond the limestone cliffs that towered over the water. He frowned. For all he knew, Chelsea might still be wandering around somewhere, or perhaps something had happened to her. He would have to swallow his pride and ask for help.

Maybe he could pass his plaid off as a towel.

He would find someone, get a ride back to the Riley ranch, and go back to Scotland. Even if he never made it to his own time, at least he would be back in his own country. Maybe someday the crystals would return to Duncan's cave. He would wait for them.

Without Chelsea. Without anyone.

"Suck it in, sweetie. The customers like their women slim and trim."

"Isn't it great to know that some things never change."

Chelsea stood in one of the bedrooms over Lola Valanti's saloon in a daze. At a poke from the woman dressing her, she sucked in her breath for the hundredth time.

The woman, who'd introduced herself as Elmira, gave a hard pull on the cords hanging down the back of the corset Chelsea wore, making her usual twenty-nine-inch waist suddenly twenty-four inches. The room spun as Chelsea wondered what torturous lunatic had invented such a contraption. The Spanish Inquisition had certainly missed out on a guaranteed implement of agony.

"I—can't—breathe!" she gasped as Elmira knotted the cords.

"You'll get used to it," Elmira said, unconcerned. "Now raise your arms and I'll slip the dress over your head."

Chelsea obeyed, too exhausted to protest. Miss Lola, as everyone called her, according to Elmira, had graciously given her hitchhiker water and food and allowed her to sleep in the back of her wagon all the way into town, which wasn't Wimberley. The town was San Marcos, a bustling settlement of several hundred people. Wimberley, it seemed, consisted only of a mill and a few ranchers and farmers.

Once in San Marcos, Lola had driven around to the back of her establishment, the Double Dollar Saloon, then had gone inside and brought back a real blanket, soft as swan's down. She'd wrapped her guest in it and hustled her inside. Chelsea had been treated to a luxurious bath in a deep, clawfoot bathtub filled with scented herbs, and had scrubbed herself with soap that smelled of lavender. For a while she'd felt as though she had somehow stumbled into a fairy tale or a lovely dream.

Then she'd woken up.

Lola had introduced her to Elmira and told the girl to "fix up the new girl" with a proper dress so she could "entertain the customers" that night. Apparently, Miss Lola really thought Chelsea was the new saloon girl recommended by her old friend Cactus Pete, and Chelsea hadn't had the nerve to correct her. If the saloon keeper threw her out on the street, where would she go and what would she do? There probably wasn't a big demand for women scientists in the year 1882.

1882. She still found it hard to believe. It was one thing to hear Sam and Jix and Griffin talk about traveling through time; it was quite another to actually find herself in a different century. It felt a lot like she was losing her mind.

She'd racked her brain ever since she arrived at Miss Lola's, trying to remember what had happened after she dove into the well, to no avail. But now as her mind wandered she started to remember.

Angry at Griffin after his latest rejection, she'd jumped into the water at Jacob's Well. Beneath the surface she'd reached out and touched something sharp. Green crystals. Her head whirled for a second, and she had to consciously steady herself as the full memory returned. The green crystals. Of course, how could she have forgotten? Green crystals—like the ones in the rock shop? Like the ones Griffin had described? Green crystals like the one in Jamie's sword?

If she went back to Jacob's Well and touched the crystals again, maybe she would return to her own time. But how had she landed here in the first place? Why 1882?

Duncan Campbell. Her memory was fuzzy, but she remembered thinking of Griffin and his intention to travel back in time to help his cousin.

The room began to spin again, and dark, cloying fingers seemed to be cutting off her oxygen. If only she could approach this scientifically, she thought as she gasped to fill her lungs, fighting yet another fainting spell. If only she could set aside her emotions and approach this as simply an interesting experience, yes, just as she had decided to approach her time spent in Miss Lola's.

Another gulp of air and her head began to clear a little. There was no use in dwelling on the fact that she might be trapped here forever. Now she had some hope. Tomorrow she'd find a way to leave Miss Lola's and get back to the well. Tomorrow she'd go home. With that comforting thought in mind, she released her pent-up breath and tried to act interested in her new friend's ministrations.

Elmira had slipped the dress over Chelsea's head and pulled it down, smoothing the silk over her hips and lacing the dress up the back.

"Miss Lola told me to tell you about her rules," Elmira said as she began to work on Chelsea's hair. Apparently she was the unofficial "stylist" for all the women who worked in the Double Dollar Saloon.

"Rules? Sure, what are they?" Chelsea was surprised to find there was any kind of discipline in a place like this.

"She don't allow no carousin' with the customers," Elmira said as she swept Chelsea's tresses up into a French roll and anchored it with a beautiful tortoiseshell comb.

"Uh, okay," Chelsea said. "What does that mean, exactly?"

"Oh, you know . . . she don't want the girls letting the men get all handsie. She don't think it's proper, leastways not down in the saloon. And if you do decide to take one up to one of the rooms, you'll have to give her half of what you make."

"Take one up to the rooms?" Chelsea frowned, then widened her eyes as the meaning sunk in. "Oh, all right. But, er, what if I don't want to take any men to the rooms?"

Elmira grinned at her, pulled a few wisps of Chelsea's hair to curl around her face. "Then you won't be making much money, sugar. But Miss Lola, she don't insist on the girls going upstairs. If you wanna just dance and sing and push the drinks, that's fine. 'Course, now that Mr. Peyton's her partner, that might change."

"If I just want to *what?*" Chelsea cried. "Now wait a minute, no one said anything about—"

"My, you clean up nice," Elmira said, turning Chelsea to face the full-length mirror in the corner. "Wish I looked as pretty as you."

Chelsea's protests died in her throat as she gazed at her reflection. A beautiful woman stared back at her. A beautiful woman with large, round eyes, the gray irises accentuated by muted blue-gray shadows painted on the lids. Her lips, stained a light pink, were parted and inviting. Her cheeks, painted a soft rose, hollowed out her cheekbones, sculpting her face. The curve of her breasts thrust upward from the confines of the low-cut blue silk dress, plump and alluring. The silk clung to her waist and her hips, then flared out briefly before descending in riotous ruffles halfway to the floor. Her legs looked great in sheer black stockings even though the two garters were biting into her upper thighs.

The combination of the corset, the dress, and the makeup had made her into a voluptuous siren, and Chelsea stood in stunned amazement. All of Jix and Sam's makeovers had never come close to this.

She glanced at Elmira, who stood looking at her proudly. She was a thin, gangly girl of no more than seventeen or eighteen, with lank brown hair hanging halfway down her back, held back on either side with ugly brown clips. She was extremely plain, with an overbite that made her look rather like a demure pony.

Chelsea's heart went out to the girl; then, selfishly, she dismissed Elmira's problems and turned back to gaze at the wonder of her own image.

If Griffin could see me now, would he still run away and get sick?

She pushed out of her mind the image of Griffin standing mesmerized by her new makeover. Griffin was back in her time, and she was trapped here. How and why, she didn't know. Maybe later, when she had a chance to catch her breath and think about everything that had happened . . . but later she wouldn't be catching her breath, she'd be dancing for Miss Lola's customers.

"I don't think so," she muttered under her breath.

"What's that, sweetie?" Elmira asked.

Tess Mallory

"I said, you are an artist, Elmira."

"Thanks." Elmira beamed back at her. "Anything else I can do for you?"

"Uh, yes. I really need to talk to Lola."

Elmira frowned. "Gosh, sugar, she's down in the kitchen talking to Chin, the cook. I don't think you'd better talk to her right now. She's awfully perturbed at him."

"Chin?" Chelsea said, distracted. "That's an odd name."

"He's Chinese, and the best cook we've ever had. His food is odd, but so good!" She rubbed her tummy. "And what's funny is, he don't speak hardly a word of English, but somehow he and Miss Lola do just fine."

Chelsea's innate curiosity got the best of her and she turned away from the mirror. "I didn't think there were many Chinese in Texas in the 1880s. I mean . . ." She stuttered to a stop. "That's interesting. Does he run into a lot of prejudice?"

Elmira gave her a questioning look. "Prejudice? Like name-calling and such? Well, there's always some that will do that, but mostly everyone likes Chin. He knows how to make fireworks," the girl added, excitement creeping into her voice. "Come July the Fourth, he'll be putting on a great show. He does it every year."

"So why is Miss Lola mad at him?"

The girl lowered her voice. "You know, Miss Lola is the best, she's just wonderful to us girls, but she calls the shots around here." She hesitated. "Well, mostly. And Chin wants to change the menu. They serve supper here most nights, you know. She's down there right now telling him how the cow ate the cabbage."

Chelsea smiled at the colloquial phrase. "Lola didn't look like someone who would yell," she said.

"Oh, it won't be Miss Lola doin' the yellin'," Elmira explained. "Lord, no. But Chin . . . well that's another thing." She shook her head. "You'd best wait."

"Thanks, Elmira," Chelsea said, "but I guess I'll have to take my chances. I really need to talk to her." She started forward, only to trip and fall flat on her face. She lay still for a minute, trying to find the energy to stand up.

"You ain't very graceful, are you, sugar?" Elmira asked brightly, leaning down to give her a hand. "But don't fret about that. Men don't care if you're as clumsy as a cow in a dress shop, long as you let 'em slide you the zucchini, if you know what I mean."

Chelsea blushed furiously as Elmira helped her to her feet, and the girl noticed the sudden color in her face.

"You're blushing, ain't you?" she said, shaking her head. "Well, if that don't beat all. A saloon girl blushing. I never heard tell of such a thing."

Somehow Chelsea found her voice at last. "That's what I need to talk to Miss Lola about. I'm not a saloon girl. There's been a mistake."

Elmira frowned and shook her head, her lank brown hair swinging slightly. "Gosh, I hope not. Miss Lola's real short-handed, and there's a bunch of politicians in town up from Houston. I was really countin' on you to pick up some of the overflow tonight."

Chelsea blinked. "Are you one of the, uh, the saloon girls?"

"Well, sure, what did you think? Last time we had a convention I made a ton of money. There was this one senator that liked to pretend he was one of the girls and . . . there you go again, blushing. My goodness, sugar, maybe you'd better go talk to Miss Lola, because if you ain't helpin' out tonight she's sure gonna be mad, and that's a fact."

"I'll go talk to her," Chelsea said, carefully picking up her skirt this time before she headed for the doorway. "And thanks, Elmira, for . . . for . . ." She glanced down at the dress, realizing she felt sexier and more beautiful than she ever had in her life, even if she did look like a first-class hooker. "Thank you."

Chelsea hurried down the hallway and down the back stairs leading to the kitchen. Women stood on the landings and on the stairs, most of them clad only in chemises, the thin, short-sleeved undergarment worn under the corset. Some had feather boas draped over their shoulders, some wore filmy robes that hid nothing whatsoever. Still others wore corsets without the chemises, and Chelsea felt the heat in her cheeks as she stopped outside the kitchen door. A man's voice, loud and angry, from the other side of the door made Chelsea hesitate.

But she had to straighten out this miscommunication with Lola and find some decent clothes and somehow get back to Jacob's Well and get back home.

How? Her logical side asked bluntly. *What if the crystals aren't there?*

Don't be negative, Chelsea answered. *You'll just have to find a way.*

Panic flooded over her suddenly like a rushing wave of water, and she closed her eyes against the tide.

"It's okay, it will be okay," she whispered. Forcing her anxiety aside, she took a deep breath and pushed open the kitchen door. A pot whizzed through the air, narrowly missing her head, slamming into the doorjamb, as a flood of screaming Chinese greeted her.

A small Chinese man wearing a short red silk kimono, loose trousers, and a small round hat brandished a heavy pot as he shouted at Miss Lola, who stood with hands on her hips and ice in her eyes.

"I said we'll stick to the regular menu, Chin," Lola said calmly. "Your sweet and sour chicken is a favorite around here."

"No sweet and sour! No sweet and sour!" he shouted. Chelsea blinked as he threw the pot against the wall. "Chicken flied steak! Chicken flied steak!"

"Maybe another time, Chin," Lola said. "But tonight we've got a lot of politicians, and they all love your sweet and sour. In fact, Senator Gibbs asked me particular if you were going to prepare it for him tonight."

The compliment somewhat mollified the man, but he continued grumbling and slamming pots around the kitchen. He threw a handful of greens on a butcher-block table and took out a huge cleaver. Giving Lola one last narrow-eyed look and spewing what had to be a Chinese oath, he brought the cleaver down in the middle of the greens, making Chelsea jump and cry out.

Lola turned and caught sight of her. "Well, hi there, honey. It's Chelsea, right? Funny name. I'm sorry for the commotion. This is Chin, our cook."

The man ignored the introduction, and Lola sighed. "Don't mind him. He's in a snit today. He's tired of fixing Chinese food and wants to make chicken fried steak. And he's complaining because he needs some help in here." She gave a critical glance around the kitchen. "I suppose he's right, at least about the help."

"How did you ever end up here?" Chelsea blurted, then slapped one hand over her mouth, aghast. "I'm sorry," she hurried to say behind her fingers. "It's none of my business. It's just that you seem so . . . so—"

Lola cut her off, her red lips twisted in cynical amusement. "So capable? So smart? How did a nice girl like me end up in a place like this?" She laughed, totally at ease. "Sometimes life turns out differently from how we planned, doesn't it? Now, what can I do for you?"

Chelsea swallowed hard and tried to smile. "I hate to cause you any trouble, because you've been wonderful to me, but I think there's been some confusion. I'm not a . . . a . . ." She floundered for the right word.

"A courtesan? A prostitute? A whore?" Lola's blue eyes went icy again, and Chelsea gulped.

"A singer," she said, hoping against hope that Lola would understand. "Or a dancer. I have two left feet and couldn't carry a tune to save my life."

Lola chuckled. "Oh, hell, honey, if that's what's bothering you, don't worry. The Double Dollar Saloon isn't known for its musical talent. We sell cheap drinks to men who want to get drunk and look at pretty girls who don't have on many clothes. Some of them like Chinese food. Don't worry."

"Don't get me wrong," Chelsea went on. "It's just that I've never sung a note in my life." She cast around desperately for a way out. "You said Chin needs help," she said, seizing on the idea, "and since I have no talent at, er, the other, why don't you hire me to help him? Then you could find someone who's good at . . . well, at the other."

Lola fixed her with a piercing stare for a full minute. Chelsea bit her lower lip as she waited for her response.

"You aren't from Cactus Pete, are you?" she finally said. "He didn't send you."

"No," she admitted. "I—I was just lost on the road. Thieves had taken all my clothes and my horse and—"

"Save it, honey," Lola said, the ice returning to her eyes. "I don't really care how you got here, but I'll tell you what I do care about—lies. I don't trust people who lie to me, and I can always tell when they are." She narrowed her gaze. "Now, did that really happen?"

Chelsea swallowed and shook her head.

"Can you cook worth a damn?"

Chelsea hesitated and shook her head again.

"Can you wash dishes without breaking them?"

"I think so," Chelsea said quickly.

Lola released her breath in a long sigh. "I'll tell you what, honey. You dance and sing tonight, and if you really can't cut it, I'll give you a crack at helping Chin. I'll have Blake keep a special eye on you and keep the men from bothering you too much."

"Blake?"

"That's my bouncer. You'll meet him later."

"Oh—okay, I guess I could try it one night, but I've never even been on a stage before and—"

"Then this will be something new for you, won't it?" Lola paused on her way to the door and glanced back at Chelsea, one hand on her ample hip. "Honey, I have a feeling that deep down inside of you there's an adventuress, a woman aching to break free of the bonds of society and really experience life."

Chelsea's mouth dropped open. "How did you—I mean, yes, I really want to stop being so shy and inhibited."

Lola spread her hands apart. "Well, then, it seems to me that you're in the right place."

Chelsea took a deep breath. "But I mean, the way I look and all, I couldn't pull it off."

"Oh, nonsense, it's simple. All you have to do is smile. You don't even have to sing, just mouth the words and move from side to side holding your skirt above your knees. Surely a pretty girl like you can do that."

"Well, you see, I . . ." Chelsea stopped in mid-sentence and cocked her head to one side. "What did you say?"

Lola tapped her foot impatiently. "I said that surely a

pretty girl like you can handle this. Now what do you say?"

"Pretty girl?" Chelsea felt numb all over, then hot, then extremely happy. "Yes," she said, "yes, a pretty girl like me could do that."

Lola gave her a perplexed look but held out her hand. "Then it's a deal. Treat me fairly and I'll do the same for you."

Chelsea took her hand and shook it enthusiastically. "Thank you, Lola—I mean, Miss Lola. You won't be sorry."

Lola glided toward the door, her taffeta petticoat rustling beneath her dress. She paused in the doorway, looked over her shoulder, and in true Mae West fashion said, "I better not be."

As soon as she was gone, Chelsea collapsed into one of the wooden kitchen chairs. Well, at least she had a place to stay for a little while. And all she had to do to pay for it was get up on a stage in front of complete strangers and sing and dance and smile like she was having a wonderful time.

"Adventure, here I come," she moaned. "Oh, Griffin, if only you were here to see me, this might be worth the agony."

"Excuse me."

Two men squatting down in front of a small campfire turned at the sound of Griffin's voice. The smell of meat frying and the possibility of breaking his fast made the Scot's mouth water. He'd been walking all night, stumbling about in the darkness and now, even though the sun was well up, he found he was completely lost. Stopping to ask directions was quite humiliating to a man who regularly made his way back to Meadbrooke Castle in the middle of the night with no light to guide him, but he was in foreign territory and had no choice.

As the men swung around to face him, and laughter kindled in their eyes, Griffin had a moment's regret. Perhaps he should have kept walking and found his own way. The jaws of the dirty men dropped open and they began to guffaw loudly.

"Well, what in the hell," the older one said. "Is it a man or a woman? I ain't quite sure, Joey."

The younger, blonder one stopped laughing abruptly and nudged his companion. "He ain't laughing, Dead Eye. Maybe we shouldn't oughta fun him."

The one called Dead Eye, a fat, grubby man with a strange wandering eye, stood and rested his hands on his hips. He had some kind of firearm strapped to his thigh, and Griffin suddenly wished fervently for his own sword. He'd best get the information he needed and leave the two barbarians alone.

"I only wondered if either of ye could point me in the direction of the nearest house," Griffin said, his voice even.

"He talks funny too." Dead Eye slipped the shiny weapon from its leather sheath and smoothed one hand over its surface.

Jamie had spent a little time acquainting Griffin with modern weapons, including guns. If he remembered correctly, this was a Colt 45, known for the exceptionally large holes it left in people. And the amazing thing was, a person could be a good distance away when he did the injury. Gunpowder was the key, Jamie had explained. Griffin glanced around looking for something he could use to defend himself.

"C'mon, Dead Eye, ain't we had enough trouble for one day?" Joey said.

"Shut up, kid. I'll take care of Lola later, but right now I'm going to teach this girlie man a lesson." He took a step toward Griffin, weapon in hand. "A real man don't wear no skirt, hombre, don't you know that?"

"It's a kilt," Griffin said, fighting to keep his temper. There was a large stick on the ground. If he could get close enough to Dead Eye, the stick might be of some use. He took a step toward it. "I'm from Scotland, and kilts are part of our customs."

"Scotland?" Joey stood, and Griffin saw he was very young, perhaps fifteen or sixteen. "Like over across the ocean?" he asked eagerly.

"Aye. This is my first visit to Texas."

"And it'll likely be yore last," Dead Eye said, pointing the gun he held directly at him. "I don't cotton to strangers, and I sure as hell don't cotton to funny-talking, skirt-wearing strangers."

"Isn't that a coincidence?" Griffin took another step toward the stick on the ground about a yard from Dead Eye's feet. "I don't 'cotton,' as ye put it, to unkempt, stupid louts such as yerself. So I guess we're even."

Dead Eye's face turned beet red. "You shouldn't oughta said that, girlie man. I was only gonna have some fun with you. Now I'm gonna shoot you dead."

"He'll do it, mister," Joey said from behind him, his voice anxious. "You'd better apologize."

Griffin met the furious man's gaze and slowly shook his head. "I dinna think so, laddie. Of course, since I'm only a 'girlie man' and ye are a 'real' man, ye won't object to an evenly matched battle between us. Hand to hand? No weapons?"

Dead Eye hesitated, and Griffin went in for the kill. "Of course if ye're afraid . . ."

"Afraid?" Dead Eye holstered his gun. "Hell, I ain't afraid of anything, and I surely ain't afraid of a girlie man like you."

"Good." Griffin smiled, then frowned at the other man's boots. "Och, look at that—your spurs are all muddy."

"Huh?" Dead Eye looked down and Griffin leaped into the air, both feet landing squarely in the middle of the man's stomach, taking him to the ground. He staggered back to a standing position, and Griffin slammed another kick into his belly and followed it with a swift chop to the back of the man's neck. Dead Eye went down for the count—as Jamie would say—while Joey stood nearby, grinning with admiration.

"That was purely something," he said. "Where did you learn how to fight like that? All that footwork?"

"In karate class," Griffin told him. "Maybe next time he willna be so hostile to strangers."

"Ka-rah-tey—I ain't never heard of that," Joey said with a shrug; then his eyes widened. "What did you say? Dead Eye nice to strangers? Hell, no way. Dead Eye, he's just mean and that's all there is to it."

Griffin knelt beside the man, getting a good whiff of his stink as he made sure he was still breathing. "He'll be all right." He rose and glanced over at the boy. "Why are ye ridin' with him? Is he yer kin?"

Joey shook his head. "Nope. I met up with him in Fort Worth. My folks got killed in a Comanche raid out in Parker County and I was left on my own. He invited me to come with him, but I didn't know how mean as an ol' snake he was. Still, I ain't got nowhere else to go."

Griffin frowned, both at the boy's emotionless telling of his parents deaths, and at they way they had died. "Comanche raid? Do ye mean Indians? Like on the tellievision? I dinna think there were hostilities between them and Americans any longer."

"Oh, hell, yes," the boy said. "Them Injuns hate us. Broken treaties and such. Can't blame 'em sometimes."

Griffin ran one hand through his hair. He was tired, hungry, thirsty, and weary of walking. Two horses stood munching grass nearby. He nodded toward them. "Are those yer horses?"

"Yep, mine and Dead Eye's."

Griffin thought for a moment, and then made up his mind. "Ye want to come with me? I dinna have much to offer, but I have friends that can help ye." He glanced down at Dead Eye, his voice rich with contempt. "I can promise ye a better life than what this animal could give ye, one without bloodshed in it."

Joey's face lit up. "You mean it? Could I go to Scotland with you?" he asked.

"Perhaps," Griffin said cautiously. No sense promising something he wasn't sure he could do. "We'll ask my friends about the possibility."

"Who are yore friends?"

"The Rileys and MacGregors, out on the Riley ranch. Do ye know them?" Joey shook his head. "Well, no matter, if ye'll just lead me into town, I can get in touch with them." He would introduce Joey to them and ask them to find him a place to stay and a job. Perhaps he could even get some schooling. Griffin knew Jix would be glad to help the lad.

Dead Eye groaned, and Griffin stepped on the pudgy man's rear end as he walked toward the horses. "I'll just borrow Dead Eye's horse as a lesson in good manners. You can bring it back to him later on."

The color drained out of Joey's face. "You're gonna take his horse? Dead Eye won't like that."

"Dead Eye's lucky I don't press charges with the local law officers," Griffin said, growing impatient. "Now, are ye with me or no?"

Joey looked at Dead Eye, then at Griffin, then back at Dead Eye. "Yep, I'm with you, but you'd better go ahead and kill ol' Dead Eye right now,'cause once he wakes up, he's gonna come after you with both barrels."

Griffin laughed shortly. "I'm no' afraid of the man, nor his weapon. Now, do ye know the way to town, and once there do ye know of a good place to eat?"

"A restaurant?" Joey frowned thoughtfully. "Well, there's the Double Dollar Saloon. It's got pretty good eatin' and bad women."

Griffin lifted one brow. "Really? I dinna know whoring was legal in this day and age."

"Well, sure it is," Joey said. "This is still pioneer country. We got to have our bad women 'cause there ain't enough good women to go around. 'Course not all the girls at Miss Lola's go upstairs, but most of 'em will for a couple of dollars."

Griffin caught the reins of the horse and considered. Maybe he'd been going about this thing all wrong. Maybe the way to overcome his malady was not to seek the help of a lady like Chelsea. Maybe the answer lay in *hiring* a woman to help him overcome his problem. After all, if he was paying a woman, she couldn't very well laugh at him, could she? And maybe, just maybe, he'd be able to conquer this sickness once and for all. Then he could take Chelsea in his arms and make love to her, confident that he wouldn't shame himself or her.

Won't it shame her if I lie with a prostitute first? a nagging voice in his conscience asked. Griffin steeled himself against the thought. He had no choice. If he wanted to remain with Chelsea, in her time, he had to find a way to touch her, to kiss her, to make love to her, without losing his supper.

"Lead the way, laddie," he said. He had a feeling it was going to continue to be a long day.

Chapter Fourteen

Chelsea stood once again looking at herself in Lola's full-length mirror, her heart pounding with nervousness and anticipation. If anyone had ever suggested that one day she'd be wearing a corset, trussed up like some kind of Jezebel, feathers in her hair, dancing and singing in front of a crowd of shouting men, she'd have laughed herself silly.

Now that was exactly where she was and exactly what was happening. How on earth was it possible?

She took a deep breath trying to remain calm. Her ribs pushed against the whalebone stays of the corset, reminding her that once Elmira had heard she was going to be part of the show, she'd insisted on giving her a different dress to wear. Unfortunately, the new dress had a waist slightly smaller than the blue one. Elmira had tightened the corset until Chelsea saw stars, stripes, and a whole parade, but once she caught her breath again she had to admit the new dress was exquisite. She studied her reflection once more, admiring her new svelte figure.

Made of satin, the gown was emerald green with silver trim around the low-cut heart neckline. The trim brought a luminescent quality to her own gray eyes, while the green made the blond highlights in her hair brighten, and once again the corset did its magic to her body. The long skirt was drawn up on one side, revealing a silver petticoat, and was fastened at the waist by a cascade of silver cloth roses. The hem of the dress reached to just below her knees, considered quite scandalous by the rest of the town, Elmira told her.

Long, green-tinted feathers adorned her hair, and Elmira had retouched her makeup, darkening it for what she called "evening wear," and adding pale green shadows to her eyelids.

Chelsea had to admit that while she still looked like a first-rate hooker, she also looked great, in a Marilyn Monroe kind of way. Although the makeup was heavy, it was once again expertly applied, and Chelsea wished with all her heart that Jix and Sam could see her now. Not to mention one very tactless Scot.

She tilted her head, appraising her new image. Would her friends even recognize her if they saw her? How fun it would be if she could fool Jix and Sam into thinking she was someone else! Maybe when she got back to her own time she'd . . . the thought trailed away. At the moment there was no way to return to her own time. She pushed the thought aside. Tomorrow. She'd worry about it tomorrow.

In the meantime she would focus on her new scientific experiment—herself. After Lola had left her in the kitchen earlier, Chelsea had decided to use the experience at the Double Dollar Saloon to test out a new personal hypothesis, i.e., if a shy, inexperienced woman was dressed like a bold, experienced woman of the world, (a) would men treat her differently, and (b) would said woman react differently to said men if they did?

Why not use this opportunity to try out some truly uncharacteristic behavior? Chelsea mused. After all, no one back home need ever know what she had done.

Not that she planned to become one of Lola's upstairs girls. She wasn't going to take things that far, but she could at least try her wings a little and learn how to flirt, couldn't she?

A knock came at the door, jarring her out of her thoughts.

"Come in," she called. The door swung open and Elmira stood there, looking excited and flushed. She wore a deep red satin dress, and her lank dark brown hair had been curled and coiffed into an elaborate creation on top of her head. Her makeup was as expertly applied as Chelsea's, and except for her unfortunate overbite, she looked quite nice.

"Show time, sweetie," Elmira said. She linked her arm with Chelsea's and pulled her toward the door. "Let's go kick up our heels."

Sweat rolled down Griffin's back and chest, tracing a path through the dust caked on his skin, and he wished, not for the first time in the last hour, that he had taken Joey's advice and stolen Dead Eye's clothes and left his horse behind.

A few miles away from where he'd left his attacker, the beast had lost a shoe and thrown Griffin on his head. Then the ill-tempered nag had stepped on a small rock, imbedding it so far into the tender part of the hoof that Griffin had to lead the gelding the rest of the way.

It had taken most of the day to walk the distance to San Marcos, but Joey had been patient in spite of the delay, keeping pace with the Scot. Now as the sun set behind them, Griffin walked down what appeared to be one of the main streets of the town, his mount trailing wearily behind him, Joey humming along beside him atop his perfectly healthy horse. The soft sound of the clip-clop of hoofbeats mingled with the dust rising from the road and with the sound of people talking. Griffin glanced to one side and suddenly realized there were several people staring at him from the wooden sidewalks in front of the buildings lining the street.

Two young women with ringlet curls trailing down their backs from beneath bonnets covered their mouths to hide their laughter, their eyes gleaming at him as an older woman gave him a horrified look and hurried the younger ones along.

Men pointed and laughed outright, while some glared and began talking to others in loud, angry tones.

"Outrageous! What's the world coming to?" one said.

"Look, Mommy," a small boy cried. "That man is a-wearin' a skirt."

Griffin felt the heat rising to his face but grinned and waved at the child. The mother, clad in a gray, long-sleeved dress that reached the ground and a small hat perched on her head, covered the child's eyes and led him away.

Griffin didn't blame her. He glanced down. He looked like the worst kind of barbarian. His chest was bare, covered with dirt and sweat, and his plaid was wound loosely around his hips, the end flipped over his shoulder, the hem hanging raggedly above his knees. He gave the waist a tuck, hoping the cloth wouldn't fall off, making his humiliation complete. The cowboy boots were incongruous and had begun to pinch, so now Griffin was limping right alongside his horse. So much for the modern conveniences of the twenty-first century.

The twenty-first century.

Griffin slowed his pace, taking a good look around. On his way to Samantha's ranch from Austin they hadn't passed through San Marcos, but he'd seen enough of modern towns by now to know what to expect.

This wasn't it.

He stopped and looked back the way they had come. From where he stood, he could see that San Marcos was a bustling little place and in his day and age would have been considered a good-sized town. But in the year 2003 he knew it wasn't. A huge structure sat in the center of what Joey called "the square," and a plaque proclaimed it to be the Hays County Courthouse. A variety of establishments bore signs claiming to be sellers of "Dry Goods," "General Merchandizing," "Drugstore," as well as businesses called "The Hofheinz Hotel" and "The Exchange Hotel." Still, Griffin knew that something was wrong.

"How much farther to this place ye keep blatherin' about?" he said, more to distract himself than because he cared.

"Just around the corner here." Joey smacked his lips. "Miss Lola's got the best fried chicken. But first we'll stop in at Jake's for a bath."

"We're going to get a bath?" Griffin frowned in surprise. As far as he knew, Joey didn't have relatives or friends in town. How did he expect to bathe?

"Sure thing. There's a place that only charges a nickel for a bath and two bits for a haircut." He shut one eye and looked speculatively at Griffin. "Looks like you need both."

"If ye say so," Griffin said. He ran one hand through his long hair and frowned. Its length had been the mark of a warrior in his day and age. Should he cut it now? Would Chelsea like it if he did? Would it help him fit in better? A curious ache began in the center of his chest. Chelsea. Where was she, and what was she doing now? Had she gotten back to the ranch? Was she bringing help even now to Jacob's Well?

Perhaps he'd been wrong to leave the place. How would she ever find him? He released his breath explosively. He was exhausted, hot, hungry, and irritable. He'd take care of those needs first and then worry about getting back to the Riley ranch. Surely someone in this town could give him directions or perhaps let him use their tellie-phone. Funny about tellie-vision and tellie-phones. One had nothing to do with the other. Somehow that didn't make sense.

Right now, nothing seemed to make sense.

He stopped walking abruptly, even though that gave the people staring at him the opportunity to really get a good look at the strange visitor to their town. But it also gave him the opportunity to take a good look at them.

Women in the twenty-first century did not wear dresses that reached the ground. At least not in everyday situations. He knew this because he had been constantly amazed and intrigued by the fact that women in the year 2003 seemed to wear so little but no one thought it unseemly. Watching tellie-vision had been quite an education in itself. Especially something called "Victoria's Secret commercials." As far as he was concerned, Victoria, whoever she was, had no secrets left whatsoever.

And the buildings. The sidewalks. They were all wooden and appeared somewhat familiar, but not right. He'd seen something like them, though, so perhaps he was being foolish. He started walking again, ignoring the titters and laughter of the people he passed. His boot kicked a rock, and it tumbled across the dusty road. Griffin stopped again and stared down.

In Scotland, roads like this weren't uncommon, either in his time or in modern times. Even in Texas, he'd seen such byways, in isolated areas and on the ranch. But San Marcos was supposed to be a large town, a small city, with a university. Would such a town have dirt roads? Something wasn't right. He glanced around at the square again and suddenly remembered where he'd seen such a place.

On a tellie-vision program called *Gunsmoke*, a show about the Old West.

He was puzzling over it when he happened to catch sight of a hat displayed in a store window. It was a silly affair with a wide straw brim and a cluster of pink roses on one side. A large pin protruded from the middle of the creation, and at its end was a ball of green glass, cut into gleaming facets.

The crystals. The memory slammed back into his brain so suddenly it left him breathless. He'd dived back into the well looking for Chelsea, but instead had found the green crystals exactly like the ones in Scotland. He'd touched them, thinking of Duncan and Chelsea, and he'd ended up here, wherever "here" might be.

"Everything okay, Scotty?" Joey asked from behind him.

"Aye," Griffin whispered, then cleared his throat. "I'm ashamed to be seen like this. I should have taken Dead Eye's shirt at least."

"Ah, heck, don't pay them no mind." Joey sneered at one woman who had stopped to stare, and she hurried away, her long dress dragging across the wooden sidewalk, her bonnet bobbing irately.

Griffin's mind raced even as his feet began to move again of their own accord.

"Do ye happen to know what the date is, Joey?" he asked, keeping his tone casual, slowing his pace until he strode beside the boy's horse. Joey scrunched his eyebrows together thoughtfully.

"Well, let's see. Yesterday was Tuesday and a week ago

Tuesday I remember it was June seventeenth so that would make it June twenty-fourth."

Griffin nodded and cleared his throat. He tossed Joey a smile. "Och, I hate to admit it, but I canna seem to keep track of the days. Must be getting old. Speakin' of age, how old would ye be, lad?"

"I'm seventeen years old," he said. "And don't start talkin' about why ain't I home with my mammy or in school."

"Don't worry, I won't." Griffin walked along in silence for a few minutes, then spoke again. "I'm no' so good at my figures," he said. "What year were ye born, do ye know?"

The young man snorted. "Do I know? 'Course I know what year I was born. Know the date too. April 14, 1865. I was born just before the end of the War Between the States."

Griffin stopped in his tracks. Joey pulled up beside him and frowned. "You okay, Scotty?"

Am I okay? Ye just told me that I've traveled through time again, to a place even more foreign to me than Chelsea's, for at least there, she was around to guide me.

Duncan. If it really was 1882, his cousin might still be alive.

"Aye," he said after swallowing hard, "I'm fine." He started to move forward again, trying to ignore the slight tremble of his knees.

"Yo're an odd fella, ain't you, Scotty?"

Griffin no longer wanted to talk. He wanted silence in which to sort out his thoughts, but he could hardly ignore the only friend he had in this century. "In what way do ye mean?" he said.

"I mean," Joey went on, "you really weren't afraid of ol' Dead Eye, were you? Even when he had the drop on you with his gun."

Griffin shrugged. If he kept his mind on Joey's questions maybe he wouldn't—what was it Jix called it?—freak out.

"Nay, I've faced worse, I suppose," he managed to say. "In my time, that is, in my country, ye must learn to be prepared."

"Huh." Joey was silent for a few minutes, then turned

back to Griffin again. "Could you teach me how to do that kay-rah-tey stuff? I wouldn't tell Dead Eye this, but I don't cotton much to guns. Never was much good with them, to tell you the truth. And what good are they if somebody gets the drop on you first?" He shook his head. "Seems to me that what *you* can do is a sight more practical than toting a gun—which, by the way, seems to just invite folks to call you out so's they can see if they's faster than you."

"I'll be glad to show ye a few of the moves," Griffin said, half listening, "though I'm really new at it myself."

Joey glanced his way, and Griffin saw the faint glimmer of hero worship in the boy's eyes. "Aw, I 'spect you know more than you even realize yourself."

Griffin blinked, surprised out of his reverie. He wasn't used to outright adoration from anyone, let alone from a young lad like Joey. Not knowing how to respond, he stayed silent.

"Let's go get our bath and haircut and find you some new duds."

"All right, laddie," Griffin said, stifling a sigh. "But is there any way to get a drink of something first?"

Joey frowned. "I thought you were worried about how you're dressed—or not dressed, I mean."

Griffin shook his head. "I've got bigger problems than a bare chest, laddie. Lead on."

Chelsea was having the time of her life.

Standing on the stage beside Elmira, her arm linked with the dark-haired woman on one side and a redhead on the other, she smiled and kicked first one leg and then the other, dancing for all she was worth.

Her first performance an hour or so ago had been terrible. She'd been one step behind everyone, petrified with fear. Lola had pulled her off the stage and shown her the routine, slowly, over and over, until she got it down. The artfully madeup madame had shoved her back onstage and whispered loudly, "Have a good time, honey!"

And in that moment, Chelsea remembered her experiment. She was going to employ different behavior if it killed her. And when she first started dancing in the high-heeled shoes Elmira had given her, she thought it just might. But after that first awkward performance, she'd thrown herself into the spirit of the whole experience and soon was amazed to find she was having a great time!

As she danced and kicked and tried to sing, she saw something strange in the faces of the men looking up at the women. Admiration. Lust, of course, but also admiration. And all at once she cast aside her presumptions about this place and this time. This was pioneer country. These people had survived against all odds. Who was she to criticize or condemn them for the way they had done it? She wondered if all of the women of Lola's Double Dollar Saloon enjoyed their work. Especially the upstairs girls.

The thought of prostitution dimmed her enthusiasm slightly, but she pushed it away and gave another high kick to the sound of hoots and hollers.

She felt wonderful. The satin dress slid against her body like a second skin, and the short bloomers Elmira had given her were much more modest than the bathing suit she wore to the public pool in her own time. Two silver petticoats danced over her knees as she swished the fabric back and forth to the delight of the men watching. But the sexiest part of her costume, besides the low-cut neckline, were the thin, black, thigh-high stockings held in place by lacy black garters.

She'd never felt so absolutely desirable in her life.

The music of the piano player behind them grew faster as the women sashayed back and forth across the stage, laughing and shrieking between verses, their legs kicking high over their heads.

"You're a natural at this, girl!" Elmira shouted to her over the music. Chelsea grinned back, feeling foolish to be taking so much pleasure in a silly thing like song and dance.

She twirled with the rest of the girls and kicked, twirled, and kicked again. When she ended up facing the audience, breathless, the door to Lola's Double Dollar Saloon opened and in walked a young man, barely showing the fuzz of his first beard. He looked somehow familiar, but Chelsea couldn't place him. She twirled again and kicked, then froze in place as a tall, broad-shouldered, bare-chested mountain of a man walked in, his white-blond hair streaming past his shoulders, his ice-blue eyes registering shock as he caught sight of her.

He wore a dirty piece of plaid material around his waist and a pair of cowboy boots and nothing else, and Chelsea didn't know whether to laugh or cry with relief.

Griffin.

Griffin Campbell. Her heart started beating a quick tattoo against her chest as their gazes locked and she knew without a doubt it was no other than the tactless Scot she loved so much. A soft smile curved his lips.

"Griffin?" she whispered to herself.

"C'mon, Chelsea, you're fallin' behind!" Elmira said, prodding her with one elbow. Chelsea resumed her position in line and started dancing again, stunned by Griffin's appearance. How had he gotten to this time period? Had he jumped into the well after her? Of course he had! He'd gotten worried and thought she'd drowned. Here she'd been wishing he could see her dressed in her finery and, *voilà!* He appeared as if in answer to her prayers!

The men sitting closest to the door nudged each other and started laughing as the Scot passed them. A tall, thin man in a dark suit leaned against the long oak bar and gave Griffin a piercing look, then moved to follow him.

Chelsea's heart felt as if it might burst as she watched Griffin make his way toward her, a stunned expression on his face. Finally when he was only a few feet away she couldn't stand it any longer. She danced to the edge of the stage and jumped down to the floor below.

"Griffin!" she cried and threw herself into his arms.

"Chelsea?" He held her, and his arms felt so strong, so familiar, so wonderfully safe. She clung to him, so happy to no longer be alone in a strange time period that all the fears she'd held down, all the terror she'd denied, suddenly came bubbling up inside of her, spilling over in glad, glad tears.

She smiled up at him, wiping away the moisture with the back of her hand. "Oh, Griffin, I didn't think I'd ever see you again, I really didn't! I mean, I thought even if I went back to the well, what if the green crystals weren't there anymore, like they weren't for you in Scotland? And then I'd be stuck here and—"

"Shhhh, dinna fash yerself," Griffin said softly. The commotion of the women on the stage dancing and laughing, and the men shouting and bellowing, and even the sight of the tall man in the dark suit standing very close to them, faded as Griffin leaned toward her, and Chelsea closed her eyes to at last receive his kiss.

"What the hell do you think you're doing?"

Chelsea jumped at the sound of the loud, angry voice and bumped her mouth on Griffin's chin. Opening her eyes, she glared at the tall, thin man now practically in their faces. He glared right back.

"What are you doing down here instead of dancing?" His face was pale and lined, made stark by the lank black hair lying against his cheekbones and over his forehead. A long mustache curled from lips clamped tightly around a cigar.

Before she could ask who he was, his long, thin fingers closed around Chelsea's wrist and he jerked her away from Griffin, pulling her against him. He smelled of cigar smoke and licorice, and the combination made Chelsea want to retch. His black eyes bore into hers, and she shrank away from him as far as his grip would let her. She had no idea who he might be, but there was not an ounce of humanity in those eyes.

"There'll be plenty of time for whoring after the performance is over," he snarled around the cigar. He shoved her toward the stage. "Now, get up there and get to work."

"Whoring?" Griffin narrowed his eyes and took a step toward the man.

"No, no, Griffin, it's all right," Chelsea said hastily. "It's fine. I need to get back to work. I'll explain later." She hurried around to the steps leading up to the stage, hoping to head off an out-and-out brawl. "It's okay, look, I'm dancing, I'm dancing!" She did a fast shuffle and joined the front row where she could keep an eye on Griffin.

The tall man glowered at the Scot. "And you." His gaze swept over the half-naked man. "What the hell are you supposed to be? The next act?" He laughed and gestured toward Chelsea. "Keep dancing, you little bitch," he called to her loudly, "and maybe I'll let you give me a private performance later."

Chelsea blushed but kept dancing, then groaned as she saw the blood and fury rush into Griffin's face.

"Here we go," she muttered, just as the Scot's right fist connected with the tall man's jaw.

Chapter Fifteen

The man fell to his knees, but Griffin jerked him back up and slammed him against the side of the stage, pressing one muscled forearm against his throat.

"How dare ye speak to her that way?" he demanded. "How dare ye?"

"Get off of me!" The man choked out. "Do you know who I am?"

"Dinna know, dinna care." Griffin bent him back over the stage until he was practically lying under the dancers' feet. Chelsea shot Elmira a startled look, but the girl just shrugged and kept dancing, so Chelsea did likewise.

Besides, she thought, still warm from Griffin's defense of her, *that man needs a lesson, and Griffin is just the one to give it to him.*

Hiram, the piano player Chelsea had met earlier, picked up the tempo of the song as the man's arms started flailing. He swung his fists into Griffin's back and shoulders. Chelsea noted smugly that he might as well have been punching a rock for all the impact it made on the Scot.

"Ye will apologize to her!" Griffin roared over the music, while the men around him laughed and cheered and lifted their mugs of beer in drunken approval.

"Yeah, that's right, apologize!" Joey called out.

Chelsea beamed at both of them and kicked for all she

was worth, her foot coming close to the bully's head over and over again. She caught his eye and smiled down at him sweetly.

"Let this be a lesson to you," she shouted. "Don't judge a book by its cover!"

She laughed and twirled into the next song. She felt wonderful. She felt beautiful. She felt like a different woman—bold, brassy, and unafraid. Griffin was here, she was dancing on a stage in front of him, and he had just saved her from a masher. This mess was finally turning into the adventure she'd hoped for! She paused to toss the back of her skirt up in perfect unison with the rest of the girls, when all hell broke loose.

Griffin's captive suddenly reached back over his head and grabbed Chelsea's ankle with both hands. Still bent halfway over, Chelsea stumbled to one side and collided with Elmira, who in turn fell against a red-haired girl called Flossie, who shrieked and threw out both arms, knocking the twins, Matilda and Sarah Jane, into the piano player's lap, sending Hiram crashing into the ivory keys headfirst.

Hiram stood, holding his head and stumbling from side to side as the girls tried to right themselves. The disoriented musician took one step too many and fell off the stage, directly on top of a table surrounded by five very serious poker players. The gamblers jumped to their feet and started swinging. In a matter of minutes, the entire bar was in an uproar, with bottles and furniture flying. Chelsea crawled over to Elmira, still lying flat on her back.

"What's happening?" Chelsea cried. "Why are they all fighting?"

"It's Friday night!" the younger girl shouted back, looking as though she was enjoying the respite. "Just lay low and you'll be all right!"

Chelsea closed her eyes and groaned. Why had she ever believed she could do this? And how awful that Griffin had seen her awkward tumble after he had defended her so bravely. She clasped her hands over her head against the sounds of glass breaking and men shouting and women screaming. She groaned again as Hiram, who must have suffered brain damage, started playing the piano again.

"Come on, sugar," Elmira said, rolling to her knees. "If we start dancing again it may calm 'em down."

Chelsea shook her head and grinned. "Sure," she said dryly. "Why didn't I think of that?"

"Chelsea?"

She looked up at the sound of Griffin's voice. He stood bending over her, his eyes filled with concern.

"Here, lass, let me help ye up." He took her by the hand, but Chelsea couldn't seem to stand. Her knees were too weak just because he was so near. She gazed up at him and smiled.

"Oh, Griffin," she said. "I'm so glad to see you."

He answered her smile, gesturing toward the chaos. The tall, thin man was stretched out on top of a table, moaning, while the rest of the bar patrons cheerfully pummeled one another.

"That one was no' so happy to see me," Griffin said; then his expression softened as he returned his gaze to hers. "I'm glad to see ye, too, lass."

Chelsea curled her fingers in the palm of his hand and felt her lips tremble with longing. He rubbed the back of her hand softly with his thumb, and it took every ounce of discipline she had to keep from returning the caress by touching her tongue to his bare knee, just inches from her face. That would be silly. Wouldn't it? Of course it would be. So instead she did nothing, just kept looking at him, unable to move, unwilling to lose the heat of his hand.

The brawl had begun to die down a little, with about half the customers lying unconscious or groaning on the floor, while others stumbled toward the door that led to the street.

"I think I've done enough lesson teachin' for one night," Griffin said with a wink. "What do ye say we find a quieter spot for our reunion?"

Chelsea nodded eagerly, when a familiar voice cut through the fading sounds of destruction.

"Hey, girlie man in the skirt! Ain't none of us wanting to see yore naked butt! Get out of the way and let them whores back on the stage."

Griffin straightened slowly and turned to look down at the man.

Chelsea closed her eyes. Dead Eye. Oh, brother. And things had just started to calm down.

Griffin shook his head. "In my country we dinna let mad dogs run loose."

"C'mon, purty boy, I wanna see the whores dance. Let's start with that one sitting right there."

Griffin paused and glanced down at Chelsea. "Let me see, how would Jix put this?"

Chelsea shook her head, confused. He smiled and turned back to Dead Eye, whose cock-eyed gaze was fixed on them, a leer on his ugly face.

"I have already kicked yer ass once today, laddie," Griffin said, "but I would be more than happy to open another can of"—he frowned thoughtfully as he folded his arms across his wide chest—"whoop ass in yer honor."

"You tell him, purty boy!" one of the men cried.

"Don't be callin' him that," the young man who had come in with Griffin said. Chelsea suddenly remembered him. It was Joey, Dead Eye's partner. But from the look on the boy's face, things had changed. Apparently, he was on Griffin's side now.

"Why not?" another drunk asked. "He is awful purty. Just as purty as a whore in—"

Joey threw a punch and caught the man squarely in the jaw, and the bar exploded into a free-for-all once again. Griffin dove off the stage and tackled Dead Eye at the waist, taking him down to the floor, while the girls on stage started dancing and singing at the top of their lungs. Chelsea scrambled out of the way of their kicking feet and sat on the steps, watching as men with cut lips and bruised faces started swinging again. Women not engaged in dancing screamed, and some were tossed over brawny shoulders to be carried upstairs, while more tables were turned over and bottles flew right and left. Chelsea shook her head in amazement, and then gasped as a bottle came flying straight toward her.

Someone intervened and knocked the bottle to one side

before it could strike her. Chelsea looked up into Griffin's smiling eyes.

"This is just like back home," he said joyfully, scooping her up in his arms. He held a long piece of wood that looked as though it had once been a table leg.

His sword, Chelsea realized as he carried her to the back of the stage. Even in this time period, Griffin remained who he was—a fierce Scottish warrior, a commanding chieftan. How could she ever have imagined he would be content in her time?

Some of the other girls had retreated from the stage and were cowering behind the curtain. Griffin swung Chelsea to her feet beside them. "Stay here!" he shouted, and headed back into the fray.

Chelsea made a grab for him but missed. She started forward only to find she couldn't move. She looked back and saw Elmira holding the skirt of her dress in both hands.

"Don't go out there, honey," she said. "When them men get this way, nobody's safe!"

"Where is Lola?" one of the other girls moaned. "Where is Blake? She never let's a fight last this long! Blake always rescues us!"

Chelsea pulled the middle of the curtain back and glanced out at the melee. Griffin was right there in the thick of things, and what was she doing? What she had always done—she was hiding. She jerked her dress from Elmira's fingers.

"Sorry, girls, but I refuse to be rescued!"

She lifted the hem of her skirt and charged back out on the stage, straight for Griffin. In spite of the fifty or so people fighting and slugging it out in the saloon, Griffin wasn't hard to spot. His bright blond hair danced around his muscled shoulders as he stood on top of a round table, swinging his wooden "sword." Four men lay unconscious on the floor, and Dead Eye stood confronting him, a broken bottle in his hand.

Chelsea sent up a quick prayer of thanks that Lola always made everyone check their guns at the door, and looked desperately around for a weapon. At the far side of the stage jutting out from the wall was a three-foot-high version of the Texas flag, complete with a heavy metal eagle screwed on at the top. Three more men now surrounded Griffin, while directly below Chelsea a man with an extremely large knife in his hand started toward the Scot as well.

She grabbed the flag by the pole and started across the stage, running at full speed. When she reached the edge she leaped with all her strength across the short expanse to land on the back of the knife-wielding adversary.

"Remember the Alamo!" she shouted, bringing the flagstaff down on the head of the man. He howled and fell, but another man grabbed her by the hair, flipping her over his head to land flat on her back amid the broken glass.

Chelsea opened her eyes in time to see a large blade plummeting toward her, and she screamed and rolled, the knife barely missing her, imbedding in the floor instead of her chest. Jumping to her feet, furious and pumped with adrenalin, she swung the flag around and caught the man across the back of the head with the metal eagle.

He went down with a groan, and she headed for Griffin. A heavy-set man grabbed her around the waist and tried to kiss her, but she jerked out of his grasp. Unfortunately, he didn't let go of her dress. She heard the tear but didn't stop, stepping out of the torn skirt to fight in her silver petticoat. Then suddenly Dead Eye stood in front of her, and she did stop. He had a gun, in spite of Lola's rules, and it was pointed right at Griffin.

Chelsea cried out and slammed the flagstaff across his wrist, sending the firearm spinning across the floor. The man turned, furious, and started for her, when Griffin brought the wooden table leg he held down across the back of the man's neck. Dead Eye fell like a sack of potatoes to the floor.

Two blasts rang out, and the fighting stopped as suddenly as it had begun. Every head turned toward the doorway. Lola Valenti stood with a smoking shotgun in her hands and fury in her eyes. A man taller than Griffin, at least six foot five, his skin as black as ebony, stood beside her, huge arms crossed over his chest, dark eyebrows glowering over black eyes that promised retribution if Miss Lola wasn't obeyed.

Griffin jumped down from the table and pulled Chelsea into his arms. "Chelsea, lass, are ye all right? Why did ye come out here? Didn't I tell ye to stay where it was safe?"

"Well, you see, there's something you need to know about Texas women, Griffin," she said softly, happy to be in his arms again. "We all have minds of our own."

"Aye, I can see that." He hugged her again, and she slipped her arms around his waist. He was sweaty and less than aromatic, but Chelsea didn't care. His warm, hard muscles throbbed beneath her hands, and she wanted nothing so much in that moment as to kiss him. She reached up and brought his head down to hers. But before their lips could touch, a loud voice intervened.

"What in the Sam Hill is going on here?"

A short, balding, overweight man had replaced Lola and her companion in the doorway. He stood with his hands on his hips, his guns slung low and the badge on his chest shining. Behind him hovered another man, a larger copy of himself, obviously his deputy.

The tall, thin man who had started the whole fight was back on his feet. He stumbled toward the sheriff and spoke to him in a low, terse voice, then moved to stand beside the law officer. Chelsea felt a wave of premonition sweep over her. He was obviously someone of means. Dressed in a black pin-striped suit that even she could tell was expensive, he bent and picked up a black bowler-style hat from the floor. He slapped it against his hand to push out a dent and gazed around at the chaos, fury in his haughty black eyes. He stepped forward, picking his way through the destruction until he reached Lola's side.

"So is this the way you manage my business, Miss Valenti?"

His business? Chelsea hadn't known Lola very long, but she would have bet that the woman wasn't afraid of anything. She would have lost. Lola looked up at the man with terror in her eyes.

"I don't know, Mr. Peyton," she whispered. "I wasn't here. I—"

"You weren't here?" his voice boomed down at her, and she shook her head. "And *why* weren't you here, Miss Lola? Isn't it your job to be here?" She nodded, twisting her hands in front of her, not meeting the man's eyes. "We shall discuss this later." He turned, his hard gaze sweeping the room again. "Sheriff Adams, I want you to arrest the man responsible for this."

"Be glad to, Mr. Peyton," the sheriff said, his voice deferential. "Now 'fess up, boys," he called out to the sagging group of men. "Who done this?"

"You don't have to ask," Peyton began. "I can tell you—"

A low moan interrupted him as Dead Eye crawled out from under a table and looked blearily up at the two men.

"Was it you, Dead Eye?" Adams asked, shaking his head. "Hell, I told you that if you busted up another saloon I was gonna lock you up and throw away the key."

"No, Sheriff, it weren't me," Dead Eye whined, cradling his arm. "It were that furriner." He pointed at Griffin with his good hand. "And that ain't all. He stole my horse. When I came in here and told him to give it back to me, he hauled off and hit me."

Chelsea looked at him in outrage. "That's not true!"

"I was about to tell you, Sheriff," Peyton interjected dryly, "that the wild-looking man over there started the whole thing. I didn't know about the horse theft, but I'm not surprised." He lifted one dark brow. "He's obviously a barbarian."

Chelsea felt like slugging the man as he moved to lean arrogantly against the bar. A glint of something on the floor caught her attention, and she saw that the gun she'd knocked out of Dead Eye's hand had skidded under the edge of the bar, almost out of sight. She edged closer to it, careful to make the move look casual.

"All right, Dead Eye, you'd better come along too if you want to press charges," the sheriff said. "And as for you . . ." He frowned at the bare-chested Scot. "Didn't your mama ever teach you not to go out in public like that?"

Griffin's face turned red but his voice remained calm. "Sheriff, this man—" he gestured toward Dead Eye—"attacked me earlier. After I made him realize the futility of his attempt, I borrowed his horse to ride into town. I planned to return it."

The sheriff shook his head. "You ain't from around here, are you, son?"

"I'm from Scotland."

"Scotland? Well, boy, you're gonna wish you'd stayed with the sheep, because in Texas you don't take a man's horse and leave him stranded out in the middle of nowhere without water."

Griffin frowned. "We were near the river. I knew he'd be fine."

"Mr. Peyton here says you accosted him. What you got to say about that?"

"He insulted one of the ladies. I was simply defending her honor."

Peyton removed the cigar from his mouth. "Ladies? There are no ladies present, so obviously your story is a lie."

The Scot took a step toward the man, his fists clenched. "Dinna call me a liar, laddie, or what I gave ye before will be like a wee tap." He moved forward, but the sheriff stopped him with the flat of his hand on his chest.

"All right, son, come along quietly."

"Sheriff, wait, you have to believe him," Chelsea said, breathless. "I can vouch for every word he's said." She spread her hands apart, trying to think of some way to convince the man not to arrest Griffin. The sheriff seemed somewhat intelligent. Surely if she appealed to his logic he would understand.

"You have to realize that he's just unacquainted with Western ways," she said. "He's the most honest man I ever met, and if he says he borrowed the horse, then he did."

The sheriff stared at her for a long minute, then bent over, laughing so hard he cried. One corner of Peyton's mouth quirked upward while the other men in the saloon began to guffaw and shove one another. Griffin grew tense, his hands flexing into fists.

"Well, hell," the sheriff said, wiping his face with the back of his hand, "if one of Lola's whores vouches for him, then he must be all right. Don't tell me—you're the whore he was defending."

Chelsea bristled. "I am not a whore." She put her hands on her hips and lifted her chin. "I am an entertainer."

He started laughing again but finally got himself under control as Chelsea glared at him and Griffin glowered. The sheriff wheezed a couple of times and shook his head, wiping his eyes. "Whoo-ee, that's rich. C'mon, son, I'm going to have to lock you up."

Griffin glanced at Chelsea over the sheriff's head, a warning in his eyes, and she suddenly realized it was really going to happen. Griffin was going to jail. And he didn't want her to do anything to stop it, because, she was certain, he didn't want her to get hurt, or get jailed with him.

"I'll go with ye, Sheriff," Griffin said, confirming her thoughts. "I'm sure we'll get this all settled in no time at all."

Dead Eye narrowed his eyes and grinned at Chelsea, his crooked, dirty teeth making her almost visibly shudder. "Don't let him get yore hopes up, darlin'," he said. "Yore man here is gonna rot in jail awhile and then dance at the end of a rope. And you'd better keep yore mouth shut or you might be joinin' him."

"Leave her out of this," Griffin said, his gaze dark and threatening.

Dead Eye grinned. "Who's gonna make me, purty boy? You?"

The sheriff stepped between them. "All right, that's enough. Let's go, son." He led Griffin toward the door, and as Dead Eye's laughter echoed through the destroyed saloon, Chelsea bent down and slid her fingers under the edge of the bar. The cold barrel of the gun was within reach, and she inched it out until she could grasp the butt of the weapon. Her hand closed around it and she ran across the room, stopping just opposite the sheriff at the door. She raised the firearm level with his chest.

"Hold it right there, Sheriff," she said, proud that her

voice only trembled the slightest bit. "I think you've got something that belongs to me."

Griffin glanced over at Chelsea. She sat on her horse, her hair still held up in curls by a comb, dark against the waves. She gazed at the moon, now high above them, and although he couldn't see the blush rising in her cheeks, he knew it was there. Water rushed by them just a few feet away. They'd ridden quite a way. Moments before, Chelsea had informed him that they had reached Cypress Creek. They couldn't be too far from Jacob's Well, and once they reached the pool, he would have yet another decision to make: Would he return with Chelsea to her time—and she was going back if the crystals were there, that much he was sure of—or would he stay and try to find Duncan?

What a lass. After she had surprised the sheriff by flashing Dead Eye's gun, Griffin had seized Adams's weapon and he and Chelsea had escaped on Joey's and Dead Eye's horses. It had been a grand getaway, but he felt certain the sheriff and his men were chasing them. They'd been lucky to reach a source of water, and now the best thing they could do was make camp and try to find their way to Jacob's Well in the morning. Her words to the sheriff came back to him and made him smile.

"Something that belongs to ye, did ye say?" he asked, a lilt in his voice. Even though they were running for their lives, knowing they were together in this made him extremely happy. Silly fool of a man that he was.

"I'm sorry about that," she said, her voice faint. "I guess I was just feeling a little . . . oh, I don't know . . . smug."

"I dinna mind," he said softly, wishing he could tell her how much he wished he could belong to her. He smiled in the darkness, remembering the way his shy and gentle Chelsea had danced and sung and fought—saints, but she could fight like a wildcat. He frowned. "And now I hope ye don't mind if I ask ye . . ." he hesitated. He didn't want to insult her, didn't want to make her think he didn't trust her, but he had to know. "No one hurt ye, did they, lass?"

"Hurt me? Oh, you mean because I was dressed like that,

dancing at the Double Dollar?" She was silent for a long moment, staring straight ahead. He was about to speak when she answered. "You know, those girls are there because they have nowhere else to go. They do the things they do to survive. It isn't their fault."

"Och, I understand that," he said. He watched the sparkling water flow past, his heart sinking. Did that mean she had done whatever was necessary to survive? "I just want to make sure ye're all right."

She turned to him and suddenly smiled. "I'm fine. In fact, I'm better than I've been in a very long time. You didn't know I could sing and dance, did you?"

He laughed, though his mind was still far from at ease. "Nay, I did not. Lass, did anyone . . . did any of those men force ye to, to do anything . . ." He broke off, unable to voice the question torturing him. If anyone had dared to touch her, to hurt her, he would kill them with his bare hands.

"No," she said softly. "Thank you for asking."

Griffin felt a great weight lifted from his shoulders. "Good, that's good." He could smile now. "Ye are a bonny singer and dancer."

"Thank you," she said, her cheeks flushed with color. "I never in my wildest dreams imagined I could do either! I've always been shy, but now I've realized . . ." She hesitated, and he nodded to encourage her.

"Aye, lass, what?"

She bit her lip, then rushed on as if she had to get the words out. "I've realized the shyness is just a way to hide, to protect myself. Inside, I want to have fun, I want to tell people exactly what I think, but I'm afraid, afraid they'll laugh at me or get mad at me or stop lov—stop being my friend."

"Ye have great insight. They say that realizing ye have a problem is half the battle," he said, pulling his horse closer to hers.

His words brought a sudden grin to her face, and the sight sent a wave of joy through him.

"You watched way too much television in Scotland," she said with a laugh.

Griffin fell silent, letting the moment wash over him as the companionable quiet between them and the soft sound of the water soothed the tumult in his soul.

He wanted to say more. He wanted to tell her how beautiful she was, how spirited, how incredibly smart and brave. But now he was the one afraid. All at once he realized how very much they were alike. He had always been afraid to hurt his father by telling him he didn't want to be chieftain of the clan. He had been afraid to tell Chelsea the truth about his problem with women. But no longer. If Chelsea could travel back in time and make it alone by overcoming her innate shyness, then surely he could find the courage to tell her the truth.

"Was I really okay?" she asked, glancing his way for the first time.

"Aye," he nodded. "Though I must say I like ye better without all the paint and furbelows."

"Really?" She lifted one hand to touch her curls, her gaze a trifle anxious. "I don't know, I kind of like it for a change, though it did take a little courage to walk around looking like this." She looked away, then back again. "To tell you the truth, this is the first time in my life I've ever felt . . . well, pretty."

Griffin met her eyes and there it was again, that indefinable something darting between them, lacing the air and making him want to hold her, touch her, taste her. But not yet. Then her words permeated his consciousness.

"Och, Chelsea, love, ye are beautiful, with or without adornment. And verra brave," he added. "Ye have inspired me. I have decided to be just as courageous."

Chelsea frowned. "What are you talking about? You're the bravest man I've ever known."

He shook his head and looked up at the moon. "Nay, I am not. I have been a coward in one verra big way, and yer words convince me all the more to make this confession to you."

"What is it, Griffin?"

He hesitated. "Let us stretch our legs and walk a bit." He swung down out of the saddle, picking up the reins and patting the horse absently on the neck as he circled around to Chelsea's mount. In her silver petticoat and emerald-green bodice she looked like some woodland fairy, and Griffin's heart filled with love. She slid both legs over to the left side of the saddle, and he reached up to lift her down.

The satin bodice slipped beneath his fingers, and instead of lowering her slowly from the saddle, his hands lost their grip and with a soft cry she fell hard against him. He caught her awkwardly, his arms clasping her beneath her round bottom, her breasts flush with his chin, her head resting on top of his as she draped her arms over his shoulders to brace herself.

Griffin began to shiver. His stomach began to roil.

Oh, God, please, he prayed, trembling, unwilling to move and spoil the warmth of the moment. *Please release me from this torment. I want to make this sweet lass my bride, but however can I if I canna act as a man?*

The picture flashed through Griffin's mind, as clearly as if it had happened yesterday. His father, hairy and naked, grunting like an animal between the legs of one of the scullery maids in the stable, her face flushed with passion, the cries of Griffin's dying mother echoing through his five-year-old brain as he watched his father break his wedding vows.

As if a light had switched on inside his head, Griffin suddenly had his answer, suddenly knew what he must do. Suddenly he broke free of his self-made prison.

He let Chelsea slide down his bare chest, relishing the feel of the satin dress, growing hard as the soft skin above her bodice touched his, all the time keeping her close, holding her against him, letting her feel how much he wanted her, showing her there was no doubt that she was the one he wanted, the only one he loved.

"Griffin?" she whispered, her voice trembling.

"Och, lass, it's all right now. Now I know what I have to do, what will end my torment. I need not burden ye with my problems."

Griffin drew in a sharp breath. Chelsea's hands were resting against his chest, and she moved them up to encircle his neck, the moonlight turning her gray eyes to silver.

"Chelsea, love," he said, running his thumb gently over her bottom lip. "Will ye marry me?"

Her eyes widened. "Will I—marry you?"

Griffin bent his head to hers and captured her lips with his mouth, letting the fire spring up between them, giving full rein to the passion flooding his soul, because soon, very soon, he knew he would be able at last to possess the woman he loved, and let her possess him. But at the moment . . . he broke the kiss and dragged in a deep breath of air.

"Will ye, lass?" he asked again, this time through gritted teeth.

"Griffin, I hardly know what to say. I—"

His stomach churned and his fingers tightened unconsciously around her waist. "Lass, 'tis simple," he said, his voice strained. "Just say yes—and please hurry!"

Chelsea opened her mouth and closed it, twice, and Griffin almost groaned aloud. Then at last she smiled.

"Oh, Griffin, of course I'll marry you."

As the bile rose to his throat, Griffin let her go so fast she almost fell.

"Grand," he choked out. With one hand clasped over his mouth he ran to the creek and dove in headfirst.

Chapter Sixteen

Griffin broke the surface and gasped for breath, feeling happier than he could ever remember being in his life. God had answered his prayer and given him the means by which to release himself from his bondage. He tossed his head and laughed out loud, relishing the coolness of the water trickling down his face and hair. He stripped off the sodden plaid from his waist and gave it a mighty heave toward the shore, then plunged beneath the water again, reveling in his newfound freedom.

When he came up again he swam for the bank, pulled himself up onto dry land, and sat directly next to the tapping feet of Chelsea Brown. He draped his plaid over his lap before glancing up at her and grinning. She didn't smile back. She sat on a large rock, her arms folded tightly across her chest. Her legs were crossed, nicely showing the black stockings and a hint of black lace garter. One foot swung freely, one tapped impatiently, or angrily, he wasn't sure which. She cleared her throat, and he dragged his gaze from her legs and back to her face.

Angrily. Yes, she was tapping her foot angrily, that much was for certain.

"Chelsea, love, is something the matter?" he asked as he reached up and squeezed water from his long hair.

"Why, whatever could be the matter?" she said sweetly.

A little too sweetly perhaps.

Griffin cocked his head toward her. "Aye, I dinna know," he said, frowning a bit. "That's why I'm asking."

Chelsea stood and began pacing back and forth on the bank behind him, her hands clasped behind her back. "Why should anything be the matter?" she asked him, her eyes shining brightly in the moonlight.

A little too brightly perhaps. Griffin was beginning to feel uneasy.

"Chelsea, love—"

"I mean, whatever could be wrong?" She walked faster, the rhythm of her voice increasing at the same time. "I mean, you wait your whole life for the man of your dreams and you think you'll never find him, not ever, and then, whoosh!" She spread her arms to the sky. "There he is, dropped into your lap from another time, another place, and you think—no way, no way he could ever like me, let alone love me—I'm too plain, too ugly for him."

Griffin started to protest her words, but she held up one hand, palm flat toward him, and kept talking.

"But then this man, he looks at you as if you're beautiful." She dropped her gaze, and Griffin's heart began to ache. Surely the lass knew how he felt. Surely she knew he thought she was the fairest flower in the world.

She looked up, her eyes burning with passion. "And for a minute you think maybe you are beautiful, at least to him, and his eyes are so soft, so gentle, and his hands . . ." She spun away and began pacing again. "His hands make you crazy, and then he kisses you and . . ." She broke off and covered her face with both hands.

Griffin fastened the plaid around his waist and stood, not moving, watching the woman he loved, waiting for whatever it was she was experiencing to pass. She began to shake, and with a pang so sharp it almost tore him in half, he realized she was crying. Because of him?

"Lass, I dinna—"

"And then he freaking throws up!" she cried, turning around to face him, her hands knotted into fists. "Every time he kisses you, he runs away and throws up! No—*he* doesn't—not some hypothetical person—*you* do it—you,

Griffin. You're the man I've waited for all of my life, and every time you kiss me you vomit! And now you ask me to marry you—and you vomit!" She began trembling again. "So you tell me, Griffin Campbell, what the *hell* is going on? What kind of game are you playing?"

Griffin felt stunned. Was it possible she had been blaming herself all this time for his sickness? Could she possibly think that he found her so repugnant that it made him ill?

He groaned aloud. "Och, lass, forgive me. Forgive my ignorance. Forgive my selfishness."

Indignant eyes brimming with tears shone in the moonlight, and Griffin cursed himself for a fool as he walked up the bank and took her in his arms.

"It isna because of ye," he whispered against her hair. She didn't slip her arms around his waist. Didn't respond at all, just held herself stiffly beside him. He tried again. " 'Tis a malady I've had most of my life, since I was a young lad. It has nothing to do with ye, lass." He cupped her face between his hands and gazed down into her eyes. "Don't ye know how much I love ye? How much I have loved ye almost since the first moment I saw ye?"

Chelsea stared up at him, the tears disappearing, replaced by stunned amazement. "No," she whispered. "No, I don't know."

He shook his head helplessly. "Och, Chelsea Brown, I love ye so much that at times it seems my heart will burst from the lovin'. I love ye so much that every time I am close to ye I want to lay ye down and touch every inch of ye and caress ye and kiss ye and make ye completely mine."

Her mouth parted and her voice was breathless. "Then why haven't you?"

"I love ye so much," he went on, "that when I dove into Jacob's Well and saw the crystals, in my mind I knew I should help Duncan, but in my heart I wanted to stay with you."

"Oh, Griffin," she said, melting against him, her arms moving to slide around his waist. "I love you, too, so much. But then, why? What's wrong?" She looked up at him, and the longing in her eyes was almost his undoing. He wanted to kiss her, to make good on his words and lay her down beside the river and make love to her. He had hoped to do better by her, but perhaps she would want him as much as he wanted her, and agree.

"Lass, will ye marry me, right now, right here?"

Chelsea reached up and touched his face, her gray eyes dark with love. "Aye, laddie," she said. "I will."

"But first I want to explain, so ye will never, never doubt that I love ye, that I think ye are the most wonderful, incredible woman I have ever known."

He spoke quickly, quietly, gazing down into her eyes. He told her about the night his mother cried out, about looking for his father and finding him in the stable with one of the maids, about his mother dying alone, about the malady that had plagued him ever since. It was over in a matter of moments, and Griffin felt the weight of his secret roll off of him as Chelsea's loving eyes told him she understood.

"Oh, Griffin," she said, "do you mean to tell me that you're a virgin?"

Heat rushed to his face, and for a second he was tempted to lie. But no, he would not start his marriage with an untruth. He would never lie to Chelsea.

"Aye, lass," he said softly. "I'm sorry, but this is why I wanted to tell ye first. Ye'll no' be coming to a bridegroom with experience, but a man who isna even a man yet."

Chelsea moved to him, pressing the palms of her hands against his chest, sliding them up to his shoulders, her head tilted back, her eyes shadowed in the moonlight. "Oh, Griffin, you darling, silly man. I'm a virgin too. Does that disappoint you?"

Griffin slid his arms around her waist, feeling his heart leap with joy at her words. "Nay, love, of course not. A man wants his wife to be pure, to know she waited for him."

"And that's what a woman wants too, don't you know that?" Chelsea shook her head at him. "Do you think I would have more respect for you if you had bedded every woman in Scotland and had all of this 'experience' as you call it? Don't you think I like knowing that when we make love it will be something special and sacred, for both of us?"

Griffin opened his mouth, then shut it and smiled. "I never thought of it that way," he said at last. "I dinna know women even thought of such things."

She laughed. "This is the twenty-first century, laddie." She caught herself. "No, this is the nineteenth century, but when we get back home it will be the twenty-first and I promise you, women think of such things there! And they think of them here too, they just aren't allowed to talk about them, except maybe at Miss Lola's."

"I think ye'd better give yer notice at Miss Lola's," he told her, but she lifted her mouth to his and he groaned and crushed her to him, forgetting everything but the fact that he loved Chelsea and the sooner they married, the sooner—his stomach rolled and he pushed her away gently.

"Griffin, I will help you with this problem," she said. "As long as I know you love me, we can work through this. You don't have to prove your love by marrying me."

"Well, ye see, I have this theory," he said, and quickly explained it, his admiration for her growing as she began to nod, falling into her scientist way of thinking.

"Yes, that makes sense to me." She glanced up at him, her eyes bright and filled with her open love for him. "Shall we try it?"

"We could wait until the morning," he said, "but I dinna know how long we may be able to evade the sheriff and his men, and, och, love, I dinna want another night to pass without you in my arms and I dare not try before I make you my bride."

Chelsea took his hand. "Well, then, what did you have in mind?"

"I know every woman wants a grand celebration," he said, smoothing his hands over her waist, "and I know that in your time there are papers and certificates and such, but in my time if a man and a woman love one another and there is no parson or priest close by, they pledge their love to one another in a handfasting and consider it binding before God and man."

"Oh, Griffin," she whispered, "that sounds lovely, but I can't do it."

He stared down at her in dismay. "But, lass, ye said—"

"If we're going to do this, we have to do it right. Do you see that hill behind you?"

Griffin frowned and turned in the direction she pointed. "Aye."

"That's Mount Baldy. I know where we are." She grinned. "And we're going to be married someplace very, very special. Will you trust me?"

"Only with my life, lass," he said softly, dropping a kiss on the end of her nose.

"Good, then get on your horse and follow me."

With a sigh Griffin helped her back on her horse and mounted his own. He had no idea what the lass had in mind, but after all, she wasn't getting a grand wedding in a church. She deserved so much more than he could give her right now, and so wherever she was leading him, he would gladly follow.

It didn't take long on horseback. Chelsea pulled up on her horse, and Griffin realized all at once how much more easily she seemed to ride. She had more confidence, for some reason.

"We're here," she said, sliding out of the saddle before he could dismount and help her. She held out her arms and spun around in a circle. "I just hope it's here."

"Hope what's here?" he asked as she started running up a nearby incline.

"Come with me," she called.

Releasing his pent-up breath, he followed, wishing he'd at least managed to steal some clothing before heading out of San Marcos. When he reached Chelsea halfway up the large hill, she stood smiling at a large oak tree. He glanced up to see what had so mesmerized her and blinked. The tree was smaller, the branch forming the "hole" just beginning, but there was no mistaking it. It was the Betrothal Tree. Even the rock was there beside it, giving a footstool to her lovely feet as she jumped up on it and thrust her hand through the opening. She looked back at him, so happy it made his heart sing.

He rounded the tree and took her hand, bringing it to

his lips for a brief, wonderful moment before he asked her the all-important question again.

"Chelsea, will ye marry me?"

She gazed into his eyes, her hand small and warm in his.

"Yes, Griffin, I will marry you."

He reached up and pulled a long green ribbon from her hair. He released her hand and pulled her down to kneel beside him, wrapping the ribbon around their wrists.

"Then before God," he said, his throat tight with emotion, "and beneath this, the Betrothal Tree, I give my promise to ye, Chelsea, that I will love ye, and honor ye, and treat ye as a good husband should, and give ye joy." Her eyes sparkled at that, and he smiled, lifting his hand to caress the side of her face. "I vow my love to ye tonight, forever, and always."

"Before God," Chelsea echoed, her voice soft, "and beneath this, the Betrothal Tree"—she hesitated as if trying to remember his words, then smiled and went on—"I give my promise to you, Griffin, that I will love you and honor you, and be a good wife to you, and give you joy." She lifted her hand to his face. "I vow my love to you tonight, forever, and always."

"Oh, my love," Griffin whispered as her mouth drew closer to his. "What God has joined together, let no man put asunder."

Their lips touched, and for a fraction of a second Griffin felt the old familiar fear, then Chelsea opened her mouth to his and heat, dark and dangerous, flooded into him, and the fear and everything that came with it melted away and disappeared.

Chelsea felt stunned as Griffin's lips touched hers, felt afraid as the kiss deepened, expecting him to pull away at any moment and reject her. Instead he pulled her closer, into his arms, caressing her mouth, her jaw, the hollow of her throat, the edge of her collarbone, tracing it all with the heat of his tongue even as his hands slid over her shoulders, slid the satin straps down her arms.

"Oh, Griffin," she moaned, and he caught the words with his mouth, brushing his fingers against the softness of her skin, moving them beneath the satin edge of her bodice. She pressed herself against his touch, and he cradled the weight of her as his thumb rubbed lightly over the satin, tracing the sensitive skin through the cloth.

Her head fell back as he kissed a path downward from her lips, his tongue caressing again, darting into the crevice between her breasts, flicking over the exposed flesh, tantalizing her with the promise he could not deliver because of the layers between them.

He half lifted her to her feet and she followed him, mindlessly, helplessly. Eventually she realized he was leading her away from the Betrothal Tree, down the hillside, to a place where there was soft grass and bright moonlight.

They knelt down together, and impatiently Chelsea slipped her arms out of the satin straps and tugged downward on the bodice, pulling it to her waist, exposing the tight corset beneath and the swell of her breasts now free of all restraint.

Griffin gazed at her bareness for a long moment, then bent and touched his tongue to her skin. Chelsea closed her eyes and shuddered, feeling like a pagan moon goddess as his mouth found her and took the offering she freely gave to him as his wife. She slid her arms over his shoulders, urging him on, when Griffin suddenly pulled away. Chelsea drew her arms around her nakedness and shivered. Her heart pounded as she opened her eyes, afraid she would see Griffin turn and run away from her, as always.

Griffin met her fearful gaze, blue eyes dark with desire and triumph as he stood and stripped the plaid from his waist. Dried after their short ride across the countryside, he placed the cloth on the ground and offered her his hand. Trembling, she took it. He pulled her to stand in the center of the plaid, his naked glory making her mouth turn dry.

He turned her away from him and began unlacing the bodice still bunched at her waist, freeing her from the satin. The silver petticoat came next. It slid to her ankles, and she stepped out of it and kicked it aside. Then there was only the corset and the black lace garters binding the sheer black stockings to her thighs. The corset was quickly undone and discarded, and Chelsea expected the stockings to come off next.

Instead Griffin slid his hands down the front of her thighs, caressing her as he kissed the delicate skin behind her ear, sending a flood of desire coursing through her body, making her feel infinitely precious. This was what she had been aching for, longing for, and she hadn't even known it. The love of a man like Griffin. His hands moved over her, and she leaned back against him, allowing him to touch her anywhere he chose, trembling beneath his gentle exploration.

"You are so beautiful," he whispered as he drew his fingers over the soft curves of her waist and her hips, lifted his hands to caress each breast, then turned her in his arms to face him. Chelsea rested both her hands on his chest, smoothing his muscled skin. She leaned toward him and traced a path with her tongue down the center of his chest.

"I've wanted to do that for so long," she said.

Griffin groaned and drew her against him, his mouth hungry as he kissed her, plunging his hands into her hair, burning his need for her against her lips. She met him passion for passion, her breath coming quickly as his hands grew less gentle and more urgent and he pulled her down to the plaid beneath their feet.

Chelsea closed her eyes and sank to her knees, turning her back to him again. He pulled her close to him, and she felt his chest hair soft against her skin, tantalizing her. She arched backward as his hands slid over her breasts, across her ribs and hips, down her thighs, smoothing the softness of her skin, pressing his hardness against her, finally finding the sweetness he sought. She caught her breath as Griffin touched her, gasped as his long fingers began to move in a soft, sensuous motion.

Then she was lost to the flooding waves of need sweeping over her and she spun around, taking possession of his mouth, running her hands over his shoulders, his arms, his back, molding her body to his. Griffin leaned her backward and stretched her across the plaid, holding himself above her and looking down at her with such love in his eyes that Chelsea felt like crying. Her gaze turned misty as he bent and touched his lips to hers, caressed her face with his mouth, possessed each breast, and finally, finally slid into the dark passion awaiting them both. Moving past the chaste barrier she'd held sacred for so long, Griffin Campbell made her his wife, claiming her forever as his own.

Chelsea yielded her virginity gladly to the man she loved, the one man, the only man. Griffin whispered her name as he moved first gently, then more urgently, taking her with him into the hot, bright warmth. Flames, white-hot, coiled inside her and she pressed her hips upward allowing Griffin to claim her, possess her, burn his love into her flesh and her innermost being.

She opened to him, baring not just her body but her soul, letting him fill her and make her part of him, one with him, forever. Over and over he joined with her until Chelsea couldn't think, couldn't breathe, could only move and feel and climb, higher and higher toward the moon and the stars with Griffin, only Griffin, taking her upward to a place she'd never been before. His light exploded into the nexus of her universe, his energy consuming hers, hers shimmering into his, until there was no longer he and she but a sharp, shattering joining as the two became one.

Chelsea cried out and Griffin called her name and became part of her forever, and then there was nothing but peace, sweet peace, as her husband held her in his arms.

Griffin cradled his wife as they lay beneath the stars, and he thanked God for the love that was now his. Soft, feathery clouds blew across the face of the moon, and for the first time in his life he felt perfectly whole, perfectly content. Chelsea slept, one hand on his chest, her beautiful head pressed against his shoulder, her sweet lips half parted as if waiting for his kiss.

Their first experience in making love had been everything he'd hoped it would be. He closed his eyes. He was so grateful that his sickness was over. How wonderful that all it had taken was to make love to a woman within the bonds of wedlock. How wonderful that all it had taken was Chelsea's love.

She snuggled against him, lifting her leg over his and rubbing her foot down his shin, giving a little sigh. The moonlight turned her hair to silver and cast shadows across her bare breasts. He bent to touch his tongue to one shimmering tip, and she sighed again. He drew the sensitive nub into his mouth, and she opened her eyes and lifted both hands to his head.

"Is that my husband?" she asked softly, caressing his long hair, raking her fingers through the slight tangles.

"Aye," he said, raising his head from her softness. "I've come knocking once again at my lover's garden. Will ye take me in?"

"Aye," she whispered, pulling him toward her. Griffin rolled her beneath him and spent several long, achingly wonderful moments memorizing her body with his tongue and his hands, until Chelsea pressed her hips against him and he could no longer wait to be consumed by the sweetness of his wife. Griffin rocked into her and almost wept with joy as she arched and clutched him, her eyes closed, her lips parted in pleasure as he made love to her. She yielded to him, and he to her, as moonlight turned to starburst in the center of his soul.

As he drifted back to earth with his beloved in his arms, Griffin realized that from that day forward no matter where in time he might end up, as long as Chelsea was with him, he was home.

Chapter Seventeen

"So I guess I would be safe in assuming I don't make you sick anymore?" Chelsea asked.

Griffin kissed her mouth gently. She swept his long hair back from his face, and her touch made him realize all over again how much he had gained in just one night.

"Aye, lass," he said, and chuckled. "I think it would be safe to say." She shivered in his arms, and he pulled the ragged edge of his plaid tartan around her shoulders. They lay naked listening to the creek, watching the dawn arrive above the hills, streaks of gold dissipating the last vestiges of the night, fingers of pink paving the way for the dazzling glow of the rising sun.

"Isn't it beautiful?" Chelsea asked, snuggling against his shoulder.

He held her closer, feeling more fortunate than any man had a right to be. She was warm and soft in his arms, and he gazed down at her, memorizing every curve of her face, every variance of color in her eyes, and realized he wanted her again, would want her forever.

"Aye," he agreed, " 'tis the most beautiful thing I've ever seen in my life."

Chelsea glanced up at him and blushed. "I meant the sunrise," she said, running her hand across his chest and down. Her eyes widened, and she smiled. "Again?"

"Och, lass, 'tis yer own sweet fault." He kissed her throat gently, touching his tongue to her skin, delighting in the way she shivered at such a small gesture of his love. He covered her body with his, feeling a surge of joy so intense that he couldn't be slow or tender, he had to express the happiness raging inside of him.

Chelsea opened to him eagerly and he filled her, making love to her as the sun rose, the only sounds around them the birds welcoming the morning, the creek rushing to the river and the river to the distant sea, and his wife's soft moans of pleasure as he made her his own once again.

When they were both sated, Griffin pulled her on top of him and wrapped the long plaid around them both. She rested her head on his chest and whispered, "I love you, Griffin. Please don't ever leave me."

His arms tightened around her, and he closed his eyes. "Never," he said fiercely. "Not while I have breath in my body."

"Well, hell, that won't be too much longer, will it, Sheriff?" a voice above them said.

Chelsea screamed and Griffin's eyes flew open. Sheriff Adams stood above him, Peyton at his side.

"Sorry to interrupt your fun," Sheriff Adams said, pressing the barrel of a rifle against Griffin's throat. "But it's time for you to pay the piper, boy."

"Griffin—" Chelsea said, her voice tight with fear.

"It's all right, love." He sat up, bringing her with him, making sure she was covered by the plaid. "Could ye turn yer heads and let my wife dress?"

"Wife?" Peyton laughed. "That's a new word for it."

The sheriff rubbed one hand across his face. "You two married? We been tracking you for hours."

"Aye, we were wed last night," Griffin said. "Now look away."

"It's a trick." Peyton pulled his own pistol from his holster. "You won't get away twice. If you try it, I'll shoot you down like the dog you are."

"I think ye must have me confused with yer other friend," Griffin said dryly. "Sheriff? Ye look to be a man of common decency."

Adams shrugged. "Sorry, son. It's obvious you can't be trusted."

Peyton laughed again, and Griffin stood, sweeping the plaid around Chelsea, protecting her from the view of the other two men. She stumbled to her feet and clutched at the material around her shoulders. Griffin retrieved the soiled remains of her dress and handed it to her.

"Dinna fash yerself," he told her, keeping his voice low. " 'Twill be all right."

"As long as we're together, nothing can be wrong," she said. He smiled and peeled the plaid from her shoulders, holding it in front of both of them as a curtain, keeping his eyes on the sheriff and Peyton as she quickly donned her clothing. When she'd finished and stepped away from him, Griffin wrapped the tartan around his waist and threw the long end of it across his chest and over his shoulder.

"So, gentleman," he said, one arm around Chelsea. "Now what?"

"Now you rot in jail until the circuit judge comes by," Peyton said. "Then you hang for being a low-down horse thief."

"He isn't a horse thief!" Chelsea said, taking a step toward the man. Griffin pulled her back, and she trembled beside him.

"I'll go with ye," Griffin said, "and peacefully, but only if ye promise to let my wife go free. She has nothing to do with this."

"Nothing to do with it?" Peyton demanded. "She's the one that pulled the gun on us!"

"She was only doing what I'd told her to do," Griffin said, hoping the sheriff would buy the lie.

"Oh, hell, Mr. Peyton, the girl ain't no never mind," Adams said. "Joey said he lent her his horse. But Dead Eye is pressing charges against you," he said to Griffin. "If you'll come along peaceable, she can go on back to Lola's."

"Griffin, I'm not letting you go to jail without me," Chelsea said, her gray eyes brilliant with unshed tears.

"Shhh, lass, trust me." He tilted her mouth to his and pressed a brief, sweet kiss on her lips.

"But, Griffin—"

"It won't be for long, lass," he said, tightening his fingers on her shoulder in warning. He knew enough about men like Peyton to know that if he tried anything the man wouldn't hesitate in shooting them both. The tall man obviously owned the sheriff, and even though Adams seemed to have a few scruples, and was willing to let Chelsea go, he doubted that the law officer would dare oppose Peyton if the man insisted. If Chelsea was on the outside instead of locked up with him, they might still be able to figure a way out of this.

"Enough of this polite chit-chat," Peyton said with a sneer. "The girl rides back with me to make sure there isn't another escape attempt."

Griffin set his jaw as the man pulled her from his arms. Chelsea struggled at first; then she caught Griffin's eye and he shook his head imperceptibly. She seemed to understand his meaning and with a sigh mounted Peyton's horse and winced as he swung up behind her. The dark-haired man slipped one hand around Chelsea's middle, tugging her back against him with a laugh. Griffin steeled himself not to attack. He knew that was exactly what Peyton wanted. Then he could shoot the prisoner and have a perfect excuse for it.

"C'mon, c'mon," Adams said, prodding Griffin toward Dead Eye's horse. "Let's go see your brother. I'd have thought that the trouble he's in would be enough to make you want to steer clear of San Marcos."

Griffin stopped walking. "My brother? What are ye talkin' about?"

Adams returned the frown. "Ain't you kin to that other furriner I got locked up in my jail? You look just like him."

Griffin shook his head slowly. "I have no relatives here."

The sheriff shrugged. "Sorry. My mistake."

"Adams, you idiot, stop apologizing to your prisoner," Peyton shouted as he turned his horse away from the river.

"I ain't apologizin'," the sheriff said. "It's a figure o' speech." He wrapped a piece of rope around Griffin's wrists. "I gotta tie you this time," he grumbled. "Can't take no more chances."

The sheriff helped Griffin mount his horse, then swung himself up into his own saddle, keeping Griffin's reins in his hands. Adams sent his horse into a fast trot, pulling Griffin's pony into the same pace. Peyton was already several yards ahead of them, and as Griffin watched the woman he loved being held by another man, a man with evil intent, his jaw tightened and he pressed his lips together in a grim, straight line.

Surely even in this time period, in this barbaric place, there was some degree of chivalry. Even in his time, women were treated decently. Well, most of the time.

As the sun blazed above the horizon, sending the temperature soaring, Griffin made a solemn vow. If Peyton hurt his wife, it would be the last thing the bastard ever did.

"Here you go," the sheriff said. He opened the jail cell door with a long key and swung the door open. "Ben, put him in while I start the paperwork."

The deputy pushed his prisoner toward the cell. Griffin didn't resist, though he was tempted. He wanted to think things through first. There would be another opportunity to escape. For one thing, he noted there was no place to relieve himself in the cell and he would at least have to be taken out for that little matter. He glanced down at the soiled plaid he still wore.

"Sheriff," he said as the deputy slammed the door shut behind him. "Would ye be so kind as to find me some clothing?" Griffin looked pointedly at his half-naked body. "I'm growing a wee bit chilled."

The sheriff grunted again but put the paper he was holding down on the desk. He crossed to a wooden closet and opened it, dug around for a few minutes, then emerged holding a bundle of clothes.

"Here," he said, shoving the clothes through the bars. "I don't know what all is in there, but maybe something will fit."

"Where did you get them?"

"Off the last six men we hung. County provided suits for 'em to be buried in."

Griffin swallowed hard. Wearing the clothes of a dead man, a man hanged to death, wasn't high on his wish list, but he couldn't afford to be squeamish. He shook out a pair of black trousers and held them up to him. They were long enough and looked like a close fit, so he pulled them on. Except for a little extra room in the waist they were fine.

All the shirts seemed to be either white or black so he chose a black one. It was a little too tight across the chest, but he didn't care. His choice of black clothing was intentional. When he made his break out of this place, he would be harder to spot in the darkness.

He turned to survey his cell. An iron bunk bed sat against the far wall. Above it, near the top of the twelve-foot-high walls, was a small window. The bed measured about three feet wide and six feet long and held a thin striped mattress, no sheets, and only a bare pillow. Next to the bed sat a battered stand holding a pitcher of water and a bowl. That was it. He turned and gazed out at the rest of the jail.

It was comprised of a single huge room that contained four cells, two on either side of the room, taking up half the space. Each set of cells shared one barred wall. Outside the cells near the front door were a chair, a hatrack, a gunrack, and the sheriff's desk stacked high with papers. In one corner sat a small stove, cold and dead. It was a humid night, so all four windows were open, as was the front door, which led onto a wooden porch.

In the cell next to Griffin a man lay stretched out on his bunk, one arm over his face as he snored quietly. His "brother," no doubt, that the sheriff had been blathering about. He probably just had a foreign accent of some kind and Adams considered all "furriners" to be the same.

Griffin ignored the other prisoner. Now that he wasn't distracted by Chelsea's presence, he could figure out what to do. The deputy, Ben, was exceedingly dumb. Slack-jawed, hollow-eyed, he had about as much spunk as a dead lizard. He wouldn't be hard to overcome. The sheriff would be harder, but not impossible.

Ben gave Griffin a nervous look as he stood staring at his prison. "I don't trust him," he said to the sheriff. "He's got shifty eyes."

"Hell, he's a horse thief," the sheriff answered. "What do you expect? Don't fret yourself." Adams sat down behind his desk and frowned at the pile of papers in front of him. "I'll stay the night and you can take over in the morning. See if you can rustle up some supper for him and the other one."

Ben shot the prisoner another look and nodded. "All right, Jack, but you watch yoreself with this one."

"Sure, sure. Go on now."

"So I'm goin' to get fed, am I?" Griffin asked from his cell.

" 'Course. We don't starve the prisoners." The sheriff pulled a sheet of paper off the top of a stack and peered at it.

"What's my companion over there in for?"

Adams looked up from his papers and glanced over at the other cell. "You don't be messin' with him. He's a bad 'un. He talks as funny as you do, but leave him alone."

"What's he in for?" Griffin insisted.

"Murder." The sheriff picked up a quill pen and dipped it into a small inkwell. "In the first degree. Now, what's your name, first and last?"

Griffin spent the next few minutes giving Adams his personal history, slightly altered, and watching the man in the other cell. He was awake. Griffin could tell even though he continued to snore lightly. His breathing had changed, the rhythm, the movement of his chest. Why was he pretending to still be asleep? Griffin squinted in the dim light and suddenly realized the man was wearing, of all things, a kilt.

"How are ye over there?" he called. "Is it a Scot ye are?"

"I told you to leave him alone. He's got a bad attitude and he don't take kindly to anyone," the sheriff said, pulling a pack of cards out of his desk. "If you wanna play a little poker to pass the time—"

"I'll play cards with the lad," the man in the cell said. He still lay on the cot, one arm over his face.

"Are ye from Scotland?" Griffin asked, watching the other prisoner closely. "I'm from the Highlands."

The man lowered his arm and slowly swung his feet off the bunk to the floor as he sat up. Griffin moved to the wall of bars between them, and his breath caught in his throat as the man stood and walked toward him. His lower face was covered with several days' beard stubble and his sun-streaked dark gold hair curled slightly around his face and at the base of his neck. His eyes were bright blue, and for a minute Griffin felt as if he were looking into a mirror.

"Duncan," he whispered.

The man grinned and reached through the bars with both hands, grabbing Griffin by the shirt collar, pulling him flat against the iron separating them, their faces inches apart.

"Hello, cousin," he said softly. "What the hell are ye doin' here?"

"Duncan," Griffin said again. "Thank God ye're alive."

The man laughed, but there was no warmth in the sound. "Aye, in the flesh, at least for a little while longer." He frowned, and his fingers tightened on the front of Griffin's shirt. "Och, but ye shouldn't have come here, lad. How did ye get here, or need I ask?"

Griffin shook his head, drinking in the sight of the familiar face that he'd thought he'd never see again, the face so much like his own except for slight differences, in particular the long, thin scar running from eyebrow to jaw down the left side of Duncan's face.

Griffin had given Duncan that scar when he was six and his cousin almost ten. They'd been sparring with their wee wooden swords, which they both agreed were for babies. Griffin had gotten the idea of taking a couple of daggers from his father's cabinet. The two boys had stolen the sharp weapons and sneaked into the woods where they joyfully fought "like real men" until Griffin, in a passionate attack, had sliced his cousin's face open.

The resulting blood, terror, and punishment of slopping the village hogs for a month had cured them both of fighting with sharp objects until they were a few years older. Griffin had never quite forgiven himself for marring Duncan's handsome face, yet now it was the scar that convinced him it was, indeed, his cousin smiling back at him from his jail cell.

"I'm that glad to see ye," Griffin said, reaching through and clasping the man's shoulders.

"But what are ye doin' here?"

Griffin raised one brow and grinned. "I've come to save ye, laddie."

The dull look in Duncan's eyes faded away, and a spark of familiar belligerence returned. He clapped the back of Griffin's neck with one hand and shook him.

"Aye, that will be the day! After I left the only thing I regretted was that ye probably wouldn't live to grow up without me there to look out for ye."

"Is that so? Well—"

"All right, you two, just step back from the bars," the sheriff said, interrupting the poignant reunion. "I don't allow no hoochy-coochy stuff between prisoners."

"Och, shut up, ye damned old twit," Duncan shot back. " 'Tis my cousin. If ye had half a brain ye would have at least known that we both hail from the same country."

"I told him that I had his brother locked up. He swore he didn't have no kin in these parts." The sheriff narrowed his eyes, hands on his hips, until the men moved apart, both still grinning. Adams shook his head and returned to his work, muttering under his breath. "What can you expect from damned crazy skirt-wearing furriners?"

"Tell me," Griffin said to Duncan, his voice low. "How did ye get here? Is this where ye've been all this time?"

His cousin ran his hand through his tousled hair and cupped the back of his neck, looking tired and thoughtful, yet not a day older than the last time Griffin had seen him, five years before.

"It's a long story," the man said, his weariness evident.

Griffin spread his hands apart. " 'Twould seem I've got plenty of time."

"Time." Duncan glanced up at him, and his smile faltered. "Funny ye should mention that fickle female. Aye, time . . ." He nodded and walked over to a straight-backed chair near his bunk. "Pull up a chair and I'll tell ye."

Griffin looked around the cell. "I dinna have a chair."

"Sheriff," Duncan called, "my cousin needs a chair."

"Damned furriners," the sheriff grumbled, but he rose and picked up a chair and carried it over to the cell.

Duncan tensed as the sheriff neared the door. The Scot gave Griffin a meaningful glance. Griffin knew he was encouraging him to jump the sheriff if he got the chance, and he prepared to do exactly that. Unfortunately, Adams was no fool. He pulled his gun from its holster and held it on his prisoner.

"Back away from the door now, son," he said. Griffin complied, and the man opened the door, shoved the chair in, and locked the cell again.

Griffin pulled his new furniture item over to the bars and sat down facing Duncan. His cousin shot the sheriff a bitter look and then slung his own chair up closer to the bars between the cells and straddled it backward, his arms resting on the curved wooden back.

"So what happened?" Griffin asked, anxious to hear the story.

"Ye obviously found my cave," Duncan said, keeping his voice low.

"Aye. And the crystals. They took me to the year 2003."

"Shhh," Duncan cautioned, glancing around. The sheriff appeared to be busy pouring coffee into a battered tin cup. "Ye cannot trust him. He isna as stupid as he might seem." He frowned. "2003? Then what the bloody hell are ye doin' here?"

Griffin shook his head impatiently. "Time enough for my story after I've heard yers."

"Verra well." Duncan bowed his head for a moment, then drew in a deep breath and lifted his gaze back to his cousin's. "I've been traveling through time for the last five years."

"By that I take it ye mean ye've traveled to more than one time period."

"Aye. In all, I've gone to ten different times in four different countries."

Griffin leaned back in his chair, overwhelmed. "Duncan, how . . . ?"

"I've discovered that the crystals exist in many time periods, in many countries," Duncan said. "Scotland, Europe, Asia, the Americas. And it's our minds that control the wee green monsters," he added.

"Our minds? What do ye mean?"

"Our thoughts," Duncan explained. "Apparently, the crystals will take ye backward or forward to any time period ye can think of, but only within the country in which the crystals reside. And I've discovered that ye must be thinking either of the time itself—that is, the year—or of a particular person." He paused, staring down at his hands for a long moment, before continuing. "The crystals will take ye either to the time ye're thinking of, or to the person."

"I suspected as much," Griffin said thoughtfully. "When I touched the crystals in 2003 I was thinking of ye—I'd seen yer ugly mug in a history book—but in my heart I was thinking of Chelsea. Lucky for me, the two of ye were in the same place." Duncan frowned at his words. "She had already gone back ahead of me," he explained.

"Chelsea?" A slight smile crossed Duncan's face. "Dinna tell me that ye finally conquered yer fear of women? Who is she, and why is she running through time with ye?"

Griffin inwardly groaned. He'd forgotten that once, after having a few whiskies with his cousin, he had told Duncan a little about his problem, though not the whole story.

"She's a woman I met in the year 2003," he said, ignoring the man's knowing look. "I got there by accident. But she and I . . . well, we were swimming at a place near here called Jacob's Well."

"Aye," Duncan interjected, " 'tis how I came here myself, from a future time."

Griffin nodded, tucking that information away for examination at a later time. "Chelsea dove into the spring and apparently touched the same kind of crystals that had brought me to her time. If what ye say is true, she must have been thinking about this time period, and that's what brought her here, and in turn brought me."

Duncan nodded. "Aye, that's the way of it. I've ventured to far ancient times and even to the distant future. For what good it did me." A darkness shadowed his eyes, and Griffin was quick to note it.

"Are ye all right?" he asked.

"Aye." Duncan rested his chin against the back of the chair. For the first time Griffin noticed the lines at the corners of his cousin's eyes and around his mouth, saw the few gray hairs at his temples. He'd thought nothing had changed about Duncan, but apparently he'd been wrong. And it was more than physical appearance. The Duncan he'd known had been full of life, adventurous, always smiling, always laughing and joking. This man was somber, serious, and Griffin detected a bitter and cynical edge to his comments.

"Dinna lie to me," Griffin said with a frown. "I ken ye too well for that."

Duncan shrugged. "Aye, well, perhaps ye did ken me in the past—in our own time, I mean—but I am no' the same person now, lad."

Griffin waited, watching his cousin as the man looked away. The silence stretched between them, and still he waited, certain that Duncan would confide in him when he was ready. At last the man laughed, a short, harsh sound, and lifted pain-filled eyes to meet his.

"I'm dyin', laddie," he said. "And I want to see Scotland, and my own time, before I go. But I dinna have the energy to try. I am doomed to die here, away from the green hills of Scotland." He sighed and looked up at Griffin, his gaze dismal. "And so are ye, lad. So are ye."

Chapter Eighteen

The next morning Lola scolded Chelsea for staying out all night, but when she explained that she had run away to get married, and that Griffin had been arrested, Lola was all sympathy. It helped that Chelsea had spent the last few hours cleaning Chin's work area.

"Would you be willing to let me help Chin for a while instead of dancing?" Chelsea asked. "I'm not sure Griffin would want me to keep performing—as much as I've enjoyed it," she added hastily.

"Sure, honey, I understand." Lola looked around at the spotless kitchen. "He'll be real happy to see this. Maybe he'll shut up for a change. I swear, that man could singe the hair off a cat at twenty paces."

Peyton had dropped Chelsea off at the saloon after bringing her back to town. She was surprised he hadn't tried to take advantage of her, but she supposed he had bigger fish to fry, mainly Griffin. She'd jumped down off the horse before he could dismount and had run down the alley beside the saloon and around the back to the door Lola kept unlocked.

Once inside, nervous with worry over Griffin, she'd quietly gone into the room she shared with Elmira. Her roommate was fast asleep, but Chelsea managed to find a soft dress made from blue gingham to replace her soiled and tattered green satin. She put it on, glad to be wearing clean clothes, wishing there was time for a bath, and headed downstairs.

She had tackled the dirty kitchen and by the time Lola appeared she had done everything but polish the coal bin. Now she and Lola chatted companionably as they fixed breakfast for the ravenous women starting to drift downstairs in varying states of disarray. Chin, it seemed, didn't do breakfast.

"I oughta be mad at that husband of yours," Lola said as she expertly flipped the bacon frying in a wide iron skillet. "Not only did he break up my place last night, but he's taking one of my best girls off the stage."

"Thank you," Chelsea said. "But he really didn't start the fight. It was that tall, thin man, the one the sheriff called Peyton." She shook her head. "He's evil."

Lola fell silent, and for a few minutes there was only the sound of the bacon frying and the glasses chinking as Chelsea dried them and placed them side by side on a clean cloth.

"You want to steer clear of Mr. Peyton," Lola said at last.

"He said something last night after the fight that I didn't understand," Chelsea said, brushing one long lock of hair back from her face and tucking it back into the bun she had fashioned at the nape of her neck. "He said something about the saloon being his business. I thought you owned it."

Lola speared a piece of bacon and moved it smoothly to a plate, her too-dark brows puckered thoughtfully.

"Isn't this your business?" Chelsea asked, pressing the question. "He seemed really mad."

The woman laughed sharply. "He's always mad. And yes, it's my business. That is, it was until I had to take out a second mortgage on it from the bank. Ezra Peyton is the president of the Hays County Bank, and after I fell behind on a few payments, well. . . ." She turned to Chelsea, her expression grim.

"He took it from me. He says that if I do what he says, he'll give me a chance to buy it back from him, but if I don't, he'll just turn me back into one of the girls." She smoothed one hand over her tousled hair, a lost expression in her eyes. "I'm too old for that anymore. In fact, I think sometimes maybe I'll leave San Marcos and try to start over before it's too late."

"Oh, Lola, you aren't old," Chelsea said sincerely. "What are you—thirty-five? Forty?"

Lola's brows darted upward and she looked stricken. "I'm twenty-five."

Chelsea winced. "I mean, gosh, well," she stuttered, groping for words, "you've—you've just had a hard time, that's all—just like the rest of the girls here."

"The girls." Lola looked out the window over the sink, her gaze on something far away. "I regret ever buying this place. I regret leading these poor girls into this life. I was young, I thought I was doing them a favor. Easy work, easy money." She laughed, but the sound was laced with bitterness. "I know someday I'll have to stand before my Maker and answer for it."

"Oh, Lola." Chelsea reached over and patted the woman's plump arm. "How did you get into this, er, business? If you don't mind my asking?"

Lola moved back to the frying bacon, removing the rest before it burned. She didn't say anything for so long Chelsea thought she had offended her.

"I'm sorry," she began. "I shouldn't have asked."

"I was sixteen," Lola said, still facing the stove. "I thought he loved me. He was a lot older, almost forty. He told me my mama would never consent to our marriage, so I ran away with him." She looked up, her eyes filled with remembrance and pain. "When we got to San Antone I found out he was already married. He never intended to do right by me, he just wanted me like the randy bull he was."

Chelsea's heart burned with fury. The bastard! Had he hurt Lola? How awful, how desperately awful.

"He took me to a sleazy room and had his way with me," Lola went on, her voice dead. "I screamed, but in that place no one cared." She sighed and turned back, finally lifting her gaze to meet Chelsea's. "So I came here and I became what I am." She shrugged. "End of story."

"That bastard," Chelsea said. "I hope he rots in hell."

"Oh, he's rotting in hell already." Lola's tender eyes turned hard. "I sent him there that night while he was sleeping. Of course, I truly believe that's one sin that the good Lord will forgive."

Chelsea blinked, stunned by Lola's confession, but still outraged by what had happened to the woman. It shocked her, the way she felt. She'd been an avid opponent of the death penalty for years, but she didn't blame Lola for what she had done.

"I don't blame you," she said aloud, patting Lola's arm gently. "But you know, you're wrong, Lola."

"About what?"

"This doesn't have to be the end of your story," she said, her mind racing as she realized the strange similarities between her life and Lola's. She'd become a lonely scientist and thought that she no longer had any choices left to make, that she was destined to be alone with her work. Until Griffin. No—until she had decided she wanted her life to be different. Griffin had only been the catalyst that set the change into action. And what a sexy catalyst. She turned back to Lola.

"Just because that's the way it's always been doesn't mean that's the way it has to be. Believe me, I know," she told her. "I never thought in a million years I'd be here and be married to a man like Griffin."

Lola glanced up and smiled, a real smile that lit her face and took ten years off her age. "You know, I used to think about opening a restaurant, a real honest-to-goodness restaurant. I love to cook, just don't have time."

"Why don't you?" Chelsea said enthusiastically. "That's a great idea. The girls could be the servers and—"

"Peyton would never let me. He'd say there's not nearly as much money in a restaurant as a saloon. I don't have the money on my own, and he sure wouldn't let me borrow any more. Besides, the people in this town would never patronize the restaurant of a former whore."

"You might be surprised," Chelsea said thoughtfully. "This isn't right. Peyton is an awful man. He's the reason Griffin's in jail. I think the sheriff would have just let him return that stupid horse to Dead Eye, but Peyton insisted on Griffin's arrest. He says he'll hang for it." Lola didn't respond, and Chelsea's throat tightened with premonition. "That's not true, is it?"

Lola sighed and picked up a cream-colored mixing bowl with a wide blue stripe around the middle. She poured cornmeal into it and broke an egg and began to stir it with a wooden spoon. Her face looked suddenly old without her makeup and in the pale light of morning.

"Oh, honey, I just don't know. Stealing a horse is a hanging offense in this part of the country, but it depends on the judge."

"I can't count on that," Chelsea said, moving to the window and looking out.

She could see the stone jail from where she stood. It was a large, two-story affair, almost castlelike in design. Definitely forbidding. She already missed Griffin so much. All morning long she'd stopped while washing dishes or sweeping the floor as suddenly the memory of his hands on her skin, his mouth on hers, broke into her thoughts. There was no way on earth she would let Griffin stay in that awful jail another night. She had to break him out, but how? One thing for certain, she couldn't do it alone.

Chelsea glanced at Lola and decided to take a chance.

"Lola," she said, "I need your help."

"What do ye mean, ye're going to die and so am I?" Griffin said, leaning against the bars and keeping his voice low. "I never felt better in my life."

Duncan gave him a half smile. "I hate to burst yer bubble, laddie, but yer health may be a wee bit in jeopardy. The penalty for horse thievin' in these parts is hangin', but that's not what I'm talkin' about."

"Then what?"

He sighed. "It's the time traveling. It does something to yer body, I dinna know what—ye're the man of science, not me," he added with a rueful laugh, shaking his head. "I only know it's killin' me, and 'twill kill ye too if ye keep travelin' back and forth."

Griffin looked at him, suddenly realizing the impact of what his cousin was saying. It had never occurred to him that time travel could be physically dangerous.

"I dinna intend to keep travelin'," he said, his brogue deepening.

"Nor did I, but alas, my wanderlust entreated me and I followed."

"Ye aren't really dyin', are ye?" Griffin asked, half afraid to hear the answer.

"Aye, I fear I am," Duncan said. He brushed a lock of dark golden hair from his face. "Each time I traveled I grew more fatigued, more weary, and now . . ." He pulled back his sleeve, exposing his arm. Griffin drew back in horror. His cousin's flesh looked shriveled, atrophied, almost as though his body was decaying before their eyes.

"My God, Duncan," Griffin said, his heart constricting. "Why did ye no' stop if it was doin' this to ye?"

"The fatigue had been coming on for some time, but I dismissed it as minor." He indicated his arm. "This dinna come about until I came here. It was then I began to feel the worst of it, and realized what was happening to me."

"But ye dinna know for certain that it will kill ye," Griffin insisted.

"Aye, nothing is for certain in this life, but every day I feel more of my life ebbing away." He nodded, almost to himself. "I am weary, cousin, but I feel I have one more trip left in me. I want to go home, not die here for a murder I dinna commit."

Griffin wanted to help him, wanted to assure him that he would make it home again, that he would take him to Scotland, but he would not make promises he couldn't keep. Not to Duncan Campbell.

The silence stretched between them for a long moment until Duncan seemed to rouse himself and turn to Griffin again. "And what about yerself? If ye get out of this, will ye return to Scotland, to our time?"

The question struck Griffin with the force of one of the automobiles so popular in Chelsea's century. Chelsea. He'd married her. He loved her. He just hadn't thought it through to the point of realizing that by doing so, he'd effectively condemned himself to never returning to his own time. He could never ask her to live in the past, in a primitive time, when her own time held such vast wonders.

"No," he said. "I may go back to Scotland, but I canna return to our time. Last night I married the woman I love and I must get her back to her own century and find our destiny there, together."

"Married?" Duncan grinned and reached through the bars to shake Griffin's shoulder in congratulations. "Is she a bonny lass? Did she make a man of ye finally?"

"Aye." Griffin ducked his head, a little embarrassed. "But more than that, she's sweet and smart and gentle, and I'm the most fortunate man in the world."

"I'm happy for ye, cousin."

Griffin heard the sadness in Duncan's voice and looked up. His cousin's eyes were shadowed, filled with pain.

"What is it?" he asked. "Ye have such darkness in yer soul, Duncan. 'Twas never so before."

"Ah, laddie," the Scot said softly, clapping him on the shoulder again, "I have lived a dozen lifetimes, it seems, and I have seen far too much. Too much sorrow. All I want is to return to Scotland, to my own time, and die in peace."

"Dinna talk that way." Griffin gripped the hand at his shoulder, and Duncan met his eyes. "There is still more ahead for ye, cousin."

"And what makes ye think so?"

"Until ye meet the girl of yer dreams, there is still life to be lived," Griffin said, speaking passionately. Duncan had so much to give. His time could not be up.

Duncan laughed and shook his head. "I had forgotten what a romantic ye are, Griffin. I dinna believe there will be a 'dream girl,' as ye put it, for me. I just want to go home."

"Aye. Well, then, first things first. We need to get out of here. Tell me about these charges against ye."

Duncan shrugged. "Och, they say I killed a man."

"And did ye?"

"Nay, though the man deserved the killin'. 'Twas done by that scum, Peyton. Do ye know the man?"

Griffin frowned. "Aye. Then why are ye sittin' here instead of him?"

Duncan stood and stretched, darting a glance toward

the sheriff, who sat contentedly snoring, his legs crossed at his ankles, propped comfortably on the desktop.

"Because Peyton owns this town, and the law," he said, glaring at Adams across the room. He lowered his voice and turned, leaning his back against the bars. "And the man had it in for me because I wouldna tell him where the crystals were."

"The crystals?" Griffin stood as well, gripping one of the bars between them, his knuckles white. "How did he find out about the crystals?"

"I was in my cups a few weeks ago, trying to convince one of Lola's girls to go upstairs with me and let me pay her later. She'd have none of it. So like a fool I told her that if she'd stay with me the night I'd bring her a beautiful emerald crystal the next morning. Peyton overheard me."

Duncan paced to his bunk and back to the bars, raking one hand through his hair as he whispered the rest of the story.

"The girl turned me down, but that night on my way to the boardinghouse, Peyton stopped me and beat the hell out of me, tryin' to get me to tell him where the crystals were. Seems he is convinced that they are emeralds, and worth a fortune. A woman was robbed of an emerald necklace a month or so ago, and he thinks I did the thievery."

"Can ye imagine if one such as he used the power of the crystals?" Griffin said softly.

"Aye, my thoughts exactly, which is why I was willin' to take a beatin' rather than tell him. Although I must say I gave as good as I got," Duncan said. "But the man is still fair obsessed with the thought of finding such a treasure. He murdered Willard Jenkins—a common criminal, no great loss—and blamed it on me. He told me he'd clear my name if I'd tell him where the crystals are. Otherwise, when the circuit judge comes by, I'll likely swing."

"Damn," Griffin said. "We've got to get out of here."

Duncan nodded. "Aye. The question is, how?"

The rest of the day passed with the languid slowness of a snail. Someone from the saloon came by at noon and brought the men strange but delectable food.

"Chinese," Duncan told him, his mouth full. "The cook at the saloon is damned good."

The deputy came and relieved the sheriff a little later, staying the afternoon; then the sheriff returned at six to stay with the prisoners until ten o'clock. Griffin and Duncan passed the time playing poker and discussing in low tones the best ways to break out of jail, but eventually they ceased talking.

By around nine o'clock, according to the big clock on the wall, Griffin felt distinctly uneasy. Chelsea had not come to see him since he'd been arrested. Something was wrong. It had to be; otherwise his wife would've been there, pleading with the sheriff to let him go, arguing why he shouldn't be hanged.

A smile curved his lips. In the few short hours they'd been apart he'd missed her so much, and he knew she must be missing him just as much. He couldn't wait for her to meet Duncan. His smile faded. Where was she?

"Sheriff," he called as Adams put a fresh pot of coffee on the wood stove in a corner. "I need to talk to you."

Adams adjusted his trousers and crossed the room, looking his usual disgruntled self. "What is it?"

"My wife hasn't been here to see me today and I'm worried about her. Have you seen her?"

The sheriff ran one hand over his grizzled face. "You don't say? No, I ain't seen her. That's kind of strange isn't it? Maybe she took off." He smiled a big toothy grin. "Maybe she decided she don't want a jailbird for a husband."

Griffin shook his head. "Dinna be ridiculous. That Peyton—he hasn't been botherin' her, has he?" The thought of the evil man putting his hands on Chelsea sent a wave of terror through Griffin that he could scarcely control. Why hadn't he thought of this sooner? What if Peyton had hurt Chelsea? Griffin knew she'd gotten safely to the saloon because he'd wheedled the information out of the deputy, but what if Peyton had returned later that night? He'd wanted Chelsea. Griffin had seen it in his beady eyes.

Fingers of panic tightened around his throat, and Griffin stood and crossed to the bars. "I need to know where she is, Sheriff," he said, his voice growing louder. "I need to know she's all right!"

"Lad, calm yerself." Duncan moved to stand beside him on the other side of the bars. "Yer lass is fine, else Peyton would've been in here braggin' about it, believe me."

Griffin clutched the bars and leaned his head against them. "Duncan, if anything happened to her . . ."

"It won't," his cousin said grimly as the sheriff stood staring at the two of them. Duncan smiled at Adams, and Griffin noted there was no liking lost between the two men, though he himself thought the sheriff was not such a bad one. "Sheriff, dinna pay him any mind. His bride is probably still recoverin' from her traumatic experience, ye ken?" He glanced over at Griffin and winked the eye away from the sheriff. "Dinna ye think so, laddie?"

Griffin frowned but took the bait. "Oh, aye, aye, I hadna thought of that. No doubt the poor girl was restin' today."

He almost laughed aloud. The poor girl was more likely plotting some way to break him out of . . . His eyes widened, and he shot Duncan a questioning look. Did his cousin know something he didn't know? He pulled his chair next to the bars again.

"Are ye up for some more poker, cousin?" he asked loudly.

"Aye, don't mind if I do." Duncan pulled his chair close and dropped into it, glancing casually back over his shoulder as he did. The sheriff had shaken his head and returned to his coffee-making, his back to them.

"All right, what's goin' on?" Griffin demanded in a hushed voice as Duncan slapped down cards on the small table between them on his side of the bars.

"Did ye no' see the huge black man that came by today at lunch with the food?"

"Aye."

"He's the bouncer at the saloon."

Griffin frowned. "Aye, what of it?"

"Did ye no' see the way he was lookin' at the inside of this place while the sheriff was taking the best of the food for himself? Measurin' the windows with his eyes, he was, givin' ye a grand few minutes' stare, too. Mark my words, somethin' is afoot."

"Chelsea," Griffin said, nodding. "She's what's afoot. That's why she hasn't been here all the day long. She's up to something."

"I dinna know, but I think we'd best be ready for anythin'."

Griffin picked up his cards. He'd enjoyed learning how to play poker while incarcerated in the jail, but he'd yet to win a hand. "All right then, laddie," he said, "what's yer bet?"

"What about if I win, we get out of here and go back to our own time?" Duncan was gazing at him, his blue eyes filled with amusement.

"And if I win?" Griffin asked.

Duncan smiled outright. "Then we get out of here and I go back to our time, alone, and ye can stay wherever ye want with yer lady love."

"It's a bet."

Duncan started rearranging the cards in his hand; then he paused, lifting his gaze to Griffin's. "Ye know I'm proud of ye, lad."

Griffin blinked. "For what?"

"For the man ye've grown to be. I always knew ye had it in ye, but I was afraid yer father would ruin ye. I'm happy to see he did not." Duncan extended his hand through the bars. "Whatever happens, cousin, I am proud to call ye my kin."

Griffin shook his hand, a brief, swift ache beginning in his heart. Whatever happened, he and his cousin would be parting ways once again.

"Thank ye, cousin," he said softly. "I am equally proud to call ye not just my cousin, but my brother, for ye are the one I never had."

"All right, you two," the sheriff called from across the room. "I don't like all this chumminess and whispering going on. What are y'all up to?"

"Nothing, Sheriff," Duncan assured him. "How can ye say that? It's a nice, quiet night." He indicated the open front door of the jail. Outside, the city streets were peaceful and quiet.

Griffin glanced down and saw he had four aces. Either Duncan had slipped him the winning hand or it was a sign. He chose to believe the latter. His luck was changing.

"A quiet night. Hell, yes, that's what bothers me," Adams uncrossed his feet and brought them down to the floor with a bang. He moved to the door and leaned against the jamb, lighting a cigarette as he cast a cautious eye down the street.

"As someone around here would probably say," Griffin cockily announced as he lay down his cards, "read 'em and weep."

Duncan grinned and slapped his own hand down. A row of hearts flashed up at Griffin, and his heart sank. "Straight flush," his cousin said. "You lose."

Griffin frowned as he scooped the cards together. "Dinna think ye will hold me to that bet," he said. "I think that—" He stopped as the hairs on the back of his neck prickled.

He spun around. No one was there, but for an instant he could've sworn he'd heard Chelsea's voice.

Chapter Nineteen

Chelsea checked the small pocket watch Lola had lent her and crouched beneath a pair of brambly bushes near the jailhouse. Nine o'clock. It wouldn't be long now. As soon as it was completely dark, her plan would be set into action.

Thank goodness I was able to talk Lola into letting me wear a pair of trousers, she thought as she knelt on the hard ground. *I wouldn't have had any knees left otherwise.*

Everything was in place. Lola had been more than willing to help Chelsea, but she knew the woman was taking a big risk in doing so. If the plan didn't work, she and her girls would suffer, Peyton would see to it. A wagon rumbled by, drawn by two mules, and Chelsea waited until the noise stopped, then peeked up over the shrubbery.

Lola and the bouncer, Blake, were climbing out of the wagon and heading toward her. Alarm rang through her body. They weren't supposed to come to her, she was supposed to go to the wagon after they left.

She hadn't had time to even go and visit Griffin in jail that day, but Lola had sent Blake with a tray of food. The big man had surveyed the room and come back with a more than adequate description of the inside of the jail, and exactly which cell was Griffin's. There had been no way to get a message to Griffin, but she knew her husband had lightning-fast instincts. She had no doubt he would fall in with her plan easily enough.

"We've got it, honey," Lola whispered, and Chelsea turned toward them. Blake stood behind the saloon madame, his huge form a dark shadow of protection. His presence made Chelsea feel less anxious, even though the continual silence of the man made her uneasy.

"Lola, what are you doing here?" Chelsea hissed. "This is too dangerous for you. You were just supposed to leave the stuff in the wagon so you can claim it was stolen later!"

"Aw, come on, honey, I haven't had this much fun since I was a girl. Besides, Blake said he doesn't trust you to set the dynamite without blowing yourself up."

Chelsea glanced up at Blake. He stared back at her solemnly, and she decided to keep her protest to herself. Besides, Lola looked pretty determined to be part of this. Maybe she needed to do it. Maybe it was her way of getting a little revenge on Peyton.

"All right," Chelsea said, "but I hope you don't regret it."

The three slipped through the trees and bushes until they reached the wall of the jail. Chelsea was surprised at how quietly Blake could move. In spite of his size, he was as agile as a much smaller man.

"I'm going to see if I can get Griffin's attention and warn him to get away from this wall," she said. "I don't want to blow him up while we're trying to get him out."

Lola looked up. There were two windows in the wall, both about twelve by twelve inches, both about fifteen feet off the ground.

"How are you going to do that?" she asked softly. "If you throw a rock, the sheriff is liable to hear."

Chelsea gauged the distance. Lola was right. She needed to somehow be able to look into the window and see where the sheriff was in relation to Griffin. She looked around for something to stand on. There was nothing, and no trees grew close enough to the jail to climb.

"I've got to find something to stand on," she began, then gasped as strong hands encircled her waist and lifted her into the air. Chelsea bit back a squeal and grabbed the back of Blake's neck for balance. The big man seated her on his shoulder, and she wavered unsteadily for a moment, righted herself, and gulped.

"Thanks," she whispered. The big man grunted. She was now only a few inches below the window. Glancing down at her human ladder, she gave him a question with her eyes. He nodded, and cautiously Chelsea swung one leg around Blake's neck and positioned her foot on his shoulder. He grasped her hands, and she managed to get her other foot under her and stand trembling on his shoulders. Blake moved closer to the wall and released her hands. Chelsea leaned against the stones, breathing heavily.

"Okay," she whispered, "now bring me to the window."

They inched their way down the wall until she was looking into the jail cell, looking down at Griffin. Her heart contracted as she watched her love, her husband, talking quietly to someone in the cell beside him. Leave it to Griffin to already be making friends with the other inmates!

"I can't see the sheriff," Chelsea said. "I'll have to take a chance." She drew in a deep breath. "Griffin!" she hissed. "Griffin!"

Griffin frowned and turned in his chair, glancing around the jail cell. He waited a second, shrugged, and swung back to his conversation.

Blake shifted under her feet, and she almost fell. "Hey!" she called in a loud whisper. "Keep it still down there."

"Blake is getting a cramp in his leg," Lola said. "Hurry!"

"Griffin!" she said, a little louder. Griffin didn't turn at all this time. Grimly she made up her mind. "Toss me a small stone," she told Lola. "A tiny one."

Lola bent to the ground and tossed her a handful of pebbles.

"Perfect." Chelsea took aim and fired. The first pebble didn't come anywhere close to him, but the second landed at his feet. Griffin looked down and frowned. He gave a slow look around the jail cell again, his expression wary.

"Griffin, you idiot, look up here!" Chelsea hissed and threw another pebble, this one a little harder. She winced as it hit him right in the eye.

"Ow!" Griffin cried.

Chelsea could hear the sheriff's chair scrape back from across the room, and she ducked down beneath the window. Blake groaned, and she started praying.

"What's the matter?" she heard the sheriff ask.

"Och, nothing," Griffin's voice drifted up to her, deep and comforting. " 'Twas just a wee spasm in my back. I have them sometimes."

"You don't say. I have some back miseries myself," the sheriff said, then launched into a dissertation about how bad his back had been ever since he'd been thrown by a bronc five years before. Blake began to tremble beneath Chelsea's feet. Lola dropped to her knees and began massaging the big man's calf muscles.

Adams probably would've gone on all night, but Chelsea gave a sigh of relief as she heard the door to the jail open and someone start talking to the sheriff, drawing him away from the cell.

"Griffin!" she called again, knowing that time was running out.

In a matter of seconds the Scot had crossed the short space and jumped onto his bunk, which brought him to eye level with the bottom of the window.

"Chelsea?" he whispered, his blue eyes searching the darkness.

Chelsea moved her face back into the square of light. "Griffin," she said, warmth spreading through her as she gazed down at him. Griffin reached up between the bars, and she shook her head. "No time, love, we're here to break you out. Get away from the bars and if you can, get under a chair or something."

Griffin's eyes widened in alarm. "What? Chelsea what are you—"

"No time! Just do what I say!"

Blake's legs picked that moment to give out. He stumbled backward from the wall, grasping Chelsea's ankles. She clapped one hand over her mouth to keep from screaming, then felt the world fall out from under her. Blake caught her before she hit the ground, and when he carefully set her on her feet, she almost started laughing. She felt exhilarated and wonderfully alive!

"Blake, do you have the dynamite?" she whispered, curtailing her excitement to focus on the matter at hand. He grunted and held up four red sticks with long fuses hanging out of them. Quickly the two of them tucked the dynamite in at the base of the wall, between cracks in the stone. Lola packed dirt around them, leaving the wicks trailing above the ground. Blake tied the four fuses together and fastened them to a much longer one.

"Do you think we have enough explosives?" Chelsea asked, glancing at Lola.

Lola shrugged. "Hell, honey, who knows? Blake?" The big man shrugged. "Guess we'll just have to hope."

"All right, then, we're set." Chelsea pushed away the sense of encroaching panic and motioned for the two to follow her. They hurried silently into the bushes, putting a good distance between them and the jail. She glanced at the pocket watch again. "Is Joey ready?"

"He sure is. Don't you worry, honey," Lola said. "You just be ready to whisk your man into the wagon and hightail it out of here."

The warmth in Lola's voice made Chelsea pause in her frantic planning. She turned to the woman and laid one hand on her arm. "But what about you? What are you going to do?"

"Well." Lola's eyes softened. "I was thinking maybe we'd just tag along with the two of you."

Chelsea felt momentarily stricken. "Oh, Lola, I hate for you to leave and let Peyton win."

Lola shook her head. "Sometimes the best thing a person can do is cut their losses and run." She smoothed a lock of platinum hair back from her face. "I've been thinking about what you said, about it not being too late for me. I want to go somewhere else and open up a restaurant, somehow. I told the girls I was closing the saloon after tonight, and I encouraged them to leave this town. I took every cent from the till, so, honey, my bridges are burned and I'm not looking back!"

Chelsea hugged the woman, feeling overjoyed. Lola hesitated, then returned the hug enthusiastically.

"All right, then, enough of this," Lola said. "We've got a jailbreak to take care of. Are you ready?"

"I'm ready," Chelsea agreed. "Blake told you that the deputy is due to relieve the sheriff at ten o'clock, right?" Lola nodded. "As soon as Adams leaves, that's when we start."

The minutes seemed to crawl by as they crouched beneath the bushes hiding from casual view. Chelsea was so tense she didn't think she could last another moment, when all at once she saw the deputy walking down the street past their hiding place. She poked Lola with her elbow and pointed. Soon they could hear Ben and Adams exchanging pleasantries outside the jail, their voices floating over to them on the sultry summer night's breeze. Then they saw the sheriff walking slowly along the wooden sidewalk in front of the jail. He paused to light a cigarette, and walked on.

"So far, so good," she whispered to Lola. "Now, where's Joey?"

"Over there with Chin."

"Chin?" Chelsea peered out into the darkness. "What's Chin doing here? I thought Joey was going to start a fight in the street."

Lola and Blake exchanged glances. "We came up with something better," she said, just before the sky exploded into a million pieces of light.

Chelsea sat back on her heels and almost laughed out loud as skyrockets burst above them, firecrackers made a pseudo machine-gun rat-tat-tat sound, fountains spewed six feet high, and Chin jumped up and down feigning a complete screaming meltdown as he raged against Joey who stood swaying, pretending to be drunk in the middle of the street. The deputy stormed out the front door of the jail, and in a second, the sheriff ran down the street and joined him.

"What the hell is going on?" Adams cried.

"Now light the charges," Lola commanded. Blake scraped a large match on a rock and lit the end of the long fuse leading to the dynamite beside the wall. Chelsea said a quick prayer that Griffin had listened to her and taken cover.

"Hunker down," Blake said, throwing himself flat. Chelsea was so surprised to hear the man speak that she hesitated. He pulled her to the ground beside him, while Lola flattened herself on the other side of the big man.

While the sheriff and deputy argued with an irate Chin and drunkenly argumentative Joey, Chelsea watched the burning tip of the fuse in the darkness grow shorter and shorter until it met with the hidden explosives. She covered her head with both arms and—

Nothing happened. She waited. Nothing.

"What's going on?" she said, pushing up to her knees and squinting toward the wall.

"Maybe the fuse went out," Lola suggested, her voice anxious. "If it doesn't blow soon, we'll have to forget it. Chin and Joey can't keep this up much longer—they'll run out of fireworks."

As if to punctuate her words, smoke suddenly filled the street. "Smoke bomb," Chelsea said, rising. "This might be our only chance to relight the fuse."

Blake and Lola shouted for her to stop, but she ignored them, darting through the acrid smoke toward the jail. A few yards from the stone wall she tripped and fell to her knees. She peered through the murky air as more fireworks exploded in the sky above. The jail was just ahead. She could make it. She stumbled to her feet and took one step forward when the world exploded and knocked her flat on her back.

Chelsea lay stunned as tiny chunks of rock showered down. Her lungs would not expand, and she fought for breath as the stench of gunpowder washed over her. Gasping, she finally managed to drag in fresh oxygen and shakily rolled to one side, hands flat against the ground.

"Griffin," she whispered, and started to rise. Something metallic and cold pressed against her temple and stopped her. Heart pounding, she looked up into the dark-eyed gaze of Ezra Peyton.

"What the bloody hell!" someone shouted from the center of the smoking debris. Griffin and another man stumbled toward them over the broken rocks, their faces blackened, their hair standing out from their heads, their clothes in tatters as they bent almost double coughing.

In the street in front of the jail, Chin, Joey, the deputy, and the sheriff had been knocked down by the blast. The deputy lay rolling from side to side, but the sheriff wasn't moving. Chelsea fervently hoped they hadn't killed him.

"How much dynamite did ye idiots use?" the man with Griffin shouted, holding one side of his head with the flat of his hand. "Ye almost blew us to Kingdom Come."

"No," Peyton said, "that will be my pleasure." He reached down and jerked Chelsea to her feet, keeping the barrel of the gun against her head. "That's far enough, boys."

Griffin and the man with him stopped, looking dazed as two men with shotguns came at them from either side. One of them, Chelsea saw with a sinking heart, was Dead Eye.

The prisoners slowly raised their hands above their heads. The gunmen near them pulled Griffin's and his companion's arms down and tied them behind their backs, then prodded them toward Peyton.

Chelsea searched her husband's face for reassurance, and he gave her a slow wink. Dead Eye shoved the two prisoners to their knees in front of Peyton, and Chelsea stared down at the man with Griffin. He glared up at his captor, and she almost took a step back. It was Duncan Campbell, or at least the man was the spitting image of the person in the photo in the Texas history book. Griffin had sworn his cousin had gone back in time, and apparently he had been right. This was the man she and Griffin had traveled back in time to save.

Well, they were doing one hell of a job.

"Kin I blast him now, Mr. Peyton?" Dead Eye whined. "You said I could if I helped."

"No, I didn't. Remember?"

Dead Eye frowned, looking perplexed, then nodded vigorously. "Oh, yeah, we're gonna hang 'em. I forgot."

"Hang them!" For a minute Chelsea thought her heart

had stopped beating. "You can't hang them! The circuit judge hasn't come to town yet."

"Really?" Peyton raised one dark brow and the corner of his thin lips quirked up cynically. "Well, you see, that is exactly the problem. The judge is taking a little too long to get here, and me and the boys think that it's time justice was served. Right, Dead Eye?"

The heavy-set man licked his lips, and Chelsea felt her stomach turn over. "You bet, Mr. Peyton," he said. "And then I get the girl, right?"

Griffin tried to stand, but Peyton's man pushed him down again. Chelsea gave her husband a quick, cautioning look, and she saw understanding flash in his somber blue eyes.

"If ye're going to hang me, hang me," Griffin said, his voice soft and dark. "But let the lass go. She has nothin' to do with this. Or do ye intend to hide behind a woman?"

"Shut up, you furrin bastard," Dead Eye said. "C'mon, Mr. Peyton, let me blast him."

Peyton laughed loud and long as he lowered the gun from Chelsea's head. His eyes gleamed in the light from the now full, rising moon as he gazed down at Griffin. "Is that what you think? That I'm not man enough to get what I want without threatening your woman? Let me show you what I'm man enough to do."

He stepped forward and whipped the pistol down, striking Griffin on the side of his head. Chelsea cried out as he fell against Duncan. She tried to go to him, but Peyton pulled her back. The touch of his hands, even through her clothing, made her feel ill, and she struggled to get away from him until he pressed the gun to her throat. She grew still, her hands tightening into fists at her sides.

Griffin groaned and righted himself. "Ye think that proves ye're a man?" he said hoarsely. "Untie me and I'll show ye what a man can do."

"Damn, I wanted to do that," Dead Eye complained.

"Get 'em on their feet."

Dead Eye and another minion hauled the two men up. Griffin swayed. Blood trickled down the side of his face, and Chelsea's throat tightened in fear. The adventure was over as far as she was concerned.

"Thanks for the tip, Lola," Peyton said as the woman moved to stand beside him.

"Sure thing, honey."

Chelsea's mouth fell open. "Lola," she whispered. "I can't believe it. But why?"

Something flickered in the other woman's gaze, but she shrugged one shoulder. "You don't think I'd double-cross Mr. Peyton, do you?" She laughed shortly. "I like living a little too well for that."

"Where's Blake?" Chelsea said, looking around for the big man. Lola's eyes widened, and almost imperceptibly she shook her head. Chelsea picked up on the small hint, and hoped she wasn't stupid to keep on trusting the woman. "Did he help you do this?"

Lola laughed. "I didn't need Blake on this one," she said. "All I had to do was hand you the dynamite and tell you where to set it."

"But why let us break out if you're planning to hang us?" Griffin asked.

"If you're killed trying to escape from jail, no one will think a thing about it," Peyton answered, tilting his bowler hat back with the butt of his gun.

"That isn't even logical." Chelsea slapped one hand over her mouth, aghast that she'd voiced her thought aloud.

"What isn't?" Peyton demanded, bringing the gun back to her again. "Go ahead, sweet cheeks, tell me about it."

"I—I—just meant that if you hang them, it will look like you broke them out so you could kill them. But if you shoot them, it will look like they were trying to escape and you stopped them." She stuttered to a stop as Duncan Campbell looked up at her from the ground, his brows furrowed.

"Lass," he said, his voice fervent, "will ye shut the hell up? Dinna we have enough trouble without ye givin' them ideas?"

Peyton's hand tightened on her waist as he laughed again. "A woman who actually makes sense. Never thought I'd see the day. But maybe we'll just string 'em up somewhere away from town. Then nobody will know who did it, and nobody will care because they broke out of jail. Besides, I like the thought of watching them twist in the wind."

Chelsea's heart went cold.

"Load 'em up," Peyton said, and gestured with his gun toward the wagon. "We're going to take a little trip and have a little talk, but not here," he said to Chelsea.

Dead Eye and his cohorts shoved Griffin and Duncan into the back of the wagon while Peyton half pulled, half dragged Chelsea around to the seat. He boosted her up and helped Lola scramble up beside her. Giving both women a leering grin, he circled around to the other side and climbed up to take the reins.

Chelsea glanced at Lola, hoping for some sign that the woman hadn't really betrayed them, that Blake was somewhere in hiding, planning to help them. The madame brushed a spot of dirt from her sleeve and ignored her, gazing instead at the moon above.

"Where are we going?" Chelsea asked. She looked back over her shoulder as the wooden wagon bounced down the rocky road. She could just make out Griffins' blond head over the edge of the wooden wagon, and the sight gave her some comfort.

"Somewhere a little more private." Peyton looked down at her, and she felt a surge of panic. Every time Chelsea had seen the man, his eyes seemed to gleam with evil, but now she saw something more in the obsidian depths.

Desire.

Chapter Twenty

"Get out."

Griffin climbed down out of the wagon at Dead Eye's command, quickly sizing up their new surroundings. The moon was high, sending illumination over the land that was almost as bright as daylight. It was both a help and a hindrance.

They had driven away from the streets of San Marcos and into the countryside, riding for about fifteen minutes before pulling up in front of a clump of oak trees. Peyton jumped down and swung a protesting Chelsea out of her seat.

Griffin and Duncan climbed awkwardly out of the back of the wagon, and several of Peyton's men grabbed them and shoved them against the trunks of two trees.

"Take the rig back to the saloon," Peyton ordered Lola, handing her the reins. "If that fool the sheriff comes by, you tell him you've been upstairs all evening with me and that I'm passed out drunk, you hear?" She nodded. He reached up and pulled her halfway off the wagon seat, pressing a rough kiss on her mouth while his other hand crudely squeezed her breast.

Griffin saw a look of fear appear on Lola's face, heard her soft whimper as the man continued to ravage her lips and body for a full minute before pushing her away. She sat for a moment on the seat, trying to repair the damage to her hair, readjusting her clothing. A glint of tears shimmered on her cheek.

Fury burned in Griffin's heart at the thought of the abuse the woman had probably suffered from the man. He'd picked up on the fact that Lola had helped Chelsea make the jailbreak, and also that she'd apparently betrayed them. After seeing the way Peyton treated her, he could understand why. She was terrified. Lola shook the reins, and the wagon rumbled away.

"String 'em up," Peyton said.

"No!" Chelsea cried.

Griffin and Duncan were led forward, and nooses, already tied, were slipped over their heads. Duncan tried to struggle, but his efforts were rewarded by a blow to the back of the head that sent him to his knees. Griffin cooperated. He wanted his wits about him. Duncan was pulled to his feet, and he stood unsteadily.

"You can't do this!" Chelsea said, tears streaming down her face. "You can't do this!"

Griffin longed to take her in his arms, to calm her, to protect her. He had to make sure that, no matter what, she was all right. "Lass, dinna fash yerself," he said, his gaze burning into hers even in the moonlight. " 'Twill be all right."

"Hell, yes, everything will be all right as soon as we stretch these here boys' necks a little." Dead Eye laughed as he led a horse over to the trees. With the aid of another man, he lifted the bound Griffin into the saddle. Then he brought another horse and lifted Duncan into the saddle as well. The men sat there, their hands still tied behind their backs, the nooses looped around their necks.

Chelsea gazed up at Griffin, her love for him shining in her eyes, her chest rising and falling rapidly. He remembered all over again the sweetness of her skin, the texture of her hair, the warmth of her mouth and her neck and a thousand other places more delicate and sensitive. To leave her now, to die now, when they were just beginning—it was unthinkable. He wasn't going to die, not in this ignominious place and time, not for a reason so pointless and vain.

"You can't do this," she whispered again.

"But I *can* do it, sweet cheeks," Peyton said, pulling her against him, his hand moving to cover her breast. "I can do whatever I want, because I have the sheriff in my back pocket. I'm the law here."

"Griffin doesn't deserve this," she whispered, not offering the man any resistance as he smoothed his hand over one breast and then the other, over and over again. Griffin thought he would explode from fury and had to close his eyes for a minute to bring the violence inside him back under control.

"I'll decide what he deserves," Peyton said. "But you can help me do that deciding. How about that?"

Griffin opened his eyes, now ready to throw himself at the man, noose or no noose.

"What do you mean?" she asked. Her clothing was that of a man, Griffin noticed, but that didn't seem to be slowing Peyton down one little bit. The bastard had undone two of the buttons on her shirt. Her face was flushed, and Griffin knew it wasn't just fear coloring her cheeks, but an anger that matched his own.

"Leave her alone!" he shouted when he couldn't stand to be silent any longer. "This is between us. Let her go."

Peyton stopped groping Chelsea. He turned and looked up at his prisoner with satisfaction in his eyes, and Griffin knew he'd been baited and caught.

"Oh, I don't think so. This little lady is going to help me decide whether you live or you die. You and your friend there." He pulled Chelsea's hand through his crooked arm and started leading her away.

"Come back here!" Griffin cried as he watched the man take his wife away from the oaks and toward the thick woods beyond. Peyton's only answer was a loud roar of laughter.

Griffin's heart was pounding so loudly he could hear it in his ears, but fear drowned out the sounds and images around him. Chelsea was at the mercy of that bastard. He had to do something. He glanced up at the branch above his head. The rope attached to the noose around his neck trailed up to the thick limb and looped over it and down. The end was in the hands of Dead Eye.

He glanced at Duncan and saw that his cousin was in an identical situation, with another of Peyton's men holding the end of his rope. Griffin caught Duncan's eye and tried to silently communicate his intention by glancing first at the branch above, then at Dead Eye, then at the horse beneath him. Duncan nodded.

Dead Eye chose that moment to saunter to Griffin's side. "So what do you think they're gonna do out there, huh? Maybe have a little tea party?" He guffawed, and the other men joined him. "Maybe she'll give him a little private show like she used to at the Double Dollar." He made several more crude remarks, but his jibes posed no problem for Griffin's control. He was no longer burning up with fury but had grown stone cold, waiting for his chance. It came with his next heartbeat.

Dead Eye turned his head to spit a stream of tobacco, and Griffin's foot lashed out and caught him in the chest. The man went down, losing his grip on the rope he held. Griffin waited until the man who held Duncan at his mercy rushed to help Dead Eye; then the Scot dug his heels into the flanks of the horse beneath him. The gelding reared up on his hind legs, and Dead Eye rolled to flee the flying hooves as Griffin urged the horse forward with his knees. For one brief second the noose tightened, jerking against Griffin's neck; then the rope cleared the branch over which it had been looped and Griffin was free. He rode away from the oak trees with Duncan close behind him, his rope flying loosely behind him, too. Duncan sported a reckless grin as they plunged into the woods in the direction Peyton had taken Chelsea.

Chelsea had never felt such panic in her life. As Peyton pushed her through the brambles and briars, her mind raced. Griffin had a noose around his neck and couldn't help her. She had to help him! Alone with this evil man, she had to accomplish two things: get him to agree to set Griffin and Duncan free, and keep him from satisfying the lust she saw in his gaze. She was terrified. She couldn't do it. She was a coward, not a bold adventurer. It had all been a sham on her part. It was easy to be bold when there was nothing to lose. Now she had everything to lose and she was paralyzed with fear. One thing was certain: The farther they went into the countryside, the harder it would be to find her way back to Griffin if she did manage to get away.

"Isn't this far enough?" she said and stumbled to a stop in a small clearing surrounded by huge post oaks.

"I guess it'll do." Peyton glanced around the area. He swung her around by the arm he held, bringing her against him. "Now, let's just see how anxious you are to save that husband of yours."

"What do you want?" she asked, lifting her chin, willing her lips not to tremble with the words.

Peyton pulled her closer, wrapping his arms around her, crushing her against him. She could feel his erection pressing against her stomach, and she thought she might faint. This man could do anything he wanted to her. He could take what he wanted or demand what he wanted and then do with Griffin and Duncan as he willed. Unless she stopped him.

"Why, sweet cheeks, what do you think I want?" He grabbed her derriere and squeezed, lifting her against his crotch. "I want two things. I want you, and I want you to tell me where those green crystals are and that I heard you talking about in the saloon. That other sidewinder mentioned those jewels too a few weeks ago, but I couldn't get any more information out of him, so I had him thrown in jail on a murder charge. But he's damn stubborn, just like your husband. Women ain't so tough." He drew his tongue down the side of her face, and Chelsea shuddered. Peyton laughed. "And I don't think you really want to see your man's bloated, blue face after I send his horse out from under him and let him dangle from a rope."

"No," Chelsea whispered, the thought making her stomach tighten. "I don't want that."

"Then first tell me where the crystals are and then, you and me, we'll have some fun."

Chelsea trembled, unable to move. She was useless. Griffin was going to die, and she would be raped and killed, or worse, raped and left alive. She closed her eyes. She was a coward, but—a sudden thought pierced her terror—she was a smart coward. What if she simply viewed this situation as if it were a scientific problem? What would she do? She would evaluate the predicament objectively and arrive at a solution. It was simple. It didn't involve any great courage. She didn't have to be Jix or Samantha. She just had to *think*.

Chelsea took several deep breaths and tried to calm her racing pulse as Peyton waited for her answer. She opened her eyes, and his dark, lustful gaze bored into her.

If she told him where the crystals were, he would likely use her, kill her, and kill Griffin and Duncan. If, however, she told him she would lead him to the crystals, but only if Griffin and Duncan were released, he might go for it. Why did he even want the crystals? Did he know of their remarkable capabilities? The thought of turning a man like Peyton loose with the power of time travel was morally reprehensible.

"I—I know where they are," she stammered, stalling for time. "But I don't understand why you want them."

"Why do I want them? Hell, woman, why wouldn't I want a fortune in emeralds? What I'd like to know is how your husband managed to steal them. That Gibbs woman was only here one night when she and the senator were passing through on their way to Houston. She went to bed with them in her room and woke up the next morning with them gone. Hell, she ranted and raved about that theft for hours before they finally left."

"Oh, of course," Chelsea said, quickly changing gears. "Well, you'll have to ask my husband about that—which leads us back to your proposal. I won't tell you where the emeralds are, but I'll take you there—if you release my husband and the other man."

Peyton pulled her against him again and licked the side of her neck with a slow, nasty slide of his tongue. Chelsea shuddered and fought the urge to do something desperate, something that would no doubt make the man hurt her.

Be smart. Another light went on. *If you make him think you're going to have sex with him, he'll let his guard down and you can grab the gun.*

"Why would I do that, sweet cheeks?" Peyton said. "You tell me where the emeralds are, and then I'll let them go."

"Why would I do that?" she taunted him with his own words, pulling back slightly and regarding him with what she hoped were sultry eyes. "First of all, I don't trust you any further than I can throw you, and second, once Griffin's out of the picture—alive but gone, if you know what I mean—then you and me can really have some fun."

Peyton's eyes lit up and the irritation in his gaze vanished. "Oh, yeah?" he said. "You sure changed your tune fast." His hand cupped her breast, and Chelsea's breath caught in her throat. She swallowed hard and slid her arms around the man's neck.

"You didn't expect me to act like I wanted you in front of Griffin, did you?" she asked, trying not to gag as the man continued to touch her. "I don't love him, but I don't want him killed either. He's a sweetie, but I'm a woman with, shall we say, voracious appetites? That's why he wanted me to quit working at the Double Dollar. That's why he insisted we get married." She shrugged and ran her fingers up into Peyton's greasy hair. "So we did, but that doesn't change anything as far as I'm concerned. I still want to have a good time," she said softly. His mouth twitched as her breath touched him. The excitement in his eyes was evident, and Chelsea felt a moment of panic. Maybe she'd gone too far.

"Hell, sweet cheeks, we don't have to wait for that," he said, tossing the gun down and scooping her up in his arms. "We'll have our fun first, and then you'll take me to the emeralds."

Chelsea started to protest, when all at once two horses burst through the thick bushes around the clearing. Griffin and Duncan, riding hell-bent for leather, nooses dangling from their necks like eerie specters, hands still tied behind their backs, headed straight for Peyton.

Peyton let go of Chelsea, and she scrambled for the gun he'd discarded moments before. Peyton found it first and backhanded her out of the way. Griffin threw himself head-first off of his horse and slammed into the man, taking him down hard. Chelsea saw the action through a blur of pain and rolled out of the way, nursing her jaw with one hand.

Duncan managed to bring his horse to a stop and slid to the ground. He ran to Griffin's side, still bound, and began kicking Peyton, his cousin using his weight to hold the man down. But Peyton still had the gun, and in spite of Duncan's kicks, he was twisting around, aiming it right at Griffin.

Chelsea suddenly realized she was sitting there, frozen, like every stupid woman in every stupid television show she'd ever seen. How many times had she sat and screamed at the helpless female who sat immobile while her hero was taking a beating to get up off her fanny and grab something and hit the bad guy over the head with it?

She stumbled to her feet and started looking about wildly for a branch, a rock, anything she could use as a weapon. She picked up a large stone and whirled around—just as a gunshot pierced the midnight air.

"Griffin!" she screamed. Griffin knelt over Peyton, a stunned expression on his face. Duncan stood above him, his eyes wide with disbelief. Griffin gave Chelsea one sharp, stricken look of apology and collapsed on top of the man who had shot him.

"All right, you furrin bastards," Peyton said, pushing the heavy body of Griffin off of him and swinging the gun around toward Duncan. "I'm through fooling around with the two of you."

"Griffin!" Chelsea ran across the clearing and threw herself down on the ground beside him. If he was dead—oh, dear God—if he was dead . . . She pulled the heavy noose from his neck and wrenched the front of his shirt open.

His chest rose and fell. He was alive. The bullet had caught him in the upper right shoulder, and from what she could tell in her hasty exam, in her inexperience, it had gone clean through. But he was bleeding profusely, and she feared he would go into shock. His hands were still tied, and she worked at the ropes binding his wrists, tearing her nails in her haste, fighting the tears that threatened to send her into hysteria.

Once his arms were free, she took off the shirt Lola had lent her and tore two large strips off the bottom. Clad in her chemise and trousers, Chelsea pulled Griffin into her lap, leaning his head against her shoulder, her heart pounding frantically as he moaned in pain. She reached across his chest and pressed the cloth against both the entrance and exit wounds, trying to stanch the flow of blood. At her touch, he opened his eyes.

"Och," he whispered, "I'm no' exactly John Wayne, am I, love?"

"Hush," Chelsea said as tears flooded down her face. "You're John Wayne, Errol Flynn, and Mel Gibson rolled into one."

He smiled; then his lips twisted and he closed his eyes. Chelsea looked up at Peyton, fury and hatred burning inside her.

"You lousy son of a bitch!" she shouted. "I told you I'd take you to the crystals! You didn't have to shoot him!"

Peyton was trembling with his own rage, and the murderous look in his eyes made her shrink back. She cradled Griffin in her arms while Duncan stood a few feet away, silently watching. He'd managed to free his hands, but he made no move to attack the man with the gun.

"So, it was all a trick," Peyton said furiously, keeping the weapon on Duncan and his gaze on Chelsea. "You do love him, and you thought you'd save him by snookerin' me till he could get here."

"I'll take you to the crystals," Cheslea said, "if you'll promise to let us go. We can't hurt you! You said it yourself—you've got the law sewn up. We just want to go home!"

Peyton darted a quick look at Duncan, then back at Chelsea. "Get up," he ordered, "and if you can get your man on his horse I'll take him with us. Otherwise I'll leave him here."

"Mr. Peyton! Mr. Peyton!" The bushes parted, and Dead Eye came riding into the clearing, pulling his horse up just before he collided with his boss. "They got away and we heard shots and—" He looked down at the three prisoners and grinned. "Aw, hell, you found 'em. I was hoping to gun 'em down while they was runnin'."

"Get down, Dead Eye," Peyton said, his voice cheerful. The man dismounted and moved to join his boss. "Why did you let them escape?" Peyton asked, his tone even.

"It was the consarndest thing," Dead Eye said, his belly shaking with his enthusiastic explanation. "There they were, sitting on the horses, tied, when all at once that one"—he pointed at Griffin—"goosed the horse and took off. The other one did the same thing, and since we weren't expecting it, they jerked the ropes clean out of our hands."

"I see." Without warning, Peyton backhanded the man across the face with his free hand. Dead Eye stumbled backward. "Don't let it happen again," the dark-haired man said, "or you'll be sitting up there beside them with your own noose."

Dead Eye wiped a trickle of blood from his mouth, his face turning dark in the moonlight. "Yessir," he snarled, "but it weren't my fault."

"Yes, it was." Peyton dismissed him without a second glance. "Now, leave me your horse and go back and tell the boys their work is over, for tonight at least. Here." He dug into his pocket and pulled out a wad of bills. "Divide it among 'em and then go to the saloon and tell Lola to give you all a drink on the house."

Dead Eye's face lit up at the sight of the cash and he eagerly took it, stuffing it into his pocket. "Sure thing, Mr. Peyton." He handed the reins of his horse to the man and hurried away without a backward glance.

"So ye aren't lettin' yer little band of outlaws in on what ye're really after," Duncan said, his voice slicing smoothly across the darkness.

Peyton shrugged. "Why should I? They got their kicks just thinkin' there might be a hangin'. Now they'll go back and get drunk and spend the money I gave them at my saloon." His oily lips spread in a smile, showing his teeth. "I can't lose."

"I need to get Griffin to a doctor," Chelsea said. Her

voice shook. She had to stay calm. She couldn't give in to the panic flooding through her, even though the cloth she held to Griffin's chest was soaked with his blood. "We've got to get him to a doctor," she pleaded.

"No, you need to get him on that horse," Peyton told her pointedly, "or else we'll leave him here to bleed to death."

All of her weakness disappeared, and she glared up at him. She had to be strong, for Griffin. "If you did, I'd never tell you where the crystals are."

"Yes, you would, sweet cheeks, because you wouldn't want this one to die." He gestured toward Duncan with the gun. "And you wouldn't want to die yourself."

"There are worse things than death," Duncan said softly, and shifted his gaze to her. "Chelsea, if he leaves Griffin behind, dinna tell him where the crystals are. We will join my cousin in death before we help this bastard."

Chelsea lifted her chin and nodded. She would never leave Griffin behind, not even if Peyton threatened to shoot her. "I won't tell him," she assured the Scot. She shot Peyton a challenging look. "If you want to find the emeralds, you'll have to help me bring Griffin along."

Peyton's thin lips pressed together for a long minute. He leaned over and spat onto the ground, never taking his eyes from hers. "I tell you what—you get him on the horse, and you"—he nodded at Duncan—"help her. Then the three of you are going to ride along in front of me. If you try to run away, I'll shoot you two furriners in the back, and torture the woman till she tells me what I want to know." A glimmer of wicked pleasure danced in his eyes. "In fact, that don't sound half bad to me right now. Why should I keep messing with you two?" He cocked the hammer of his gun and pointed it at Duncan. "I can end this right now."

"If you kill them you might as well kill me, too."

Griffin heard Chelsea's voice from far away and frowned, trying to find her in the darkness surrounding him.

"I mean it, Peyton," she was saying. "You can torture me all you want, but I'll never tell you a thing. Why should I, if you take away the only man I'll ever love? What would I have to live for?"

Torture? Someone was going to torture Chelsea? Griffin struggled back to consciousness, and his eyes flew open to find Peyton with his gun pointed at Duncan's belly. Griffin tried to sit up, but a burning pain in his shoulder sent him falling back against Chelsea's softness. He looked up at her and saw the determination in her eyes, the set of her jaw, and felt a rush of pride wash over him along with the memories of the last few hours. His wife was ready to risk death in order to protect him. She was a true Campbell, but he wouldn't allow her to remain in danger.

"I've told ye a dozen times," he whispered, gazing up at Peyton, "let her go and I'll tell you where the crystals are."

"You can tell him," Chelsea said, "but I won't leave. I'll follow you if I have to, but you aren't leaving me out of this, Griffin Campbell. This is one adventure we're going to finish together!"

Griffin patted her hand, feeling the warmth of his love for her flood over him. "All right, lass, then we'll just have to work together, won't we?"

"Get him up," Peyton said. "This is your last chance, heroes. If you try anything else"—he swung the gun around to Chelsea—"she'll be dead."

His face grew suddenly thoughtful, and Griffin caught his breath. Peyton thinking couldn't be a good thing. Sure enough, he started talking again, confirming Griffin's fears.

"Now, you know what?" the thin man said. "Maybe I've been going at this all wrong. Hell, yes." He nodded toward Duncan. "You fellas are going to tell me where the emeralds are, and right now, or I'm going to kill her."

"Ye are the dumbest bastard I've ever met," Duncan said in disgust. "If ye kill her, neither of us will help ye. It's a stalemate, so bugger off and be on yer way."

Peyton's dark eyes narrowed and he reached over and grabbed Chelsea, slamming the barrel of the gun into her ribs. She cried out with the pain. "I said, get him on his horse and show me where the damned emeralds are, got it? Last chance."

"Stop, stop. I'll show ye," Griffin said, his breath coming hard, the pain searing his shoulder. "I canna tell ye, but I'll lead ye there." With a groan he tried to stand, but it took both Duncan and Chelsea to help him to his feet and get him on the horse.

Chelsea insisted on riding with him so she could help hold him in the saddle. Once seated behind him, she repacked his bandage as well as she could with the rest of her torn shirt. He didn't like her state of dishabille in the thin chemise, but their first priority was survival. Peyton's plans for her were obvious, and no amount of promises would convince Griffin that he and Duncan wouldn't be dead before sunrise. He had to beat the man, and he had to beat him fast.

"I'll lead him to the crystals," Griffin said wearily. "Then we'll go home, aye, lass?"

Chelsea tightened her arms around his waist. She leaned her head against his back, and he almost broke down. She was so trusting, so precious. All she'd wanted was a little adventure. It would not end in her death—nor his. He would see to it.

In spite of his aching shoulder, Griffin managed to get the group headed in the right direction. He knew that in a matter of hours fever might set in, and he set a fast pace for the four of them. The sooner they got to Jacob's Well, the sooner they could overpower Peyton and get back home again.

Half the battle was won. He and Duncan were no longer tied and no longer had nooses around their necks. Of course, he could only use one arm and he might bleed to death before they reached the well, but that wasn't in his plan.

"Griffin . . ." He heard Chelsea's soft whisper against his back.

"Yes, love?" he said, hoping the steady clip-clop of the horses' hooves effectively hid their voices in case she wanted to confide a plan.

"I love you," she said, and he could feel the pressure of her lips against his shirt, knew she kissed the place bleeding through in the back.

"Och, lass." He squeezed her hand curled over his taut stomach. "This isna the end. Dinna be saying goodbye."

She kissed him again. "But even if it is, it was worth it, just to be your wife. Just to have made love to you and to be loved by a man like you."

"Shut up that chatter!" Peyton yelled from behind.

Griffin lifted her hand from his waist and kissed her palm. " 'Twill be all right," he whispered. "Do ye know I am verra proud of ye?"

Chelsea didn't speak, but the pressure of her arms around his waist and the softness of her face pressed against his back was answer enough.

They rode for what seemed like hours, but Griffin knew from watching the stars twinkling above that it had only been about forty-five minutes. It was fortunate that he had made some sharp mental notes when he and Joey traveled from the well to San Marcos. In his time he was pretty well known for his tracking abilities, another reason he'd been embarrassed when he and Chelsea had gotten lost on the Riley ranch, but he'd been so enamored with the lass, he just hadn't paid attention at the time.

Griffin's shoulder ached and it was hard to concentrate, but he forced his mind to the task at hand. When he thought he couldn't go another yard, he looked up and realized they were almost there.

"It's just through this glen," he said, bringing his horse to a stop.

"All right, get down and we'll walk." Peyton dismounted and stood a good distance away from the three, his gun leveled and steady. "I want the three of you to walk abreast, so I can keep an eye on you."

"We can do that for a bit," Griffin said, but farther on we'll come to the creek and then we'll be walking single file."

Peyton walked over and took Chelsea by the arm. "Then she'll be walking with me." His dark eyes glittered in the moonlight as he squeezed her against him, and Griffin felt his hatred for the man deepen. "Don't try any funny stuff."

"I assure you," Griffin said, turning to lead the way, "funny stuff is the last thing on my mind."

Huge oak trees sheltered the path leading to the limestone ledges above the creek, and as they neared them, Griffin felt a wave of apprehension. What if the crystals weren't there? Peyton would think he had lied to him. He glanced at Duncan, walking beside him.

"Laddie," he whispered, "if the crystals aren't there . . ."

"Dinna fash yerself," Duncan said. "I ken what to do."

"No talking!" Peyton shouted. "You two walk apart from each other, and if there's any more talking I swear to God I will shoot this sweet little thing's left foot plumb off."

Griffin's jaw tightened. He had to end this, now, before anything happened to Chelsea.

Chapter Twenty-one

The path curved and sloped downward. Griffin thought he could use the unevenness of the terrain to dupe Peyton into taking a false step, but the man was as surefooted as a mountain goat. Besides, he had the gun and he had Chelsea.

Griffin rethought his urge to act hastily. He wasn't about to take a chance until he knew the odds were in his favor. He wouldn't risk Chelsea's life.

"Up here," Griffin called back to them. They had reached the limestone and he and Duncan began to climb with Peyton and Chelsea close behind them. At last they all stood on the outcropping, gazing down at the deep pool known in Chelsea's time as Jacob's Well.

"So where are they?" Peyton demanded, the moonlight carving stark shadows into his long, ruthless face. "Why would you hide them out here?"

"I'm afraid they aren't exactly the jewels ye were expecting," Griffin told him, "but I assure ye they are just as valuable."

"What the hell are you talking about, pretty boy? I know you and him and her stole the emeralds that belonged to the senator's wife. What else could you have been talking about when you mentioned green crystals? Now, where are they?"

Griffin shrugged. "Have it yer way. They're down there." He pointed into the water. Peyton's face fell.

"In there? Down in the water? Hell, why would you hide them down there?"

"Because stupid little twits like ye wouldna think to look there," Duncan said.

Peyton's eyes narrowed. "You'll be sorry for that comment," he said. "All right, get down there and bring them up. And you"—he waved the gun at Duncan—"you sit over there on that rock so I can keep an eye on you."

"Griffin can't go down into the water," Chelsea said, jerking her arm away from their captor. She stood with her hands on her hips and glared. "You shot him, remember? Duncan will have to get them, or me."

"Not ye, lass," Griffin said. She was right about him, of course, but it galled him to admit it. His right arm was useless and he'd lost a great deal of blood. It would take a man's full strength to swim down to the crystals.

"I don't give a damn who gets them," Peyton said, grabbing her arm again. "But somebody better get in that water quick."

"Duncan, can ye do it?" Griffin asked, remembering his cousin's withered arm beneath his billowing shirtsleeves. He didn't want to reveal the man's weakness, but he had to be sure his cousin was fit enough.

"Aye," Duncan answered, his eyes dark and dangerous.

Griffin frowned. Once his cousin reached the crystals, if he touched them—if indeed they were there—he would be sent spinning through time again. That would likely be the best way to escape this situation, but how could he be sure that after Duncan had disappeared, the crystals would still be there for him and Chelsea to use? The magic associated with them was sporadic and unpredictable.

"Hurry up," Peyton ordered. "I'm getting short on patience."

Duncan stripped off his shirt and kilt. Chelsea stared as he bared himself, and Griffin couldn't help but smile, even in this tense situation. His cousin had somehow in his travels procured a pair of plaid boxer shorts. Then Griffin saw his wife's gaze light on Duncan's arm, saw the compassion enter her eyes. How had he ever lived without her?

"Maybe you could learn a bit from your cousin," she called to Griffin. "About fashion."

"Och, ye liked the leather chaps and ye know it," he said, giving her a wink before turning to Duncan. "Wait, lad," he cautioned, "ye cannot just go down there and start grab-bin', ye ken my meaning?"

"Aye," Duncan agreed.

"What?" Peyton moved toward them, dragging Chelsea along. "Why not? What's going on?" He jammed the gun into her side. "You two better not be trying to trick me again."

"Calm down," Griffin said, his mind running over every possible plan of action. "I'm no' trickin' ye."

Duncan picked up his discarded shirt. "I'll get them," he said. "Ye just take care of yerself and Chelsea."

Griffin nodded. He knew what his cousin meant. He needed to get close to Chelsea. When the time came, they would all have to be in the water at the same instant. They might not get a second chance.

Duncan started climbing down the limestone cliff. There were natural stepping stones leading down to the water, but Griffin leaned over the edge of the outcropping. If he had to jump, he and Chelsea could easily land in the middle of the pool. But first he had to get Chelsea in his arms again.

"He's goin' down," he said, turning to Peyton. "Would ye let my wife look at my wound? It's broken open again."

Peyton gave him a wary look. "I told you, I don't want no funny business."

Griffin shook his head. "No funny business. Ye have the gun. I wouldn't risk her life. After all, we're here, we're getting the emeralds for ye, and then ye're going to let us go. Why would I pull something now? Besides, I haven't the strength."

"Remember that, sweet cheeks," Peyton said with a leer. "How's a lily-livered weakling like that going to please you? She was telling me just a little while ago, pretty boy, that she had an appetite too big for you to fill." He shifted his attention back to Chelsea. "Maybe you'd better think about coming with me. I'll even let you wear the emeralds."

"I'll think about it," she said. Griffin heard the forced calm in her voice and longed to rush to her, longed to destroy the man endangering her. "But let me check his bandage. If he faints, he'll be awfully heavy to carry back to the horses."

"Hell, if he faints, we'll just dump him in the well. Good riddance." The man shrugged. "Go ahead, tend his wound, but I want the two of you to sit over there on that rock where I can keep an eye on you."

Chelsea walked casually over to Griffin, but when she lifted her eyes to his, he saw the relief and love in her gaze. He guided her to the rock, and they sank down on it together. She lifted his shirt and began tending the bloody hole in his shoulder. She ran her fingers gently down the middle of his back, and Griffin sucked in a sharp breath of air.

"Oh, Griffin," she whispered, "I've missed you so much."

"Aye, lass," he said softly. "Every minute apart from you has been like an eternity. It's time to go home."

"Home?" she asked, a lilt in her voice. "You know, we've never talked about it," she gave a little half laugh. "We haven't had a chance, but are we going to be together"—she lowered her voice—"in my time?"

Griffin released his breath slowly. He pictured life in her time—automobiles and tellie-vision, malls and cell phones. He pictured life in his own time without Chelsea. Without her sweet lips. Without her golden hair. Without her warm body next to his on the cold and lonely nights.

"Och, lass," he said, "I will live anywhere, at any time, to be with ye. Ye are my heart's delight."

"Now, isn't that sweet?" Peyton stood over the two of them, his lips twisted into a sneer. "What a teat-sucking bastard you—"

"Griffin! I canna find them!"

A chill streaked down Griffin's spine, and he stood and crossed to the ledge. Below, on the limestone rock beside the pool, Duncan stood shaking his head.

"Ye must have hid them too well," Duncan said.

Griffin considered his cousin's words. Either Duncan

was telling the truth or this was part of his ploy to get Griffin and Chelsea to the water. He suspected the latter.

"Aye, I must have," Griffin agreed. "I'll have to come down and direct ye." He motioned for Chelsea to come to him, and she hurried to his side.

"Where do you think you're going?" Peyton asked, blocking their way.

"Ye heard Duncan. I've got to go down and help him."

"But the girl stays here."

Griffin shot Chelsea a swift look. "Nay, she comes with me. I . . ." He reached up and held his shoulder. The bleeding had almost stopped, but his shirt was soaked with blood. "I need her to help me get down to the pool. I canna support myself with this arm, and Duncan canna support me with his withered limb." He sent his cousin a silent apology.

Duncan held up his arm for Peyton to see.

Peyton hesitated. The man was no fool, but he had to realize that the suggestion made sense. The only other possibility would be for Peyton to help Griffin and give up his advantage with the gun.

A half smile touched Griffin's lips. "Or ye could help me," he said. "But I dinna think ye can climb and aid me with yer gun. Ye could leave it here and Chelsea could promise not to touch it."

Peyton's eyes narrowed and his dark brows drew together. "What kind of idiot do you take me for?" He jerked his head toward the water. "Help him down there," he told Chelsea, "but I'm watching all of you. If you try to swim downstream, I'll pick you off one at a time like ducks in a barrel. I can always find someone else to swim down and find the emeralds."

"Fair enough," Griffin agreed, suspecting the man would have already shot them if he felt sure the "emeralds" were there and not hidden elsewhere. "Come on, love, give me yer hand."

They were halfway to the water when something whizzed by them.

"Get down!" Duncan shouted. "Someone's shooting!"

Chelsea threw herself against Griffin and pushed him

back against the stone. He realized she was trying to protect him, and he swung her around, shielding her with his body. He lightly touched her nose. "I'm the man, lass, dinna forget it."

Chelsea stuck out her tongue even as she tried to pull him down under the limestone outcropping now directly above them. "That doesn't mean I can't try to save your backside, laddie. Get under here!"

"Who's there?" Peyton called out from above them. Griffin peered across the water in the direction from which the shot had come. In the bright moonlight it should have been easy to see who was standing there shooting, but all he could make out was a shadowy figure.

"Who's there?" Peyton said again. "Show yourself or I'll start shooting. I don't care about those people down there. I'll be up here behind the rocks."

"Nice guy," Chelsea muttered.

"A real prince," Griffin agreed, then leaned forward. "Look."

From behind a huge cypress tree, one of the many growing on the edge of the stream, someone stepped out and walked toward the water.

"Don't shoot, Ezra," a woman's voice said. "It's me."

"Lola?" Peyton's startled laughter echoed across the silent creek. "You scared the hell out of me. Thought someone was trying to shoot me. What was that shot about? You aiming for the furriners?"

Another, taller shadow stepped out into the moonlight. Blake. Griffin saw that the big black man held a rifle. The bouncer handed Lola the gun, and she lifted it to her shoulder.

"No, Ezra," Lola said, her voice soft yet distinct, "I was aiming for you." She pulled the trigger.

The loud retort rang against the limestone cliffs, and Griffin moved from beneath the outcropping in time to see Peyton grab his chest. Blood spurted between his fingers, staining his shirt as he stared at the wound, looking stunned.

An artery. Griffin had been in enough battles to know the man would die within seconds.

Peyton looked down at one blood-covered hand, then across the creek where Lola stood. He lifted his gun, took a stumbling step forward, and pitched headfirst over the edge of the limestone cliff. When he hit the water, a wave surged up over the limestone ridge where Duncan stood. The Scot immediately dove in after the man. He dragged the floating body to the side, a bright stream of blood trailing after him. Duncan hauled himself out of the water and pulled Peyton's sodden mass to lie across the limestone.

"He's dead," he announced.

Griffin glanced over at Lola. She had a grim but triumphant expression on her face.

"I'm sorry, ya'll," she called softly across the creek. "But now I've made it right."

"Lola, don't forget what we talked about," Chelsea said. "There are still choices to be made."

"I know, honey. I plan to make a few." She turned to Blake, and tears of gratefulness brimmed in her eyes. He nodded down at her, and the two turned in unison and silently walked away.

"Thank goodness it's over," Chelsea said lifting her hair in both hands and letting it fall back against her neck.

"Aye," Griffin said, moving to slip his arms around her waist. " 'Tis over at last."

"I wouldn't say that."

Griffin groaned aloud and pushed Chelsea behind him again. Dead Eye stood on the other side of the creek, not far from where Lola and Blake had been. The man had obviously kept himself hidden until he saw how the scenario played out.

Duncan looked up at Griffin from the ledge below. "What the hell is this? Grand Central Station?"

Chelsea frowned. "You know about Grand Central Station?"

He nodded. "I've been around. What do ye want, Dead Eye?"

"I want them emeralds I heard Mr. Peyton talkin' about. He didn't know that I knowed about them, but I did and I followed him out here. I figured he'd get 'em and then

kill the lot of you, and then I could kill him and take 'em."
He jerked one thumb over his shoulder. "But good ol' Lola
took care of it for me." A wide grin stretched his ugly face
as he raised a shining silver revolver. "So now I guess I'll
just kill y'all instead."

"Wait a minute," Griffin said. "If ye kill us, I promise
ye'll never find the emeralds. They're so well hidden my
cousin couldn't even find them. I know ye must have heard
Peyton say that."

"I heard him. But I figured it was just a trick. Just between you and me and the doorpost, Mr. Peyton weren't
the sharpest nail in the barn."

"No, he wasn't," Griffin agreed, starting to move down
the limestone rock toward the pool of water, leading Chelsea carefully behind him. "But we've known all along that
ye're much smarter."

"That's right," Chelsea chimed in as she tightened her
grip on his hand. "I told Griffin just yesterday that if Peyton
didn't watch himself, you might just take over his whole
operation."

"You did?" Dead Eye grinned again, his dingy teeth looking almost green in the moonlight. "Well, hell, you were
right. I had this planned all along."

"And because you're smarter than he is," Chelsea went
on, "you know that we are so sick and tired of this whole
thing that we'd be happy to give you the emeralds just so
we could get out of here. Of course, if you killed us, then
there'd be all the trouble and mess of getting rid of the
bodies and running from the law, when all you have to do
is let us get the emeralds, give them to you, and be on our
way."

Dead Eye looked a little puzzled, and Griffin almost
laughed out loud. He gave Chelsea a hug as he swung her
off a ledge and down to his side. They were beside the
pool now, and he exchanged glances with Duncan.

"Let me and Duncan get the emeralds," Griffin said,
starting to shed his shirt. "I promise I'll bring them right
back up to you."

"You're bleedin'," Dead Eye said.

"Right. That's why I need Duncan. But I have to show

him where they are." He gave Chelsea a quick kiss. "Be ready," he said under his breath. Duncan jumped into the water while Griffin sat down on the rock and eased into the icy water.

Griffin still didn't know if the crystals truly were not under the water or if Duncan had been simply stalling for time, but he would soon find out. His cousin slipped his strong right arm around Griffin's waist and helped pull him beneath the surface, through the pressurized water, toward a limestone shelf where an eerie green light glowed.

The crystals.

They gleamed in the moonlight, mocking Griffin, taunting him with their nearness. Their emerald-green shards invited him to touch them, to travel anywhere in time he wanted. He reached out to them, but Chelsea's face, soft, loving, darted swiftly into his mind, wiping out the hypnotic emerald light of the crystals. He jerked his hand away.

Nodding at Duncan, Griffin pointed upward. They would have to insist that Chelsea join them. He could say the "emeralds" had slipped into a small crevice and their hands were too large to reach them. Duncan gave him his arm again and together they rose to the surface. When they broke the water, however, Dead Eye stood at the edge of the pool, his arm around Chelsea, his gun thrust into her side.

"You know," she said softly as Griffin and Duncan treaded water, looking up at her helplessly, "I am getting very tired of this. Hai!"

She slammed her elbow into Dead Eye's side, brought her knee up into his stomach, and as he doubled over, took the gun from his nerveless fingers.

"Bye-bye," Chelsea said, and pushed the dumbfounded man into Jacob's Well.

"No!" Duncan shouted, and dove under the water.

"Come on, lass!" Griffin yelled. "This may be our last chance!"

Chelsea's gray eyes widened, and without hesitation she jumped in, feet first. Griffin put his good arm around her, cursing the injury that made it necessary for her to help him. The two plunged beneath the surface.

In the depths below, Duncan struggled with Dead Eye, who was reaching for the crystals. Griffin released Chelsea and using his good arm, swam to his cousin's side.

Dead Eye fought like a man possessed, stretching his fingers toward the crystals. Duncan had him around the neck, and Griffin grabbed his feet. As Griffin held on, he watched in alarm as Duncan's forearm tightened against Dead Eye's throat. Duncan intended to kill the man.

A flood of thoughts raced through Griffin's mind. He abhorred violence, especially violence that could be avoided. Granted, Dead Eye deserved to die. He was like a rabid animal and should be put down. But at the same time, Griffin was not so hard as to believe that it was his job to take the life of a man in cold blood.

He saw a movement out of the corner of his eye and turned to see Chelsea, her hair shimmering around her like a mermaid's. She was swimming toward Duncan, and he saw the determination in her eyes. He let go of Dead Eye's legs and pushed himself toward Duncan. His cousin's grip on Dead Eye was like iron, but Griffin managed to get him to relax his hold on the man's throat a little. There was fury in Duncan's eyes, even beneath the water, and Griffin watched it flare and fade as Dead Eye's eyes bugged out and his face began to turn blue.

The two cousins swam the stricken man to the surface and together pulled him out. Chelsea was right behind them.

"What were you thinking?" she shouted at Duncan. "You don't drown a man if there's no reason!"

"There was a reason," he said, water pooling around him as he pushed on Dead Eye's back, trying to pump the contents of the pool from his lungs. Griffin knelt beside him.

"He was goin' to shoot ye," Duncan reminded her, "or have ye already forgotten that, ye daft girl?"

"But you had him, you didn't need to—"

Dead Eye coughed, and water flooded out of his mouth. He was breathing, and Griffin stood. He grabbed Chelsea's hand and hauled her to her feet.

"All right, lads and lassies," he said, "there's no time for arguing. We'll settle it on the other side."

"We can't just leave him here," Chelsea said. "Just because he's breathing doesn't mean he's all right!"

"Are ye plannin' to sacrifice all of us for the sake of this blackguard?" Duncan demanded.

"That's enough, Duncan," Griffin said, his good hand coming down on his cousin's shoulder. "Ye were wrong, and ye know it." He smiled over at Chelsea. "We'll tie him up, and when we're sure he's all right—"

"You gonna tie ol' Dead Eye up?" said a voice from behind them.

The three turned. Joey stood at the edge of the creek, his hands balanced on his hips, a broad grin on his face. Chin stood beside him, holding what appeared to be a handful of bottle rockets.

"This *is* Grand Central Station," Chelsea said, raising both arms in exasperation. "What are you doing here?"

"Oh, me and Chin came out here to shoot off some more fireworks." His grin faded as he caught sight of Peyton's body on top of the limestone, his blood pooling in a stark puddle beneath him. "Uh-oh. Looks like you had some trouble." The grin returned. "Hell, guess Miss Lola will be glad to hear this."

The three exchanged glances. "I guess she will," Chelsea said. "But it wasn't us, Joey. Someone else killed him. Listen, is the sheriff all right? I've been worried."

"Hell, yes, he's just got a bad headache. But if I were y'all, I'd hightail it out of here. He's madder'n an old wet hen."

"That's exactly what we planned to do," Griffin said, "but Dead Eye came along and tried to stop us."

"What did ya do, try to make him drink the whole creek?" He laughed, and beside him Chin grinned widely, exposing a set of pearly white teeth inside a huge mouth. The effect was slightly disturbing.

"Joey," Chelsea said, excitement in her voice, "this is perfect. Will you take Dead Eye back to town for us? We've really got to be going."

"Sure, I'll take him. Just as soon as me and Chin get

through. We're going to go down the creek a little ways. There's a perfect spot on those limestone cliffs to shoot off some more fireworks. Then we'll take him to town." He started walking away and turned back. "Say, did you know Chin's gonna teach me how to cook and then we're heading out to California? It's gonna be great."

"That's wonderful, Joey," Griffin said, happy for the youngster. "Just remember how bad guys end up and stay on the straight and narrow."

Joey nodded. "I'll remember. And maybe someday I'll come over to Scotland and visit you, Scotty. You still going back?"

Griffin looked down at Chelsea and slipped his arm around her waist. "Perhaps someday, if my wife wants to go."

"So long!" Joey lifted one hand in farewell and headed off down the creek bank, with Chin following close behind him. As they disappeared around a bend, Griffin sighed and hugged Chelsea tightly.

"All right. Shall we try again?"

Duncan gave him a nod, but Griffin saw the uneasiness in his cousin's eyes. Understanding dawned swiftly.

"Duncan," he said. "Forgive me. We haven't even said goodbye." He held out his good arm to the man, but Duncan shook his head.

"I'm no' sayin' goodbye, lad," he said, frowning. "Do ye no' ken that the crystals work only once at any given time? And all who touch it must be focusing on the same place, else it will not work at all."

"How do you know?" Chelsea asked.

"Believe me, I know. So, unless ye're planning on leaving me behind to face the wrath of Dead Eye over there"—he raised both brows—"I suppose ye're going to have a house guest for a while."

Griffin was overwhelmed with joy. He'd hated the thought of losing his cousin again. Now perhaps the two of them would have some time to catch up. As if reading his mind, Duncan added, "But I'm still going back to Scotland."

Griffin drew in a deep breath. He'd forgotten about

Duncan's malady. He'd been so happy to discover an end to his own sickness, he'd put aside Duncan's belief that he didn't have long to live.

"Aye," Griffin said. "We'll bide a while and then Chelsea and I will take ye home to Scotland, whenever ye're ready to go."

Chelsea gave him a questioning look, and he kissed the end of her nose, a promise to tell her later. Griffin took her left hand and Duncan, with a rare smile, took the right.

"Then we'll all be thinking of the year 2003," Griffin said. "And of a certain few people who dinna know they'll be getting another guest from the past. On the count of three." Griffin gazed down into Chelsea's adoring eyes. "One . . . two . . ."

Fireworks exploded above them, brilliant flowering stars glimmering beneath the huge orb of the moon. Griffin threw back his head and laughed.

"What's so funny?" Chelsea asked, smiling up at him.

"Ye wanted an adventure, lass. Well, I'd say ye got it, and more!" He kissed her hand. "Three!"

They jumped. The icy water closed over their heads, and as the three swam toward the glowing crystals, Griffin focused on Chelsea's time. But more, he focused on her warm hand curled inside his, and suddenly he knew . . . he was going home.

Chapter Twenty-two

"Where are the stuffed crabcakes? Jamie! Jamie Mac-Gregor! Did you take the stuffed crabcakes?"

Chelsea could hear Jix storming through the Riley ranch house calling for her husband, shouting orders to the caterer and demanding to know where in the hell the preacher was.

"Jix is, er, feeling her ninth month of pregnancy," Samantha Riley said, popping another stuffed crabcake into her mouth.

"No kidding. But really, Sam, I think we should tell her we have the darn crabcakes," Chelsea said.

"Let her rant a little bit longer. She enjoys it."

Chelsea turned back to the mirror. The two women sat in Jix's bedroom. Chelsea had taken a long, luxurious bubble bath, dried her hair, perfumed and lotioned her body, and had just sat down at the wide dresser to do her makeup before putting on her wedding dress.

Leave it to Sam and Jix to insist that the handfasting she and Griffin had performed in 1882 was not legal and binding. And besides, Jix said, she and Sam couldn't be there and they hadn't been waiting all this time for Chelsea to get married only to miss out on the ceremony!

And leave it to the strange crystals to twist time into a pretzel so that when they returned, they discovered they'd been gone for seven months instead of just seven days!

Jix and Sam had actually cried when she and Griffin showed up at the ranch after their whirlwind return to 2003, with Duncan in tow. And when the women had begged to give them a wedding, Chelsea couldn't help but give in. Although she couldn't imagine feeling more married to the love of her life than she already did, she was secretly pleased by the attention her two best friends were showering on her.

Even her parents had shown up, arriving the night before and expressing their warm, if formal, welcome to Griffin. She'd wished that just once her mother and father could unbend, smile, have a good time. She knew they loved her, but they were just so darned . . . scientific. By the time they had gone to bed in one of the Rileys' many guest bedrooms and Chelsea and Griffin had retired to theirs, she'd been on the verge of tears.

She smiled. Her tears hadn't lasted long. As soon as the door closed behind them, Griffin had swept her up in his arms and tossed her into the middle of their king-sized bed where he proceeded to love every single bit of sadness out of her body.

Now she was here, getting ready for her wedding. If someone had told her a year ago that she'd be marrying the most handsome man in the world, who also happened to be a time traveler, she'd have laughed herself silly.

Chelsea smiled into the mirror. Maybe she would anyway. It was a day for laughter, for joy, and for happiness. Her smile faded, and a slight frown suddenly marred her reflection.

She'd awakened, later in the night, to face a sudden, terrifying thought. In her wildest dreams, she could have never imagined marrying a man like Griffin, let alone the crazy adventure that had bonded them together forever. Now that they were in her time, there would be no more adventures, no more bad guys chasing them or threats of death or fireworks when you least expected it.

What if Griffin grew bored with her? she'd worried. What if the only reason he'd fallen in love with her in the first place was because they were experiencing such excitement together? Now that it was over, would he stop loving her?

"What's the matter, lass?"

His deep, wonderful voice had cut through her fear and she had turned to him, to his arms. If she couldn't spend the rest of her life with Griffin Campbell, she didn't know what she'd do. But she had to make sure he understood what living in her time would mean. She couldn't bear it if he became unhappy or resentful.

She had taken a deep breath and voiced her fears. "I was just wondering if you'll eventually resent being in my time instead of yours, or if you'll get bored with me."

He sat up beside her and switched on the lamp beside the bed. Her heart had contracted as she remembered that day not so long ago when the mere switching on of a lamp had caused Griffin, newly arrived from 1605, to panic. He had adapted. Would he continue to adapt? Concern shadowed his blue eyes.

"Bored with ye? Lass, ye're jesting with me."

She had shaken her head. "No. I know that when we were in the past together it was more exciting—I was more exciting. And now that we're here . . . well, I know I'm not beautiful, and let's face it, I doubt that we're going to be chased by outlaws any time soon and . . ."

Her voice had trailed away. Griffin slid his arm around her shoulders and pulled her against him. She cuddled up to him, amazed as always at the perfect way the two of them fit together.

"Chelsea," he had said softly, "do ye not know that ye are the most beautiful woman in the world to me? Do ye not understand that the excitement ye bring me, just by being who ye are, is more than enough for me for the rest of my life?" He had dropped a kiss on her head and laughed. "And I dinna know how ye feel about it, but I'm perfectly content to live without people chasin' me, tryin' to kill me!"

"But will you be happy here? You're a warrior."

Griffin had been thoughtful for a moment. "I have ye and that's all I need," he'd said at last. "But beyond that, to set yer mind at ease, I have Colonel Riley's promise that

I can play cowboy here to my heart's content, and that makes me very happy." He had grinned, looking like a small boy, and Chelsea loved him more. Would it always be like this, she had wondered, always finding new ways to love him?

"And ye know," he'd gone on, "I plan to attend the university as soon as Jamie helps me arrange it. Do ye know what it means, lass, for me to obtain higher learnin'? To not have to face every day with a sword, nor battle to keep Scotland free?" He'd shaken his head and cuddled her closer. "I was a warrior because I had to be, no' because I liked it."

Her smile returned full force as she remembered what had followed those reassuring words. His words, his touch, had settled everything once and for all in her mind and heart, and she knew that she would never doubt his love again.

Or herself.

Not only had their adventure given them one another, it had given her something more—courage and self-esteem. Now as she looked into the mirror she saw what Griffin saw—a beautiful, strong woman, content in her own skin, ready to face life with new spirit, new joy. She straightened and with renewed enthusiasm unscrewed a tube of mascara. She'd come full circle, and this time she knew she didn't need a makeover.

"You're really happy, aren't you, Cookie?" Sam asked suddenly. She took another stuffed crabcake but didn't eat it. She rolled it between her fingers, her eyes downcast.

Chelsea watched her friend in the mirror, wondering what was wrong. Sam was usually either cracking sarcastic jokes or criticizing something. She was seldom introspective.

"Yes, I'm ecstatic," Chelsea said, "but you don't look so hot."

Her friend shrugged. "I was just thinking about when Jix and I gave you that makeover." She looked up and smiled. "You know, the one that made you look like the Night of the Living Dead?"

"Oh, that one," Chelsea laughed. "I remember."

"We were such idiots."

Chelsea's smile faded and her heartbeat quickened. In all the years she had known Sam she'd never once heard her apologize for anything.

"You and Jix meant well," she said softly, "I knew that."

"But we sapped what little self-confidence you had." Sam put the crabcake back on the tray. "You know, when you disappeared with Griffin, we were really scared. Jix and I talked a lot about it, and we realized that not only had we left you out of a lot of things we did together, but we took you for granted. And we were condescending poops."

Chelsea opened her mouth to say, no, they didn't, they weren't, and it was all right, really, when all at once she realized she wasn't going to do it. That was what the old Chelsea would've done. The new Chelsea saw that brushing off this apology would be the worst thing she could do for Sam, or for herself.

The silence stretched between them for a long moment, and finally Sam looked up, a wry smile on her face. "You aren't going to let me off the hook, are you?"

Chelsea shook her head. "Nope. Ya'll were condescending poops. But I let you treat me that way, so I'm partly at fault, too." Their eyes met, and she saw something soften in Samantha Riley's gaze.

"I'm sorry. I promise that from now on Jix and I will treat you with the respect you deserve." Sam paused, the shadow back in her eyes. "You know, it's funny, I've always been the one with all the answers, but look." She spread her hands apart and looked around the room. "I'm the one that's still alone."

"Oh, Sam—"

"No, no, don't offer comfort to the woman in the middle of the gigantic pity party, you'll only encourage her."

Chelsea wanted to say something, anything, to make her friend feel better, but she didn't know quite how to handle it.

"Do you want to help me with my makeup?" she asked tentatively.

Sam jumped up and gave her a quick hug. "You'll do fine all by yourself," she said. She headed for the door but stopped with her hand on the knob, looking back at the bride-to-be. Chelsea was shocked to see that her friend was crying.

"I missed you, Cookie," Sam whispered. The door closed behind her, and Chelsea sat back in her chair, feeling stunned and happy and amazed all at once.

"Wow," she said. "The miracles just keep on coming."

A few seconds later the door slammed back open and Jix stood in the doorway, her red hair sticking out all over her head, her green eyes wild. She had on her matron-of-honor's dress, which was a bright emerald green, and in her very pregnant condition she looked like a watermelon about to explode.

"Chelsea Brown Campbell!" she shouted. "Are you eating those crabcakes?"

Chelsea reached over and took one of the hors d'oeuvres and brought it to her lips. She smacked loudly and took a bite.

"Yes, Jix," she said around the delectable morsel. "Yes, I am."

Griffin stood at the front of the wee chapel, which was decorated with flowing green ivy and tiny white flowers. He smiled. In a few moments he would once again make Chelsea his wife, this time with all of her friends present to wish them well. He wore a Campbell kilt, borrowed from Jamie's uncle Angus, topped with what he considered a rather feminine black velvet jacket and ruffled shirt. But according to Jamie this was the Scottish style now and besides, it would make Chelsea happy. That was all that mattered. He rested his hand on the hilt of his sword, shined to brilliance and strapped to his waist. When Jamie and Samantha had come searching at Jacob's Well for them, they had found the claymore and kept it until his return.

Griffin took a deep breath as the pastor of Jix's church joined him with a nod, and Duncan and Jamie took their places beside him as best man and groomsman. He met his cousin's approving gaze and smiled. Duncan's arm was steadily improving thanks to therapy provided by Samantha Riley. In time, she said, he would have full use of it once again.

Time. Griffin's smile widened. Time, it seemed, had a way of taking care of everything, sooner or later.

Piano music filled the chapel as first Samantha, then Jix, walked in studied cadence down the aisle, each holding a tiny bouquet of red roses tied with emerald-green ribbons that matched their dresses. Chelsea had told him that Jix and Sam had been thrilled they were getting remarried so close to Christmas, allowing the two women to decorate in red and green.

Griffin didn't care if the chapel were painted purple and Jix and Sam danced down the aisle naked; he just wanted to remarry Chelsea and start spending the rest of his life carving a wonderful life for the two of them in this brave, new world. He would never discount their first wedding beneath the Betrothal Tree, but he understood her need for another ceremony among her family and friends.

He smiled as Jix turned and took her place opposite him. She was so terribly huge with child that he was amazed she'd agreed to be Chelsea's matron of honor. But this was a different time, with different ways, and the relaxed attitude toward things in general was something he would have to get used to, very quickly.

Jix suddenly released her breath in a sigh so loud that half the guests probably heard it. Her face turned bright red, and Griffin gave her a sympathetic smile.

"Dinna fash yerself," he whispered across to the woman who had started this whole journey for him so many centuries ago. "Ye look lovely."

Jix's dismayed expression was replaced with a smile. "You've come a long way, too, baby," she whispered back. "I take it there's no need for the Squash Lady to make a return?"

It was Griffin's turn to blush, and he shook his head just as the woman playing the piano began to pound out a new tune.

Everyone in the chapel rose, and Griffin turned to see Chelsea, his Chelsea, walking down the aisle toward him on the arm of her father. No, she didn't walk, she floated like the angel she was, dressed in white, her gown flowing in her wake, her hair swept up in a mass of soft curls. A band of small white roses held the gossamer veil at the crown of her head, but inserted between the flowers were tiny tufts of purple heather, the bonny flower of Scotland.

She looked up at him shyly as she approached, and he saw more heather tucked into the bouquet of open white roses she held. His gaze softened as she stopped beside him. How amazing that Chelsea would think of honoring him with the very flowers she carried.

Her father placed her hand in Griffin's, and she looked up at her husband, her gray eyes filled with a joy that made his pulse quicken.

"Ye are a vision," he whispered, folding her hand between the two of his, "and thank ye for the flowers."

Her eyes lit up more, if it were possible, and they turned to face the pastor.

"Dearly beloved," the preacher began.

Griffin was mesmerized by the words the man of God spoke, describing the union of Christ and the church and how the union of husband and wife was the earthly illustration of the same. He'd never heard such a comparison, and suddenly the love he felt for his wife seemed even more sacred than before. Then all at once he and Chelsea were repeating vows, promising to love and honor one another all the days of their lives.

They exchanged rings—a wedding gift from Samantha—fashioned from white gold in a beautiful Celtic knot design. He slipped the symbol of their timeless love on Chelsea's finger and gazed down at her, making a silent vow to never do anything that would take away the look of pure happiness shining in his bride's eyes.

"And now," the preacher said, "you may kiss the—"

"Oh, no!"

Griffin and Chelsea turned at Jix's outcry. The matron of honor stood staring down at the floor, her bouquet crushed to her chest, a look of shock and pain in her eyes. The hem of her hunter-green gown was turning dark and wet. She looked up at the bridal couple, a horrified look on her face.

"My water broke!" she said in a loud stage whisper. "I think I'm in labor! Jamie!"

Her husband was at Jix's side in two long steps. He tried to pick her up, but she cried out, "No, no, don't pick me up!"

"How long have you been having contractions, Jix?" Samantha demanded. Chelsea crossed to Jix's side and helped her friend sit down on the top step of the altar.

"About six hours."

"How close are they coming?"

"About every—every—" Jix gripped Jamie's hand and squeezed her eyes shut. "About every couple of minutes. I've been fighting them. I didn't want to ruin the wedding!" She wailed the last word.

"Oh, honey, you should've told us," Chelsea said, hugging her tightly.

Samantha tossed her bouquet aside and started shooting out orders. "Pastor Jim, get these people out of here! Duncan, you and Griffin pull that cloth off that table and hold it up for a curtain so I can examine her. Chelsea, give me your veil!"

The whole bridal party stood in stunned silence until Jix let loose another loud moan.

"Well, what are you waiting for, people?" Sam demanded. "Let's move!"

The four moved out at her command and in a matter of minutes had the room cleared. Chelsea sat beside Jix, her veil removed and clutched tightly in her hands. Jamie sat on the other side of his wife, holding her hand as she panted according to Sam's instruction. Griffin and Duncan held the cloth stoically in front of Jix, their backs to the women.

"Ye're goin' to be fine, love," Jamie told her. "I love ye, sweetheart, ye are the light of my life."

"Yes, well, that's what got me into this, isn't it, you sweet-talking Scot!" Jix shouted, then groaned again. "Here comes another one!"

"My gosh, Jix." Sam looked up from examining her, her expression one of outrage. "You're dilated to ten centimeters! You must have been in labor all night!"

"No, I swear it didn't start until this morning and—oh my gosh!" her eyes widened. "What was that?"

"Chelsea, give me your veil! Jix, it's time to push."

Chelsea handed the soft gossamer to Sam. Jix grabbed Chelsea's arm. "I can't do this! I'm not ready to be a mother!"

"Of course you are, silly," Chelsea told her, taking her friend's hand and holding it tightly. "Don't you know you've been mothering all of us for years?" She kissed her on the forehead. "You're going to be wonderful."

"But I ruined your wedding!"

Chelsea glanced up at Griffin. "No, you didn't." She grinned. "It's just one more adventure, Jix, in this long adventure called life. Now, are you going to push or is Sam going to have to really get tough on you?"

"Chelsea," Jix said, her breathing labored. "Sam told me you two talked, and I just want to say"—she grimaced and held her taut belly with both hands—"I'm sorry, too!"

Samantha stuck her head up over Jix's knees and glared at the two of them. "You're going to be sorry if you don't start pushing, because I'm going to turn a candlestick into a forceps and go in after this baby myself!"

"Stop bossing me around, Sam!" Jix cried.

"Then stop being such a wimp. Push!"

Chelsea held her best friend's hand, and in a matter of minutes a new little MacGregor made his arrival known to the world. He started crying almost immediately, shaking his tiny fists to protest being taken from his mother's nice warm womb. Samantha quickly wrapped him in Chelsea's veil and laid him on top of Jix's stomach, then took the cloth away from Duncan and Griffin and covered her with it.

"There, that'll do until the EMTs get here," Sam said, dusting her hands together, looking smug about her accomplishment. "But if you ever do that to me again, Jix MacGregor, I swear I will kill you."

"And I'll help ye," Duncan interjected as he gave Sam a look of admiration. "Good job, lass."

Jamie cradled his wife in his arms, and Jix looked down at her baby, tears running down her cheeks.

Tess Mallory

"Isn't he perfect?" she whispered. "Isn't he just perfect?"

"Aye," Jamie said softly, "just like his mother."

Chelsea stood and turned away from the couple to give them some privacy. Griffin was waiting for her and he opened his arms. She ran to him, laughing and crying at the same time, throwing her arms around him with the sheer joy of living.

"Well, there's one thing for certain," Griffin whispered as he held her close. "This is one wedding day yer friends have made sure we'll never forget."

Chelsea slid her hands up the front of the crisp tuxedo, drinking in the sight of her husband smiling down at her.

"I don't know why I ever thought it would be dull to come back here," she said. "It never is."

"And it never will be," he promised. "Not if I have anything to say about it. Now, what was this something called a 'honey moon'? I dinna quite understand."

Chelsea saw the devilish gleam in his eyes and pulled his head down to hers, kissing him gently.

"Come with me, laddie," she said. "I'll explain it to you if it takes me all night."

Epilogue

The night was incredible. The moonlight painted sparkles on the water as Griffin watched Chelsea floating across Jacob's Well. In the distance firecrackers were popping, in anticipation of the Fourth of July celebration in the nearby town of Wimberley. As he stood on the limestone ledge above the water, he imagined all the families together on this night, children with their parents, creating memories that would last a lifetime. He smiled, confident in the knowledge that one day he and Chelsea would be joining them, with their own children, their own family.

Shaking his long, wet hair back from his shoulders, Griffin stretched his arms above his head, naked and wet, feeling utterly and completely content.

"You look like a Celtic god," Chelsea said softly, bringing his attention back to her, where it belonged.

She lazily glided toward him in the green-blue pool, the moonlight casting silver shadows across the water, turning the night enchanted. He caught his breath.

"Och, no, lass," he said, " 'tis ye who are the moon goddess this night."

"Then come down here," she commanded, "and ravish me, lowly mortal."

Griffin grinned and dove into the pool. He swam straight to her and gathered her into his arms.

"Gladly." He dropped a kiss to her willing mouth, then drank in the sight of her, loving the way she fit against him, loving her. "Chelsea, darlin', the last six months have been the finest of my life," he said as he gazed down into her moonlit eyes.

After Jix's baby had arrived on their wedding day, they'd skipped the reception, as did most of the guests, and hurried to their honeymoon cottage at Dancing Water Inn, where their second wedding night was every bit as glorious as their first. Now, six months later, they'd taken a break from their studies—Chelsea from her dissertation on time travel, and Griffin from his work on his bachelor's degree in anthropology—to return to their favorite place.

Of course, Griffin had suggested that they not bother with swimsuits at all, but Chelsea insisted they at least wear them on their walk down to the pool. He'd agreed, but just for old times' sake he'd worn his plaid. At least to the water's edge.

The first thing they'd done, just to be safe, was check for the crystals. As they'd both expected, the crystals weren't there. Jix had always insisted that the crystals were not only magical, but had a mind of their own. As a scientist, Chelsea had resisted both ideas all along, but after their grand adventure even she had finally admitted that magic had to figure into the equation somewhere, along with a Higher Power. It was all there in the first draft of her dissertation entitled "Time Travel—Magic, Science, or Reality?"

What a fortunate man he was, to have a wife so sweet, so beautiful, and so amazingly intelligent.

Griffin kissed the side of Chelsea's neck as the spring water buoyed them in place. "And what about ye, lass?" he asked, sure of her answer. "Are ye happy?"

"Well, I don't know." She touched the tip of her tongue to her top lip and gave him a sultry look. Heat coiled inside Griffin, dark and extremely volatile. She grinned, knowing exactly what she was doing to him, and continued primly, using what he called her "scientist" voice.

"I'm *relatively* happy. I mean, for example, if I was standing *outside* a train, watching the train go by and there was a clock on the station wall, and you were *on* the train throwing me kisses and—"

Griffin laughed and stopped her teasing reference to Einstein's theory of relativity by capturing her mouth with his. When they paused for breath, Chelsea leaned her head on his shoulder, and he marveled at the way a single look from her, a tiny gesture, could send such an urgent need through every fiber of his body.

"Um," she said, and licked his water-dappled skin. Griffin drew in a sharp breath, growing very still as she smoothed one hand over his chest and down across his rock-hard abs. "More," she whispered.

It was all he could do to keep from taking her right there in the water, but instead he cocked one dark brow at her and shook his head. "I dinna know; perhaps ye'd rather discuss some of Einstein's other theories. I mean, after all—"

Chelsea ducked his head under the water and he came up sputtering. He gave her a wicked grin and reached for his squealing wife. She tried valiantly to swim away, but Griffin caught her and held her captive against him.

"Now I'm goin' to have to pay ye back for that," he said, sliding his hands across the smoothness of her shoulders.

"Are you?" she asked, sounding breathless.

"Aye."

"But I was going to make it up to you, laddie."

"What do ye have in mind?" He cupped her face between his hands and took his time devouring her mouth for several mesmerizing minutes before she pushed away from him. He watched her swim a few feet away, wondering what she was up to. She treaded the water, keeping her gaze locked with his. Seconds later she triumphantly held up the lower part of her swimsuit and tossed it behind her to slap wetly on the limestone rocks at the pool's edge.

"Oh, I don't know," she said, sliding first one strap of her swimsuit top and then the other off her shoulders. "Maybe this?" She held the top up and tossed it behind her.

Griffin sliced through the water, scooping her into his arms. "Never let it be said that I was an unreasonable man," he said, waiting for her next move. He was sure there had to be one.

"I know we've already had two wedding nights," she said, tracing her finger up the side of his neck, her eyes lowered innocently, "but since this is our six-month anniversary"—she lifted her gaze to his, and the passion in her gray eyes sent a surge of desire through him that was a physical ache—"can I please have one more?" she finished, batting her lashes and pouting her lower lip, looking so cute and completely sexy that he conceded the game.

Griffin pulled her across the water to the bank of the creek, where he lifted her onto his plaid, spread across the soft grass. He began to make love to her, to his wife, beside the place where so much had happened, so very long ago. With every touch he told her that he loved her, and with every caress and fevered breath she told him the same. And when they found each other across the burning sea of their passion, Griffin knew they reached for something more, something beyond the reckless need and the sweet pleasure of their hands and lips on one another; they reached for that perfect union of man and woman, of husband and wife, and found it.

"Look up," Griffin said after they'd drifted back to earth and lay replete in one another's arms.

Chelsea opened her eyes. Above them the heavens exploded in a dazzling display of fireworks lighting the darkness, bursting in reds and greens and golds and silvers against the midnight sky, shimmering in smooth reflection on the moon-bright water.

Griffin lifted Chelsea's face to his and kissed her, knowing the celebration had only just begun.

ABOUT THE HISTORY OF JACOB'S WELL, WIMBERLEY, AND SAN MARCOS

Jacob's Well is a real place in Texas, as is the Dancing Waters Inn, both owned by a real person, David Baker. Please don't go ringing his doorbell asking if there really are time-travel crystals in the mysterious pool. There aren't any; well, at least none we know about. Of course, the crystals only seem to appear when someone needs them, so you never know.

"Jacob's Well is a perpetual artesian spring, pumping thousands of gallons of fresh water per minute to form Cypress Creek. Considered a sacred place by native Americans and the heart of Wimberley by early settlers, today Jacob's Well supports a habitat rich in wildlife and plant life, including several endangered species."
    —www.dancingwatersinn.com.

The very real present-day village of Wimberley, Texas, is basically the way I described it—a great little town nestled in the Texas Hill Country. I've mentioned a few real places like The EmilyAnn Theatre (www.emilyann.org) and some of the shops around the quaint village square. Although I wanted to keep the story in Wimberley, I needed a saloon, so I traveled to San Marcos for the exciting finale to Chelsea and Griffin's adventure. I gleaned a great deal of historical information about that fair city from *Clear Springs and Limestone Ledges* by Frances Stovall, and I hope that good lady will forgive me for some of the poetic license I have taken.

One thing is certain: Texas is full of wonderful places and wonderful people, so why don't y'all come and see us sometime?

—Tess Mallory
tessmallory@yahoo.com

TESS MALLORY
HIGHLAND DREAM

When Jix Ferguson's dream reveals that her best friend is making a terrible mistake and marrying the wrong guy, she tricks Samantha into flying to Scotland. There the two women met the man Jix is convinced her friend should marry—Jamie MacGregor. He is handsome, smart, perfect . . . the only problem is, Jix falls for him, too. Then a slight scuffle involving the Scot's ancestral sword sends all three back to the start of the seventeenth century—where MacGregors are outlaws and hunted. All Jix has to do is marry Griffin Campbell, steal Jamie's sword back from their captor, and find a way to return herself and her friends to their own time. Oh yeah, and she has to fall in love. It isn't going to be easy, but in this matter of the heart, Jix knows she'll laugh last.

__52444-9 $5.50 US/$6.50 CAN

THE PLEASURE MASTER

NINA BANGS

Stranded by the side of a New York highway on Christmas Eve, hairdresser Kathy Bartlett wishes herself somewhere warm and peaceful with a subservient male at her side. She finds herself transported all right, but to Scotland in 1542 with the last man she would have chosen.

With the face of a dark god or a fallen angel, and the reputation of being able to seduce any woman, Ian Ross is the kind of sexual expert Kathy avoids like the plague. So when she learns that the men in his family are competing to prove their prowess, she sprays hair mousse on his brothers' "love guns" and swears she will never succumb to the explosive attraction she feels for Ian. But as the competition heats up, neither Kathy nor Ian reckon the most powerful aphrodisiac of all: love.

___52445-7 $5.50 US/$6.50 CAN